Prais

Veronica

'Wow, wow, WOW. Her best

JILL MA

'Uplifting, inspiring and guaranteed to make you hungry'

SARAH MORGAN

'Family secrets, a beautiful Cornish setting and a beach like no other . . . I was swept away!'

LUCY DIAMOND

'I absolutely loved it!'

KATE EBERLEN

'A delicious, dreamy, joy of a book'

LIBBY PAGE

'Gorgeously romantic'

JO THOMAS

'I loved this gorgeous, hopeful story of second chances'

LIZ FENWICK

'The perfect weekend read. I was so captivated I didn't notice I was turning the pages'

FANNY BLAKE

'Captivating and romantic. I completely fell in love with Speedwell'

HEIDI SWAIN

'Full of warmth, joy and a brilliant cast of characters'

ALEX BROWN

'Irresistibly romantic and bursting with joie de vivre. I adored it'

PHILLIPA ASHLEY

'A sumptuous, joyfully indulgent treat of a book'

CRESSIDA McLAUGHLIN

'Such wonderful characters and the perfect setting'

CARI ROSEN

Veronica Henry has always been involved in storytelling, from her first job typing scripts for *The Archers* to being writer-in-residence on the Venice-Simplon Orient Express. She was a scriptwriter for many years, working on some of our best-loved dramas including *Heartbeat* and *Holby City*. She has written over twenty novels, all published by Orion. She lives on the North Devon coast where she loves walking on the beach, swimming in the sea or watching the sun set with a killer negroni.

Also by Veronica Henry

Thirty Days in Paris
The Impulse Purchase
A Wedding at the Beach Hut
A Home from Home
Christmas at the Beach Hut
A Family Recipe
The Forever House
How to Find Love in a Bookshop
High Tide
The Beach Hut Next Door
A Night on the Orient Express
The Long Weekend
The Birthday Party
The Beach Hut
Marriage and Other Games
Love on the Rocks
An Eligible Bachelor Wild Oats

THE HONEYCOTE NOVELS
A Country Christmas
(previously published as Honeycote)
A Country Life
(*previously published as* Making Hay)
A Country Wedding
(*previously published as* Just a Family Affair)

A Day at the Beach Hut (short stories and recipes)
A Sea Change (Quick Read)

The Secret Beach

Veronica Henry

ORION

First published in Great Britain in 2024 by Orion Fiction,
This paperback published in 2024 by Orion Fiction,
an imprint of The Orion Publishing Group Ltd
Carmelite House, 50 Victoria Embankment,
London EC4Y 0DZ

An Hachette UK company

1 3 5 7 9 10 8 6 4 2

A CIP catalogue record for this book is available from the British Library.

ISBN (Paperback) 978 1 3987 0319 3
ISBN (eBook) 978 1 3987 0320 9

Illustration by Leonie Wharton

Typeset at The Spartan Press Ltd,
Lymington, Hants

Printed and bound in Great Britain by Clays Ltd,
Elcograf S.p.A.

FSC www.fsc.org MIX Paper | Supporting responsible forestry FSC® C104740

www.orionbooks.co.uk

The Secret Beach

Prologue

Twenty years earlier

Nikki stood at the top of the steps. They were precarious at the best of times, let alone in a high wind with the rain almost horizontal, driving little needles straight onto her eyelids. The television and radio had been rife with severe weather warnings all day. No one with any sense was out in it. You'd have to be mad. Maybe she was? She sometimes thought so. But she hadn't seen him for over a week, what with one thing and another, so here she was, scrambling down, her sneakers slipping on the wet stones, the shale at the edges providing no purchase, nothing to cling on to but a few scrubby branches of gorse.

When she'd left town earlier, the waves were coming up over the harbour wall, hurling themselves over the railings in a spectacular display of petulance. The wind careened around the winding streets as if hunting someone down, relentless and unforgiving, letting out a high-pitched moan. Speedwell was battening down its hatches, shops shutting early, sandbags in doorways, cars moving away from the edge of the quay. Everyone knew the drill. No one ignored the warnings.

People often mistook August for a month of glorious sunshine and high temperatures, but it could bring the worst storms, sudden and unexpected. No doubt tomorrow, it would be as if nothing had happened. The sun would come out and the sea would be tranquil and nonchalant. The tourists would emerge, eager to make up for a day spent indoors on jigsaws and holiday paperbacks. The tills would ring merrily again: postcards and fudge and ice creams.

But for today, the storm raged on.

At the bottom, she jumped onto the sand. The sea was a murky, bruised blue, swirling and surging at random. It didn't seem to know where it wanted to go, as dangerous and unpredictable as a drunk at throwing-out time. She put up a hand to wipe her face. It was impossible to know what was rain, what was salt spray and what was her tears. When had she started to cry again? She mustn't. She had to hold it together, or he would take her in his arms and kiss those tears away and her resolution would crumble.

She'd made up her mind. It was the solution with the least collateral damage. He wouldn't be able to argue with her logic. Sometimes in life you had to make a sacrifice. You had to do the noble thing.

She took in a gulp of air to try to calm herself, pressing her body against the cliff as she edged along towards the rocks that formed their hiding place. She knew the shoreline like the back of her hand, even though it changed with every turn of the tide, every phase of the moon, the sand and the rocks shifting and morphing, the colours melting into each other. She knew its smell, that hit of briny, brackish air like opening an oyster. The feel of the sand that branded the soles of your feet in the midday summer sun but would be cold and hard as iron if she stepped on it now. The noise of the waves: now a menacing boom, but on a warm night they would whisper gently as you drifted off to sleep. She tried not to think about the fact that this was the last time she would see him like this.

In secret.

On their secret beach.

I

Now

A spectacular position with unrivalled panoramic views, it said on the details. *This former coastguard's cottage on the rugged coast of North Cornwall would make the perfect clifftop retreat.*

Living in a small town had its advantages, especially if you knew the right people. When her friend Joel told her the house of her dreams was about to come on the market, Nikki was the first in line. She watched as Joel fished the keys out of the pocket of his waxed coat and aimed for the lock, shutting one eye then booting the bottom of the door with a well-aimed kick that made her wince.

'Stuck again,' he said. 'You should replace it with a UPVC one. It's the salt.'

No way, thought Nikki privately. That wouldn't suit the cottage at all. Built of a soft grey stone, it was identical to its three adjoining neighbours, with a slate roof, a porch in the middle and four sash windows. Above the door was a window light with 'Number Four' written in black and gold cursive.

All the door needed was a bit of sanding and a lick

of paint, she thought. Perhaps royal blue, rather than its current dingy white. They went through the porch with its wooden benches – perfect for tucking boots and shoes underneath – and stepped straight inside a large room. All the furniture had gone and the carpet was curling at the edges. Nikki was itching to pull it up, for she could see there were pine floorboards underneath.

'It was all re-wired backalong,' Joel told her, snapping on a light. 'And the owner's family had central heating put in for him a few years ago.'

The smell of damp suggested they hadn't bothered to put it on since he'd passed. It wouldn't take much to warm the place by lighting a crackling fire in the inglenook fireplace. Nikki was trying not to smile. It was everything she dreamed it would be, even if it was half the size of her current house. She didn't need so much space anymore. She didn't need to be walking distance from the school. The advantages of an empty nest. And she already had a buyer lined up. Joel had a hot box of people wanting to buy property in Speedwell. She was good to go.

Through an archway was a small dining area at the foot of the stairs and through that was the kitchen. Eek. Fifty shades of brown. Beige lino, fake-mahogany units, fawn tiles, paint the colour of burnt porridge. There was a very old under-the-counter fridge and an electric hob with spiral burners, the kind you'd have lit your cigarette on back in the day. But Nikki wasn't fazed. There was an Everhot range that just needed going over with a tub of Astonish. And from the window, beyond the wall at the bottom of the garden, all she could see was miles and miles of pewter ocean, shifting and shimmering. Who cared about grotty old kitchen units when you had that view?

She had to have it.

She told herself she mustn't get too excited. This house would be catnip to second-homers. The asking price was just a lure to get people in through the door.

'Handy toilet.' At the back of the kitchen, Joel clicked the latch of a tongue-and-groove door to reveal a pink loo with no seat. The smell suggested the owner's aim hadn't been terribly accurate.

'That'll have to come out,' said Nikki. 'It'll make a perfect larder.'

She imagined it lined with wooden shelves with all her groceries in perfect rows.

Joel shut the door with a smile. 'Shall we see upstairs?'

They headed up the narrow wooden staircase. There were two double rooms, one single and a bathroom with an avocado suite.

'I'll let you have a look around,' said Joel, and he pulled his phone out of his pocket, scrolling through his emails.

In the back bedroom, Nikki pressed her forehead against the window. From up here, the view was even more spectacular, a silver carpet leading to infinity. Her gaze drifted down to the garden. An untouched tangle of grass and brambles, an empty washing line drooping across the middle. A dry-stone wall marked the boundary, and behind that, across a swathe of scrub, the steps she'd been down so many times. At the bottom, surrounded by towering rocks, was a beach made from millions and millions of crushed shells, known to the locals as Devil's Cove. To Nikki and her friends, as teenagers, it was known as the secret beach. From time to time, winter storms caused a landslide and the steps crumbled away, to be gradually reformed. You needed nerve and stamina to go down, but it was worth it.

She felt a thrill of excitement at the thought of being so near the place that had been such a big part of her life, but she told herself to stay calm. The chances were slim. Her pockets weren't as deep as some.

She glanced at the garden next door. It was the opposite of this overgrown wilderness, landscaped in limestone slabs, white pebbles and teak decking, with drifts of soft grasses rustling in the breeze. By the boundary wall was a raised terrace screened by a row of black bamboo, and on it was perched a wooden hot tub. She imagined sitting there on a starlit night, gazing up at the sky.

She left the room and went to find Joel.

'Who lives next door?'

Joel rolled his eyes. 'Londoners. It's a holiday let,' he said. 'They must be raking it in.'

Nikki didn't rise to the bait. They were all making money from out-of-towners. Even – especially, arguably, as an estate agent – Joel, but it was habit for the locals to complain about them. Nikki tried not to partake. She'd certainly done well from them herself. As a wedding planner, the majority of her clients were people from away who dreamed of getting married by the sea. You didn't bite the hand that fed you.

She felt downhearted all of a sudden, knowing the amount of money a property like this could make as a holiday let would mean she'd probably lose it to an investor. For a moment, she wished she hadn't taunted herself by coming to view it. It was everything she'd ever wanted. Every time she'd gone down the steps to the secret beach, ever since she'd been at school, she'd looked at these cottages and thought *one day*. Was it really within her grasp?

Why not? She worked hard. Saved hard. She deserved to live here as much as anyone. And this, as they say, was 'her' time. She thought of her lovely Bill, swinging in a hammock in Bali, working on his laptop, happy as a clam. She'd have her son back home in a heartbeat, but she accepted he'd had to fly the nest. And this could be her reward, for the pain of losing him to a tropical paradise. He'd flit back in and out of her life, of course he would, but in the meantime, she couldn't just sit and wait for him to reappear. She needed to make a new future for herself. Could a house replace a person? Probably not. Yet she had fallen in love with this little cottage and how it made her feel.

She loved the way the silvery ocean light crept into every corner.

She loved the way it felt good about itself, even though it was a little worn at the edges.

She loved the way it already seemed like home.

She realised Joel was looking at her.

'It's yours, if you want it,' he said.

'What?' She wasn't sure she'd heard properly.

'The vendors say their dad wanted it to go to someone local. And they want a quick sale.' He spread his hands. 'I can call and tell them, if you offer the asking price.'

'They could probably get more.' She couldn't believe she'd said that.

'Maybe,' said Joel. 'But he's left all his money to charity, so they don't care.'

'Oh.'

'Some of it's going to the lifeboat.' Joel knew this

would mean a lot to Nikki. After all, she was crew, and the lifeboat depended heavily on donations and bequests.

Her heart was pounding. She hadn't thought she was in with a chance, but now it was within her grasp, she felt a bit overwhelmed. She had to go for it. 'Absolutely. Asking price it is. We've got a deal.'

She stuck out her hand. Joel smiled, and they shook. They went back a long way. He'd been two years below her at school; played football with her brother Graham. The family company, North Property Management, had always looked after his rentals, fixing things at a moment's notice, so she knew he would make this deal work.

'Is it OK if I have a look around the garden?'

'Stay as long as you like. Far as I'm concerned, it's yours now.'

She knew Joel would go back to the office happy. A short chain with no complications was worth its weight in gold. And with a fair wind, she'd be in Number 4 Coastguard Cottages before summer got underway.

2

Nikki headed around the side of the house, pushed the squeaky old gate and walked through the long grass. The sea air rushed up to her in excitement, as if it had just heard the news. She breathed it in, the salty breeze that swept in over the barnacled rocks. In Speedwell, the air was tinged with diesel and fish from the boats in the harbour; frying chips and roasting coffee. Here, just a quarter of a mile along the coast, the gusts that came in from the Atlantic were pure and untainted but for the faint drift of seaweed.

Amidst the overgrown grass, she spotted pale yellow primroses, white narcissi and a drift of purple crocuses, and she felt a wave of sadness for whoever had planted them. Their heart must have been lifted by their arrival every spring, just as hers was now.

For a moment, she wondered if her deal with Joel had been a dream. It wasn't every day that the thing you had been working towards came true. For a while now she'd craved seascape and solace – not isolation, but the ability to be by herself and enjoy her own company and have the choice of when to see other people. Her life, by anyone's standards, was busy, and life in a small town meant everyone knew your business. Often before you did.

She pulled out her phone and pressed the FaceTime button, checking there was enough signal. She still couldn't get over the fact that she could see Bill in Bali at the touch of a button even though he was on the other side of the world. It was early evening there now, so hopefully she'd catch him.

And yes! There he was. Her heart never failed to leap when she saw his smiley face, so like his dad.

'Hey, Ma!'

He was in a tight tank top, his arms butterscotch brown, his hair almost to his shoulders. Probably on his way out to a beach bar. He was a digital nomad, doing fiendishly clever things on his laptop from a country where he could wear flip-flops all day and swing in a hammock. It was what was known as a no-brainer.

'Guess what I've just bought!'

'You got it?'

She held up crossed fingers to the camera, then flipped it to show him the view.

'This will be the view from your bedroom next time you come home.'

'That's so cool, Ma.'

'It's way smaller than your old one.' It still worried her. They both knew he didn't need his own space anymore, but as a mum it was counterintuitive to get rid of your child's bedroom so she would keep that little third one for him. But she knew he wasn't likely to come home permanently. All you could ask for at this stage in your child's life was for them to be safe and well and happy, and Bill was all of those things. She'd worried about him not going to uni at first, but now she had to admit he had his life sorted. There was no point in structuring her life around his any longer. It was a weird feeling. Bittersweet. Freedom at a price.

'I've still got my room at Dad's, remember. As long as I've got somewhere to crash when I come and see you.'

'You definitely have.' She knew she'd go to pains to decorate it, even though he'd only be in it a couple of days in any given year. It was called being a mum. 'All good with you?'

He gave her a thumbs-up. 'Golden.' That was the most she'd get. She probably didn't want to know too much. She kissed her fingertips at him and gave him a wave. 'See ya, Mum.'

He was gone. Off for a sundowner with some long-limbed girl with intricate tattoos, no doubt. Lucky boy.

She waded through the garden, scrambled over the wall at the bottom, then dropped down onto the path that ran behind. She headed west, away from the cottages, until she reached a small gap in the thick hedge. If you didn't know it was there, you'd miss it, for there was nothing to indicate the magic that lay below.

She pushed her way through the gap and assessed the state of the steps. Over winter, anything could have happened, but to her expert eye it looked manageable. You needed to be surefooted and have no fear of heights to climb down, for the drop was sheer and the steps scarcely wide enough to hold a shoe. But she'd done it so many times she had the knack of planting her foot firmly in the middle, and not looking down.

As soon as she started her descent the wind began to pummel her, no longer the benign breeze she'd enjoyed in the garden. And when she got to the bottom, she saw the waves were wild – the tide was in, leaving only a narrow strip of beach. She stood, breathless from her climb, exhilarated by her surroundings. The dark slate of the cliffs, the pale wet sand, the steel-grey of the sea, topped with brilliant white foam. She was mesmerised by the swell of the waves and their capricious nature. If you thought you had their measure, you were a fool. You were never safe.

No one knew that better than she did.

In summer, the sea would be lazy and beguiling, the water jade and the beach a rosy pink, warmed by the sun. Then, this little cove would be a haven for anyone who ventured down here. You could hide here all day, unseen. Nikki remembered long, hot summers, lugging a rucksack full of cans of cider and ham rolls and suntan cream, battered Jackie Collins paperbacks and a portable CD player. It was the time and place she had felt happiest, for everything had seemed so simple then. She and her friends had sunbathed and swum and danced until the sun went down leaving a streak of burnt orange across the horizon. She remembered firm bronzed skin and freckles and salty hair; carefree laughter and no responsibility except being up in time for school or work the next morning.

And she shivered, remembering another time when this had been her refuge. Cold hands, white puffs of icy breath, a shared flask of fiery rum. Her hopes being raised and then dashed like the sea against the cliffs. A storm of emotions: joy and despair, passion and horrible, horrible unending doubt. Nikki, always so certain, had been crippled by her inability to know what was the right thing to do. And in the end, she had known the right thing to do was to walk away. But it had been too late.

With a swoosh, the waves came up to her, nibbling at her trainers. She danced away from them, then jumped onto the flat rock where they used to line up their cans and bottles – a makeshift bar. She held her arms out and let the wind batter her. She wasn't going to dwell on the past. She had a successful business, a son who was making his own way in life and, now, the house she'd been waiting a lifetime for.

'The world is my oyster!' she shouted out loud. She hoped nobody was watching, as she must look like a mad woman, screaming like a banshee. But the world *was* her oyster, finally – and it was up to her to make pearls. As many as she could.

3

Just over two months later, on a bright, breezy May morning, Joel handed Nikki a set of keys and a welcoming wicker basket with scones, raspberry jam and clotted cream.

'It's probably the last thing you want,' said Joel. 'But I give them to all my clients. And then remind them it's cream first in Devon, jam first in Cornwall.'

Speedwell was right on the border. The town itself was in Cornwall, but half a mile up the coast you stepped over into North Devon. So nowhere was the cream or jam debate more fierce.

Nikki tucked the scones in her bicycle basket. 'I don't mind which comes first,' she said, grinning. 'And thanks, Joel. I know how much you helped make this happen.'

'And people say estate agents are the scum of the earth.' Joel grinned and raised his hand. Nikki gave it a triumphant slap. There'd be a bottle of champagne on its way to him by way of thanks.

She pocketed the keys then rode hell for leather out of town on her e-bike and up the winding hill that followed the coast. As the cottages came into view, she felt a surge of excitement. The same excitement she used to feel as a teenager, filled with the anticipation of an afternoon of fun and laughter and music with her friends, wondering who would be there and what might happen. She pulled off the road and onto the gravel path in front of her lawn. Her lawn, her garden path, her front door.

The cottage stood out crisply against a pale blue sky, the sun softening the grey stone.

The breeze was a light skittering scented with brine and something herbaceous. Nikki paused for a moment, looking at the Sold sign, filled with pride that she'd had the courage to take this risk. She still couldn't quite believe it was hers as she put the key in the lock and pushed the door open, holding her breath. What if she'd made a terrible mistake?

It was even more wonderful than she remembered. The sunlight reached into every corner, and rather than highlighting any flaws it seemed to soften them. As she walked through the rooms, she fancied she could feel the cottage sigh with relief. At last, she imagined it saying, here is the person who will cherish me. And she would. She was itching to get started – and she'd begin with the carpet she had longed to pull up the day she had been to view.

There was already a skip on the drive, with North Property Management emblazoned on the side. Her brother Graham had dropped it off, and later he was bringing over some of her furniture in one of the company vans. Most of her stuff was in storage. For now, all she needed was a bed, a little table and chairs and an armchair for flumping into at the end of a long day. She was going to camp out here while she did the renovations, safe in the knowledge her mum would give her a bed at their family home, Mariners, if the dust and grime got too much.

She threw open the back door and looked out into the dew-drenched garden. It was even wilder than before, a tangle of green tendrils with little shoots of colour here and there. Beyond the tangle was the glassy sea. She would never tire of the sight of it, all hidden depths and shape-shifting and changing moods, like a film star with a million guises. There wasn't time to moon over it now. The sea wasn't going anywhere and there was work to be done.

Two hours later, Nikki lugged a pair of bin bags out to the skip. Even though the house had been emptied there was rubbish to get rid of: grimy net curtains to take down from the windows, bits of old carpet from around the loo, layers of newspaper lining the shelves in the airing cupboard. As she worked her way through the house, she began to understand it: which rooms had the best view and the most light. She began to imagine how she might live in it and where all her possessions would go.

As she hurled the bags over the side of the skip, she noticed a station wagon had pulled up and parked outside the house next door. A big old silver Saab, with the boot open, crammed with stuff. Holidaymakers, probably. They must be staying at least a fortnight, judging by the amount they'd brought with them. The front door was open and she peered inside to see if she could see anyone, but there was no sign of life. Until a brown streak shot out of the house and straight over to the tiny patch of grass in front of her house – theirs was paved with immaculate limestone – where he proceeded to leave a hefty deposit.

'Oi!'

The dog looked up at her, unashamed. He was long legged, with a handsome head and a rough coat. She had no idea what breed he was, but he was very appealing, and despite his misdemeanour she was taken by him. It wasn't his fault if his owner wasn't keeping an eye on him.

She went inside for a plastic bag, scooped up the offending deposit then marched up to the open door.

'Hello!' she called, and rapped on the tastefully painted wood. It was dark aubergine. No one in Speedwell had a dark aubergine door. It was rich and dark and glamorous and inviting.

'Hello!' a voice from within sang back and the next moment a man appeared.

He was slim, with thick hair swept back from his forehead, and large enquiring eyes behind tortoiseshell glasses. His dark blue shirt was French-tucked into jeans. A drift of the most delicious cologne smelled of warm nights somewhere exotic.

'A present for you,' said Nikki, holding out the bag and nodding her head towards the dog, which had slunk back inside sensing something was up and had disappeared.

'Oh my God,' he said, and his voice was like melting treacle. 'I am so sorry. Let me take that.' He stretched out an arm and took the bag from Nikki without flinching. 'I can't apologise enough. People who let their dogs crap on other people's lawns are the worst.'

'They certainly are.'

'What can I do to atone?'

Nikki was disarmed. She wished she hadn't been quite

so abrupt now. She gave a smile and a shrug. 'Just make sure he doesn't do it again.'

He looked concerned. 'I don't want us to get off on the wrong foot. I was going to ask you in for a drink, since we're going to be neighbours, but now Gatsby's kind of ruined the moment.'

'Neighbours?'

'Yes. I'm finally making the big scary move down from London.' He held out his hand. 'I'm Adam. Adam Fitzroy.'

'Oh! I'm sorry. I assumed you were on holiday. Hello.'

She took his hand. It was warm, and his clasp was tight. Not in an aggressive power-play way, but a friendly, welcoming squeeze. Behind him, the guilty party hove back into view and sat by his owner's feet, the picture of innocence.

'Gatsby,' Adam said, 'you have a lot of work to do to make up to—'

He turned to Nikki with an enquiring smile, and she realised she hadn't introduced herself.

'Nikki,' she said, cursing herself for her gaucheness. 'Nikki North. I've moved in today. I got the keys this morning.'

Gatsby looked up at her with beseeching brown eyes.

'I find it impossible to be cross with Gatsby,' said Adam. 'But I totally understand if you can't find it in your heart to forgive him.'

Nikki smiled, despite herself. 'What is he?' she asked.

'A wire-haired Viszla. I'm afraid he doesn't live up to his name, though. He has never so much as raised a paw to make me a cocktail.'

Nikki laughed. 'You're a Scott Fitzgerald fan, then?'

She'd read *The Great Gatsby* only a couple of years ago, when a couple wanted a Gatsby-themed wedding.

He paused for a moment.

'My wife named him. Ill advisedly – I think Gatsby was a terrible person. But she thought it was glamorous.'

'Oh.' She looked around. 'Is she moving down too?'

'Er – no.' He looked at the ground, awkward. Nikki sensed she'd made a faux pas. 'I'm afraid my wife passed away.' He looked back up at her. 'Right at the beginning of Covid. She was a consultant anaesthetist working on a frontline ward.' He gave a little shrug which meant that Nikki was to fill in the rest of the blanks.

'I'm so sorry.' Nikki put a hand to her throat. She could feel it tighten with emotion. 'I'm *so* sorry. That's terrible. I . . .'

She trailed off, mortified now she had been so confrontational.

'Sometimes I think I should wear a badge, to stop people being embarrassed.' He tapped his chest. 'Saying *recently bereaved* or *widower* or something. Because I really hate this bit, when people don't know what to say.'

'I can imagine,' said Nikki. 'It must be really bloody awful.'

'It is.' He gazed at her earnestly, and gave a little helpless shrug.

'I'm sorry for your loss,' she said, only too aware how insufficient her words were. 'What was your wife's name?'

He looked surprised. It was rare for people to ask questions. They usually wanted to change the subject as soon as they could. 'Jill.'

'Jill.' Nikki wanted to acknowledge her existence by saying her name.

'Jill Chesterton. She didn't take my name when we got married. Because of her job, I think. Not that I minded. I mean, I'm not one of those men who thinks a woman should have his name. Obviously. Because that's . . .' He trailed off, looking sheepish. 'Sorry. I'm babbling. I always feel really awkward talking about her because I know it makes people feel awkward.'

'I don't.'

'No, I can see that. It's very unusual. And I really appreciate it.'

He smiled at her. Nikki suddenly wished she wasn't standing there in a North Property Management boiler suit with the legs rolled up and her hair in a bandana, like a dishevelled member of Bananarama.

'I understand,' she said softly, for she knew exactly how important it was, to be able to talk about the one you'd lost. What a release it must be to be able to share memories, the things you had loved most about them, the little moments that had meant so much, your fears for their safety now they had gone, your fear that you might forget them or betray them in some way.

She'd never had that luxury.

Silence hung between them, but it was a comfortable one. He swept his left hand through his hair, and Nikki noticed how it fell back into place straight away. It was slate grey, the colour of wet rocks on the beach below.

'Listen,' he said, 'I'm sure you've got stuff to be getting on with. Why don't I make us a cocktail at around six? Are you new around here too?'

Nikki recognised the need to change the subject, the bright tone that was slightly forced. She knew how much energy that took.

'Gosh, no. Speedwell born and bred. But I've wanted one of these cottages for as long as I can remember. I've spent half my life on that beach.'

She nodded her head towards the clifftop.

'I can't wait to explore properly. Maybe you can give me some inside knowledge?'

'Of course. I'll see you at six.' She bent down to fondle Gatsby's head. 'And you are forgiven. See you later, Gatsby.'

She headed back up the path with a fizz inside her that hadn't been there before. She felt pleased she was going to have a proper neighbour, rather than a rotation of holidaymakers. They often had no consideration for whoever was next door to them. Noisy children, loud music, endless barbecues belching smoke, barking dogs: they could be tricky, and by the time you'd complained they had gone back home, to be replaced with the next lot.

Adam Fitzroy. For a moment she was tempted to google him, but she decided that was a bit stalky and she could find out what she needed to know from the horse's mouth. She wouldn't google his wife either. He could tell her everything himself in good time.

She was pretty sure he wouldn't be boring. Adam seemed like the epitome of a certain type of man – urbane and charming, a silver fox with a hint of the dandy. Suave but not arrogant. Confident but not brash. As if Richard E. Grant had a long-lost brother, with a bit of Alan Rickman thrown in.

Steady on, Nikki, she told herself with a grin. It was easy, when you lived in your home town, to be overwhelmed by the novelty of newcomers.

As she headed back into the house, she noticed there was a pile of post in the little wire cage on the back of the front door. She fished out the post and leafed through it. A Lidl leaflet, charity letters, what looked like the gas bill. And a postcard. A plain white old-fashioned postcard, with a message written on the back in black italics:

There are no secrets in a small town

She felt a spike of fear, and her heart tripped over itself. With a dry mouth, she turned the card over to see if there were any clues, but there was no such thing as a postmark anymore, just a purple first-class stamp in the right-hand corner. It was addressed to her personally, in capital letters – Nikki North – in the same black ink as the message. It didn't look like a flyer, but she was on a lot of mailing lists, so she often got enigmatic mail from companies whose marketing messaging was more baffling than intriguing. Perhaps she'd receive a follow-up in a week or two and all would become clear.

She took it inside, grabbed her reading glasses from her handbag and looked more closely. It was definitely handwritten. She looked out of the window, as if the sender might be standing there.

The trouble with guilt was that it made you paranoid.

She saw him for one second, in her mind's eye. Then she brushed away the memory. No one could possibly know. They'd made sure not a soul in Speedwell had an inkling.

On a sudden impulse, she ripped up the card and put it in the bin. She wasn't going to let it ruin the excitement of moving in. It didn't mean anything. She was reading too much into it. Instead, she grabbed a Stanley knife. She wanted to get the living-room carpet into the skip and see what the floorboards underneath were like.

Cocktails with her new neighbour would be the perfect reward.

4

At half past five, the sun began to wander downwards to the sea, floating as light and as free as a dandelion head. Nikki poured a cap of Olverum into the ancient bath then filled it with hot water to wash away the dust of the afternoon. She'd managed to cut up the carpet, rolling it up in sections and chucking it into the skip. It was filthy work, but she'd been delighted to find the floorboards underneath undamaged. The stair carpet was next, but that could wait until the morning. She could feel grit in her hair and teeth and she'd need at least half an hour of soaking. Baths were her luxury, where she did her unwinding and her thinking.

She felt her muscles start to unknot as she lay in the fragrant steam, eyeing up the small window with its thick frosted glass. How much would it cost to knock it out and enlarge it so she could have a view of the sea while she bathed? What she really wanted was her ultimate dream, a clawfoot bath in the middle of the room, but that would be way out of her budget. She had to take this renovation slowly and buy things as she could afford them. For now, she was going to have a cheap kitchen and bathroom put in, and a few cosmetic tweaks, then paint everything white. Mike and Jason, two of the fitters from North Property Management, were standing by to fit everything as soon as she'd gutted it.

She'd managed to banish all thoughts of the mystery postcard to the back of her mind while she was working, but as she sank under the bubbles, it floated back into her thoughts. Logic told her there was no substance to her fears. No one knew her secret. No one would have any reason to remind her of it. It had given her a momentary jolt, but she wasn't going to let the past – the distant past now – overshadow her achievement and her joy.

Afterwards, she stood in her towel and surveyed her limited choice of clothing. She had only brought scruffy stuff with her, and a couple of the floaty floral dresses she wore to meet clients. She'd adopted them as a kind of uniform, the sort of dress she thought people would expect a wedding planner to wear. She'd have to wear one of them as she couldn't turn up for drinks in leggings and a sweatshirt. The rest of her wardrobe was hanging in one of the spare rooms at Mariners, and it was too late to go and grab anything. She pulled on the less formal of the dresses with her Converse high tops. The only mirror she had was over the sink in the bathroom so she couldn't see the full effect, but she hoped she looked cool rather than dowdy. You had to be careful in your mid-forties to hit that sweet spot between mutton and frump.

She'd had the foresight to remember her hairdryer, so she coaxed her pixie crop into tousled imperfection. Chopping off all her hair a year ago had been liberating. She'd done it the day after she'd dropped Bill at Heathrow, to take her mind off her aching heart. Her hairdresser had persuaded her into going ice-blonde the same day, and she'd come out feeling invincible. It might be high-maintenance colour-wise but it meant the sneaky strands of grey went unnoticed.

'Bloody hell, you look ten years younger,' her older sister Jess had told her, and she'd then forced her to go and have her brows done properly. Jess took these things very seriously. 'You have to, at our age,' she told Nikki sternly, but Nikki wasn't as worried about losing her looks as Jess was. Perhaps because she wasn't as striking in the first place. Jess, with her heart-shaped face and flashing green eyes, had always turned heads.

Now, with lashings of mascara and a slick of lip-gloss, Nikki thought she'd scrubbed up all right. She was barely recognisable from the scarecrow of earlier. Not a head-turner, perhaps, but not bad.

Adam had the good grace not to look too startled by her transformation when he answered the door to her. She held up her hands with a smile.

'I'm really sorry – I've got nothing to bring as an offering.'

'Oh, don't worry at all. Come in.' He bent forward to kiss her and she felt the fleeting warmth of his cheek on hers. He'd changed out of his blue shirt into a white one with pale blue piping around the undone cuffs. He was still damp from a recent shower, his wet hair swept back, his feet bare.

'What would you like to drink?' he asked, leading her into the living room, which was the mirror of hers, the fire place on the left, the arch through to the back on the right. 'I can do whatever you like, but I'm mad for gimlets right now. Gin and fresh lime, basically. It'll stop you getting scurvy.'

'That sounds great.'

He headed over to a bar area built into the wall to the right of the fireplace. Ranks of open shelves bore rows of glasses in all shapes and sizes, and underneath was a white marble work surface with everything needed to make cocktails. He grabbed three limes from a wire basket which he began to squeeze into a shaker, adding a handful of ice, before free-pouring a generous serving of Hendrick's Neptunia.

Nikki looked around the room. The walls were a bright acid yellow – a perfect foil for the furniture, which all looked as if it had been bought on holiday in Provence or Puglia and shipped home. A bookcase spilled Booker Prize-winning novels, fat cookery books and autobiographies. A multicoloured rug ran underneath two beautifully worn suede sofas and a low coffee table. This hadn't been your run-of-the-mill holiday let, thought Nikki. It must have been thousands a week to rent.

'This is amazing,' she said, and suddenly her plans for next door seemed very unambitious. This was a lifetime of accumulation, presented with an expert touch.

'It's all Jill. She "*curated*" it.' He put quote marks round the word with his fingers. 'It was her dream to live in Cornwall. We were supposed to move down full-time once we'd done it up. She had a job lined up at the hospital in Truro. But then . . .' He sighed. 'When she died, I handed it straight over to an agency because I couldn't cope. It hadn't been our plan to rent it. It's taken me this long to sort my head out, sell the house in Ealing, get my act together . . . but at last I'm here.'

'I hope you'll be happy. And that you find peace.'

He nodded his thanks. 'I'll try. I know that's what Jill would have wanted. I keep imagining her bossing me about, telling me where to put things.' Adam vigorously shook the cocktail shaker for a few moments, then poured the contents into two coupes and handed one to Nikki. 'Hopefully I won't make the place look like a trashed Travelodge too quickly.'

They clinked glasses.

'Welcome to Speedwell,' said Nikki.

Adam gestured to one of the two sofas for her to sit down and she sank into it. It was incredibly soft and luxurious. She'd never be able to get up.

'So, you're a local?' he said.

'I've lived here all my life.' She gave a wry grin. 'I didn't even go to university.'

He shrugged. 'Why would you want to be anywhere else?'

'It's a very small town, which isn't always a good thing.' The incriminating postcard flashed into her mind again and she took a sip of her drink to chase it away. 'Though it can be. We do all stick together when the going gets tough.'

'When the tourists start playing up?'

'Not so much that. The tourists are our bread and butter.' She hesitated. 'You know about the lifeboat disaster, right?'

He nodded. 'Twenty years ago, wasn't it?'

'Twenty years this August. I lost my father.' Like him, she felt the need to get the tragedy out in the open.

'Oh God.' His face looked anguished.

'And my sister Jess's husband.' She had to force herself to say his name. 'Rik.'

'That's terrible. I'm so sorry.'

'It was a pretty tough time.' Nikki managed a smile. 'But we stuck together. And the town's got big plans to commemorate the anniversary this summer. I'm on the committee, for my sins.'

'It's important, isn't it? Not to forget. I've been to the museum. It was very moving.'

There was a tiny museum on the harbour front. For the tenth anniversary, a special exhibition had been unveiled. Lifesize photos of all of the men who'd been lost – five from the lifeboat and two from the fishing vessel they were trying to save – with their biographies, and testimonials from their loved ones, so they would never be forgotten.

'My mum was instrumental in organising that. I think it helped her.'

'I guess you never really get over it.'

Nikki shrugged. 'You just have to carry on.' Even today she wasn't sure how she'd managed to. But she'd had to, for her mum and Graham. And Jess. Especially Jess.

'Yes,' he said quietly, 'you do.'

There was silence for a moment while they contemplated their respective losses. Nikki stared at a painting of a stormy sea propped up against the wall. There were three of them, presumably waiting to be hung. Nikki pointed her glass at them.

'Those are wonderful.'

They were large, with bold brushstrokes, showing the same view of the sea at three different times of day: one dark navy, one pearl grey and one blushing with pinks and purples.

'Jill painted them. The last time we were down together. I thought they'd look good in here.'

'They're spectacular. She's captured the view perfectly.'

'I need to find someone to hang them.' He looked embarrassed. 'I'm an absolute klutz when it comes to DIY.'

'I can do it for you.'

'Honestly?'

'I'm the DIY queen.' She grinned. 'I can go and get my drill, if you want.' She put her glass on the coffee table. 'I'd better not have any more of that, though, or they won't be straight.'

'That would be amazing. You put me to shame.'

'I was born with a spirit level in my hand.'

'The perfect neighbour. I'm afraid I'm useless at anything practical. Though I can cook.'

She spread her hands. 'Well, I can't. I can eat though.'

'Looks like we're well-matched, then.'

'Give me five minutes.'

Back at home, she headed for her toolbox to find a power drill, a tape measure and some proper picture hooks. As she gathered together what she needed, she mulled over Adam. He was obviously still deep in the grieving process. She would do her best to look out for him, for he might find it difficult from time to time, being in a strange place.

And no one knew the vagaries of grief better than she did. How very lost you could feel. How desperate you could be for a hand to reach out and grab you, even if you shunned it at the time.

5

When she came back, Adam was staring down at the paintings.

'Which order?' he said. 'I think it should go pink, grey, blue – sunrise, middle of the day, night.'

'That makes sense to me. But they're the same size so you can swap them around if you want to.'

'She painted them in real time, you know. On the same day. Out on the decking at the back.' He mimed standing in front of a canvas with a paintbrush. 'Bish bash bosh.'

'That's incredible.'

'I'm a complete underachiever in comparison.'

'What *do* you do?' Nikki was curious. She couldn't hazard a guess. It was difficult to pigeonhole him. He was quite posh, but not gratingly so. Smart, but not a know-it-all. Artistic, but not totally bohemian.

'Nothing very glamorous, I'm afraid. I'm an accountant. For creatives. Not a creative accountant – that's something very different.' He laughed. 'Artists, musicians, writers – a motley crew who have one thing in common: they hate numbers. So I hold their hands and try and make their life easier.'

'That sounds interesting.'

'It can be. Though they don't tend to want to talk to me about their work. More about what they can claim on expenses. You wouldn't believe what they try and get away with.'

Nikki laughed. She'd run her tape measure across the wall and marked out where she thought the paintings should go. She held one of them in place so he could assess.

'I reckon that's about the right height?'

He stood back and looked at it. 'Perfect.'

'OK. I'll get drilling. If you're happy?'

'Let's do it. We can always patch it up if it doesn't look right.'

A little while later, the picture hooks were up and the two of them manoeuvred the pictures into place. Nikki had to admit they looked very striking against the yellow. She would never have dared choose it as a colour, but it worked.

Adam took them in, his eyes roaming over every last detail.

'Thank you,' he said. There was a slight tremor in his voice, and he pushed at his glasses. 'Right, I think you deserve another drink for all that endeavour.'

He hurried over to the bar and made himself busy. Nikki brushed up the dust from the drill holes and tidied away her things, setting them by the front door. On a console table under the window, she noticed a wedding photograph: Adam looking considerably younger, his hair raven-black, in a cream Nehru jacket, gazing at a woman who must be Jill. She was tall and elegant, wearing a silk embroidered kimono, her pale blonde hair piled up on her head, her eyes warm and laughing.

'Here we go.'

Adam turned from the bar, holding out a fresh glass.

'Thank you. That's a beautiful photo.'

'It was a beautiful day. We got married at Kew Gardens.'

'I'm a wedding planner, so I'm a bit obsessed with wedding photos.'

'A wedding planner? Wow. You must be a romantic.'

Nikki went to sit back down on the sofa. She took a sip of her drink, pondering his statement. Was she? She did love her job. Nothing gave her more joy than seeing a happy couple enjoy a perfect day with their friends and family, then head off into the sunset to start a new life together. But a romantic?

'Maybe,' she said, but there was doubt in her voice. 'Though I always think it's ironic I've never been married.' She laughed. 'I sort of did things in the wrong order. Had a baby with my childhood sweetheart, and we were going to tie the knot but then realised we weren't really meant to be together.' She always felt a rush of fondness when she thought about Woody, Bill's dad. 'But the lovely thing is we're still great friends. People keep asking me if I've found anyone else yet. They don't seem to understand that I'm quite happy on my own.'

Apart from anything, thought Nikki, she didn't have *time* for anyone else in her life.

Adam rolled his eyes. 'People ask me that too. I find it really rude.'

'I know! As if you're incomplete without another person.'

'I can't imagine having anyone else in my life. I've got

my kids, of course, but Eva's in Berlin, ensconced in the art world. She inherited her mum's talent. And Oscar's working in finance in New York. My head for figures, I guess, but much better than me at making money.' He ran his foot along Gatsby's back. 'Meanwhile, I've got Gatsby. He's all I need. For the time being, anyway.'

'I'd love a dog, but I'm out of the house too much. It wouldn't be fair.'

'I don't know where I'd be without him, to be honest.' Adam jumped up. 'Let me get something to snack on or we'll be footless.'

He disappeared off towards the kitchen, Gatsby shadowing him. Nikki sank back into the sofa, sipping her gimlet, feeling herself relax. It was bliss, after the last few days of chasing solicitors and poor Joel, wondering if the sale would go through or collapse at the last minute for some unforeseen reason, plus panicking she had over-stretched herself and would regret buying it. It was an investment, she reminded herself, and the happiness it was bringing her already was worth every penny.

Adam came back with an earthenware bowl of home-made hummus, lemony and garlicky and strewn with pine nuts and fresh coriander. Nikki realised she was ravenous as she picked up a triangle of warm pitta and dug in.

'Oh my God,' she said. 'This is the food of the gods.'

'It's my weak spot,' said Adam. 'It's about a million calories a teaspoon but I could live on it.'

'God, me too.' Nikki hoped she didn't seem greedy as she scooped up another dollop.

'Fill your boots. It'll stop me eating it. I really miss having someone to cook for.' A shadow flickered over his face for a moment. 'I could give you some to take home.'

'I might have to get you to supply us for our grazing platters.'

'What's a grazing platter?'

'You know, a big wooden board covered in charcuterie and cheese and fruit and dips and . . . well, anything you can think of, really.'

'Maybe that could be my side hustle. Or I could just give you the recipe. Do you do all the catering?'

'Not me. I'm a hopeless cook. I use a company that have a unit next to me. Though my mother does the cakes.'

'What a lovely job that must be. Wedding cakes.'

'Don't underestimate the stress. There's a lot of high emotion. But she loves doing them. It's what gave me the idea for the business. She was getting swamped with orders, and we realised loads of people were coming here to get married. So, I set up The Seaside Wedding Company.'

'Smart move. Smart name.'

'Lots of people have jumped on the bandwagon since. But I was the first and I like to think I'm the best.'

'Well, I'm sure you are.'

'In the meantime, whatever you need, just let me know,' she told him. 'Chimney sweep, window cleaner. Log delivery. I'll make sure you're not ripped off. People can take the mickey if they think you're from up country.'

'And who can blame them?' said Adam. 'I'll take you up on that. I might need someone who can look after Gatsby if I go up to London. I'll need to go and meet clients once or twice a month.'

In response to hearing his name, Gatsby rolled onto his back on the Moroccan rug and waved his legs in the air.

'My niece Juno is a dog walker,' said Nikki. 'She gets very booked up but I'll put in a good word.'

'I can't believe I've moved in next to *the* person to know.'

Nikki looked at her watch and realised it was nearly nine. The time had flown by. She jumped up.

'I'd better go. I need to get up at the crack of dawn and fill the skip. If you've got any rubbish you want to chuck in, feel free.'

Too much gin was making her babble. She didn't have much head for booze these days. It was definitely time to go.

Adam walked with her to the door. She picked up her tools.

'Thank you so much for a lovely time.'

'You're very welcome.'

He opened the door, then leaned in to kiss her as he had when she arrived. On both cheeks this time. It was a very London gesture. In Speedwell, no one kissed you unless they wanted something more.

'I think,' he said, 'I'm rather lucky to have you as a neighbour. If there's anything I can do in return . . .'

'Cocktails is just fine,' said Nikki hastily, backing out before she made an idiot of herself.

By the time she got home, she felt a bit swimmy. The gimlets had basically been neat gin with an afterthought of lime juice. It was too late to cook so she drank a big glass of water before getting ready for bed. Her first night in her new home. The bedroom she'd chosen was the largest one at the back. She jumped under the duvet while the anaesthetic of the gin was still going strong. Hopefully she'd fall asleep straight away.

She didn't. The unaccustomed alcohol and the rich hummus meant her mind was doing overtime. She was still awake at midnight when a wild wind got up, whipping itself into a frenzy around the little house, screeching and keening. As hard as she tried not to feel unsettled, it unlocked memories. And with the memories came guilt, guilt she had long since buried. Or was it shame? It was hard to distinguish between the two. Whichever it was, it seeped into her, filling her body with a thrumming anxiety that kept sleep at bay.

She thought of the card she'd received, ripped up into little shreds. The words still imprinted on her memory. *There are no secrets in a small town.* She sighed and turned over for the hundredth time, smoothing her pillow.

What if she hadn't been in the harbour that morning, the day he arrived? Would everything have turned out differently? There was no way of knowing, so she should stop torturing herself. She'd asked herself that question often enough. She breathed, in for four, out for four, and let her mind float back in time.

Sometimes she let herself remember the beginning. Just enough detail to keep it as a dream, reliving the good bits and stopping before it all went wrong.

6

Twenty years earlier

Rik Mahoney-Chambord sailed into Speedwell harbour on a summer's morning as the sun rose, gilding his salty bleached-blond locks. He stood at the helm in a pair of cut-off Levi's, and scanned the quay as if searching for a girl he'd left behind long ago. His father was from Cork and his mother from Toulouse, which was how he'd come by his charm, his warm blood and his preposterous name. It was hard to know which was drawing more attention: his lean torso the colour of the golden fudge sold in the Candy Cabin, or the gleaming wood and brass of his vintage yacht.

The harbour was calm as he docked, the waves lapping a gentle welcome, the early morning light dancing off the water. You could feel something shift in the little town; an alertness, a wariness. They welcomed strangers every week, but this one felt different. From the wheelhouse, Kris Kristofferson sang about coming down on a Sunday morning. Glances were exchanged. Eyebrows raised. And Nikki North, on her way back from the mini-market with a fresh loaf and a packet of bacon, stopped in her tracks. She lifted up her sunglasses and smiled.

'Well, hello, sailor,' she sang under her breath, then went and sat on the harbour wall to see what he did next. She hadn't meant to stay out so late, because Sunday would have been much better spent without a hangover, but there'd been a great band on and then a lock-in and once you'd got past midnight at the Neptune you were in for the long haul. She looked down at last night's clothes: cargo pants and a cropped singlet that exposed her tanned stomach, and a denim jacket. Could be worse.

The boat was called *The Lady Stardust*, and she watched her captain jump onto the pontoon and stride along it, pulling on a sweatshirt and shaking out his shaggy locks as his head popped out of the neck. She could hear him whistling 'Brandy (You're a Fine Girl)' and immediately her interest in him doubled, for the seventies' classic was their pub anthem. Someone would put it on the jukebox and they'd all join in, roaring away with gusto, then go back to their drinking and talking as the last note faded, as if nothing had happened. Her eyes followed him until he reached the quayside and she began to sing along.

He stopped, put his hands in his pockets and grinned at her. Nikki felt as if the sun had just come out, even though it was already shining.

'My favourite thing about that song,' he told her, 'is how many girls have been named after it.'

'Really?'

'Yep. And if I wasn't like the guy in the song, and actually managed to stay ashore long enough to settle down, I'd call my daughter Brandy.'

'Never say never,' said Nikki, feeling a sudden rush of boldness. 'You might not have met the right girl yet.'

'Maybe.' His gaze swept up and down the parade of

shops on the seafront. 'What are the chances of getting some breakfast around here, do you think?'

'It's a bit early yet.' Nikki hoped her mascara wasn't smudged. If there was any left at all. 'But if you wait here, I can bring you a bacon sandwich.'

She held up the carrier bag containing her hangover cure. Please say yes, she thought.

He looked pleased. 'That would be amazing.'

'Ketchup or brown sauce?'

'Brown sauce,' he said. 'Thank you. It's not often you get a welcome like this in a strange town.'

'Welcome to Speedwell,' said Nikki, and they locked gazes. His eyes were the pale denim-blue of his shorts, and she found herself drowning in them, momentarily at a loss for what to do or say. Then gathered herself together and pointed at the bench overlooking the harbour. 'Wait there. I'll be back in ten minutes.'

Exhilarated by her encounter, she ran along the seafront with its cafés and sweet shops and funny little emporiums that kept the tourists happy, then dived off between two buildings. Speedwell was full of secret passages. A warren of cobbled walkways leading to walled gardens and court-yards and hidden houses. And right in the heart of this maze was Mariners – square, white, Georgian, rambling – the North family home.

She burst into the kitchen where her dad was sitting at the table with a brown pot of tea in front of him. He looked up and raised an eyebrow with a smile. It was usually her sister Jess who strolled in at this time, not Nikki.

'Good night?' he asked. He was in his usual plaid shirt and jeans, and she felt a burst of affection for his solid, grounding presence. It brought her back down to earth, for she feared she had lost her head. She went to give him a hug. He smelled of tea and toothpaste and beard oil. Reassuring.

'It was fun,' she said. 'A classic Neptune lock-in. Want a bacon sandwich?'

'I've had my breakfast.' He watched as she grabbed a frying pan to put on the stove.

'Mum still in bed?' she asked.

'Yes. I'll take her up something in a minute.'

'I can do some extra bacon for her?'

'I think she'd just like a cup of tea. She was still asleep when I got up.'

'She deserves a lie-in.' Nikki peeled off two thick rashers and placed them in the pan.

'I know. She does too much.'

'She wouldn't have it any other way, Dad. You know that.'

Her mum Helen rarely stood still. She helped with the family business, made wedding cakes, raised funds for the lifeboat station and was always there to pull something delicious out of the oven at seven o'clock. It was probably why all three of the North children, Nikki and Jess and Graham, were still at home. At twenty-three, Nikki had somehow forgotten to leave, and was still working for her dad five years after leaving school.

'Morning, campers.'

Nikki looked up from the stove to see her sister Jess saunter in. She was dressed in a short satin dressing gown with a tiger embroidered on the back, her dark hair wild, her legs long and brown.

'Hey.'

'Who's that for?' Jess eyed the bacon with longing.

'I'm making a sandwich for Woody.' The lie was effortless but necessary.

'Where is he? Can't he make his own?'

'We were watching the sun come up. In the harbour.'

'Oh.' Jess gave her a knowing look. 'How romantic.'

Nikki rolled her eyes. 'There's nothing between us.'

'Yeah, right.' Jess reached out to steal a rasher of bacon.

'Oi.' Nikki flicked her with the fish slice. 'Hands off. Make your own.'

'I've got to go to work! I'm due on shift at eight. Saving lives!'

Nikki knew that if she didn't give in there would be hell to pay. Jess was an A & E nurse, in the hospital in Tawcombe, a small town three miles up the coast just over the border into North Devon. She slid the bacon between two slices of bread and handed it to her sister, then lay two more pieces in the pan, praying her beautiful stranger hadn't been side-tracked while waiting for his breakfast.

'Say thank you,' William said to Jess.

'Thanks,' said Jess, with her mouth full, glaring at her dad and giving Nikki a thumbs-up.

Five minutes later, brown sauce liberally applied, Nikki wrapped her sandwich in tin foil and patted her dad on the head as she headed for the door.

'See you all later.'

'See you, love.'

'Send my love to Woody,' sang Jess, and Nikki wasn't sure if she detected a note of sarcasm in her voice. Thank goodness she was heading to work and wouldn't be swinging by the harbour. The last thing she wanted was her sister getting in on the act.

*

To Nikki's relief, the new arrival was still sitting on the bench when she got back. She had never felt this kind of urgency before. She wasn't given to chasing men. Not that she was chasing him, exactly, but she was beguiled. She slowed to a walk as she approached, catching her breath, wishing she'd had time to shower and change. He was leaning with his arms stretched along the back of the bench, his blond hair touching the neck of his sweatshirt, one long brown leg crossed over the over.

'One bacon sandwich with brown sauce.' She leaned over the back of the bench and waved it under his nose.

'You angel!' He smiled up at her. 'You've got no idea how much I've been craving this.'

She sat next to him on the bench as he began to eat. He couldn't get it in fast enough.

'I should have made you two.'

'No, this is perfect. Want a bite?' He proffered the uneaten half.

'I'm fine,' she said, even though the prospect of sharing his sandwich was quite appealing.

'You're a pro. This is just the right amount of crispy, just the right amount of sauce.'

She laughed. 'I'm highly trained.'

In two minutes, it was all gone. Nikki panicked that would be it, that he would thank her and slip out of reach.

'So what are you doing here? In sunny Speedwell?'

'I was told the most beautiful girl in the world lived here.'

He was looking at her, his eyes teasing. There was a smear of brown sauce on his top lip. She longed to reach out and wipe it off.

'Ha ha,' she replied. 'But beauty isn't everything, you know.'

'No,' he said. 'The ability to make a decent bacon sarnie is far more important.'

She paused, then pointed at his face.

'You've got a blob of brown sauce, just there.'

He tapped his face till she nodded, then wiped it off.

'Better?'

'Yep.'

There was silence for a moment. Nikki scrabbled for what to say next. Her conversation so far hadn't been scintillating, and he wasn't very forthcoming.

'Do you need somebody to show you around?' she managed finally.

'I usually prefer to explore by myself.'

'Fair enough.'

'Usually,' he said, standing up. 'But I get the feeling you might be a fun tour guide.'

'Whatever you want, I'll make it happen.'

'That's quite a promise.' His eyes glinted. There seemed to be sparks of copper amidst the blue.

Nikki laughed. 'Within reason. This is a quiet seaside town. Basically, if you want chips, or a tattoo, you're sorted.'

'Right now, all I really want is a decent cup of coffee.'

'Tony's should be open by now.' She nodded her head along the front. 'Though define decent.'

'I'll make do with hot and wet.'

'You'll be fine, then. Come on.' She jumped up, and started heading along the cobbles of the quay. There were more people out and about now: early tourists, people heading for their boats, shop owners opening up. She could see her companion getting admiring glances – next to him, she felt insignificant, for he was dazzling. He walked like a rockstar, a carefree, confident saunter.

'What's your name, by the way?' she asked as they passed the Candy Cabin. The sugary, buttery scent of fudge was already filling the air as the first batch went into the copper vat.

'Rik,' he said. 'Without a c.'

'Snap. As in without a c. I'm Nikki. With two ks.'

'I know.'

She stopped in her tracks and stared at him.

'How?'

'I asked one of the fishermen while you were making my bacon sandwich. Asked him if there was anything I should know about you. He said you were all right.'

'All right?' She put her hands on her hips in indignation.

'In a nice way,' he went on. 'Said you were sound. He said the one I wanted to watch out for was your sister.'

'Oh,' said Nikki. 'Yes. Jess is . . .'

She didn't want to be disloyal. She didn't want to talk about Jess at all.

'Jess,' she managed finally, and pushed open the door of Tony's Café.

For years it had been a greasy spoon but when the eponymous Tony had died, his daughter took over and gave it a re-vamp. Now it was all paninis and hot chocolate with squirty cream on top. They took a seat right by the window so they could look out to sea, and Jess put her fingers up to order two coffees from Melinda, who gave her a double thumbs-up which could have been recognition of the order, or approval of her companion, or both.

'Seriously,' Nikki said, putting her head in one hand. 'What are you doing here? Speedwell isn't the kind of place you just happen upon. You have to make an effort to get here.'

The coast around Speedwell was notoriously tricky to navigate, with its hidden rocks and capricious tides.

'I've got a job with a boat builder in Tawcombe for the summer,' he said. 'I've been in the South of France since October and I wanted a change of scene.'

'I'd love to go to the South of France,' sighed Nikki. She tried to imagine it: azure seas and cocktails on board fancy yachts.

'I could take you there one day.' Did he mean that? Probably not. It was an easy offer to make

'Do you live on that boat, then?'

'Yep. It's the only thing I've got in the world. My dad left it to me when he died.'

'Oh.' She wasn't sure what to say.

She went to put a hand on his. He looked into her eyes as her fingers touched his skin. He smiled, and she blushed, and she didn't know what to do next. Luckily, Melinda brought their coffees over. Behind Rik, she looked at Nikki with wide eyes as she put their cups down on the table.

'Enjoy,' she said, and Nikki knew what she meant. She took her hand away and grabbed her cup.

'Thank you,' she said, trying not to grin.

Rik pulled his coffee towards him, picking up a packet of sugar and shaking it. 'I spend my life sailing from one place to the next, picking up work. One day I might find somewhere that feels like home.'

He seemed wistful. Nikki's heart buckled a little, wondering what he'd been through.

'Maybe Speedwell will be the place for you,' she joked. Suddenly it became a personal challenge, to make sure he stayed.

He looked out of the window. Today, the harbour was coquettish, picturesque, with its gaily coloured houses painted pink, yellow and blue, the cobbled quay, the cliffs rising up in the distance, seagulls circling. The sun threw droplets of silver onto the water, sparkling so brightly it made your eyes hurt.

'Maybe,' he said eventually.

'I'm heading to the secret beach for a swim later,' she said. 'If you want to come?'

'The *secret* beach?'

'Yep.' She put her finger to her lips, her eyes dancing. 'If I show you, you have to promise not to reveal its whereabouts to anyone.'

He nodded solemnly. 'I'm very good at keeping secrets.'

'Then you can come. We just need to grab some picnic stuff.'

'I need to get some provisions anyway, for the boat.'

'Let's go to the mini-mart, then.' She tapped her hands on the table to seal the deal, nodding to Melinda for the bill.

Wandering around the shop with Rik had a mundane intimacy that was strangely thrilling. Nikki threw Pringles and Cheesy Wotsits and pork pies into the basket as he took milk and coffee from the shelf then lit upon a packet of custard creams with glee.

'You can't get these in St Tropez.'

Nikki laughed. 'I wouldn't know.'

He dug her in the ribs with his elbow.

'Ow,' she protested, laughing. He inspected the contents of her basket, frowned, then walked off and came back with a French stick, salami and tomatoes, and grapes and oranges. Nikki realised they were being stared at by the other customers in the shop. She was mesmerised by how lightly he wore his allure, oblivious to the looks and the nudges as he wandered amidst the shelves, picking things up to examine them, rejecting some, tossing others into the basket.

When he took it from her and went to the till to pay, she protested.

'I insist,' he said. 'I'd have paid a hundred quid for that bacon sandwich.' He pulled out a battered wallet, refusing to let her contribute.

Kind, too. Did it get any better? She bent her head so he couldn't see her smile. She was fizzing inside like a sherbet dip dab.

'Come on, then,' he said, picking up the carrier bag. 'Show me this secret beach of yours.'

7

'Bloody hell!'

Nikki's heart swelled with pride as Rik stood at the top of the cliff surveying the view beneath them. The beach was looking its very best, the cliffs outlined in black against the bluest of skies, the sea twinkling an invitation, the sand glittering in the sunshine as if it had been scattered with diamond dust. There was no one else in sight. A private paradise.

'I mean, the coast of Ireland is wilder than wild and the South of France is out of this world, but this is better than both of them.'

'It's pretty special,' said Nikki.

'Do a lot of people come here?'

'Not really. It's such an effort to get to. We usually have it to ourselves.'

'So it really is a secret beach?'

'Yes.' In a moment of impulse, Nikki put a hand over his mouth and whispered in his ear. 'You're never to breathe a word, remember, or I'll have to have you keelhauled.'

She could feel the warmth of his mouth on her palm.

She could tell he was smiling. She took her hand away, surprised by her own boldness at such an intimate gesture.

'Come on. Let's get in the water.'

She led the way, bounding down the steps, and he scrambled after her, surefooted even though he hadn't had the benefit of years of practice like she had.

They spent ages in the sea, swimming until they were out of their depth. Rik moved effortlessly through the water, lithe and streamlined, his skin gleaming gold. Despite his perfection, Nikki felt no self-consciousness next to him, even though her skin was pale against her red swimsuit. She was a strong swimmer and easily kept up with him. They lay floating on their backs and looking up at the vast expanse of sky.

'I could lie here forever,' said Rik.

'You'll get wrinkly fingertips,' said Nikki, but she understood why he might want to. Out here, with nothing to do but float, life seemed easy and uncomplicated as any worries drifted away on the tide. Not that she had many, but she worked hard and it was the place that always relaxed her and made her forget lists and schedules.

Afterwards, they stretched themselves out on the flat rock that was just big enough for two and let the sun dry the water on their skin. Behind it were a series of interlinked caves, just about head height. No one would know you were in there unless they knew about them. Centuries ago, they were used by smugglers to store brandy, though you'd have to know the coastline well to make your way in by boat without coming to grief on the rocks.

'I'd do anything for one of those grapes right now,' said Rik, his arms behind his head.

'Anything?' Nikki sat up, rummaged in the shopping

bag and found the bunch he'd bought earlier. She pulled them off their stalks and dropped them into his mouth, one by one, laughing. He kept his eyes shut, but he was laughing too.

'Enough!' he pleaded, opening his eyes wide. He put his hand up to hold her wrist, and she felt a jolt as his fingers touched her skin, and his grip tightened around her. They froze for a few seconds, him gazing up at her, her looking down at him, then he released her and put his arms behind his head again.

She sat beside him, her heart hammering. All she wanted to do was roll on top of him, feel the full length of her body against his, but she had no real idea if he was into her or if this was just two people enjoying an afternoon on the beach and messing about.

Instead, she pulled two cans of cider out of the bag and passed him one, resisting the urge to press the cold metal against his skin to make him jump.

'No, thanks,' he said. 'I don't drink.'

'Oh.' She hastily put the cans back in the bag. 'Sorry.'

'There's no need to be sorry. It's just . . . my dad died of *the drink*, as they say. It's kind of put me off.'

'I guess it would. I'm really sorry,' she said, aware she was repeating herself.

'It was his own fault. He'd had enough warning. But I worry it's, you know, in the blood. So I just avoid it.'

'That makes sense.'

'I always wonder what my life would have been like, if he hadn't been such a slave to it.' He stared up at the sky. 'My mum and dad met in the South of France when he came to deliver a yacht. They had a passionate fling, and my mum came back to Kinsale with him, thinking she was going to live the Irish dream. They got pregnant with me, and it all fell apart pretty quickly. My dad refused to marry her and she was gutted.'

'I'm not surprised.'

He shrugged. 'He was young. He didn't want to get tied down. And I think he knew he couldn't cope with the responsibility and things would turn bad.' He mimed drinking from a glass. 'So Mum went back to Toulouse. I spent my childhood bouncing between the two of them. He'd come over to France to get me, take me back to Kinsale, and I'd spend the summer there. Dad would throw me the odd ham roll and the odd sausage. He wasn't great at looking after me but he taught me a lot about boats. I loved it. Come autumn, I had to go back to school in France. I went back to Kinsale when I was sixteen to live with him, but I realised my dad was falling apart. The drink was making him pretty sick.'

'Oh dear.'

'Yeah.' He was silent for a moment. 'He died a couple of years later. I didn't cope very well. I went back to France, fell out with my mum because I was drinking too. Then I got my act together, went and collected *The Lady Stardust*. And I've been drifting about ever since. Trying to find my place in the world. Trying to find my people.'

'Oh,' said Nikki softly, her heart going out to him. 'That's a sad story.'

'I spent my life wondering why I wasn't enough to keep them together. Why he loved drinking more than he loved me.'

Nikki felt tears spring into her eyes. She wanted to reach over and hug him, but she didn't quite dare, for he seemed a little tense, as if there was a barrier round him. He turned to look at her, his eyes half closed in the afternoon sun.

'Your turn.'

'Oh. Um – really boring. Mum and Dad were born and bred here and are as happy as anything. There are three of us. My older sister's a nurse, and I work for my dad, and my brother will probably take over from him when he finishes college. Dull as ditchwater.'

'No.' Rik sat up. 'You've got it cracked. You're all in it together, in the most beautiful place on earth.'

'Speedwell?'

'Can't you see that?'

'It's pretty, but it's not very exciting. Not very glamorous.'

'Trust me, I've seen glamorous in the South of France. All they worry about is money and being thin and who's got the biggest boat.'

'Oh.'

'Here seems much more real.' He propped himself up on his elbows. 'Though not this. This is *un*real. Maybe I could bring the boat round and moor it out there and we could live here all summer.'

Nikki felt a thrill rush through her. *We*. She pictured his boat out in the bay, the two of them on deck as the sun set, then snuggled up in a wooden bed in the cabin, falling asleep in each other's arms.

'I'm not sure if you'd be allowed to moor out there all summer,' she said.

'I was only kidding,' he said, batting her leg with the back of his hand.

Her heart fell, and she felt embarrassed she'd taken him seriously. What an idiot. And now she didn't know what to say, so she bundled up her jacket as a pillow and lay down beside him. They stayed silent for a few minutes, basking in the afternoon sun, then she looked over and realised he was fast asleep.

She stared at him, his dirty-blond hair spread out on the rock, his long lashes resting on his cheek, his perfect mouth. It was as if an angel had fallen from the sky and landed next to her. When he woke, they went for another swim, then shared an orange, dividing the segments between them.

Just before sunset they walked up the steps and back into town, sun-kissed and sleepy. The harbour was always magical at night. Moonlight lit up the cobbles and outlined the houses, while a cool breeze fluttered, setting the halyards clanking their plangent, atonal symphony. The water shimmered between the boats, lapping the harbour wall in a soothing rhythm.

'Thank you for a perfect afternoon,' he said.

Perfect. Nikki felt her very bones fill with syrupy pleasure.

He nodded his head towards his boat, and lifted up the shopping bag.

'I can do you a coffee, if you want. With custard creams.'

Nikki hesitated. She really wasn't sure what was behind his invitation. If he meant more than coffee, or if he was just being polite. She didn't think she could take the pressure of wondering whether he'd make a move. And if he did, and one thing led to another, she would then have the agony of the whole of Speedwell seeing her coming off his boat tomorrow morning. And then she would spend the next day wondering what it had meant, and if it would go any further, or if he would move on to someone else. She wasn't certain enough or confident enough to put herself through the torture.

You're a coward, she told herself. Jess would be up the pontoon before you could say one-night stand. And if it was just a one-night stand, she wouldn't care. But they were very different.

Besides, she really needed to get to bed because they had a big scheduling meeting at North Property Management first thing tomorrow and she needed her wits about her.

'I'd better not,' she said. 'School day tomorrow.'

He clicked his fingers and pointed at her. 'You're right. I've got to get up early and get the bus to Tawcombe. Let's be sensible. Another time.'

Her stomach flipped at the thought of another time. Of not being sensible.

'Night, then.'

He stepped forward for a hug. His sweatshirt was soft around her. He smelled of salt and the orange they'd eaten. She wanted to turn her face to his and taste that orange on his lips. She wasn't sure if she could bear another moment of the bliss of being in his arms, so after a few seconds she stepped away, then suddenly felt cold.

'See you soon,' he murmured, and turned away.

She watched him head back along the pontoon, swinging the shopping bag. Then he jumped on board his boat and disappeared from view. She felt overwhelmed by the memory of the afternoon, how he had opened up to her, how close they had felt, even though nothing had happened. She wanted to run after him, jump on board the boat and fall into his arms.

But instead she turned away and walked back home to Mariners.

8

Now

Early on Sunday morning, Helen North sat in the quiet of the kitchen. She'd already put the pork in the Aga – it was a six-hour Jamie Oliver recipe, a family favourite – and was about to make a lemon meringue pie. But first she was going to sit down with tea and a croissant and mull over the realisation that had crept up on her over the past few months.

It was time to find someone to share her life.

She sat in her husband's chair, a comfy, worn old wheelback made of oak, and looked over at the photo of him that stood on the third shelf of the dresser: William outside the Neptune in his big navy jumper with the roll neck, clutching the handle of a pint glass, the harbour wall behind him and the glittering water beyond. She wondered how he would look now. His beard would be all white, probably, because the last time she had seen him there had been glints of silver. He would still be fit, because he never stood still – there would be no unsightly paunch. Perhaps he would wear glasses? He'd still be working, she knew that. Retirement would bore him. Which would drive their son Graham nuts, probably! She smiled at the thought of them squabbling, over what Graham would call interference and William would consider helping. Though maybe she would have been able to persuade him to take a back seat and go and see a bit of the world? They'd rarely had time for holidays, with the family and the business and the lifeboat. William always said who needs a holiday when you live in Speedwell, and Helen had mostly agreed, but sometimes she'd felt a pang of longing for a different sun, a different view, a different language.

And now, at the age of sixty-seven, she had come to the realisation that she was longing for something even more. It had crept up on her gradually, this urge, and it took her a while to identify what it was she craved. It was companionship.

Widowhood had been tough, but it had never been lonely. There had been too many people around for that. People who needed her as much as she needed them, for she was not the only one to lose a husband that day, and her children had lost a father. They had clung together, bewildered and bereft, and moments alone had been rare.

She hadn't been ready before now. Twenty years was an awfully long time, she supposed, but there were no rules about how long it took. She would never find anyone like William. He was irreplaceable. She wanted someone from out of town, because she knew all the available men in Speedwell, and none of them were what she was looking for.

Whoever he was, he would need to share some of William's qualities. He would need to be confident. Comfortable in his own skin. Independent. Solvent.

Kind. A family man, preferably, for it was important for a partner to understand that family often came first.

But there were other qualities she needed this time. She wanted someone who would give her the confidence to step out of her comfort zone. William had been physically adventurous, but he had never wanted to stray far from Speedwell. He'd had no interest in foreign travel, or cities. And Helen had found herself hungering for both of those lately. She dreamed of wandering the streets of Venice or Vienna or Istanbul. Of devouring *cacio e pepe* or *sachertorte*. Seeing the sun rise over the Bosphorus.

There were companies who catered for single travellers, but somehow that didn't appeal. She wanted someone to plan with, to debate the merits of which city to choose, which hotel to stay in. To wander out on a warm evening and stroll until the perfect restaurant presented itself.

It wasn't too late, was it?

She knew she had to be proactive if her wish was to come true. Mr Right wasn't going to knock on the front door and say, 'Pack your bags! I've booked us into the Hotel Cipriani.' And online was the modern way.

She'd tentatively signed up to a dating app for widows and widowers called Sunshine After the Rain. You put up your profile, and you could match with other people whose interests you shared, then meet up for no-strings walks or cinema trips or whatever you had in common. And it seemed that quite often companionship led to romance, if the testimonials were anything to go by.

Robert and I hit it off straight away. After a few lovely months getting to know each other – woodland walks, trips to the theatre, candlelit suppers – we are engaged to be married! I never thought I would feel like this again . . .

Helen felt her heart melt as she read similar stories. Was there someone out there who would be her partner in crime, and egg her on to do something out of the ordinary? Nothing too wild. She wasn't about to hare off to Argentina to take up tango. But she really should expand her horizons before it was too late. She adored her house and the sea and the coast and her job and her family, but she knew there was more out there. And now was the time. Another five or ten years and it might be too late. If she didn't act now, she would never know what other wonders the world held.

She had played around with writing her profile, agonising over how to present herself. She'd pored over other women's profiles, with their solo trips to Mexico and their award-winning business ventures and their charity challenges. In the end, she decided to go with the truth. And now she just needed to find some photographs. There was one of her blowing out the candles on her cake on her last birthday, but it wasn't very flattering as her cheeks were all puffed out. She'd tried taking selfies, but she couldn't get it right at all, not like Juno, who always looked like Angelina Jolie when she took one. Helen just looked as if she was grimacing, or her eyes seemed to cross. It was so frustrating. She didn't want to look airbrushed and glamorous, for she didn't want to present a false image – but she wanted to look nice.

Maybe she should have some professional shots done? There were examples of women her age looking like something out of a magazine – wandering through an autumn wood dressed in cream cashmere, curled up by a roaring log fire holding a glass of wine, riding along on a mint-green bicycle with a basket on the front. But the photos looked completely staged and had obviously been touched up, leading to disappointment in real life. And the last thing she wanted was to see someone's face fall as she turned up for their first meeting.

She sat for a moment considering her options. She was going to have to ask for help. Nikki and Jess would give her some advice. She wasn't sure what they would think, whether they would be thrilled to bits and cheer her on, or if they would think it was disrespectful to their dad.

She looked up again at the photo of William. Twenty years since she had felt his strong arms around her, felt his beard brush her cheek as he had kissed her goodbye before heading out into the storm that afternoon. She imagined what would have happened if that dreadful day had gone differently, and he'd walked back into the room a few hours later. She would have taken off his wet things and hung them up, found him dry clothes and sat him down in this very chair while she got him a shot of warming whisky and a plate of food, like she'd done countless times after a shout. She'd have listened to his tale of how the rescue had gone, the risks they'd taken, the bravery they'd shown . . .

She sighed. She had enough common sense to know she wasn't betraying William. She knew he would think she should have ventured out of her shell a long time ago. He had never been a jealous man. He had been practical, and would have known full well it didn't mean she didn't still love him, for she always would.

'Go for it, Helly,' she heard him saying now, in that broad burr redolent of sea and shipwrecks. 'You're a wonderful woman. Find someone who deserves you and will look after you. Just don't settle for second best.'

9

After her evening with Adam, Nikki woke much later than she intended. It was gone eight o'clock and she should already be hard at work, but she'd lain awake for hours and had then fallen into a velvety dark blue slumber.

She lay still for a moment, not sure which of her emotions to deal with. Her veins were buzzing and her stomach was flittering, not with butterflies but something more menacing. Black moths. She had been so looking forward to waking up in the cottage with that special new-house feeling, but the postcard had taken the shine off her excitement.

She dragged herself out of bed and went to the window. Last night's storm had died down, and everything outside looked slightly the worse for wear, the grass and hedges flattened, the trees hunched sideways. The sea looked swollen, the surface rolling like a drunken sailor after a night on the rum. But the sun was peeping through, and she was tempted to head down the steps to the beach for a swim. The silkiness of the water on her skin would lower her heart rate as she gave herself up to it, becoming weightless, cradled like a baby. But she wanted to get the stair carpet up and into the skip before she went for Sunday lunch at her mum's. Besides, she was on call today for the lifeboat, and this was just the kind of day people might get into trouble in the water, fooled by the sunshine. She got dressed quickly, checked her pager and stuck it on her waistband.

She headed to the kitchen to make a coffee. Her mouth was dry and her head throbbed: too many gimlets and a bad night's sleep were probably the last thing she had needed, but she didn't regret them. She felt comforted by the thought of Adam and Gatbsy next door. Both of them were a rather reassuring presence, offsetting her uncertainty.

She started a list in her head, of who could possibly be behind the message. It was impossible to imagine who had kept quiet for so long and chosen to speak up now. She'd thought that no one knew her secret, except Woody, and he would take it to his grave. Never in a million years would he betray her, the mother of his son. In a funny way, they loved each other even more than when they'd been together, albeit not in a romantic way. It was a love based on mutual respect and trust and their adoration of the boy they shared. It was unbreakable.

Wasn't it? For a moment, Nikki's belief in their bond wavered. But what possible reason could Woody have to cause her such anguish? He was a straightforward soul, not given to jealousy or bitterness or revenge. She refused to believe he'd have it in him, plus his handwriting was awful. This card wasn't his style at all.

Of course, she could be jumping to conclusions by assuming what the sender was alluding to. Perhaps she was guilty of some other transgression? Weddings were a high-octane business – had she slighted a bride somewhere along the way? She couldn't think of any instance where her clients were anything other than delighted. She had a drawer full of effusive thank-you letters in her office. They gave her confidence when she felt as if she was losing control, when all the loose ends were still loose and looking in danger of staying that way. Of course, everything was tied up in the end, in a beautiful bow, but it was always a race to the finishing line. And she was a perfectionist. Nothing was left to chance.

A terrible unease gnawed at her as she went from telling herself she was over-reacting, that no one could possibly know, to full-blown panic that her whole world was going to fall apart. She would be shunned, by her family, by the whole town. Her business would collapse. She would be thrown out of the lifeboat. They wouldn't want her as part of the team if they knew what she'd done.

She felt nauseous as she took a sip of her coffee. She probably needed food. A few scoops of hummus – admittedly the most delicious she'd ever had – wasn't really enough sustenance after the long day she'd had yesterday. She jammed some bread in the toaster and was shocked to find she was on the verge of tears. This should be a special moment, her first breakfast in the house of her dreams. She should be wandering out into the garden with her mug and enjoying the view, the breeze on her face. Instead, she wanted to slink back to bed and hide under the covers. Your past always catches up with you in the end, she thought. And it wasn't as if she'd ever been in any doubt that what she was doing was wrong.

The toast popped up, making her jump. She told herself

to get a grip. She had a lot to get through. She put on the radio to distract her then slathered butter and Marmite onto her toast. Being hungry and slightly hungover was always bad for anxiety.

She steeled herself for pulling up the stair carpet. It was filthy, and stubbornly stuck to the treads, and the nails savaged her fingers as she pulled at the edges, but it was absorbing work and her anxiety faded as she concentrated. It took ages to lever up the battens, but by midday, it was all in the skip and she was back in the bath, soaking away the grime.

She didn't have the energy left to cycle to lunch, so she took her van. She suddenly felt self-conscious, for her business name was emblazoned on the sides: The Seaside Wedding Company. It had never bothered her before, that people might know her movements, but she suddenly felt the need for anonymity. Who might be watching her, with knowing eyes, tracking her every move?

The vestiges of her dreams were still clinging to her, images and memories flashing into her mind. She remembered the first time she'd taken Rik to Mariners. How he had fallen under its spell.

Everyone always did.

10

Then

After their afternoon at the beach, Nikki didn't see Rik again for nearly a week. It wasn't for want of trying, for she kept her eyes peeled for a glimpse of him as she went about the town, but she supposed he was getting up early and coming home late from the boatyard. At last, on Thursday evening, she spied him on the deck of *The Lady Stardust* and felt her tummy turn over. She couldn't find the courage to walk along the pontoon and say hi. She just didn't have the confidence. Even though she and Rik had spent a lovely day together last Sunday, and she had felt quite close to him, it suddenly felt as if that counted for nothing.

Her worst fear was the prospect of him looking at her, slightly puzzled, as if trying to remember where he'd seen her. And then smiling politely, but clearly wondering how he could get rid of her. Even worse, she imagined some lithe creature in a see-through kaftan coming up out of his cabin and looking at her, then him, as if to say, 'Who's that?'

She resigned herself to accepting that she would stumble across him, in time, somewhere, and she would have to take it from there. But she couldn't get him out of her thoughts, how comfortable they'd been with each other, how it felt as if they'd known each other for ever. Or was she getting carried away? Had she had a little too much sun that afternoon and read too much into it?

Somehow, she'd built Rik up into being her little secret, and now she lived in fear of him making other friends in Speedwell and leaving her behind. Maybe she'd just served as an introduction, but now he was settling in she was superfluous? She'd have to be patient, play it cool. Anyway, she might not be his type. If he'd been living in the South of France, he was probably used to girls who were way more sophisticated than anyone he'd find in Speedwell.

Her patience paid off. On Saturday evening, she was in the Neptune sitting with a bunch of friends by the window while they all decided whether to stay in Speedwell or head over to Tawcombe where there was more going on. She looked up as the door opened and Rik sauntered in.

He had the supreme confidence that comes from knowing you will always be the most attractive person in the room. He moved like a tiger, slinking, loose-hipped, graceful. His eyes looked as if they had all the sea in them. She knew he would taste of salt. He had done up the buttons on his denim shirt wrong, just two in the middle, leaving an expanse of brown chest and brown stomach above and below.

She felt rooted to the spot as he headed for the bar.

'Who is *that*?' breathed her friend Tamsin.

Nikki watched as he put his hands up and pulled his hair back from his face, showing a lean jawline and razor-sharp cheekbones. Then he dropped his hair back down, as if the gesture had been to show everyone just how perfect he was. He leaned forwards onto the bar, giving the barmaid a dazzling smile as he ordered an orange juice and lemonade, then turned to survey the room.

She tensed, then put her hand up to wave, praying he would notice her.

Suddenly his eyes met hers and his face lit up, and he waved back and headed over to their table.

'Do you know him?' asked Tamsin.

'Kind of.'

Everything inside her was doing double time. Her heart. Her pulse. Something deep in her belly. She could feel it echoing in her ears. She prayed her cheeks weren't as pink as they felt, for her blood seemed very near to the surface of her skin.

There he was, right in front of her, looking pleased. 'Nikki. How are you doing? I haven't seen you all week. I've been crazy busy.'

'Same here,' she said.

He pointed to a spare seat at the table. 'OK if I park myself here?'

'Course! This is Rik, guys,' said Nikki, then introduced everyone else at the table. 'Tamsin, Noah, Ben, Shelley.'

Rik looked around at them all. 'I'll never remember everyone's names.'

'Just call them *mate*,' said Nikki. 'They all answer to that.'

'Thanks for last Sunday.' He was looking at her, his eyes brimming with complicity.

Nikki could sense Tamsin all agog next to her. She wanted to laugh with the joy of it all. 'It was fun.'

'We should go again.'

'Sure.'

'Maybe tomorrow? I've got the day off. Thank God. I'm knackered!'

Damn. Tomorrow was Sunday lunch at Mariners. She'd promised her parents she'd be there, because it was their anniversary. She knew they'd understand if she didn't come, but Jess was going to be at work so Nikki felt she should be there for them.

'I've got Sunday lunch with my family. But you could come? We could go to the beach after?'

Rik gave a groan. 'Sunday lunch. I can't remember the last time I had Sunday lunch. Do you mean it? Won't your parents mind?'

'Not at all. Mum always does extra.' This was true. Sunday lunch at Mariners was always open house. Every meal was open house, really.

'Amazing. Thank you.'

Rik looked as if he'd won the lottery. It was kind of sweet. And it gave Nikki the courage to reach out and re-do his buttons. He looked down.

'Oh God – I'm so tired I can't even dress myself properly.'

She could feel his skin, warm and soft under her fingers as she did them up again, then patted him, laughing. 'There you go.'

'Where would I be without you?'

Oh God. That smile. How did he do that? Make her feel like the only person in the room? He leaned back in his chair, drumming on the edge of the table in front of him in time with the jukebox. She had never seen anyone so comfortable in their own skin, so completely at ease.

'I'm going to grab a game of pool,' he said suddenly, and jumped up. As he walked away, Tamsin turned to Nikki.

'Who the hell is he? And why didn't you tell me?'

Nikki tried to shrug it off. 'I met him last week. Showed him around a bit.'

'Yeah?' Tamsin gave a laugh that was filled with innuendo.

The two of them watched as he idly chalked the tip of his cue. He played a deadly game, clearing the table in record time, earning himself a round of applause. He gave a modest bow and headed back over to the table.

'I'm going to crash,' he told Nikki. 'I'm not used to these early mornings yet. How do I get to your parents?'

'I'll come and get you. It's only down the road.' She couldn't help feeling a little disappointed that he was leaving already. Maybe it was the not-drinking thing.

'Great.' He gave her a thumbs-up, then a squeeze on the shoulder. A jolt went right through her, deep inside and to her very nerve endings.

'See you tomorrow,' she managed.

He gave a wave to everyone else at the table. 'Good to meet you all.'

Everyone's eyes followed him out of the bar. The girls stared with longing; the men with suspicion.

'Um,' said Tamsin. 'Any chance I could come for lunch as well? I won't touch him. Honestly. I'll just look.'

Her mum didn't bat an eyelid when Nikki told her she'd invited Rik for lunch. Helen automatically cooked double the amount they needed, as Jess and Nikki were always bringing along waifs and strays, William had been known to drag people back from his Sunday pint at the Neptune and if Helen went to church, she often asked people back. You never knew who might be there.

It was everyone's favourite place, the kitchen at Mariners. It was never going to win any interior design awards. The units were ancient, shiny brown with corrugated silver along the top. The mustard-yellow walls hadn't been painted for as long as anyone could remember, which was ironic, given they were in the business of decorating.

'You know what they say. Cobblers' children have no shoes,' William always said. 'I'll get round to it one day.'

The dining room was on the other side of a long breakfast bar, carpeted in threadbare maroon. The table was cumbersome and easily seated twelve on matching chairs with cracked leather seats. Generations of Norths had eaten there, for the house had been in the family since the middle of the nineteenth century, as had much of the furniture. An ornately carved cabinet had been turned into a bar, filled with dusty old bottles – Harvey's Bristol Cream, Taylor's Port, Bell's whisky and Bailey's and Tia Maria. Half of it went untouched from one year to the next, occasionally plundered by Helen to add to a trifle or Christmas cake, while the popular bottles were continually replenished. An old sideboard was topped with a turntable and speakers, the cupboards beneath filled with LPs. On a rowdy night, the records would come out and everyone would sing along to William's collection of Motown. They were all singers, dancers, performers, the Norths. The von Trapps, someone had called them once.

Nikki had finished laying the table, the ancient mats with views of Speedwell at each place. William pulled out a bottle of local beer for himself and Rik took an

Appletiser. Graham came in, red-faced from rugby training, trailing a cocktail of Radox and Timotei from his shower.

'I'm starving, Mum.'

'Say hello to our guest,' his mother told him.

'This is Rik,' said Nikki. 'This is my annoying little brother Graham.'

'Hey.' Graham gave Rik a nod as they shook hands.

'Oh my.' Rik eyed the rib of beef Helen pulled from the oven with longing. 'Will there be Yorkshire puddings?'

'There will.' Helen smiled and produced a trayful. Rik gave a contented sigh.

'The French think they're the greatest cooks in the world,' he said. 'But they can't do a Sunday lunch to save their lives.'

'So you've sailed up from the South of France, then?' William, trussed up in a blue-and-white striped apron, was putting the finishing touches to the gravy, wooden spoon in one hand, beer in the other. 'Did you go round or through?'

Rik did an upward motion with his hand. 'Up through the canals. It was touch and go in some places. I thought it wouldn't be deep enough. But I made it.'

William nodded his approval. 'Nice. How long did it take you?'

'Three months or so. I stopped in a few places. Paris.'

'Paris,' said Helen with longing.

Nikki tried to imagine being in Paris with Rik. It made her unable to breathe.

'Have you always sailed?' William wasn't going to be diverted. Cities held no interest for him.

Rik grinned. 'I was pretty much born on a boat. My

dad worked at the harbour in Kinsale. I learned everything I know there every summer, then went back to my mum in Toulouse for school. I spoke French with a Cork accent and got teased mercilessly. When I left school, me and Dad set up a business delivering boats. Did that until he died.'

'I'm sorry, lad.' William raised his bottle in a toast.

Rik shrugged. 'He lived his best life.' He clinked his bottle against William's. 'I'm working at the boatyard in Tawcombe for the next couple of months.'

'Welcome. I hope you'll enjoy it here. I think our weather is more Kinsale than Cannes, though.'

William picked up the steel and sharpened the carving knife before tackling the beef which had been resting on the side. Beautiful slices fell away, rosy-pink in the middle. Graham carried the vegetables over to the table: roast potatoes, cauliflower cheese, peas and carrots. And gravy. And horseradish.

'Sit, everyone,' said Helen. 'We don't want it going cold.'

'You have no idea how much I'm going to enjoy this,' said Rik.

Nikki watched as he piled his plate high, unembarrassed. It was almost as if he'd been here forever. He drew everyone into conversation over the lunch table. He talked about his favourite French rugby team to Graham, outlining the detail of Toulouse's last match down to every last try. He asked Helen about her wedding cake business.

And then Jess walked in, behind an extravagant bouquet of red roses.

'Darling! We thought you were at work,' said Helen.

'I swapped shifts. I couldn't miss your anniversary

lunch.' Jess embraced her father from behind. Helen took the flowers from her with a smile. Rik stared at her, his fork halfway to his mouth. And Nikki's heart sank.

No one could ever ignore Jess North. She was wild, pushed everyone to the edge, always got exactly what she wanted. Loving her was a challenge for all the family, even Helen, who was a saint, but they did, taking their lead from William, who saw no wrong in his headstrong firstborn. Somehow, he was able to laugh at her tantrums and outbursts.

'She doesn't mean any of it,' he would say, when one of the family became exasperated by her shenanigans. 'It's just Jess.'

That, in Nikki's opinion, was not a good enough reason to put up with her behaviour. The message seemed to be that if you wanted Jess to love you, you had to let her get away with anything. It was exhausting. Jess had calmed down over the years, and was less volatile now, but she was still capable of throwing her toys out of the pram – and making sure *everyone* got hit by something in the process. She pulled as many people as she could into her dramas.

Now she'd made her entrance, she headed into the kitchen to help herself. 'You pigs have eaten all the Yorkshire puddings. Who's got a spare Yorkshire pudding?'

She walked over to the table and inspected everyone's plates. The only one which still had a Yorkshire pudding on it was Rik's. He was saving it till last. Her eyes fell on it, then she looked up at him.

'Well, hello,' she said. 'I don't suppose I could have that one, could I? I'm guessing it's not your first.'

‘Madame.’ Rik put it ceremoniously onto his side plate and handed it to her. Nikki saw their eyes meet, and Jess’s widen in pleasure. Oh God, she thought in despair.

And then, when they were all devouring Helen’s towering lemon meringue pie, Woody arrived. He was a regular guest at the Norths’ table. Mariners was his second home. His parents had moved the family down to Speedwell from Macclesfield after some ‘trouble’. When he arrived at the school, Nikki had warmed straight away to his openness and his silly sense of humour, and knew he was going to be important in her life.

It had been tough for Woody, arriving in the middle of the school year, and he’d felt more of an outsider than he had anticipated. At school in Macclesfield, he’d known nearly everyone in his class since he was five, for they’d all come up through the same primary and middle. In Cornwall, no one had a clue about him and nor did they seem curious. Two weeks after he arrived, he began to find googly eye stickers stuck to his things – the sleeve of his jacket, the outside of his locker, the inside of his desk lid. It was funny at first, but then it wasn’t, because everyone sniggered in a rather spiteful way when he found them, and it started getting to him, stopped him wanting to go to school, even though he knew that was daft. His dad called him soft for caring; his mum wanted to go and talk to the head, which was the last thing he wanted because his mum would lose her rag and that was never pretty.

It was Nikki who found him pulling a row of eyes off his backpack and saw he was nearly in tears.

‘I can’t help having googly eyes,’ he said.

'They aren't googly,' she told him. 'They're the kindest, smiliest eyes I've ever seen.'

'And also,' he said fiercely, 'I don't want to have to punch whoever's doing it. Because I can tell you, I'll hurt them. And I know it will be me who gets into trouble.'

He was talking from experience. If you didn't stick up for yourself where he came from, you were sunk. But he knew that if he wanted to join the police, he had to stay out of trouble.

'Leave it with me,' said Nikki, picking off the last pair of googly eyes and flicking them into the bin.

He never knew how she did it, but there were no more stickers. And from then on, he and Nikki were firm friends. She brought him back to Mariners and he was pulled into the heart of the house. He never brought Nikki home to his, where his mum had the telly on full blast from dawn to dusk, so there wasn't much point in trying to have a conversation.

And now he was as good as one of the family, wandering in and out of the house, even if Nikki wasn't there. He'd do the quick crossword with Helen, or kick a football about with Graham, or listen to Jess's latest drama. He'd joined the police, as was his dream, and he looked out for all of them.

Now, Nikki tensed as he ruffled her hair on his way past then sat in the chair next to her. She saw Rik's eyes flicker towards them, saw a moment of confusion in his eyes. Then Jess leaned forwards across the table to grab Rik's attention.

'So,' she said, 'are we all going to the beach after this?'

'Absolutely,' said Rik. 'Once we've helped your mum with the washing-up.'

Helen beamed. Jess rolled her eyes. Nikki gritted her teeth and clenched her fists under the table. Jess hardly ever came to the beach on a Sunday these days, so why was she suggesting it now?

Did she even have to ask?

11

Now

'Oh!' Helen looked startled as Nikki came into the kitchen. She was looking at her iPad, and pushed it away, flustered. 'I didn't realise the time. How are you, darling? How's the house?'

Nikki plonked herself down at the kitchen table. She breathed in the smell of the kitchen: the base note of oil from the Aga, the joint roasting, her mum's Estée Lauder. Their dad had bought a bottle of Youth Dew every Christmas from Debenhams in Exeter, and now it was up to Jess or Nikki to make sure there was a fresh bottle under the tree each year. They all knew it was for their benefit. It was the smell of their mum. The smell of comfort.

'It's everything I dreamed of,' she said. 'But there's a lot of work. My nails are wrecked.'

'Can I pop over and see it one day this week?'

'I'd love that.'

'I'm so proud of you, darling. I know how long you've waited for one of them to come up.'

'You have to make things happen, don't you?'

'You do.' Helen squared her iPad on the table. She

looked nervous. 'And talking of making things happen, I want to pick your brain about something.'

'What?'

'I've been thinking . . . about . . .' She searched for the word. 'I think it's time. I think it's the right time. And I'm not sure what you'll think. What you'll all think. But . . .' She was flailing.

'Go on, Mum. Spit it out.'

Helen shut her eyes. 'Dating.'

Nikki wiped her brow in mock relief. 'Phew. I thought you were going to say you wanted to sell Mariners.'

'No!' said Helen. 'Never. We've had that discussion. You know I'd never let this house go.'

'Good! Well, dating. Yes. Why not? If that's what you want.'

'I need some help, though. I mean, I really haven't a clue.'

Nikki looked at her mum, her warm, gentle brown eyes that shone with wisdom, her creamy freckled skin, barely lined despite what she'd been through, the shining bright chestnut hair that fell to her shoulders. She'd worn her grief with such grace and dignity, like a lace shawl made of shadowy cobwebs, always there but barely seen. Helen hadn't ever expressed any interest in finding someone before now, but if she felt the need for someone new in her life, Nikki would support her.

'Of course I'll help. It'll be fun.'

'Will it? It looks terrifying.'

From the hallway came the sound of Graham and his family arriving.

'Don't say anything yet.' Helen panicked. 'I don't want everyone knowing.'

The kitchen door opened and in spilled Graham, his wife Suzanne, and their three daughters Mia, Meg and Molly, otherwise known as the M and Ms. Nikki was never quite sure about them all having the same initial, but that was classic Suzanne: everything in her life matched perfectly, but you couldn't hate her for it because she was kind and fun and endlessly patient with Graham, who was like a box of frogs, and always had a plan, from the moment he woke, whether he was organising a hog roast at the yacht club or going to look at a bargain he'd seen on Autotrader.

'Nik! I need your advice.' Suzanne was bearing down on her with a large folder tied with a ribbon. 'Would you look at this for me? I keep changing things and it's driving me insane.'

'I've told her to bite the bullet and hand it over but she won't listen to me, because what do I know?' Graham bent down to hug his mother. 'Hey, Mum.'

'It's my pitch for the Pier Hotel renovation.' Suzanne laid the folder down on the dining table. 'Tamara says they want to use local people for everything so I think I'm in with a chance. But I'm finding it so hard to know whether to go traditional, or industrial, or luxe, or something completely radical.'

Suzanne had an interior design business and although she'd gone from strength to strength in the last couple of years given the local property boom, this would be a huge contract for her. Tamara Lethbridge and her husband Duke had landed in Speedwell from West London a couple of years ago and were investing heavily in the town. They'd already opened a seafood café on the front, they were about to open a bar, and they'd bought the rundown Pier Hotel to do up.

'Let's have a look.'

Nikki leafed through her portfolio. It captured all the nostalgia of British seaside tradition. There were bright stripes and saucy vintage postcards blown up on the walls, and vintage memorabilia – a Punch and Judy stall in reception and a huge plaster 99 ice cream cone outside the front door.

'I love it,' said Nikki, thinking what a great eye Suzanne had. 'It's joyful and witty, and I think that's what people want. We've had years of dark sludge and moodiness.'

'I know, but is it sophisticated enough? I know Tamara wants the London crowd. Her Soho House mates.' Suzanne made a face.

'I think if the furnishings are high quality, you'll be fine. People want to have fun when they come to the seaside. Let their hair down and be a bit silly.'

'If you think it's OK...'

'Suze, just send it in.' Graham was getting exasperated. He'd probably had this conversation a thousand times. 'You've poured your heart and soul into it but it's time to hand it over.'

'I want this contract so much.' Suzanne's eyes were wide with longing. 'I really want to raise my game now the M and Ms are bigger.'

'You won't get it if you don't meet the deadline for the pitch.'

Nikki could see that Suzanne was overwhelmed. 'It's fabulous, Suzanne. Honestly. You know I wouldn't let you submit it if I didn't think it was good enough.'

Suzanne stared down at her work. 'I've worked so

bloody hard. I've come in at the right price, too. I haven't been greedy.'

'Look. You're going for it, and that's great. But if you don't get it, it's not as if you're not busy.'

'That's what I keep telling her.' Graham was indignant.

'I know, but this will take me to the next level. Proper jobs, not just flinging about a few lampshades and cushions.'

Nikki shut the folder. 'It's beautiful, Suzanne. You've worked really hard. Give it to Tamara and forget about it.'

'Easy to say.' Suzanne heaved a sigh.

'Lunch won't be long,' called Helen from the kitchen. 'Can you get the girls to lay the table?'

Nikki's heart went out to her sister-in-law. It was hard, putting your neck on the line. And she knew that Suzanne would really care what Tamara thought because she seemed slightly in thrall to the new arrivals and their entourage. The shiny new people. They were good for the town, of course, but they were slightly upsetting the natural balance because they had money and power and influence.

'Guys! Sorry we're late. Nightmare in A and E last night – I've only just got up!' Jess swept in, followed by Juno, holding up her hands with a dramatic eye roll as she dumped a bottle of Shiraz on the table and unclipped her French bull terrier. Edith, a little sack of grey velvet, immediately did a lap of the table to be greeted by everyone.

Jess and Juno were an eye-catching duo. Jess, with her dark hair piled up, a bright pink cardigan and skin-tight capri pants, had the glamour of a fifties Hollywood star, while Juno's blue hair and multiple piercings belied her sweet nature. The M and Ms tumbled over to her at once.

They adored their cousin, and desperately tried to copy her punkish style.

There followed five minutes of hugs and exclamations as Jess held court, describing last night's medical drama and filling them in on the gossip – there'd been a big fight in Tawcombe. Graham was by now outnumbered eight to one but he loved it, and served everyone drinks from the bar on the dresser. Suzanne quickly swept away her portfolio. Nikki suspected she didn't want Jess to see it. Jess wasn't always tactful, and even though she wasn't particularly qualified to judge, it was probably better not to let her have any input.

Standard Sunday lunch at Mariners, thought Nikki as the noise level rose and Edith yelped in excitement. As ever her gaze drifted over to the Cornishware mug on the dresser which had 'Dad' in black letters glazed onto the blue-and-white stripes. If he was here now, he'd be sipping slowly at a glass of the home brew he kept in the garage. And he'd have doted on Juno and the M and Ms – and Bill – the grandchildren he had never met. He would have made Suzanne feel part of the family, just as Helen did. Graham sat in his father's wheel-backed chair at the head of the table, and he was plenty big enough to fill William's shoes, though Nikki knew he worried he wasn't. For all his restless energy, Graham was insecure deep down. Losing your dad at a vulnerable age would do that to you.

'How's the new gaffe?' Nikki jumped as Jess came up to her.

'Right now? An absolute mess.'

'I've got you a housewarming present.' Jess reached

into her bag and pulled out a golden pineapple. 'It's an ice-bucket. Sorry, I didn't have time to wrap it.'

'Thank you!' Nikki looked at it with delight. It was kitsch and fun and absolutely perfect.

'Sorry I haven't been over yet. Work's been manic.'

'I'd wait, if I were you. Till I've got things straight.'

'I'll come and help when I can. I'm on nights all next week though.'

Nikki loved her sister when she was being supportive. *When* being the operative word, for she wasn't always. You never knew what angle Jess was going to take. And you had to be careful when telling her things. She could take umbrage, or judge, or she could be as nice a pie. Nikki was used to it, but it was wearing, and you had to be strategic. She wondered what she would say about their mum's latest revelation. She would definitely have views.

'Honestly, don't worry. You've got enough on your plate with work.'

'It's only fair. You helped me with mine.'

'True.' Nikki had organised the decoration of Jess's bungalow on the other side of town, ten years ago now. It was weird how her sister seemed to run the entire A & E unit at Tawcombe hospital almost single-handedly just by sheer force of her personality, but she couldn't so much as prise open a pot of paint. Though of course she *could* – it was just that Jess never did anything she didn't want to do and was very good at getting other people to do things for her.

The M and Ms were putting the finishing touches to the table, working in sync as the perfect team, while Juno was helping Helen decant all the vegetables into serving dishes.

'Graham, darling, would you carve?' Helen peeled the foil off the pork which was resting in its dish, encased in shiny salty crackling the colour of a ginger nut.

'That's sexist, Mum,' Jess said, frowning.

'OK, you do it, then.' Helen waved the carving knife at her. She never let Jess wind her up.

'No, I'm useless.'

'Let Graham do it, Jess. He's good at it.' Nikki appreciated Jess's sentiment but Graham was definitely the best at getting even slices.

Eventually the food was laid out and at last there they all were, seated at the table. Nikki gazed around at them – her mum and her siblings and her nieces. Juno had got Helen's iPad and was about to call Bill on FaceTime. She'd prop it up in the middle of the table and they'd each have a chat, and he'd insist he wished he was there with them. Even though he was living in paradise, a little bit of him probably did long for home.

Everyone was safe at Mariners, she thought. Safe as houses. Even her.

At least she hoped so. She felt a fleeting prickle of unease. She didn't want to lose the thing that was most important to her. Her family.

After lunch, everyone was in a contented slump, finishing off their wine and picking idly at a round of Camembert. The M and Ms were variously finishing off their homework (Mia), playing on Suzanne's phone (Molly) or lying on the floor cuddling Edith (Meg).

'We should get the money from the house sale in now you've completed,' said Graham.

Nikki had forgotten that's where some of the proceeds

from the sale of Number Four were going. Speedwell had an independent lifeboat station. Every penny needed to keep them afloat came from donations. Graham was the treasurer, a role he took very seriously.

'It's a good dollop in the pot,' said Helen, who was in charge of fundraising and ran the shop.

'Yes. It's confidential, by the way,' Graham reminded them. 'The family don't want people knowing about their donation.'

Jess gave a bark of laughter. 'Oh, everyone'll find out. You know what a small town this is.'

Small town. Nikki could see the words in black on the back of the postcard. She picked up her glass and swallowed the rest of her wine, trying to blot out the image. She'd had such a wonderful afternoon; she didn't want her mood lowered as she was about to head home. Why couldn't she just forget about it?

No one else was really listening to the conversation now, distracted by Juno pulling out her guitar and playing them her latest composition. Her voice was honey spiked with chilli, her lyrics haunting and full of vivid images of seaside life: waves and rocks and moonlight and uncertainty.

She was a siren, luring her audience, lulling them into a false sense of security with her sweetness then hitting them with a twist in the tale, for her songs were stories. Everyone fell silent as she sang, completely under her spell. The M and Ms were wide-eyed, in awe of their cousin and her mystical beauty. They tried to copy her style, but they weren't yet allowed piercings or tattoos or hair dye, so they settled on fishnet tights and big boots, which was as much as Suzanne would allow. Occasionally she would let them go and see Juno play, though never on a school night and never past ten o'clock.

Nikki wondered what would become of her niece. There was something of the drifter about Juno, for she cared nothing for things or status and seemed to have no aspirations nor a shred of ambition. Maybe one day she would be ready to unleash herself onto the world. In the meantime, she walked people's dogs while they were at work, pulled pints at the Neptune when they were short-staffed and did a bit of life-modelling at the college.

It drove Jess mad; she used to badger her endlessly to go on *Britain's Got Talent*.

'Don't waste the gift you've been given!' she would shout at her. But Juno would roll her eyes and shrug.

'Over my dead body am I going on there,' she would say.

'You can't wait for some big cheese to wander into the pub and give you a record deal. It's not *Fisherman's Friends*.'

'I don't want a record deal,' said Juno. 'If I did, I'd have one already.'

Jess didn't understand. Nor did Nikki, deep down, but she did know that you shouldn't push people into doing things. And actually, Juno seemed very happy, and wasn't that the point? She brought joy to everyone, with her gentle nature. Baby Juno had been the saving of them all when she was born, especially Helen. A little bundle of hope.

Nikki was always transfixed when Juno sang, searching her face for a family resemblance. For the ghost of him was there, in the curve of her cheekbone, the light in her eyes, the half-smile she remembered so well. She felt her throat tighten, and turned away so no one could see the tears in her eyes.

The ghost of someone she had loved.

Twenty years, and sometimes the longing still hit her.

12

Then

Nikki was torn about going to the beach after lunch. It would seem churlish if she didn't go, when she and Rik had agreed earlier that they would. He'd even brought his trunks and a towel. But whereas she'd been looking forward to it, now she was dreading it. Having Jess in tow made it an entirely different proposition. And Woody was coming too. It wouldn't be like last week, when she'd had Rik to herself in a private paradise.

So it was with a heavy heart that she followed the other three down the steps. There were already a few people on the beach, a gang she recognised from Tawcombe who had obviously come to take advantage of the last of the summer sun. Someone had a barbecue on the go, and Bob Marley was booming out of a ghetto blaster. To anyone else, it was the perfect picture of youthful summer fun, but all Nikki could think about was the two of them lying on the rock together in the sun. That wasn't going to happen today.

She tried not to show her disappointment. She didn't want to look sulky and withdrawn next to ebullient Jess. Within moments, her sister had stripped down to her

Wicked Weasel bikini – a few threads of fabric that left little to the imagination. With her wild dark hair and her sunbed tan, Jess always turned heads. She'd already flipped open a bottle of WKD, and was dancing to the mellow reggae, in full-on party mode.

Nikki spread out her towel on the sand and sat with her arms wrapped around her knees. She resigned herself to the fact that she couldn't control what was going to happen, but she willed Rik to come and sit next to her. Of course, he didn't. Instead, he followed Jess into the sea as Nikki watched from behind her sunglasses. Jess never went swimming these days, preferring her hair and make-up to stay pristine, but for some reason today she was all for leaping about in the waves like an extra from Baywatch, *cavorting* in front of Rik.

By the time they came out of the water, Woody had plonked himself next to her. Nikki tried not to be hostile, for he wasn't to know her feelings for Rik, or that he was cramping her style. What could she say? Bugger off, I want Rik to sit next to me? After all, he was her dearest friend. The last thing Nikki wanted to do was hurt his feelings.

'Rik's invited us back to his boat.' Jess emerged from the waves like a brunette Ursula Andress. 'What do you two think? Or have you got plans?' She raised her eyebrows suggestively.

'I'm up for it,' said Woody, who was so easy going he just went with whatever anyone wanted to do.

Nikki narrowed her eyes behind her glasses. Was Jess deliberately making it look as if she and Woody were a couple? She wouldn't put it past her.

'Sure,' she said. She was longing to see the inside of *The Lady Stardust*, and to get a peep into who Rik was.

'I don't keep booze on board,' said Rik. 'So if you want a *drink* drink, you'll have to stop at the mini-mart.'

'Oh, we can do without drink,' declared Jess airily, slinging a matey arm around his neck. 'There's nothing worse than watching everyone else get hammered around you.'

She'd ditched her bottle of WKD, Nikki noticed. Jess the chameleon, reading the signals, pretending to be something she wasn't. She could be whatever you wanted her to be, if she wanted you.

They went back to Rik's boat as the sun set. It was snug below deck, only just enough room for them all to squeeze around the table in the galley while Rik made them coffee. Nikki drank in all the details. He didn't have much, for there was barely any space for personal stuff. A small row of paperbacks in French. A photo of his dad – shirtless on board *The Lady Stardust*, a glass in one hand and a cigarette in the other, as handsome as his son. She peeped into his cabin and imagined being curled up in there under the duvet.

Dream on, she told herself. Jess had spotted an acoustic guitar, and was urging him to play. To Nikki's surprise Rik smiled, grabbed the guitar and led them all up on deck, where he serenaded them under the stars, singing 'Forget Her' by Jeff Buckley in a voice that was gruff and sweet. He seemed to be somewhere else when he sang and she wondered if he was thinking of someone who had brought him heartache.

'Oh man,' sighed Jess as he came to the end. 'That's

it. You're coming to the karaoke night. You'll win hands down.'

'I don't really sing in public.' Rik handed the guitar over to Jess for a go. 'Your turn.'

With the moon shining above her, Jess gave a heart-rending version of Mazzy Star's 'Fade into You', all dreamy vulnerability and innocence, her eyes half closed and a secret smile on her face as the night air played with her curls. Rik looked mesmerised. Nikki felt slightly sick. This was a masquerade.

At half past midnight, Woody stood up.

'I've got to go. I'm on earlies this week.'

Nikki shot up out of her seat. No way was she going to play gooseberry to Rik and Jess.

'Are you going too?' asked Rik.

She wasn't sure if he was disappointed or hopeful.

'Yep. I'd better. Thanks for coffee.'

'Thanks for asking me to lunch. It was wonderful.'

She stepped away before Rik could give her a farewell hug. She couldn't bear the thought of touching him and then him letting go. Behind him, Jess wiggled her fingers in farewell. She had clearly no intention of going anywhere but below deck.

'See you guys,' she sang out. There'd been no debate about her staying on. It was a fait accompli.

Oh, to have an ounce of that confidence, thought Nikki. To know that you were desired. That you didn't have to risk rejection. She jumped onto the pontoon and was halfway along it before Woody could catch up with her.

'You OK?' he asked.

Did he know? Had he guessed how she felt?

'I'm fine,' she said, keeping her voice bright. 'I just can't cope with Jess in predatory mode.'

'Poor bugger hasn't got a chance,' laughed Woody, and Nikki felt deflated. She'd secretly hoped she'd misread what was going on.

The moon followed her home, plump with scandal, as if eager to discuss the scenario that was unfolding, but Nikki shut the door firmly on it as soon as she got home and headed up to bed, trying not to think of Jess leaning back, her laughing eyes meeting Rik's as he bent to kiss her for the first time.

13

Now

By early evening, Suzanne and Graham had taken the M and Ms off home for the usual Sunday evening ritual of uniforms, book bags and homework. Jess, Juno and Nikki embarked on the washing-up and didn't allow Helen to lift a finger. When the last plate was dried and put away, and the surfaces wiped down, she pulled out her iPad.

'Right, hive mind,' she said. 'I need some help.'

'What's this?' Jess sat down next to her.

'I'm . . .' Helen searched for the right words. 'Putting myself out there. I think that's what they call it.'

'Putting yourself out where?' Jess frowned and looked at the screen. 'Oh! It's a dating site. Mum!' She gazed at her in part-admiration, part-amazement. 'I never thought you'd do it.'

'I just feel as if it's time.'

Jess looked accusingly at Nikki. 'Did you know about this?'

'Mum mentioned it earlier.'

Juno leaned over Jess and stared at the screen. 'Go for it, Gran.'

'What is this site?' Jess was scrolling through, dubious.

'It's for people who've been bereaved. I know it's narrowing my options but I feel more comfortable on it than on others. For now. I think. I don't know. That's why I need your advice.' Helen fiddled with the three gold bangles on her left arm, which she always did when she was nervous. 'And I need help with my profile thingy. Everything I write just sounds boring. Then if I try and spice it up, I sound like a sex maniac.'

Jess cackled. 'It's an art, Mum. Let's have a look at what you've done so far.'

Helen scrolled through to the profile page. 'I still don't know if I'll have the nerve to post it.'

Jess read it out loud:

'I am lucky to live in a beautiful part of the country, in a little town on the North Cornish coast. I have a large family whom I adore, but it's time to have time for me now they are all growing up. I have a small business making wedding cakes, and I also raise money for our local lifeboat station, working in the shop twice a week. I love walks along the coast, birdwatching, cooking, crime novels (Ian Rankin, Ann Cleeves and Susan Hill are my favourite authors) and do yoga twice a week to keep fit. I'd love to travel a bit more and see what else life has to offer.'

'Birdwatching?' said Jess, wrinkling her brow in doubt.

'Well, your dad was into it. And I've still got his binoculars and books, so I can brush up on it in case anyone asks. I felt like I needed a hobby.'

'I'm not sure birdwatching's going to get anyone's pulse racing.'

'Yes, but I don't want to send out the wrong signals.'

'What do you mean?'

'Well, you know. I don't want them to think I'm . . .' Helen shrugged, not quite sure how to articulate herself.

'You need to pimp it up a bit. This makes you sound like you wear flat shoes and elasticated waistbands.'

'Does it?' Helen felt confused and wished she'd never mentioned anything.

Nikki decided to intervene. Jess was a harsh judge, and forgot that she was an old hand at online dating so knew how to play the game. The important thing was not to frighten her mum off.

'I think it's a very nice profile, Mum, but I agree you need to make it a bit more exciting. People exaggerate all the time so you're up against stiff competition. You don't want to miss Mr Right.'

'Mr Right,' sighed Helen. 'I can't imagine Mr Right. I'm not sure I can do this.'

'Just have a bit of fun!' Jess was frowning at the screen. 'You don't have to marry any of them. But you need to attract someone who appreciates you for who you really are. Someone who'll spoil you. So up your game.'

'OK.'

'What have you got to lose?'

'My dignity?'

Jess rolled her eyes. 'Let me have a go at your profile. Then we'll get to work on your confidence. You can't go into this faint-hearted. You've got to be very focussed and clear. And be prepared to kiss a lot of frogs.'

Helen winced.

Jess laughed and started typing.

Nikki and Juno exchanged glances. Knowing Jess, she'd make Helen sound like a member of the Folies Bergères who was a helicopter pilot on the side.

'What about photos?' asked Juno. 'You need a hot photo.'

'Actually,' said Helen, 'I was going to ask if you'd do me one.'

Juno's face lit up. 'Really?'

'You take lovely pictures. Your Instagram is beautiful.'

'Let's do it,' said Juno. 'We'll get a sunny day and take some with the sea in the background.'

'Get that coastal grandmother vibe,' interjected Jess.

'Coastal grandmother?'

'You know, that expensive beachy look, like Diane Keaton in *Something's Gotta Give*.'

'Oh. Right. OK.'

'I mean, you literally are a coastal grandmother, so you own that.'

Helen nodded, trying to pretend she understood. 'So what should I wear?'

'White linen. Maybe a straw hat. Definitely a wicker basket.' Jess waved a hand. 'Don't worry. You've got all the clothes you need and we can accessorise. Right. Here we go. Listen up.'

She began to read:

'I'm a glamorous woman of a certain age (think Helen Mirren with a dash of Nigella in the kitchen) with a successful baking business. I'm also a chief fundraiser for our local lifeboat, a charity which is very close to my heart. I love going out on our family boat, The Shrimp,

entertaining and exploring the stunning coastline where I live – hiking, cycling and swimming. I'm happy in bare feet, but I love putting on my Jimmy Choos once in a while. I'm looking for someone confident, solvent, with a kind heart and a spirit of adventure. How about a trip on The Orient Express*?'*

'*The Orient Express*? That's way out of my league.'

'Only if you think it is.'

'Plus I don't have any Jimmy Choos,' said Helen. 'And I can't remember the last time I went out on a bike. And you've made *The Shrimp* sound like a superyacht. Not a beaten-up old dayboat.'

The Shrimp had been William's pride and joy, and they'd never got rid of her. She was moored up in the harbour, and every now and then someone took her out for a trip along the coast, to find seals or puffins.

'It doesn't matter. Everyone exaggerates a bit. It's about building up an image so you get the right calibre. If you downplay yourself, you'll get some dreary old bore who wants to take you metal detecting. You want someone with a bit of dash. And a bit of cash.'

'I'm not a gold-digger.'

'No. But you want someone who won't automatically go for the cheapest wine on the menu. You need spoiling and looking after. Aim high!'

Nikki had to agree. 'I think Jess is right. You deserve someone special.'

'It's just a game, Gran,' Juno added. 'It's like bargaining. You can go down but you can't go up.'

Jess saved the new words.

'Trust me. You can't oversell yourself in the dating game. You don't want to be a nurse or a purse.'

'A nurse or a purse?' echoed Helen. 'No, I do not.'

'And none of this is a lie. Except maybe the shoes. And you could get some of those with the click of a button.'

'But what if I do find the perfect match, and they're disappointed when they see me?'

The three of them stared at her. Even at the end of the day, after cooking lunch for nine without turning a hair, Helen looked radiant. Her smile lit up her face. She was a very beautiful woman and any man would be lucky to have her. She deserved the very best, and the three of them would make sure she got it.

Afterwards, as they left Mariners and headed out down the passageway towards the street, Nikki expressed her surprise at their mum's decision.

'I think it's great,' said Jess. 'Mum's so fabulous, and there'll be someone out there for her.'

'Do you think so?' Nikki was more cautious. 'I mean, look at us. We haven't exactly struck lucky.'

'Speak for yourself.' Jess looked at her sister with a mischievous twinkle. 'I've dated loads of fantastic guys – I just haven't wanted to settle down with any of them. But that's me, not them. I'm too bloody selfish now to have someone else in my life. And I wouldn't wish me on anyone.'

She laughed, and Nikki wondered if she really meant that, or if she was putting on a brave face. Her sister did seem perfectly happy to be single these days. She was a career nurse, but she offset that by partying hard and holidaying even harder, even at her age, so in some ways the convenience of occasional online dating really suited

Jess. She had the balls for it too. She was happy to take risks on someone, but she was ruthless if they didn't live up to her expectations. Nikki was sometimes shocked by her brutality. She would cheerfully walk out on a date before they'd even ordered drinks if she didn't think it was working.

'No point in getting their hopes up,' Jess would say, unabashed.

Nikki found the dating game much more challenging. Jess had often told her she overthought it, and she should throw caution to the wind a bit more. She'd met some lovely men, kind and fun and interesting, though somehow never all three qualities at once, and certainly none that had lit enough of a spark inside her to make a long-term commitment. Somehow, after three or four months, there would be a mutual parting. Never any drama. Things just fizzled out.

'I just hope Mum's built for it. Not everyone's like you, Jess,' she said now.

'We'll vet them for her. I'm not going to let her walk into a trap. And I'm pretty good at red flags.'

'True.' Jess examined potential dates with forensic precision and knew the warning signs. She could find someone's real identity in moments by clues hidden in their profiles they had no idea were obvious.

'And her generation will be different from ours. There'll be more choice, because there'll be more widowers. I think she might find somebody rather special.' Jess looked uncharacteristically misty-eyed. 'No one will live up to Dad. That would be impossible. But she definitely deserves some fun. She's run around after us lot for long enough. And been at Graham and Suzanne's beck and call.'

Jess thought Graham and Suzanne used Helen a bit too much. But Nikki pointed out that the M and Ms were her mum's *raison d'être* now Bill and Juno were independent.

'They're a *lot* of work, though,' objected Jess. 'And she's much older than when it was just Bill and Juno. And we didn't take the piss.'

'Nor do Graham and Suzanne.'

'Oh, come on. They're always out, always going away for weekends. When did we ever go away?'

'They're different from us. They love their city breaks. And they do a lot of networking.'

Jess rolled her eyes. 'Brown-nosing.'

'Whatever. You know Suzanne.'

'Yep. Social climber.' Suzanne and Jess had always been wary of each other. 'And she's turning Graham into one.'

'She just wants her business to be a success,' protested Nikki. She didn't like it when Jess judged their little brother. He'd had a big pair of shoes to step into when their dad died, and he'd done a brilliant job of expanding the business. If he wanted to reap the rewards, that was up to him. And he doted on Suzanne and was incredibly supportive of her business. They worked well together.

'Anyway, hopefully Mum will get swept away by some tech billionaire who's cashed in his chips.'

'That's not Mum's style.'

'Says who? I bet she wouldn't complain. I know I wouldn't.' Jess sighed. 'I can just see her, on the Italian lakes, soaking up the sun while some George Clooney lookalike makes her a Bellini.'

'Oh,' said Nikki. 'Wouldn't that be lovely? Let's hope so. Fingers crossed.'

Jess gave her an impulsive hug. 'We'll look out for her.

No one messes with the Norths, remember? We always stick together.'

'Mm hmm,' Nikki agreed, hardly able to breathe in Jess's tight embrace, hoping she couldn't see the flicker of guilt in her eyes. She hadn't always looked out for Jess. Far from it. But then Jess hadn't looked out for her either. She'd been *blatant* about stealing Rik.

They'd been young, though, so maybe it didn't matter anymore. What mattered was now. And their mum. So yes, they must always stick together.

14

It took Nikki just over ten minutes to cycle from her new house to work for her lunchtime appointment the following week. She locked up her bike in the parking area at the converted gas works where she had her office. Like much of the town it was Victorian, made of the same local grey stone as her cottage, with arched windows painted a jaunty blue to brighten the slightly forbidding façade. The Seaside Wedding Company was the smallest office, on the end, and next door was the unit where Helen still made wedding cakes.

It was fifteen years since her mum had complained that she couldn't keep up with the orders she had on her books. Helen had begun making wedding cakes as a bit of a hobby that she could do in the kitchen at home, a bit of fun in between doing the wages, and her cakes had proved so popular it had almost got out of hand.

'Everyone seems to be coming to Speedwell to get married these days,' Nikki had observed. The town had been popular for hen and stag weekends for a while, but lately she'd noticed even more wedding cars winding their way through the streets, and the pavements smothered in confetti. And so the idea for The Seaside Wedding Company was born.

She had felt bad abandoning North Property Management to set up her own thing, but she didn't feel as if organising window cleaning and getting burglar alarms fitted and locks changed was fulfilling her.

'I never expected you to stay on for ever,' Graham told her when she ran the idea by him. 'Off you go. We'll be fine. We'll get someone in to help.'

'But I'm irreplaceable,' protested Nikki. 'Aren't I?'

'You made yourself replaceable when you set up the new computer system,' Graham grinned. 'I expect we'll drop a few balls but we'll figure it out.'

'Do you think it's a good idea, though? Wedding planning?'

'If you don't do it, somebody else will.' Graham's prescient words spurred her on, for she knew this was true. So she and her mum had moved into the space at the old gas works, and now she was the go-to wedding planner for this stretch of coast. She was supremely organised, brilliant at budgeting, and knew every corner of the town, every venue. And she knew what people wanted from their big day: not to have to worry about a thing.

It had been nerve-wracking, as a single parent of a small boy, to set up a new business, but her gut instinct had been right. By the end of the first year, she was booked solidly for the next summer. Whether it was an elopement for two or a huge family wedding, Nikki North would make your dream come true. She organised every last detail, from the save-the-date card to the going-away car.

Now, she checked that everything was ready for her presentation. Everything was laid out on an antique table: samples and menus and brochures for venues and florists. On the wall behind was a huge white board, and at the top was written *Phoebe and Alec* and the date of the wedding in less than six weeks' time.

She saw her prospective clients pull up and park outside, then make their way to the door. She opened it with a smile.

'Phoebe and Alec?' she said, holding out her hand. 'Welcome to The Seaside Wedding Company.'

Nikki sat them down in a pair of velvet armchairs. She was always a little nervous at this first meeting. It was free of charge, but it was her chance to pitch her skills and to see if they were a good match. She was confident she was the best planner for miles around, but just as in a good marriage, there had to be chemistry.

And this was a tricky one, as their wedding wasn't that far off, which put the pressure on.

'We were going to just slip away and do it quietly,' Phoebe explained. 'But as the day got nearer we realised how important it was to have everyone we love with us. We know it's short notice but we've been told that you can work miracles.'

'I'll do my best,' said Nikki. 'But I have to warn you the most popular venues are already taken. The important thing is you've got the registry office booked.'

'It's just going to be us at the ceremony,' said Alec. 'So we want a bit of a party afterwards. Very chilled. Very relaxed. We're crazy busy right now so we just need someone to take control and arrange it all.'

Nikki looked at Phoebe. She was elfin, draped in floaty floral chiffon and a plethora of fine gold necklaces that probably weighed more than she did. Nikki had googled

Phoebe via the website at the bottom of her email and knew she was a manifesting coach. Nikki was dubious about the concept, but that Phoebe was a success was in no doubt, if her two hundred thousand Instagram followers were anything to go by. She and Alec were holding hands, clearly besotted, but Phoebe looked anxious. Nikki sensed there was something she wanted to get off her chest. There was quite often baggage around a wedding. A family issue, or a friendship dilemma.

'Are you OK?' she asked. 'Would you like some water?'

'I'm fine,' said Phoebe, then she took a deep breath. 'The thing is . . . this is my second wedding. And I hated my first one so much, because I knew it wasn't right.' Tears sprang into her eyes. 'I hated every minute of it, and I shouldn't have gone ahead with it. But I wasn't brave enough to call it off.'

'Hey,' said Alec, patting her shoulder. 'It's OK.' He smiled at Nikki. 'We just need to give you the background. So you understand why we're doing it this way.'

'Sure.' Nikki nodded.

'Charlie worked for my dad, and everyone loved him, and my parents really wanted me to marry him. I knew it was wrong, but I went ahead with it to please everyone.'

'Oh dear. I'm so sorry,' said Nikki.

'Our marriage only lasted six months. Charlie walked out. And my parents were furious. With *me*.'

'Babe, it's OK. It's all in the past.' Alec squeezed her hand.

Phoebe put her hand on her chest, breathing deeply. 'I just find the whole wedding thing a bit triggering now. And I love Alec with all my heart, and I want to make it special, but I don't want to be reminded of the first one. So I want something *completely* different.'

'OK.' Nikki nodded. 'Well, the good thing is this wedding is for you this time, right?'

'Absolutely. One hundred per cent. And my parents have refused to come. They were hoping me and Charlie would get back together. They blame Alec for everything.'

Alec gave a little shrug. 'I could see how miserable she was. I couldn't just let her suffer.'

'You rescued me.' Phoebe's eyes sparkled for a moment. 'There was something about Alec. He made me feel safe. And he made me laugh. Charlie never, *ever* made me laugh.'

'I don't think you need to know *all* of this, though,' Alec said, aware that perhaps they were tipping into oversharing. 'This is about the wedding.'

The first appointment turned into a bit of a therapy session. Nikki often thought she could write a book about some of the complicated scenarios she'd been drawn into. It had taught her a lot about how to navigate family politics.

'Don't worry. It's good for me to have a bit of background. Now we can start planning. The first thing we need to establish is how many guests.'

'I think about fifty.' Phoebe nodded. 'We're just doing close friends. None of those people you feel obliged to invite.'

'Any ideas for the kind of feel you want to go for?'

'We definitely want to keep it simple. My last one was so formal. A big hotel do, with receiving lines and table plans and endless speeches. So I want this one to be fun.' Phoebe leaned forwards. She was much more relaxed now she'd unburdened herself. 'But I *have* got an idea for a theme. Stars. Alec loves stars.'

'Oh, that sounds beautiful.' Nikki loved the idea.

'I don't want it to be all about me, though,' said Alec, looking concerned.

'It won't be. It's perfect. I love stars too. I just don't know as much about them as you do.'

'I am a bit obsessed,' admitted Alec. 'I asked for a telescope for my fourth birthday.'

Nikki smiled. 'I can definitely work with that.' Her mind was already conjuring up ideas. 'I'll have to see what's available that weekend, so we might not have much choice.'

'Whatever you can pull together in the time,' said Alec. 'As long as it's a happy day. That's all we care about.'

Phoebe clasped her hands. 'This is going to be amazing. I know you're the right person. I asked the universe to find me someone who'd understand and here you are.'

Nikki suspected it was Google who'd found her rather than the universe, but she rather liked the idea of being manifested. She'd warmed to Alec and Phoebe, and felt excited. She always knew when the chemistry was right with clients when she began to visualise their big day straight away. She couldn't wait to get started.

A loud siren made the three of them jump. Her pager.

'I'm so sorry,' she said, getting up. 'I'm going to have to go. I'm lifeboat crew.'

That was the deal when you were on call. You had to drop whatever you were doing. On the spot. Crew members had walked out of teaching classes, cutting hair, mending washing machines . . . Nikki had a caveat on her website that she might be called away at short notice.

‘Wow,’ said Alec, jumping up. ‘That’s amazing. Like Saving Lives at Sea?’

‘Exactly,’ said Nikki.

‘Come on, Pheeb.’ Alec grabbed Phoebe’s hand and they followed her to the door.

‘I’ll text you as soon as I’m back and make a plan. Is that OK?’

‘Of course! You’ve been amazing already. You’ve totally put my mind at rest.’ Phoebe looked genuinely relieved.

Nikki smiled at them both. ‘Thank you.’

She herded them out and locked the door. In five minutes, she’d be at the station, ready to find out where the crew was headed, and what to expect. There wasn’t a minute to lose.

15

Twenty minutes later, she was in the back of a RIB, slicing through the waves across Speedwell Bay. She raked her eyes across the view ahead as they cut through the choppy water, leaving the town behind them. Eddie Newell was at the helm with Dan Hedges on radar and Nikki navigating, the three of them bound by a sense of purpose, each falling into their role and preparing for what they might find ahead.

They were looking for an exhausted kayaker, separated from the rest of his group who had all underestimated the stamina needed to round the headland and paddle to the next cove. An easy enough trip in high summer, with the warmth of the sun and the calmer water, but on a cooler day the cold seeped into your bones even if you hadn't got wet, and this man had been dunked by a boisterous wave. His friends had called the coastguard for help as soon as they'd made their way to shore.

An indecisive sun bobbed out from behind the clouds to take a look at what was going on, turning the inky grey to a blue. The cliffs to the right soared skywards, craggy and imposing, topped with trees bent by the wind.

Sometimes in summer when the sky was bright and the sea was a shimmering turquoise, you could imagine you were somewhere else, somewhere Mediterranean perhaps, but right now you could only be in the chill Atlantic on the south-west coast of England.

They could see three of the men on the beach, their kayaks dragged up on the sand. They began following the search pattern relayed to them by the coastguard. With luck, he wouldn't have drifted out too far. Or worse, gone under. He had his kayak to cling on to, but if he got too cold, if hypothermia had set in, he might lose his grip.

People's capabilities in the sea were always a fine line. The fittest person might get ill or get an injury, or the elements might spring a surprise on them. And it wasn't just the foolhardy who got into trouble. The most experienced could be caught unawares. Which was why this job was so important. The crew didn't ask questions, or judge. They were there to save lives.

It had taken Nikki some time, ten years after the disaster, to find the courage to join the lifeboat crew. Not physical courage – she knew she was fit enough. It was the mental stamina, the calm, the ability to assess a situation. And trust – not her trust in others, but their trust in her. Would they worry she didn't have the grit, because of what had happened?

It turned out to be the very opposite. They trusted her completely, this motley crew made up from a random assortment of occupations – an optician, a brace of electricians, an insurance broker and a tattoo artist, amongst others, bound by their bravery and a desire to help people. They knew she had lost her dad, but somehow they valued her more for it.

They had been the saving of her. Before then, she'd been losing sight of herself and sometimes, she thought, her mind, and she wasn't proud of the person she was becoming. Too many nights in the Neptune when Bill was at his dad's. Not enough self-respect. Too much anger with nowhere to put it. She'd needed to change course, and joining the lifeboat was a kill-or-cure solution. People were surprised. It had seemed like the last thing she would want to do. But it was a tribute to her father. And her way of telling the sea it was not going to win. It was not going to destroy her as well.

Telling her mum had been difficult. Helen had been silent for a moment, gazing down into her cup of tea while Nikki held her breath. If her mum didn't want her to join, she wouldn't. Nikki didn't want to cause her any more distress. But Helen had looked up with a small smile and said, 'I think your dad would be very proud.' Nikki threw her arms around her and they both had tears in their eyes. She was glad to have her mother's blessing.

Her decision had served her well. She was a different person now from the one who had forced herself to pluck up the courage to fill out the application. It had given her the mettle to start The Seaside Wedding Company too. If she was brave enough to plunge into an icy black sea on a winter's night, she could do anything.

There! There he was, clinging to a lime-green kayak, the waves out here so high he had been hidden at first. She gave a shout. Eddie changed course and the boat surged towards him as everyone got ready for the rescue. Nikki felt the adrenaline rush she got with every rescue. You never knew how a shout was going to turn out. Things could go badly wrong; miracles could happen. There was only so much they could control.

'All right, mate? We've got you. Hang in there.' Dan and Nikki were poised to grab him under the arms from behind as soon as they got close enough. Eddie steadied the boat, a difficult task with the swell. It would all be seamlessly choreographed. They all knew exactly what they were doing.

'One two three lift!'

A few moments of effort and the kayaker was in. He stared up at the sky, stupefied as they put a lifejacket on him.

'I'm Nikki.' Nikki helped him into the double crew seat and sat next to him. 'What's your name? Can you tell me?'

There was an uncertain nod, a slow blink. 'Phil.'

'All right, Phil. We're going to get you back to shore as quickly as we can.'

'I thought I was going to drown.'

Nikki put her arm around him.

'You're all right now. We've got you.'

'Where are the others? Where are the others?' His voice rose in panic.

'They're OK. They're on the beach. It's all good.'

'Thank you.' He slumped against her, exhausted by his ordeal.

'That's all right. It's what we're here for. Do you know what the day is?'

'Wednesday? It's my bloody birthday. My fiftieth.'

'Happy birthday.'

'I could have died,' he said again.

'You could have,' she said. 'But you didn't.'

'Ambulance is on its way to the boathouse,' Dan told her.

'Ambulance?' said Phil. 'I'm fine.'

'You need checking over,' said Nikki firmly. You didn't mess about with possible hypothermia. It was deceptive, and she could tell Phil wasn't as alert as he probably should be.

'My wife's going to kill me,' said Phil. 'She's cooking a special dinner.'

'I think she'll probably be very glad you're safe,' said Nikki.

Phil's face crumpled. He was going to cry. This often happened. Being rescued was an overwhelming experience.

'You're going to be fine,' said Nikki gently. 'With a bit of luck, you'll be back in time for birthday cake.'

'My kayak. It was her present to me.'

'We've got it,' said Dan. He'd fished it out of the water while Nikki was settling him and strapped it onto the side. 'You can come and pick it up from the boathouse.'

Phil covered his face with his hands. 'I don't know how to thank you.'

Knowing they'd saved someone's life was all the thanks they ever needed. As Speedwell hove back into view, the three of them looked at each other over Phil's head.

'Nice work, team,' said Eddie.

Back in the boathouse, Eddie gave them all a debrief over a cup of tea. Afterwards, Nikki wriggled out of her layers of protective clothing and back into her own clothes as the team trickled back to their real lives, to their work and conversations and meals. Normal service resumed itself quickly. Partners and families and colleagues were used to the interruption and learned not to complain. How could you?

Before she left, she stood on the harbour by the slipway and offered up a prayer of thanks for a successful rescue. She was never quite sure who the prayer was to, for she didn't believe in God any more than she believed in Neptune or Poseidon, but she felt she owed gratitude to something and it was her ritual, a quiet moment of contemplation where she shut her eyes and acknowledged that she had only played a very small part in the outcome.

When she opened her eyes, she found the coxswain, Archie Fowler, had come to find her.

'Everything OK?'

'Yeah,' he said. 'I wanted a word, that's all.'

'What about?' She felt a flicker of anxiety. The postcard was always there, at the back of her mind. She felt a slight prickling on the back of her neck, as if someone was watching her from afar. Could it be a member of the crew who had sent it? They were all taught to observe, after all. Perhaps one of them had seen something—

'It's a good thing,' Archie said with a smile. 'I wanted to see if you'd consider going for helm. Eddie's going to be retiring soon, so I could do with an extra.'

'Me?' Nikki was surprised.

'Reckon you'd be the best person for the job. You've got a lot of experience under your belt now. It'll be tough, but I think you've got it in you.'

Nikki was silent for a moment. It had taken up a lot of her spare time to study to be navigator, and helm would be an even bigger commitment and a huge responsibility.

'You'd be the first woman in Speedwell to take the helm,' Archie told her.

She grinned at him. 'You know I can't turn down the challenge now.'

He shrugged, but his eyes were twinkling. 'Just saying.'

'You really think I can do it?'

'You know I wouldn't ask you if I didn't.'

This was true. Archie had never suffered fools gladly. He had been shore crew the day of the disaster, helping launch the lifeboat into that turbulent water, and he'd never really got over the loss of his cohorts. Nikki looked at him now, his once fair hair flying in the breeze, his brilliant blue eyes that never missed anything gazing at her as he waited for her response.

She wanted to do it. Of course she did. To prove to herself she could. To honour her dad. For the rest of the crew. For Archie, who trusted her. But was it realistic? Work was full on for the next few months, and she'd taken on the renovation. The anniversary was coming up and that would take a lot of time. Would she be over-stretching herself?

'Would you let me think about it?' she asked. 'I don't want to take it on and then find it's too much.'

'That's why I'm asking now. There's plenty of time, but you're the one I want.'

That was high praise indeed coming from Archie.

'I'll let you know, when I've had a chance to think it over properly. I wasn't expecting to be asked, and I need to make sure I can give it my best. Thank you.'

He tapped her on the arm. 'You're all right.'

He didn't need to say any more. She knew the subtext. This was about her dad. Her following in his footsteps. She knew then she would have to accept the challenge.

*

She left the lifeboat station, unable to keep the smile off her face, unable to believe that Archie had such faith in her. He knew how much it would mean to her, to be asked. What an honour it was. She would do it, she decided. She'd have to be very organised, and strict with her time. Once summer was over and the renovation was done, she'd be able to focus on her study. Of course she could do it. Why was she even doubting herself?

She slipped back into the office. She wanted to write up her notes from the meeting with Alec and Phoebe and set a date with them for a presentation once she'd done some research. Then she was due to meet her mum in the Neptune. They were going to the anniversary committee meeting together – they were in charge of catering, booking the food trucks and ice cream vans and a mobile bar. Helen had stepped down as chair the year before, and Tamara Lethbridge had taken over.

'The committee needs new blood,' her mum had said, when Nikki voiced her concern that Tamara wasn't the right person. She wasn't local, and wasn't very good at listening to the quieter members of the committee who'd been serving since the beginning. To Nikki's mind, that wasn't how a good chair operated, but perhaps she should give her the benefit of the doubt. She was certainly dynamic.

The post had arrived while she was out and she scooped it up, threw it on the desk, went to open her laptop, then froze.

There was another postcard. Face upwards on the desk, the black lettering standing out defiantly.

Who else knows the truth, besides you? And me?

Nikki squeezed her eyes shut, praying it would be gone when she opened them again. It wasn't.

This proved that she was a target, and it wasn't a random marketing message like she'd tried to convince herself it was. Whoever sent it knew where she lived, *and* where she worked. And presumably what she had done. What a fool she was, to think she could swan about, flaunting herself as a shining example of a successful woman who had it all and could do it all when actually she was living a total lie.

She felt bile rush into her stomach, and the creeping claw of paranoia. All the joy of Archie's proposition evaporated. All she wanted was to rush home and crawl into bed, pull the covers over her head and hide her shame from the world. But she couldn't miss the committee meeting and her mother would be waiting for her at the Neptune. Instead, she got out her phone and texted the one person in the world she knew she could trust.

16

'Gran! For heaven's sake, relax. You look as if you're in pain. Like someone's stuffed a broom up your bum.'

Helen took the weight off the palms of her hands. She was leaning back onto the wall overlooking the bay, and the stones were digging in. Everyone seemed to have their profile pictures taken with the pyramids or the Eiffel Tower or Machu Picchu looming behind them. The craggy cliffs of Speedwell would have to do for now – in the sunshine, she could almost be anywhere.

She was wearing a pink linen shirt, teamed with skinny white jeans with frayed hems and her chunky platform trainers. She'd blow-dried her hair so it shone like polished copper, then tousled it up with a bit of product so she looked windswept rather than groomed. A gold chain and small diamond hoops had finished off her outfit. William had given her the earrings for her fortieth birthday. She'd cried and he'd laughed at her, kindly. 'If I'd known they were going to make you cry, I wouldn't have bought them.'

The last thing she'd done before Juno arrived was take

off her wedding ring. She always wore it, but she probably shouldn't have it on in her profile photos. The skin on her finger was indented through years of wear. Anyone who looked closely would be able to see the ring's conspicuous absence, which was why she was trying to hide her hands.

'You don't think you should wear something a bit more . . .' Juno waved her hands about – 'eye-catching?'

'I want to look like me,' said Helen. 'Not a fake me.'

'Hmmm.' Juno eyed her thoughtfully, then wriggled out of the white biker jacket she was wearing and chucked it at her. 'Try sticking that on.'

Helen shrugged on the jacket and it fitted perfectly. She pulled up the collar of her shirt, then put her hands in her pockets and smiled.

'How do I look?'

'Foxy!' Juno was snapping away on her phone. 'This is great. This is much more like it.'

She stopped for a moment, put her head to one side, then rummaged in her bag. She came over to Helen with a red lipstick and before she could protest, was putting it on her.

'Not with my hair colour!' protested Helen.

'Shhh,' said Juno. Then she put her hands in Helen's hair and ruffled it up even more. 'There. Now you look like you've just come out of your trailer after hot sex with Colin Farrell.'

Oh God. That wasn't the look she was going for at all. That was the best way to get all kinds of inappropriate approaches. Helen cleared her throat, smoothed down her hair and tried to look wholesome.

'No! You look like a Sunday school teacher.'

'It's fine. I'm sure what you've done is fine. Let's stop.'

She couldn't bear it a moment longer. As long as she had a couple of half-decent snaps, that would be enough.

'Come on, then.' Juno was obviously relieved. 'Let's go and get a drink.'

The Neptune stood on the end of the quay, built of white-washed stone, its name painted in black letters over the latticed windows and a mural of Neptune climbing up its side, bearded, crowned – and stark naked. There had been uproar when it had appeared overnight five years ago, like very posh graffiti. There had been letters of protest from more straight-laced members of the community, but people came to see it from miles around, so, all in all, Naked Neptune was good for the town, and Belle and Gloria, the landladies, were delighted. They'd recently moved down from Manchester to take over the pub, and many people suspected they'd set up the whole thing, but now it was history and no one cared.

The Neptune was always busy, for the food was renowned for its robust simplicity: mussels in cider or fish pie or scampi. Triple-cooked chips and peas on the side. Gloria made her famous tartare sauce fresh every morning – mayonnaise studded with gherkins, capers, tarragon, dill and parsley – and they got through bowls and bowls of it on a weekend.

Juno and Helen pushed through the crowds and made their way to the bar to order the Neptune's signature Bloody Mary, a concoction of chilli-infused vodka, sherry, horseradish, celery salt and tomato juice that came with a fat prawn hanging off the rim of the glass.

Whenever she came in, Helen looked at the bar stool where William would have sat having his pint on his way home. Always just the one, which he savoured, and which he'd been having in here since he was fourteen and his own father brought him in. There was always a moment when she thought she might see him there, and he would turn, and his face would break into that gentle smile and he would nod to whoever was behind the bar to bring her a glass of white wine. But he never was.

Somehow over the years her body had absorbed the grief and it had become part of her. It was something she had got used to because she had to. It didn't mean she was any less sad, or that she didn't miss William as much, because she wished he was here every minute of the day. She had simply learned to live with the pain, as human beings did. Gradually other experiences layered themselves over the top of that terrible day, like emotional scar tissue covering up a wound, and she learned to be more than her grief, and not to let it define her. But it was hard to think of herself as anything other than William North's widow.

'Widow' felt like such a final word, as if she had been buried with her husband, as if it was her fate to carry around her widowhood like the woman in the black hooded cape in the advert. She wanted to shake it off and become someone new. She had been without William almost as long as she had been with him, which seemed like a turning point. She would never forget him, or stop loving him with all her heart, but time was running out.

She wanted someone for herself. Someone who knew she preferred Sauvignon Blanc over Chardonnay. Someone who would catch her eye at a party, see she was bored and come to rescue her. Someone who would surprise her with tickets to go to see Tom Jones and book a lovely hotel so they didn't have to face a long journey home afterwards.

And someone she could spoil and look after and care for too, for Helen was a nurturer.

And then there was the obvious. Although it made her curl up a little inside to think about it, she missed physical intimacy. The little sparkles that zinged through you in anticipation. The pure heaven of being curled up in someone's arms afterwards as your heart rate slowed down and you both drifted off to sleep. William had known her so well and had always been able to surprise her, tease her, take her breath away. Was there someone out there who could do that for her? Would she have the courage to reveal herself to another man after all this time?

If she didn't try, she would never know.

While Juno got the drinks, Helen mingled amongst the regulars. She couldn't move without being greeted by someone, for these were her people. Their people. The fishermen who faced the high seas every day to bring back the lobster, the brill, the turbot that graced the restaurant tables. The shop owners who met the wants and needs of the tourists who descended on the little town in summer. The ordinary folk – the hairdressers and cleaners and electricians with businesses that sometimes struggled in the off season but found new hope come spring.

No one knew the rhythm of life in a seaside town better than the Norths. Their maintenance company serviced most of the properties in Speedwell, for they had a crack team of workmen and labourers. Quite a few of them were in the pub now, and they all had the utmost respect for Helen, for they knew she was the quiet influence who made sure they were looked after and paid well, the one they turned to for sage advice and sympathy when things went wrong in their private lives. Illness, injury, money trouble, marriage problems.

'Hey, Mrs N. Looking good.' Jeff, their chief electrician, tweaked the sleeve of the biker jacket. 'What's all this?'

'It's Juno's,' laughed Helen. 'How's Nina?'

Jeff's wife had recently had a knee operation.

'She's getting there. It's going to take a while. I've promised to take her back a portion of Gloria's mussels.'

'If you need any more time off, just say.'

'I'm all good. The kids have been golden. But thanks.'

Juno arrived at her side and pressed a Bloody Mary into her hand and the two of them worked their way around the pub. The air was filled with chatter and the scent of woodsmoke from the enormous fireplace and cooking from the kitchen, and when Gloria brought out the first copper serving dishes filled with crispy-topped fish pie, Van Morrison sang out her name. Gloria did a little dance, holding up her tray, and everyone cheered.

I love my home town, thought Helen, and everyone in it, and if only William were still alive, everything would be perfect. But he's not and it's not, and it's up to me now to start a new chapter, before it's too late.

Juno was flicking through the photos on her phone with a smile.

'Look,' she said, holding it out. 'I think I got the money shot.'

It was a photograph of Helen, head slightly back, laughing, her smile wide, her eyes sparkling, the collar of the white jacket turned up.

'You've been taking pictures in here!' Helen said accusingly.

'Yes. Because when you didn't know I was taking pictures you actually relaxed, and I got photos of the real you.'

'Thank you,' said Helen, pleased, for she thought she looked just right. Like a woman you might want in your life, if you were a man of a certain age.

She looked up and saw Nikki approaching their table. They were both going to the committee meeting, which was held in the function room above the bar. They'd been held there since the very first gathering.

'Hi, darling,' she said, reaching out her hand for her daughter's. Nikki bent down to kiss her cheek.

'Hi, Mum. Hey, Juno.'

'What do you think?' Juno held up her phone for Nikki to see Helen's photo. 'For her profile picture.'

'Smoking!' Nikki looked at the picture then back to her mum in admiration. 'You'll be beating them off with a stick.' She looked over at the bar. 'I'm just going to grab myself a glass of wine before we go up.'

Something in her tone alerted Helen. Her daughter looked a little weary tonight. She was usually so bubbly and upbeat but there was a marked frown between her brows, and she seemed on edge.

'Everything OK?' she asked.

'Yes, fine,' said Nikki. 'I had a shout this afternoon, that's all. Everything was good, but it's always full on. And it interrupted my appointment with some new clients.'

'Oh no.'

'They were fine about it. But you know, it messes up the flow, so I need to catch up with them.'

She headed off to the bar. Helen watched after her. Nikki had too much on her plate, she thought, though maybe it was just the stress of the new house and the hectic summer season coming up. Nikki was so determinedly independent, rarely calling on anyone for help.

She reflected for a moment on how different her two daughters were. Jess had always been demanding. From the minute she was born, she'd come out screaming for attention. She still was demanding, even now, whereas Nikki never rocked the boat. How could two people with the same parents, same upbringing, be the complete opposite of each other? Not that it meant she loved one of them more than the other. She loved all of her children equally, but differently. Jess the hellraising diva, Graham the amiable enthusiast, and Nikki the appeaser who never put a foot wrong.

She'd keep an eye on her. Rally the rest of the family to help out. Nikki was always on hand to help without being asked so it was only fair they should repay her generosity. She made it too easy for everyone to assume she was coping.

Now she was back again, with a glass of Pinot Grigio. 'Shall we go up?'

Helen looked at the clock and realised it was nearly seven. The meeting was about to start. For a moment, she wondered if she should still be going, now she'd stepped down as chair, but she found it hard to let go.

Twenty years. It was difficult to believe it had been so long. She remembered the very first memorial, one year on. It had been at her instigation, and it had been word of mouth – a call to meet on the harbour as dusk fell. There had been a special church service that morning, but Helen wanted something for the non-churchgoers, something less formal than the sombre singing of hymns and a sermon. This was to be a celebration of everyone they had lost. A chance to share memories. And tears. And hugs.

She hadn't expected a big crowd, but when she got there, half the town had turned up. And at eight o'clock, strings of fairy lights wrapped around the front of the Neptune came on. The landlord Keiran and his staff came out with trays of hot buttered cider to warm everyone's hands. And their hearts. Someone else passed around a bucket to raise money for the lifeboat, and by the end of the evening it was heavy with coins and bristling with notes. Nearly a thousand pounds. Which for an impromptu fundraise was incredible.

From then on, Helen gathered together a proper committee and made the Speedwell Memorial an official annual event. It was important for the town to never forget, to come together, to share their feelings in an attempt to heal as best they could, but also to raise funds for the lifeboat station. There was a support group, too, for those who were struggling with their loss, whether for practical or financial or emotional reasons. Several had lost a breadwinner.

Helen had been lucky the family business was well-established, and Nikki and Graham had stepped into their father's shoes. She often felt guilty that Graham had been so young to take on so much responsibility, but as he told her often, it had always been his intention to take over. He'd had no intention of going to university and he insisted that he never wanted to leave Speedwell. 'Everything I want from life is here,' he told her. That first year had been hell, but everyone who worked for them had stepped up and clients had been understanding.

Helen knew how impressed William would be with how far they had come. They'd gone from strength to strength through determination. Fate might have dealt them a terrible blow, but William would have been furious if they'd let it affect the business. In fact, it had become a comfort to them all, and they'd channelled their grief into ambition. Jess was a bit of an outlier, as she had her own career, but she was still on the board, still had an input, still had dividends, and sometimes she saw things from a different angle and made them more innovative.

When Nikki had joined the lifeboat crew, Helen had mixed feelings but she was overwhelmed by her daughter's grit, and her mission to embrace what had been taken from them all and turn it to good use.

'You have to accept the sea for what it is,' Nikki said at the time. 'And I feel as if joining is the one way to prove Dad didn't die for nothing.'

Bravery. That's what every single member of the crew had. Without that courage the sea would win every time. They did their duty with no questions asked, just as William and Rik and all the rest of the men had that night. As Helen stood up to follow Nikki, she realised the twentieth anniversary was as important as the first.

17

Nikki was wary of Tamara Lethbridge. Her voice was a little too drawly, her eyes a little too wide, and her boho dresses must have cost an arm and a leg.

When her mum had finally resigned as chair of the Speedwell Memorial Committee last year, Nikki had presumed one of the old stalwarts would take over, but somehow Tamara had elbowed her way in, dazzling everyone with her contacts and her confidence. Now Nikki was wondering if she should have volunteered herself. Surely it was better for the committee to be in the hands of someone with close links? Rather than someone with a different agenda. Tamara and her husband Duke were sponsoring the twentieth anniversary, and they had poured money into the pot to make sure their company name was plastered all over everything. She had basically bought her way in.

Nikki also didn't like the way Tamara had Suzanne in her thrall. Nikki admired her sister-in-law for spotting an opportunity. She was in high demand decorating many of the houses that had been snapped up in Speedwell after the pandemic by people wanting a slice of sea life.

It had been wonderful to see Suzanne blossom and grow in confidence: it must have been tough, marrying into the North family as a bit of an outsider. Nikki knew she and her mum and Jess were all strong women and might be seen as overpowering, but now Suzanne had her own identity and was becoming quite a mover and shaker locally. Nikki feared Tamara had her dangling with the promise of the contract to do up the Pier, and worried that the job would end up going to one of her London cronies. Suzanne would be crushed.

Now the minutes were over, Tamara had taken the floor and was about to make an announcement to the committee.

'I am absolutely thrilled – over the moon, in fact – to let you know that Zak Glazier has agreed to compose and perform a special song for the ceremony. Free of charge.' Everyone looked at each other in astonishment. Zak was a chart-topping singer-songwriter who had bought a country retreat along the coast. He was seen around the town quite often, in his big coat and cowboy boots, his red curls flying out behind him.

'This is going to move things up a gear,' Tamara went on. 'It pretty much guarantees us television coverage, certainly local, maybe national. And lots of interviews in the press. Zak has taken Speedwell to his heart since he moved here, and he told me it would be a privilege to honour the memory of those we lost that night.'

Nikki felt a flicker of irritation. Tamara had absolutely no experience of or connection to those who had been lost, so how dare she say 'we'? And the committee had agreed at the last meeting to Juno writing and performing something special. Juno had been thrilled to be asked, and it had given a much-needed boost to her confidence. To have that snatched away would be a disaster.

Nikki knew the deal, though. There was money involved. Zak Glazier would pull the crowds in. Did that make it right? Yes, one of the aims of the committee was to raise funds for the lifeboat station, but it was also a very emotional and poignant event, and a very personal one.

She raised her hand, and heads turned towards her.

'I thought we agreed at the last meeting that Juno was writing a song?'

'Of course.' Tamara smiled. 'We'd still love that. Zak will need a support act. It will be great exposure for her.'

Nikki wasn't going to let her get away with this. 'I thought she was the headline? I'm sure that's what we agreed. Can we check the minutes?'

She turned to Mandy Elwell, who was the secretary. Mandy looked alarmed, and started to leaf through her folder.

'Nikki.' Tamara spoke with exaggerated patience. 'I'm sure you can appreciate this is a fantastic opportunity.'

'For who, though? Zak doesn't need the exposure.'

'It's very generous of him to give up his time.'

'Juno's giving up her time too. Is hers not worth as much as his?'

Nikki felt her mum put a hand on her arm in an attempt to calm her. Tamara's smile was a little fixed. Nikki could see she wanted to shut her down as quickly as possible.

'We can hardly ask Zak to be the support.' Tamara held up her hands and appealed to the rest of the committee. There was a ripple of nervous laughter.

'But he's got nothing to do with what happened. He's lived here for what – eighteen months? He has no personal connection whatsoever.' Nikki looked around but no one met her eye. She frowned. Was she wrong, to think that this mattered?

The smile was still there. The *I'm listening but I'm not listening* smile.

'I do understand. But we're trying to spread the net a little wider to get coverage. And with that coverage will come more funding. You know how difficult it is to get donations and this is a *gift*.'

Nikki shut her eyes. She could just see it. It would be like a roadshow. Full of screaming teenagers. Not in keeping at all. The whole point of the memorial would be forgotten. And she wasn't just being old-fashioned, or mealy-mouthed because it wasn't her idea, or ungrateful. It was because this ceremony meant so much to her and the others. It was up to her to preserve its ethos.

Or was it? Should she just let it go?

'We could put it to the vote?' said Tamara.

Nikki could see, by the fact that no one had come forward to back her up, which way that would go. So that was it, she thought. Showbiz and money trumped respect and honour. She could picture the evening news. Zak there in his big coat, hunched up and mumbling some platitude. Tamara next to him, lapping up the attention. And Juno relegated to the warm-up act. She fought back tears of frustration.

'That's not necessary.' There was an edge to her voice that people didn't hear very often. Several members of the committee looked at each other, wondering if they should speak up. 'I understand we must move with the times.'

'The last thing I want to do is upset anyone,' Tamara assured her. 'I'm trying to do my best for the town.'

Nikki could feel a red mist coming down as she thought about how she would explain the decision to Juno. She knew Juno struggled with her self-esteem and her confidence. A knock like this would prove Juno's narrative to herself: that she wasn't ever going to be good enough.

'What about a duet?' she heard herself say. 'It would be the perfect compromise. It would be a huge boost for Juno. And it would give Zak a chance to really integrate himself into the town and our story, rather than taking over and making it all about him.'

There was silence. Tamara's smile had frozen. Around her, Nikki could hear the committee murmuring their agreement, nodding in approval. A bit bloody late, she thought. But better late than never.

'I reckon that's a grand idea.' Sandy Rogers was the first to speak up.

'And me.' Mandy Elwell chimed in her support.

'How about we put that to the vote?' suggested Nikki. 'All those in favour of a duet, put up their hand.'

Of the ten people on the committee, four put up their hand. With Nikki that made five. Then Helen added hers.

'That's six out of ten,' Nikki said.

There was a moment while Tamara considered her options. She wasn't happy but she didn't have much choice.

'I'll talk to Zak and see what he says,' she said.

'Perfect,' said Nikki.

The tension in the room relaxed after that, and the agenda moved on to more mundane things. Security, publicity, litter – most of the roles were allocated to particular members of the committee and it was a well-oiled machine. Several of them gave Nikki their approval behind Tamara's back, which she appreciated, though she didn't understand why they hadn't stood up for her in the first place. Dazzled by the prospect of Zak's celebrity, she supposed. Anyway, all was well and they were set fair.

At the end of the meeting, Tamara came up to her.

'No hard feelings, I hope.'

'Of course not,' said Nikki.

Tamara was rummaging about in her capacious handbag.

'We're opening our new bar next Friday. I really hope you can come.'

Nikki looked down at the invitation Tamara handed her. It was glossy, with a beautiful illustration of a woman rising out of the sea bearing a trident.

'Salacia,' said Tamara. 'The Roman goddess of the sea. We thought that was the perfect name.'

Nikki appreciated this was an olive branch.

'It's fantastic. And I've seen the work you've been doing. Wow!'

Tamara and Duke had done a complete refurb on the old post office at the start of the quay. There was now a double-height glass frontage, with mezzanine floors and twisty lights made from Murano glass. Definitely more Soho than Speedwell.

'Do bring a plus one.'

'Thank you.' For a split second, her new neighbour flashed into her mind. It would be the perfect way to repay Adam's hospitality.

'I'm sorry if you thought I was treading on your toes earlier.' Tamara leaned into her. Nikki found herself drowning in the scent of honey and cardamom and violets. 'I didn't mean to disrespect Juno. I guess I was overexcited about Zak and what it would mean to the fundraising. I know it's a constant battle, to raise money. And how important the lifeboat is to the town.'

Nikki wondered if she'd misjudged her, and if she'd been a bit harsh, calling her out like that in front of everyone.

'I think the duet could really work,' she said. 'If he's up for it.'

'I'll give him no choice. I'll tell him that's the deal,' said Tamara with an impish grin.

Nikki was surprised. She *had* misjudged her. She must be more careful. She knew she was tense and overwound about the card that had arrived earlier. It had put her on edge, and she'd ended up behaving rather badly, which was somewhat out of character. Years of wedding planning had taught her tact, diplomacy and patience.

'I'm sorry if I was rude. I'm very protective of Juno, that's all.'

'Of course you are. I can't imagine, losing your dad and your grandad all at once. Before you were even born.' Tamara looked genuinely anguished.

'It was terrible. For everyone.'

'We're going to make this anniversary the event of a lifetime. I promise you.'

As Tamara slid away, Nikki heard a text come in on her phone. She pulled it out and read it.

I'm in the Codmother. Want chips?

She'd lost her appetite completely.

No thanks I'm good she texted back.

OK. See you on the front in 5.

She put her phone back in her bag with a sigh of relief. If there was one person she trusted with her life, it was Detective Sergeant 'Woody' Woodman. He knew everything about her. They had no secrets. He'd help her put everything into perspective, she was sure of it.

18

Nikki slid into the passenger seat next to Woody. He was parked outside the Neptune, scoffing his chips one by one, and her heart swelled with affection as she watched him.

The problem when they'd been together was that they never really saw each other. Woody's shifts were punishing and unsociable and sometimes weeks went by when they only crossed over in the wee small hours of the morning. And then Woody came home one night and cried, admitting to having feelings for the custody sergeant, Angela Lewis, whom he saw significantly more often than he saw Nikki.

Nikki wasn't cross, or upset, or even surprised. They peeled apart, gently, and she bought her house which was walking distance from his, and Bill bobbed quite happily between the two of them. They had parented him brilliantly after the split, she thought. Much better than they would have if they'd tried to stay together.

They were still the very best of friends.

In front of them, the sea was Quink-dark, the boats swaying as the tide came in and filled up the harbour. It felt calm and peaceful, as if nothing could go wrong, but Nikki knew you could never be complacent where the sea was concerned. A deadly rip, a broken-down engine, a drink too many – anything could happen. Across the harbour by the slipway, the lifeboat station kept a watchful eye. Behind them, the coloured lights strung across the front of the Neptune threw a rainbow glow across the cobbles.

Woody's car was filled with the steamy scent of vinegar. She smiled down at the chips in his lap.

'It's no wonder you're such a fat lump.'

Woody couldn't put on a pound, no matter how hard he tried. He was a string bean, all six foot four of him.

'Go on,' he said with a grin, poking a chip at her. 'You know you want to.'

Nikki dodged her head out of the way, laughing. They still teased each other mercilessly, as if they were still in the sixth form.

He aimed the chip at his own mouth instead, chomping with satisfaction. 'So what's up, then?'

She sighed. 'I've been getting these weird cards.'

'What kind of weird?'

'The first one said *there are no secrets in a small town*.'

Woody shrugged. 'Well, there are. We know that. Otherwise, I'd be out of a job.' She didn't answer. 'Why are you so worried?'

'It was addressed to me. Personally. And it felt like a threat.'

'Let's have a look.'

'I ripped it up and threw it in the bin.'

Woody tutted. 'I could have had it fingerprinted.'

'Then there was this one. It came to the office.' She

pulled it out of her bag and showed him. *Who else knows the truth, besides you? And me?*

Woody gave it a glance.

'It's probably just an advert for something.'

'I don't think so. They look as if they're handwritten.' Nikki reached out a hand and took a chip, unable to resist any longer. 'What if somebody knows?'

'Nobody knows. And even if they did, so what? It's been years.'

'It would be disastrous if anyone found out.' Nikki's tone was sharp.

'But maybe it wouldn't?' He looked at her. 'Don't spend your whole life living in fear, Nik. Sometimes that's worse than whatever you're afraid of.'

'It's OK for you to say. You've never done anything wrong.'

'Of course I have.' He sighed. 'Angela Lewis.'

Angela hadn't even lasted long, but by then they'd gone their separate ways.

'She wasn't your fault. We were doomed from the start. We should have just stayed friends.' Had she been wrong, to use him as a rebound? He'd known full well that was what he was.

He grinned. 'Yeah. But then we wouldn't have Bill. Imagine that. Life without Bill.'

She sighed. 'Do you think he's OK?'

'Happy as a pig in shit.'

'I miss him.'

'God, me too. Not his stinky trainers though. I don't miss them.'

They both laughed, thinking about the boy that had bound them for life.

'I better go,' she said now. She'd meant to get an early night and it was nearly eleven.

Woody crumpled up his chip wrapper, wound down the window and lobbed it straight into the bin.

'Try and forget about it, Nik. People are strange. People are jealous. They probably just want to make you worry.'

'Well, they've succeeded.'

'If anything happens, just shoot me a text. I'll be right there.'

She looked at him, with his tufty hair and his bright blue eyes which never seemed to blink and his infinite freckles, looking no different than the day he'd arrived in Speedwell. She rested her head on his shoulder for a moment, comforted by his presence, comforted by the knowledge that he would be there for her, in a trice. He always had been, she remembered. Right from the night the inevitable had happened, Woody had been there by her side.

19

Then

That Friday was the end-of-summer fancy dress party at the Neptune. The theme was rock stars, which everyone agreed was pretty easy, even if you didn't want to make too much effort. Mostly you just needed a wig and a pair of sunglasses. And as usual there was the karaoke competition, with a great big golden trophy that would be carried home triumphantly by the winner.

Nearly everyone in town piled into the pub. The mood was always joyful. This was the best night of the year for the locals, the chance to let their hair down. Keiran the landlord did them proud, kicking off the evening with free chicken or scampi in a basket to line everyone's stomach, because it was always a heavy night and he knew it was a fine line between jolly rowdiness and utter carnage. Experience had taught him it was best to get as many carbs into his customers as possible, so the chips were chunky and plentiful, nestled in red-and-white gingham napkins, and their saltiness made everyone buy more drinks, so he was quids in.

The first hour was always filled with laughter and shrieks of glee: the transformations were impressive. Some went for an obvious choice; others were more daring. There were loads of Elvises and Elton Johns and lots of different David Bowies in all his guises as well as several Madonnas in her different phases. Some clubbed together and came as groups: Abba and the Beatles and the Spice Girls.

Nikki had transformed herself into Stevie Nicks. She'd found a long black lace skirt in a charity shop, and wore it with high suede boots and a velvet jacket. She looked good. Sometimes fancy dress was a great excuse to be someone you weren't, and she was enjoying her alter ego, in total contrast to her usual practical jeans and sweatshirt. She was certainly getting more attention than usual and she rather liked people looking at her with new eyes.

She ordered a glass of cider and danced her way through the crowds, greeting friends, admiring outfits, feeling the tension of the working day leave her. She edged into a corner at the back of the pub where her friends had commandeered two settles either side of a scrubbed pine table. Woody was at the head, so she sat next to him. Did he suspect how she was feeling, about that night on the boat last Sunday? About the heat that rushed through her every time Rik came into her thoughts? She hadn't seen him since, but she tried to push him out of her mind. She would wake, heart pounding, in the middle of the night, having felt the touch of his hand on her bare shoulder in her dreams, burning her skin.

It was a stupid crush, she told herself. It would fade before long. It would have to, because she couldn't bear it much longer. She'd had to avoid Jess, because she didn't want to hear a word about what had gone on between the two of them. Jess wouldn't leave out a single detail. Nikki took another tentative sip of cider. Sometimes drink muffled her emotions, but sometimes it amplified them. She could never tell, so it was best to be cautious.

Gradually, she began to relax, as the cider did its work and the gossip at the table drew her in. The evening was going to be OK. She would enjoy it. It was always joyful and hilarious and heart-warming. Not for the first time, she thought how lucky she was to live somewhere like Speedwell and to feel such a part of the fabric of the town. Not everyone felt they belonged where they lived, but she couldn't imagine living anywhere else, or leaving all these people behind. They had made her who she was. She mustn't let her feelings for Rik unsettle her. Two weeks ago, she hadn't even known he existed, she reminded herself.

She dug into one of the baskets of fried chicken at the table, tearing open a ketchup sachet and squeezing it over the hot chips. She hadn't eaten anything since breakfast and that was asking for trouble, as someone had already put a fresh tray of drinks down on the table and handed her another cider. Then Tamsin arrived, causing a stir as Kate Bush – no-one ever saw her in anything but a fleece and wellies, but with her tangle of long dark hair, the transformation worked.

An hour later, just before the karaoke was due to start, Nikki headed to the loo. She touched up her black eyeliner and the burgundy lipstick, staring at her unfamiliar reflection but quite admiring it. Maybe she should have a change of image? Perhaps even go travelling? She had probably fallen for Rik because he was new blood; the most interesting person to arrive on the scene in Speedwell since . . . since forever. There must be other people just as enticing in the world. It was up to her to go and find them. You couldn't wait for the man of your dreams to turn up on your doorstep. You had to be proactive, not sit around mooning.

But what would the business do without her? How would her dad manage? She couldn't leave him in the lurch. She sighed as she turned away from the mirror. She was trapped, pinned by filial duty to a single point on the map.

Buoyed by her own pep talk, she headed out of the Ladies just as Rik was coming out of the Gents. When had he arrived? For a moment she was tempted to slide back into the cloakroom, but it was too late. He had seen her, and his face lit up.

'Nikki.' He reached out his hand, touched her on the arm. 'You look amazing.'

'Thanks.' Nikki found herself blushing, and hoped her heavy make-up would hide her pink cheeks. This was both a dream come true and a nightmare. She squirmed inside, discomfort and excitement jostling for pole position. She could smell his warm musk scent, not quite sure if it was just him or something he wore.

There was a pause, and he smiled.

'Thank you for last Sunday,' he said. 'For introducing me to everyone. It's tough, arriving in a strange town. But I felt like one of the family.'

She laughed shakily. She tried not to move, not wanting to break the spell, but not daring to look at him. Then he moved in, wrapped his arms around her, pulling her in. She could feel her heartbeat against his, a contrapuntal rhythm. She could barely breathe. What did this mean?

'You're a star,' he said.

She didn't know what to do. Was this just a hug of gratitude, or something more? Where was Jess? Had she come with him? Was she going to appear at any minute, and smirk at their embrace, knowing it meant nothing, knowing she had all the power?

Or had nothing happened between them? Had she misread all the signals and assumed Rik had fallen for her sister, because that was what she was programmed to believe: that any man would find Jess irresistible and choose her over Nikki. Did he remember their closeness that afternoon on the beach; the closeness she had been too afraid to do anything about?

And then suddenly she felt Rik let her go. He stepped away, brushing at his clothes, as if dusting her off him.

'Hey, Woody,' she heard him say.

She turned and there was Woody striding towards them along the corridor. His face when he saw them together was a mixture of shock and concern.

Rik smiled at him, appraising him with those velvet eyes. Woody was taller than him. Woody was taller than everyone. He didn't smile back.

'I'm going outside for a smoke,' he said to Nikki. 'Coming?'

Nikki knew it was an order. Woody didn't smoke. Nor did she. He was rescuing her. Not from Rik. He was rescuing her from herself.

'Sure.' She raised a hand in farewell to Rik, and followed Woody down the corridor and out onto the terrace at the back. Above them, the stars were pin sharp, and she could hear the pounding of the waves against the harbour wall. It would be high tide at midnight.

Woody looked out to the invisible horizon, his hands

in his pockets. The breeze pushed his hair about, like a hairdresser trying out styles.

'Don't fall for him, Nik,' he said.

'Don't be silly,' said Nikki, her throat tight with panic.

Woody turned and looked straight at her. 'I've seen the way you look at him.'

She tried to laugh, tried to deny it, but it came out as a sob. She breathed in, trying to hold back her tears. She couldn't break down in front of Woody. But there they were, big fat tears quivering on her cheeks. She flicked them away in fury. How dare they betray her?

She wiped them away, gulping in knife-sharp gusts of air. She hadn't spent so long on her eye make-up ever. She wasn't going to ruin it. Woody was looking at her in alarm.

'I'm fine,' she told him. 'I'm OK.' She breathed. And smiled. 'Is my make-up OK?'

'Just a bit of a smudge.' He put up one finger and ran it under her left eye.

'Thank you.'

'You know I will always be here for you,' he said, his voice slightly cracking. 'Always.'

Nikki nodded. 'I know,' she said. 'And me too. For you.'

She reached out her hand and he took hers, squeezing it so hard it almost hurt.

From inside, a big burst of music shook the walls, blaring out into the dark night.

'The karaoke's starting,' she said.

'Let's go, then.' Woody disentangled his fingers. 'Come on. I'll get you a Baby Guinness.'

He strode off. Nikki stood for a moment, shivering in

the night air, wondering how five minutes could turn her upside down like that, confusing her, making her question everything she felt and thought. She had felt so close to Rik in that moment. She had felt something between them, she was sure. An incredible, all-consuming warmth. But now she felt frozen, inside and out.

She sighed. She'd better go inside or she *would* freeze. And there was karaoke to be done.

The pub was full to bursting. The walls seemed to drip with the heat of so many people, and it was standing room only as the karaoke began. The crowd were good-natured, giving a rousing cheer to even the most tone-deaf and out-of-tune performer, for they valued participation over performance. There was no need to be pitch perfect, you just had to have a go and muck in.

Nikki wasn't sure a Baby Guinness was the best idea after all the cider she'd drunk. Sambuca topped with Baileys in a shot glass, it was the current Neptune craze. She downed it in one, and it buoyed her up to take the stage and belt out her rendition of 'Edge of Seventeen'. She might not have the voice of Stevie Nicks, but she came from a family of performers and show-offs, and as the crowd sang along, she enjoyed the limelight.

At one point she looked out into the audience and saw Rik staring at her. She met his gaze, and for a few seconds it was as if there was only the two of them in the room.

And then the door opened and in walked Jess, in satin bell bottoms, a floral shirt and a furry gilet. Her dark hair was ironed poker straight, and she had moons of blue eyeshadow. Her eyes raked the room until they fell on Rik. With a triumphant smile she bore down on him, and the next moment he was sporting a fake moustache with his hair flattened under a baker boy hat.

Sonny to her Cher.

As Nikki finished her song to riotous applause, Jess pulled a reluctant Rik through the crowds and dragged him up on stage. He was protesting, but he was laughing nevertheless, and the audience began to clap, egging them on. Rik played to the crowd, shrugging as if to say 'what can I do?', and took one of the mikes as the opening bars of 'I Got You Babe' blasted out over the loud speaker.

As duets went, what it lacked in polish it made up for with enthusiasm. Jess was hamming it up, singing to Rik as if he was the love of her life. He played it cool, but his eyes were laughing, and he had the moves and no one was left in any doubt that he could sing. For an impromptu performance, it was impressive.

Someone pressed another Baby Guinness into Nikki's hand by way of appreciation for her performance, but she pushed it away. She could feel bile rise up inside her and she needed some air, but it was impossible to push her way through the throng. She was pinned to the spot and forced to watch.

As Jess and Rik reached the last bars, the applause was rapturous. They took a bow. And then Jess threw her arms around Rik and kissed him. A proper kiss, not just a peck on the cheek. A kiss that left nothing to the imagination or anyone in two minds about their relationship.

They owned the stage. They owned the room.

They owned the world.

20

Now

On Saturday, Helen crept through the streets of Speedwell just after dawn. She could already tell the day was set fair. She could judge the weather better than a barometer, feeling in her bones and smelling in the air whether there would be sunshine or rain for the rest of the day. Today, there was a little cloud cover, but the sun was elbowing its way through and would push those clouds to one side by eight o'clock, then show the full force of her rays by mid-morning. Perfect weather for a wedding.

She let herself into her unit, feeling the usual leap of pleasure at entering her domain. She'd had it fitted out to her own specification. It was pristine and gleaming, with a state-of-the-art oven and stainless-steel work surfaces. The walls were racked with shelves containing all the tools of her trade: mixing bowls, food processors, every size and shape of cake tin imaginable, wooden spoons and spatulas, icing bags and nozzles. A large cupboard held flours and sugars and baking powder; food colouring and cocoa powder and vanilla essence. In the fridge was best organic butter and cream; next to it were boxes of free-range eggs from a nearby farm and baskets full of lemons. It was the opposite of the kitchen at Mariners, which was dilapidated and scruffy and disorganised and definitely wouldn't get a food hygiene certificate. In here, you'd be hard-pushed to find so much as a crumb out of place or a thumbprint on a surface.

Here, Helen created her masterpieces. If she was feeling flat or tense, she would come in and experiment with new flavours and techniques to add to her repertoire. She often spent the evening scrolling through Pinterest and something would catch her eye. Something that seemed impossible to recreate at first glimpse, but Helen would try and try again until she had got it just right. Her friends were used to being given the results of her trial runs, and would give her feedback in return for being guinea pigs.

Today's wedding was for a garden designer and her client. Gillian and Carenza had fallen in love over the sweet peas, and were having a simple ceremony followed by tea on Carenza's lawn. The cake they'd chosen was a single-tier sponge flecked with the zest and juice of the best Spanish oranges, then filled with passion fruit curd and meringue buttercream and coated with a white Belgian chocolate ganache. It had hardened off in the fridge overnight, and now she had to put on the finishing touches. She'd brought a basket of flowers from her cutting garden at Mariners in a gorgeous array of yellow and blue and purple: nasturtiums and borage and cornflowers; violas and pansies.

She gently laid out the flower heads, throwing away any that were torn or bruised, then spent half an hour carefully applying them to the tops and sides of the cake with edible glue. By the time she had finished it looked breathtakingly beautiful.

'Oh, Mum,' sighed Nikki, who'd arrived to collect it.

'I think this is the best one I've ever done.' Helen stood back and took a photograph with her iPad.

'They'll love it. I mean, what more could they wish for?'

Despite her enthusiasm, Helen couldn't help noticing that Nikki was more tense than usual, stressing while they placed the cake inside one of the special boxes Helen had designed to avoid disastrous mishaps.

'Is everything OK?' she asked. Nikki had seemed strained at the committee meeting too.

Nikki didn't answer for a moment. Helen felt anxious. Was there something wrong? Was Nikki unwell? Or did she have money worries? She'd always prided herself on having a very open relationship with her children. There were no secrets between them. They could talk to her about anything.

'I guess I'm just feeling my age,' Nikki joked in the end. 'The house is chaos and I'm heading into silly season. I can't remember the last time I had a decent night's sleep.'

'You should make sure you get a day off.'

'Don't worry, Mum. I'm always like this before a wedding. You know I am.'

The two of them ceremoniously carried the box out to the van, where Nikki had a special space in the back with a non-slip mat, and had the air-con running so it didn't melt.

'Today is going to be perfect,' Helen reassured her. She was her daughter's biggest cheerleader, especially in those moments of panic when Nikki feared that a wedding was never going to come together. She watched her daughter drive out of the yard, wishing her cake Godspeed and hoping it would bring joy to everyone who shared it.

Afterwards, Helen went back inside to tidy up and have a reviving cup of tea. The concentration and meticulous handiwork were exhausting. People often asked her when she was going to retire, but she didn't think she'd ever give up the cakes. It didn't feel like work. It was a pleasure from the very first glimmer of an idea to the moment she shut the lid on the box. She printed out the photo she'd taken earlier and pinned it on the wall along with all the other pictures she'd taken over the years. All those love stories. All those weddings. She was a romantic at heart. She loved to think of her icing gluing people together.

It reminded her to check the dating website. She sat down with a cup of tea and opened her iPad. She'd uploaded her profile and a few of Juno's photos to Sunshine After the Rain, but no one had caught her eye just yet, and she couldn't help feeling disappointed. There were plenty of perfectly pleasant men, but they all seemed a little bit dull. 'Looking for a lovely lady to cuddle up with on the sofa' seemed to be a constant refrain. That was the last thing she wanted to do. She had matched with a couple of them in the hopes that if she dug a bit deeper, she might find a diamond, but their repartee had been less than scintillating and they seemed very grumpy if she didn't give them the answers they wanted.

How did the young manage it? she wondered. Was there a trick, a secret code? Jess might have told her that you had to kiss a lot of frogs before you found the right one, but there was no way she was going to kiss any of the frogs she'd matched with so far.

And then a new profile caught her eye. Ralph. His brown eyes were merry, and he had a thatch of very thick grey hair that looked slightly unkempt, but only as if he'd just ruffled it absent-mindedly, not because he was slovenly. He had on a checked country shirt and a mustard-yellow tie with a dashing knot. She read his introduction.

> *I'm a pianist, ex-head of music for a school in Somerset, and I still do some composing for adverts which keeps the wolf from the door. You might have had one of my jingles rolling around your head! My glass is half full, hopefully of nice red burgundy. I have an impossibly beautiful Irish Setter, Clara (named after Clara Schumann), who keeps me company. I like, in no particular order: the smell of hot tarmac after rain, Tunnock's tea cakes, a drop of real ale, steam trains, grandfather clocks, Chet Baker, boiled eggs in front of* Antiques Roadshow, *Ian Rankin, Led Zeppelin, moth holes, my ancient Volvo convertible, big ice cubes in my gin and tonic, crosswords,* Inspector Morse, *taking off, big socks. I've been widowed for five years and I feel ready for something – I'm not sure what, but I'd like to meet someone who'll make me think, make me laugh, and make me get off my bum and have some adventures.*

Helen felt a ripple of excitement. None of the other men had piqued her interest in the least, but Ralph's words had a warmth and openness to them she found refreshingly unselfconscious. A little bit different but not too eccentric. His clothes looked comfy with a rakish edge, he had a dog (always a good sign) and a convertible, which showed a bit of spirit. They both liked Ian Rankin, which was also a good sign. She didn't feel intimidated by him, just intrigued to know a little bit more. Which was more than she could say about any of the other profiles.

A little nervous, she clicked on him to see if they might match. And there it was – the burst of fireworks to indicate that he had liked her too, so they would be able to message each other. She wondered what he had liked about her profile. Some people said that men liked every profile, in a mad frenzy to find a mate, but she didn't feel as if that would be his strategy. He seemed discerning. Thoughtful.

Of course, it was easy to romanticise and project the qualities you wanted onto someone. But Ralph looked worth the risk. She would never know unless she tried. So she plucked up the courage and typed out a message without thinking too hard. She knew if she overthought it, she'd never write anything.

> *Hello! I love your list. We have Ian Rankin in common! And who doesn't love boiled eggs on a Sunday evening? Here's a few of my likes: being up before everyone else, bubble baths, firework night, cauliflower cheese, my book club, sunset swims, watching my granddaughters dance, Meatloaf (the singer not the food!),* Silent Witness, *fresh bed linen. Have you read anything good lately?*

She knew it was good to finish your message with a question to ensure a reply. She read over her list. Did she sound boring? It was all true. She didn't want to lie because there was no point in pretending to be something she wasn't. And although he was probably a bit more sophisticated than she was, being a pianist, he didn't seem too rarefied. Quite normal really.

She could imagine him and William having a pint outside the Neptune on a summer evening. And that was a good thing.

She pressed send before she had a chance to chicken out. And afterwards, she felt a skip of excitement. If you wanted change in your life, you had to make it happen. And if he didn't answer, she wouldn't lose any sleep over it. That was one of the good things about getting older: you stopped taking things so personally.

21

Gillian and Carenza's wedding was perfect from start to finish.

Despite getting married for the first time at the age of sixty-three, practical Gillian had refused a formal wedding car. She didn't see the point when all she needed was to get to the registry office on time and her flatbed truck would do that. Nikki had spent the day before mucking it out, washing and polishing it until it gleamed and pinning a loosely tied wreath of foliage studded with roses and peonies to the front. And that morning, she'd driven Gillian to the registry office herself to meet her bride.

This was why she was the best wedding planner in town. Nothing was too much trouble.

At tea on the lawn, with a string quartet playing 'An English Country Garden', Nikki could imagine the two of them living out their days together in this beautiful setting, filled with the scent of honeysuckle and lavender. She tumbled into bed at midnight, knowing there wasn't a thing she could have done to make it any more perfect.

It was the small, intimate weddings Nikki loved doing best. They might not be the ones that made the most money, but they were incredibly rewarding, leaving her with a warm glow of satisfaction and the sense that love really did make the world go round. And she relished making them extra special. It was the tiny personal touches that made the difference, rather than extravagant displays of ostentation.

Sunday meant more skip-filling and hard work. Nikki crawled out of bed at eight, and made her way down to the kitchen to make coffee and toast and turn the radio on. The next thing she knew a face appeared at the kitchen window and she nearly dropped her mug. She pulled open the back door and Juno bounced in. She was wearing a North Property Management boiler suit too, her blue hair up in a baseball cap. She shimmied across the kitchen in time to the music and grabbed the remaining slice of Nikki's toast. 'Oh God – toast and Marmite. I'm starving.' She pulled some more bread out of the packet and put it in the toaster. 'So – what are we on?'

Nikki had offered her fifty quid cash to come and help her out. She pointed at the ugly dark wood kitchen units. 'These have got to come out.'

Next door, Nikki could see Gatsby jump up onto the hot tub platform and look out to sea. It was icy turquoise today. Nikki had already lost count of the different shades of blue that could change from one minute to the next, depending on the clouds, the sun, the temperature, the prevailing wind.

'By the way, I think I've got you a new client,' she told Juno. 'The guy next door needs someone to look after his dog when he goes to London.'

'He'll have to have an interview.' Juno was very picky

about her clients. If she didn't think they were good dog owners, she wouldn't take them on. 'What's his name?'

'Adam.'

'The dog, I mean.'

'Gatsby.'

Juno raised her eyebrows. 'That's quite a name to live up to.' The second lot of toast popped up and Juno began buttering it.

'There's something else I want to talk to you about.' Nikki still wasn't sure how Juno was going to react to her news. Tamara had phoned her the day before to tell her Zak was on board with doing a duet.

Juno turned around, taut with suspicion. 'What?'

'You know the anniversary event?'

'Don't they want me anymore?'

'Yes! A hundred per cent. But better than that.' Nikki hoped Juno would think it was better. 'Zak Glazier approached them about doing something to help get publicity. So the committee came up with the idea of you both doing a duet.'

Juno didn't answer at first.

'Me and Zak Glazier?' she said at last.

'Wouldn't that be amazing?'

'There's no way I can do that. I mean – Zak Glazier? There'll be hundreds of screaming fans. They won't want me there. I'll probably get booed off.' She shook her head. 'I'd rather do something on my own.'

Nikki could see Juno was panicking about being out of her comfort zone. It was how she lived her life. She kept herself safe and stress-free. It was why she was still at home and hadn't gone off to uni or gone travelling. Nikki could see a little bit of herself in her niece – after all, she'd never left Speedwell either. Every year that passed made it harder and harder to leave.

'Juno, I know it's a scary prospect, but it could be great for you. It's a once-in-a-lifetime opportunity, to get that kind of exposure.'

'But I don't want exposure. I keep telling Mum. I'm quite happy with things as they are. If I wasn't, I'd have done something about it.'

'But you're so talented.'

Juno shrugged. 'And?'

'You should do something with it. It's a waste otherwise.'

'Why? Not everyone wants fame and fortune. I don't.'

Did she mean that? Nikki wondered. Or was it lack of confidence holding her back? Fear of the unknown? She sighed.

'Look. You know we're trying to raise money for the lifeboat. And Zak's offer is great publicity for the event. But the committee felt strongly that your voice was more important than his.'

'Really?'

Nikki knew she was equivocating slightly, but it didn't matter. 'Yes. So a duet seemed like the perfect solution. We'll have your authentic voice, and Zak's pull. We *need* you.' Juno didn't look at all convinced. 'At least meet him. He's asked you to go to his studio to try and pull something together.'

'His studio?' Juno looked taken aback. 'But what if he hates my song-writing? Or my voice? Or me?'

'You won't ever know the answer to *what if* unless you take a risk. That's how you grow, Juno. That's how you live your best life. Avoiding *what if* is the coward's way.'

Nikki held her breath. Had she been too harsh? Juno didn't react well to pressure. Juno chewed on the last of her toast, ruminating.

'Why don't I take you to his house to meet him?' Nikki offered. 'You can have a chat. See what he's like. See if you trust him. You don't have to commit to anything. You've got nothing to lose.'

Juno nodded, eventually. 'OK. But if he's even this much of a dick,' she held her fingers a centimetre apart. 'I'm out of there.'

Nikki laughed. 'I'll get Tamara to set it up.'

She felt a surge of excitement for Juno. She shouldn't hide her songs from the rest of the world. This was a step towards getting her to come out of her shell. For a moment she fantasised about Juno and Zak going viral, the song getting to number one, a world tour – then she told herself to stop dreaming on Juno's behalf. What would be would be.

Nikki had gathered together all the tools they would need for dismantling the kitchen. She quailed slightly at the thought of being without a kitchen for the next couple of weeks while Mike and Jason worked their magic, but she would manage. She'd got a little gas ring and an air fryer which she could set up in the dining area, and she could work her way around her relatives for sustenance. And there was always the Neptune.

She watched as Juno set to with a screwdriver to take off the doors. They were all doers, the North women. Even the M and Ms could mend their own bicycle punctures, sew on a button if it fell off their school shirt and rustle up a bowl of pasta pesto with parmesan. Meanwhile, she turned off the stopcock and put tape around all the electric sockets. Her dad had trained her well.

'It's all in the prep,' he used to say, and he was right. Sanding, priming, taping, filling, checking for wires, turning off power supplies . . . all the things that people often didn't bother with.

It took just over an hour and a half to get rid of the units and the worksurface and stack it all neatly in the skip. Then they attacked the horrible brown tiles decorated with wheatsheaves, prising them off with a hammer and bolster. By midday their hair and teeth were coated in dust, but the wheelbarrow was full. They trundled it out to the skip then sat on the back doorstep with a mug of tea each.

'Can I ask you something?' said Juno.

'Course.'

'What was my dad really like?'

Juno looked straight into Nikki's eyes, and her stomach looped the loop.

'What do you mean?'

'Thinking about this song has made me realise I don't know as much about my dad as I do about Grandpa. I mean, everyone always talks about how wonderful and kind Grandpa was and what he did for the town. But they don't talk about Dad so much.'

'I guess because he hadn't been here so long.'

'Even Mum won't talk about him. Whenever I ask about him, she goes a bit funny. Just tries to shut the conversation down. Why's she like that?'

Nikki crammed the rest of a digestive biscuit in her mouth so she wouldn't have to answer straight away.

'I don't know,' she said eventually. 'You know what

your mum's like. Maybe she misses him? Or maybe she's angry with him. People sometimes get angry with people who die. I get angry with my dad sometimes, even now. For leaving us. For leaving Mum.'

'But they couldn't have done anything. It wasn't their fault.' Juno's eyes were wide.

'No. Of course not. I'm not saying it's logical. It's just human nature. You can have mixed feelings, even after all this time.'

'I get angry too, sometimes, that I never got to meet my own dad. But not angry with him.' Juno threw the rest of her mug of tea on the grass. 'You can miss someone even if you've never met them. And it's not fair that Mum won't talk about him.'

'Your mum doesn't really like talking about private stuff. She's always been the same. I mean, she'll tell you how she's feeling. You're never in any doubt about what kind of a mood she's in. But she doesn't really do . . . intimate chats.' Nikki could remember the storms of their teenage years, when the whole house was run by Jess's moods. If you confronted her to find out what was going on, she stormed off. Slammed the door in your face.

'You're telling me,' said Juno. 'She's either up, or down. There's never any in between.'

'You're not going to change her.'

'No. But I do want to find out a bit more about the person that is half of me. And I thought you must have known him quite well. What was he like? Was he the kind of person who'd make you a cup of tea without asking? Or know when you needed a hug? What did he *smell* like?'

Heavenly, thought Nikki. He smelled heavenly. Of salt and toffee and something from Provence – lavender, maybe. If she shut her eyes and closed all her other senses down, she could breathe him in now.

'Well,' she said, 'when he arrived in Speedwell, it was as if he'd brought the sun with him, all the way from France. And that's there in you, Juno. You always bring the sun.'

'Oh.' Juno thought about what Nikki had said, and smiled. 'That's nice.'

It was true. Juno was a sunbeam. She had incredible empathy, and an easy way with people, no matter what age they were. She was no walkover though. She had a certain feistiness. If she saw someone being rude in a supermarket queue, she'd call them out. And woe betide a man giving someone unwanted attention. They'd have Juno to reckon with. She didn't pull her punches.

'I know Mum got pregnant with me before they got married, because I can do the maths,' Juno went on. 'But what actually happened? No one will ever say.'

22

Then

If Nikki could have found the courage to leave Speedwell at the end of that summer, she would have. But perhaps even then there was something in her that hoped Rik's relationship with Jess would disintegrate, and that she would be there to pick up the pieces. So she told herself she couldn't possibly leave her job, that she was indispensable at North Property Management and her dad couldn't cope without her. This was not true, of course. For a start, she knew William would never have held her back or stood in the way of her dreams. And they would easily find someone to take over from her. She was good, but not irreplaceable. But that was her excuse, and she hated herself for the lies she told herself.

In the meantime, Jess and Rik were inseparable as summer turned to autumn and autumn turned to winter. They were besotted with each other. There was almost a Ready Brek glow about them, radiating an aura that made everyone sigh with envy and longing. Oh, to have that connection. That chemistry. Their arms were wound around each other, holding on even whilst talking to someone else. They were almost like one person.

Nikki tried to avoid them, but it was impossible, for there they were, in the Neptune or in the kitchen at Mariners. They were mostly living on the boat, for Rik didn't like to leave it empty, but when it got too cold, or the sea mist rolled in, Jess would insist on going back home, for central heating and hot water and comfort food.

Rik had settled into the North family, and it was as if he had always been part of them. He and William chatted for hours about boats, and he joined the lifeboat crew. It was as if he had always been a part of them too, for he was more at home on water than on land, and had that innate understanding of the sea that was so crucial when it came to saving lives. His mother, Sabine, came over from France, and they all saw where he got his magical charm from.

It was a fairy tale come true, and Nikki learned to live with the pain of having Rik so close but so totally out of reach.

There were definitely chinks, though. Nikki had heard more than one argument. Jess's voice rising in indignation made its way through the thick walls of the house. This was par for the course. Jess's relationships were always volatile, because she was demanding, and unreasonable. And inconsiderate. Nikki never heard Rik raise his voice back.

It was New Year's Eve when she saw them arguing in the hallway. Jess wanted to go to the Neptune for their end-of-year festivities, but Rik was desperate for a quiet night after a week of seasonal indulgence, and he was on call for the lifeboat. It was teeming with rain outside too.

Hot chocolate in front of the telly at Mariners seemed a much more enticing option but Jess didn't see it that way.

'I didn't realise you were so *boring*,' she complained.

'You go,' he said, quite reasonably. 'I'm totally OK with you going.'

'Oh, thanks,' Jess snapped back. 'You're totally OK with me doing what I want, are you? Good to know.'

'You know what I mean.' Rik was starting to look desperate. He looked up and saw Nikki at the top of the stairs, ready to head out for the night. She wanted to disappear back into her room and not intrude on their argument. Jess scowled, and grabbed her coat off the hook.

'OK. Sleep well, Grandad.' She stormed out of the door.

Rik looked dejected as Nikki made her way down the stairs.

'If it helps, it's not you,' she told him. 'She's always been like this. She doesn't mean it.'

'I'd better go.' Rik sighed.

'Leave her. She'll be as happy as anything by the time she gets to the pub. Jess's tantrums never last long.'

'I know,' he said. 'But . . . it can be hard.'

That was the price you paid with Jess. She was an immoveable force, an inspiration in lots of ways, larger than life, filled with energy and fun. But tricky.

'You learn to live with it,' said Nikki. 'We all have. She is worth it, I promise. She's one in a million.'

Why was she defending her, when this was a prime opportunity to put doubt into Rik's mind? Because it was true, she supposed. She loved Jess. And deep down she doubted that Rik would ever choose her over her ebullient, dazzling sister, so she didn't want to play that card.

He didn't reply at first. He seemed weighed down by the row they'd just had, his shoulders slumped. The light in his eyes had gone out.

'Nikki . . .' He sighed her name, and there seemed to be longing in it.

'Yes?'

'I wanted to say . . . I'm sorry.'

'What for?'

'I know there was something between us.' He pointed back and forwards between them. 'I could feel it. And I think you could too.'

She shook her head as if she didn't understand what he was saying. She gave him a helpless half-smile but couldn't meet his gaze, because she knew she would fold under its intensity. Was she supposed to agree? Or deny it? She ended up shrugging, but she was burning inside. He was too close. The heat of him . . .

'The thing is, I thought you and Woody were together. That day I first came to Mariners.'

'Me and Woody?' She almost laughed.

'That's why I backed off. I didn't want to cause trouble. Or come between you.'

'Me and Woody are best mates. That's it.'

'I know that now. But it's too late. And I'm really sorry. If you thought I'd behaved badly . . .' She couldn't avoid looking at him now. He was staring straight at her. 'Because I think . . .'

'What?' she whispered.

'I think I've made a mistake.'

There was silence. For three seconds. Five. She had to say something. But she couldn't.

'There's nothing I can do now. I'm in too deep with Jess.'

'Of course not.' She reached out a hand to pat his arm. It was supposed to be a gesture of reassurance, but the moment she touched him, she saw the light come back into his eyes. There was still something between them. Something powerful. He stepped towards her and she put her hands up, closing her eyes, terrified they were going to do something irreversible. Yet she longed for that to happen too.

'Nikki . . .' He whispered her name again and she felt her resolve melting. The chemistry was impossible to ignore. There was something deliciously toxic shooting through her veins that made her feel as if anything was possible, as if she was irresistible, as if—

The front door flew open. Rik stepped away from her and reached for his coat. Jess was standing in the doorway, drenched from the rain outside.

'You *have* to come. Because I've got something important to tell you.' She looked at the two of them. Nikki wondered if there was guilt written all over their faces, but Jess didn't look in the least bit suspicious. Of course not. She had never seen Nikki as a threat. And besides, she had the trump card. She smiled as she dealt it. 'I'm pregnant.' She laughed and Nikki noticed a slight tinge of hysteria. 'I'm having a baby.'

23

Now

Nikki gave Juno an edited version of events, leaving out her part of the story. Instead, she told of a whirlwind romance and Jess's surprise announcement that New Year's Eve. And Rik's subsequent proposal. Two weeks later, once the news had sunk in, he'd gone to ask William for his daughter's hand in marriage. Helen had given him her own grandmother's engagement ring, a square-cut sapphire surrounded by diamonds.

'Jess has always wanted it,' she told him. 'And it's lovely to think it will stay in the family.'

At no point did Nikki suggest that things in the garden hadn't been entirely rosy, for the last thing she wanted was for Juno to think that it was her fault; that her imminent arrival had put her parents under pressure and forced them together. Yet somehow Juno read between the lines.

'What I don't understand is what he saw in Mum?'

'What?' Nikki was startled by the question.

'I mean, I love Mum, of course I do, but we all know she's selfish and stroppy and it's all about her, most of the time. How did he put up with it?'

Nikki was at a loss for words. She stared at Juno, whose

troubled eyes were full of questions. She couldn't think what to say. She certainly couldn't tell her the truth. In the end, she shrugged, attempting a blithe smile.

'Opposites attract, I guess. And your mum isn't all bad. You know that. She's pretty wonderful, underneath it all.'

It was true. Even now, just as you'd had enough of Jess, just as you were about ready to kill her, she would grab you and tell you how important you were to her, and how she couldn't live without you, and she'd wrap you in one of her hugs, suffocating you with that intoxicating Black Orchid, and you would feel on top of the world. And the memory of whatever she'd done to enrage you would melt away and you'd fall in love with her again for the millionth time.

Nikki couldn't breathe. Everything was closing in. Too many questions. Too many memories. Too much guilt.

There are no secrets in a small town.

'Let's go for a swim,' she said. 'It's nearly high tide. We can wash off all this dust.'

'You're changing the subject.'

'I'm not. I'm dirty and knackered and I need a break. Come on. Let's do it.'

Juno knew when to drop a conversation. Ten minutes later they'd grabbed their swimming things and were clambering down the steps to the beach. The early evening sun was getting weaker, drifting downwards as if it was losing the will to stay afloat, and a sharp sea breeze snapped at their heels. Summer might be here, but she was fickle.

Halfway down, as they rounded a corner and the beach itself came into view, Nikki spied Adam and Gatsby. Adam looked like an advert for a luxury outdoor clothing company, as if he was about to conquer the coast path with a foldaway tent in his pocket, or make a fire out of driftwood and rocks. Gatsby was bounding through the shallows, having the time of his life.

'Oh my God,' breathed Juno. 'Look at him.'

Nikki knew she would be talking about the dog. Juno prioritised animals over humans every day of the week.

'That's my new neighbour.'

Gatsby spotted them and gave a bark of excitement, streaking across the sand. Adam turned to see what had distracted him, and raised his hand in recognition. Nikki felt a flicker of pleasure at the sight of him as she scrambled down the last few steps. It was a slightly unfamiliar feeling – one that had been long buried.

Juno jumped onto the sand as Gatsby came bounding over, then dropped to her knees and put her arms around him. As Adam walked over, Nikki pointed at the two of them.

'This is my niece Juno I was telling you about.'

Adam smiled down at Juno and Gatsby, who were embroiled in some kind of dog/human love-in where the rest of the world might as well not have existed.

'Hi, Juno,' said Adam. 'It certainly looks as if you two have hit it off.'

'He's beautiful.' Juno looked up at him. 'Any time you want me to look after him, just say the word.'

Nikki looked surprised. 'You're honoured. She's got quite the waiting list.'

'Gatsby will melt the stoniest of hearts. Even mine. I was dead against him. Until he nudged his hairy snout under my arm while I was watching the rugby and forced me to love him.'

'Irresistible.' Juno gave Gatsby a final rub of his fluffy

ears and stood up. 'We'd better get in if we're going to. The tide's on the turn.'

'Do you mind if I join you?' Adam pointed his thumb towards the sea. 'I don't know the water so I don't want to go in on my own.'

'Of course.'

'I bet it's brass monkeys,' he went on, gamely.

'It always is. The sea here never really warms up until late summer. Brace yourself.'

The three of them got ready, folding up their clothes and leaving their bags on top of the flat rock.

'No wet suits?' said Adam, pulling his on, but not before they had a glimpse of a flat stomach, sculpted shoulders and impressive biceps. Juno tried to catch Nikki's eye but she refused to look at her.

'We're hardcore,' said Nikki. 'We don't do wet suits. But we go in all year round so we're used to it.'

Adam nodded. 'I've told myself that's what I'm going to do.' He looked at the water doubtfully.

'Come on, then,' said Juno. 'Last one in's a pickled egg.'

The three of them raced down to the water's edge, Gatsby following and barking in excitement. In front of them, the waves pranced and cavorted like showgirls, throwing brilliant white plumes of foam into the air. The sea beneath was backlit by the sun, turning it translucent.

'Yikes!' yelped Adam as their feet hit the water.

Adam copied as the women splashed themselves, getting their skin used to the icy cold. The waves pummelled them, teasing, as if to say 'Come on'. They ploughed on through the shallows, gasping with the shock. It was always a challenge as the temperature hit you, taking your breath away. The temptation to run back out was always there. You had to push yourself, forging through the water as it crept up your body, setting your skin on fire.

'Bloomin' Nora!' Adam's eyes were out on stalks.

'Just keep breathing,' Nikki told him.

The final wave of the set approached, towering over them. It was always a thrill, this moment, as you gathered your nerve.

'Go!' shouted Nikki, and the three of them threw themselves at the base of the wave, duck-diving underneath and coming out the other side, gasping and laughing.

'I've got brain freeze,' shouted Adam, but he looked exhilarated.

It was such a strange combination of torture and ecstasy, but somehow there was nothing more liberating than floating about in the waves, letting them toss you hither and thither, controlling your breath so you could acclimatise. After a few minutes, the agony faded, and the temperature felt almost normal.

Eventually they headed back in. Nikki and Juno grabbed their fleece-lined robes, and Adam eyed them with envy.

'I'm going to have to get one of those, aren't I?'

'If you're going in on a regular basis, definitely.' Nikki shrugged hers on.

'I'm just going to dodge in there to get dressed.' Adam pointed behind the rock towards the caves, which were often used as impromptu changing rooms.

For a moment, Nikki remembered a clandestine rendezvous. It was the safest place in Speedwell to be hidden, away from prying eyes.

'Oh my God,' hissed Juno as Adam disappeared. 'He'd be perfect for you.'

'Don't be ridiculous,' Nikki laughed.

'You're blushing,' said Juno.

'I am not.' Nikki touched her cheeks. 'It's the cold water.'

'Yeah, right. Seriously, though. Why not?'

'There's just one problem,' said Nikki, pulling on a pair of thick socks. 'He's in love with his wife.'

'He's married?'

'Widowed.'

'Oh.' Juno frowned. 'How long since his wife died?'

'Three years, maybe?'

'That's long enough.'

'Not necessarily.' Nikki shoved her socked feet into her Crocs, and grabbed her bobble hat.

'How long does it take to get over someone?' Juno looked perplexed.

'I think it's different for different people.' Nikki pulled her hat down even further to cover her cheeks.

'I guess so. Look at Granny. It's taken her twenty years to even *think* about dating.'

Nikki burrowed in her bag, not sure what to say. Sometimes you never got over someone. But she couldn't explain that to Juno.

'I'm not an expert,' she said eventually. 'But I think it takes time. Or the right person to come along.'

Juno looked at her. She seemed to be scrutinising her.

'What?' Nikki wondered if her guilt was evident. Her niece was perceptive. She picked up on things other people missed.

Juno burst out laughing. 'You're never going to pull him in that outfit, anyway.'

Nikki put her hands out to one side and did a twirl as if she was on a catwalk, showing off her regalia: bobble hat, fleecy robe, socks and Crocs.

'I don't know what you mean. This is seaside chic. Everyone's wearing it.'

They were still laughing when Adam reappeared. In comparison to them he looked ruggedly cool in his cable-knit sweater and cashmere beanie. To his credit, he didn't seem disconcerted by their get-up.

'Hey, I just thought,' he said, 'I'm making burritos later if you'd like me to bring you some round.'

'Burritos!' Juno's eyes lit up.

'It'll save you cooking. You've been working hard, if the skip's anything to go by.'

Nikki hesitated. She didn't want to set a precedent, for she couldn't repay the favour any time soon, but she didn't want to hurt his feelings either. And who didn't love a burrito?

'Are you sure?'

He nodded. 'I always make way too much. Force of habit. Still can't get used to cooking for one.'

It was only a vague allusion to his status, and he certainly wasn't self-pitying, but Nikki's heart went out to him.

'That's very kind. Thank you.'

'I'll bring them round. Your own personal Deliveroo.'

'That'll be a luxury. We don't have Deliveroo around here.'

He looked shocked. 'You don't have Deliveroo?'

'We do not.'

'Uber Eats?'

Nikki laughed. 'Not even Uber.'

Adam blinked in shock. Juno patted him kindly on the arm.

'Welcome to Speedwell. And don't worry – you'll get used to it. Everybody does in the end.'

Good as his word, Adam turned up on the doorstep at seven o'clock with a tray bearing two plump burritos, a bottle of Cholula hot sauce and two salt-rimmed glasses.

'Virgin Palomas,' he said. 'Grapefruit, lime, agave syrup, no tequila. Though I do have some, if you want a shot.'

'I could get used to this,' said Nikki. 'It's like having my own private chef.' As she took the tray from him, she saw the glint of a wedding band on his left hand. She hadn't noticed it there before. Had he put it on as a warning, to keep away any unwelcome overtures from the spinsters, widows and divorcées of Speedwell? 'You have no idea how grateful we are. We were going to go into town for chips.'

'No worries. Just drop the things back any time.' He melted away into the evening before she could ask him in.

Nikki and Juno sat at the garden table she had put in the dining area. Everything looked a bit bleak, lit by a naked light bulb, the walls empty, the floorboards bare. And now the sun had gone it was chilly. But Nikki lit a couple of candles and found the soundtrack from *Chef* to accompany their feast. It wouldn't be long before everything was transformed, she told herself. Pink walls perhaps for the eating area, she decided, as she tucked in. A hot, zingy Mexican pink.

The burritos were out of this world – spicy black beans, melted cheese, guacamole, piquant coriander and lime zest stirred through nutty brown rice, all wrapped up in the softest tortillas.

'Is your neighbour for real?' asked Juno.

'He's very kind, isn't he?' Nikki knew she sounded prim.

Juno gave her a hard stare. 'Very kind,' she said. She picked up the Cholula bottle meaningfully. 'And very hot.'

'Oh,' said Nikki. 'Do you think?'

She took a gulp of her Paloma and spluttered.

'Cough it up,' said Juno. 'It might be a gold watch.'

'Sorry. It's quite tart. Freshly squeezed, I think.' She put the glass down. 'Thank you, for helping me out today.'

'You're doing it again.'

'What?'

'Changing the subject.'

Nikki sighed. Juno wasn't going to let it drop.

'Yes, he's very attractive,' she told her. 'But I'm not interested. Number one, like I told you, he's widowed. Two, he's my neighbour. It wouldn't be appropriate. I don't want to blur the boundaries. Or be too embarrassed to say hello if it all goes wrong. I have to live next to him, don't forget.'

'I guess.' Juno tried to look convinced. 'But it's been a while since Whatshisname.'

'Callum?' Callum had been Nikki's last boyfriend. Very nice, but so dull no one had ever been able to remember his name, so he'd been nicknamed Whatshisname. He was a physics teacher at the college, and when he'd got a new job as head of science for a school in Cheltenham, neither he nor Nikki had suggested a long-distance relationship. And somehow she'd never dipped her toe back into the dating scene.

She valued her independence and didn't want a massive commitment, yet there was something unfulfilling about a fling. She no longer had any appetite for brief encounters. Besides, there weren't many candidates in Speedwell. She knew everyone that lived there, and she wasn't inclined to have a dalliance with any of the holidaymakers that descended each summer. She didn't want to be relegated to a fleeting memory; a sun-drenched, booze-fuelled conquest to be forgotten as quickly as the sunburn faded.

She could, of course, expand her horizons. There were other people further afield, and one of them might be perfect for her. But she never seemed to have time to look, between the business and the lifeboat and now the renovation.

And what was so wrong with being single anyway? Why was the world so obsessed with putting people into pairs? Nikki was quite content to be on her own. She was never bored. And apart from anything else, she had got so used to stretching out in her luxurious queen-sized bed, she couldn't imagine sharing it with anyone.

Juno began stacking the plates and glasses.

'I'll wash these and take them back,' she said. 'And make sure he knows I'll have Gatsby any time he likes.'

Because she was adamant about being happy with her single status, Nikki was surprised to find herself mildly vexed that now she wouldn't get the chance to speak to Adam herself. It would have been the ideal opportunity to ask him to be her plus one to the opening of Salicia. It would be the perfect thank you for the burritos.

'No,' she said. 'Leave them there. I'll take them back.'

'Oh yeah?' said Juno, smirking. 'Not interested, eh?'

Nikki stuck out her tongue at her niece, but she couldn't help smiling.

24

On Monday morning, Nikki woke just after daybreak. She had left her curtains open now the weather was getting better, for she loved the moment when a pale blue light began to creep into the bedroom, waking her gradually, preferring that to the shrill intervention of an alarm. Besides, the birds provided their own wake-up call. Sometimes she couldn't believe how loud the dawn chorus was. No one could hope to sleep through it. She lay there for a moment, listening to every trill and chirrup, taking her energy from their uplifting chatter.

Mondays were usually her day off, as she inevitably worked weekends, but today she wanted to crack on with sanding the floorboards so they could be finished at the same time as the kitchen. Then she could start painting and move everything in properly.

She decided she was going to have to get up at five from now on to fit everything into her life. If she went to bed by ten, she could still get a decent amount of sleep. It was the only way she was going to survive: wedding season was always insane, and to throw building work into the mix was even more insane. It didn't have to be for ever, she reasoned. The madness would be over by autumn. Although autumn weddings were becoming a thing – September and October were pretty full already. She could draw breath in November, when she was due to go to Bali to visit Bill. It seemed a lifetime away. But at least there no one could send her threatening postcards. She still couldn't work out who could possibly be behind them or what their motive might be. Despite Woody's reassurance, she felt exposed and more than a little anxious, but there was nothing she could do except get on with life.

She rolled out of bed, ready to prepare the house for the arrival of her renovation team now the kitchen had been gutted, making lists of what she might need to buy and reconsidering every decision to make sure it was the right one. Jason and Mike were golden, but she still had to oversee everything. She wasn't micro-managing: she was the one who had to live here so she wanted everything to her specification, and no workman appreciated being asked to move something – a plug, a switch, a light-fitting – after the event.

She spent the day on her knees with the sander. The floor was going to be beautiful: pale golden wood that she would cover with a light wax. By five, Jason and Mike had gone – they liked to start and finish early so they could be propping up the bar at the Neptune by six – so she jumped into the shower then put on her jeans and a white linen shirt that she'd brought back from Mariners, conscious that she was trying to dress down but at the same time look . . . what? Alluring? Hot? Or just presentable? She ruffled up her damp hair, put on the merest hint of mascara and briefly checked her reflection in the cheval mirror she'd got out of storage.

She couldn't quite look herself in the eye for she knew what she was up to. You're just taking back his stuff, she reminded herself, as she grabbed Adam's tray, headed out of the front door and round to his before she had second thoughts.

She had to admit it was kind of fun, feeling the light buzz of anticipation and caring what she looked like just a little bit more than usual. She'd even put on decent underwear – not that she had any fantasies about things going that far, but somehow it made her feel better about herself, to have on a matching bra and knickers that weren't grey from over-washing.

Adam smiled as he answered the door. 'Hey.'

'I've brought your things back.' She held out the tray with the plates and glasses.

'That's perfect timing,' he said. 'I wondered if I could pick your brains?'

'Of course.'

'I need a bit of local knowledge.'

'Sure.'

'I'd be really grateful. I could give you a bowl of pasta in return?'

'I already owe you gimlets and burritos.'

'I'm not counting.'

'I'll reciprocate when I've actually got a kitchen. It shouldn't be long – Mike and Jason reckon they'll have it in by the end of the week.'

He gave her an easy smile.

'Hey. No rush. I told you; I love having someone to cook for. Come on in.'

This time, Adam ushered her straight through the living room and into the kitchen. She couldn't help gasping as she walked in. It was an open-plan extension with a slanting glass roof and folding doors which were half open, letting in the briny sea air. There was a big island topped with slate, a bright orange range cooker and thick, chunky shelves from floor to ceiling, which held painted crockery and bowls and glassware, more cookery books and a host of pans and kitchen utensils. Tongue-and-groove units painted in off-black hid the fridge, freezer and dishwasher. And all over the walls, more art, all with a food theme – the butchery cuts on a cow, a vintage Guinness sign, framed restaurant menus with the date scrawled on them. It was bold and bright and utterly mouth-watering. A place for friends and laughter and dancing.

'Wow,' was all she could think of to say. 'I mean, really wow.'

'Trust me, I still pinch myself whenever I come in here. I know how lucky I am.' Adam smiled, pouring pale yellow wine into a long-stemmed glass and handing it to her.

'I shouldn't.' Nikki took the glass anyway.

'It'll take the taste of dust away. It's only light. Albariño.'

Nikki took a sip. The zesty lemony-ness filled her mouth as she looked around the room, doing her mental arithmetic, wondering just how long it would take to save up and do the same. She wouldn't be able to afford such a high-end finish, but with Suzanne's help she could do something slightly less ambitious. Suzanne was clever at sourcing cheaper options and getting a luxe effect on a tight budget.

Adam pulled up a stool for her to sit at the island. All across it were spread a sheaf of pen-and-ink drawings on thick white paper, coloured in with a watercolour wash.

Adam tapped one of the drawings.

'You recognise it?'

'Of course! It's our beach.' The secret beach. It was captured perfectly. Nikki recognised every rock and stone, the curve of the sand, the familiar waves. 'And those plants – those are the flowers that grow on the cliffs.' She recognised sea buckthorn and samphire; gorse and thrift, all intricately drawn and coloured in with a wash of pink and green and yellow. If she shut her eyes, she could imagine their herbaceous scent. The perfumed air here was intoxicating. 'They're very different from the paintings.'

'She was very talented. It would have been annoying if she hadn't been so self-deprecating. She called them her little scribbles.' He picked one of them up. 'I want to get them framed and give one each to her friends. A little piece of Jill to remember her by. It's taken me till now to sort through them.'

He stared down at the drawing he was holding. It really was exquisite, capturing the wildness of the cove and its windswept beauty with just a few deft strokes of a pen.

'She was incredibly talented. You must be so proud . . .' Nikki tailed off, realising that Adam was trying his hardest not to cry. 'Oh God. I'm sorry.'

'No. It's fine.' His voice broke. 'It's just . . . oh shit . . . this wasn't supposed to happen.' He choked on a half-sob, tried to laugh, then swore again.

Nikki put a tentative hand on his back. For a moment,

he tensed, and she was about to take her hand away, thinking she had crossed a boundary. Then he relaxed, and she held it there, for reassurance while he gathered himself together. She could feel the warmth of him under the soft cotton of his shirt, his muscles coiled and defined, and for a moment wondered what his skin felt like. Stop it, she told herself. Don't go there.

'Thank you,' he said. 'Sorry. That was embarrassing. But you never know when grief is going to jump out, do you?'

'I know,' said Nikki. 'But I always think it's best to give in. Don't fight it. Kind of like being caught up in a rip tide. It will spit you out eventually. Exhausted, but on the other side.'

'I like that.' Adam nodded. 'Ideally, I'd have a good blub every morning, to get it out of my system. But that's not how it works.'

'Honestly. I get it.' She was all too familiar with the heavy lump you carried with you. The sense of despair on waking. The struggle to pretend. The awful, awful desolation when you didn't think you could bear the pain a moment longer. Somehow, you carried on. And gradually, very gradually, you got used to the burden. It never left you, but you learned to live with it.

Even now, it was there, deep inside her. Her grief, her longing, her sadness.

'Anyway, I didn't drag you in here to cry all over you,' said Adam. 'I wondered if you knew of any office premises to rent? I don't need anywhere huge. And it doesn't have to be glamorous.' He sighed. 'I thought I was going to be able to work from home. But the more time I spend here, the less I want to sully it with paperwork and figures and all the office crap.'

'I think it's important to separate home and work when you've got your own business. Otherwise, you never switch off.'

'Exactly.'

'I'll ask my brother. And my mate Joel, who sold me Number Four. Between them they know everything that's going on in Speedwell.'

'Thank you. I think it would make a huge difference.' He clapped his hands. 'Anyway. Pasta puttanesca do you? Otherwise known as tart's spaghetti? Capers, olives, tomatoes, bit of chilli?'

'That sounds perfect.'

Moments later the air was filled with the scent of frying garlic. She sipped the rest of her wine and watched as Adam moved around the kitchen, grabbing jars, knives, bunches of herbs, chopping with an impressive speed and precision, throwing things into the heavy frying pan on the hob and shaking it by the handle. He lobbed sea salt into a pan of boiling water and a drizzle of olive oil.

Before she knew it, he placed a bowl in front of her filled with a coiled nest of spaghetti topped with a glistening rich sauce.

'Are you a trained chef?' she asked.

'God, no. Just an obsessive eater. I'm really only happy when I'm feeding people.' He wiped a splash of sauce off the rim of his bowl with a finger. 'Strictly speaking we should be having a big glass of red with this, but I know you need to be up early so I won't tempt you.'

'I can't think of anything I'd love more, but you're right. I've only got the guys for two weeks so I've got to make the most of them or Graham will kill me. Technically they work for North Property Management.' She dug her fork in and twirled the pasta until she had the perfect amount. 'Oh yum. This is perfection.'

'It's my go-to quick supper. It lifts my heart. Salty, spicy, punchy.'

'Well, I really appreciate it. I'd have been making cheese on toast otherwise.'

'You're not a cook?'

'I can cook. I'm just not very good at cooking for myself. Which, as I'm on my own most of the time, means I don't experiment in the kitchen much. But maybe I should. I mean this took you, what – fifteen minutes?'

'Exactly. Don't get me wrong – there's nothing wrong with a cheese toastie every now and then. But you should nourish yourself properly. I mean, if you don't care about yourself, who will?'

He was looking at her intently. Nikki liked the feeling of someone being concerned about her.

'I've never thought of it like that.' Now was not the time to mention the stack of ready meals she kept in the fridge. Or the fact that if she was really in need of feeding up, she just went to Mariners, or the Neptune for fishcakes and mushy peas.

'I could give you a few recipes for instant gratification.' Adam raised his glass to her and there was a twinkle in his eye replacing the earlier tears.

Was he flirting with her? His demeanour was naturally flirtatious, though not in a creepy way. He was charming and generous of spirit and quick-minded, which, combined, was rather irresistible.

And confusing.

She put down her fork.

'That was so delicious. Thank you. But I'd better go – I've got to hoover up the living room before bed now the dust has settled.' She hesitated, then took the plunge. 'By the way, a friend of mine is opening a new bar on Friday night, if you'd like to come? It's the most glamorous thing to happen in Speedwell since . . .' She tried to think. 'Well, ever.'

He smiled, and she loved the way his eyes crinkled and his face lit up. 'I'd love that. It might give me a chance to meet a few new people.'

Nikki felt a bit lightheaded. 'Exactly.'

'Is there a dress code?'

'We don't really do dress codes in Speedwell. Just . . . clean?'

He laughed. 'I think I can manage that.'

'Can I help you clear up?'

'No!' He laughed at her. 'It's two bowls and a couple of pans. I can manage.' He leaned forward to kiss her on the cheek. 'See you Friday.'

As she felt his cheek brush hers, her heart quickened and a shot of something pierced her belly. Whatever it was, it slid further down her insides like hot coffee poured over ice cream. Oh help, she thought.

She had read somewhere that, physiologically, it could take less than a second to fall for someone, if the chemistry was right. Of course, there were other steps to the process, but the trigger could be there from the start. A bright flame that was almost impossible to ignore. And she recognised it. That mood-lifting, pulse-raising, spine-tingling sensation that, if it went unchecked, catapulted into euphoria and then you were done for.

'Are you OK?' Adam was peering at her, concerned.

She jumped off her stool.

'Oh, fine. Just my to-do list whizzing through my head. Thank you so much for the pasta and I'll let you know about the office space.'

She needed to leave before she made a fool of herself. She headed home on a cloud of Albariño and something in her veins she couldn't quite identify. As she stumbled up the stairs to bed, she suddenly remembered what it was.

Lust.

25

The problem with wedding themes was they could get out of control and become too gimmicky and a bit trashy. It was about balance. Enough of a touch to make people smile, and for everything to feel held together, but not overdone and twee.

Later that week, Nikki was fine-tuning her presentation for Phoebe and Alec, trying to make sure she wasn't running away with the celestial brief and turning their wedding into a theme park. She was with her mum at Mariners going through cake options. Jess was there too – she had a late shift so she'd come to join them for coffee and a catch-up.

'I think I've narrowed it down to three,' said Helen, who'd spent all night on Pinterest. 'Individual white fondant fancies with a silver new moon on top, a traditional round cake with dark blue icing and hand-painted constellations, or several layers with gold stars sprinkled on the sides. They might have their own ideas, of course.'

'Oh, I love the fondant fancies,' said Nikki. 'But they'll probably want a statement cake.' She could picture Alec and Phoebe in front of a towering tier, their hands clasped over a cake knife. She could usually predict what people would go for, but sometimes they surprised her. She dropped the three images into her presentation document. 'Thanks, Mum.'

'In the meantime, girls,' Helen was trying not to smile too much, 'I think I've found a match. Someone I might actually have something in common with.'

Jess looked up from the magazine she'd been reading. 'Who?'

'Hang on.' Helen tapped into the app to find Ralph's profile. 'Here we go. What do you think?'

She held up Ralph's beaming, kindly face.

'He looks adorable,' said Nikki. 'Like Richard Briers from *The Good Life*.'

'He does a bit,' Helen agreed.

Jess was scrutinising more heavily, scanning Ralph's photos for clues.

'Right,' she said, 'tell me everything you know about him and let's do a deep dive.'

'But do you think he looks nice?'

'Yep. He looks very nice. But you need to do your due diligence.' Jess grabbed the iPad. 'Name. Where does he live? What's he told you? What have you told him?'

'What is this? The Spanish Inquisition?'

'Yes, Mum. You have to be careful. I'm not letting you meet up with any old randomer.' Jess frowned. 'You haven't met him yet, have you?'

'No! We've just exchanged a few messages.'

'Have you gone to WhatsApp yet?'

Ralph had suggested coming off the dating app and exchanging numbers. Helen felt a prickle of anxiety.

'Yes, actually, as a matter of fact.'

'Jess. Go easy.' Nikki could see her mum was getting agitated by Jess's interrogation. She felt caught in the middle. Jess was right to be protective, but Helen was capable of looking after herself and they shouldn't patronise her.

'It saves disappointment in the long run.' Jess's fingers were racing over the keys. 'There's always something people keep back, and it's usually a deal-breaker. I should know.' She grimaced. She had a chequered internet dating history littered with married men and bankrupts. 'Give me his number. And do you know his address? Where he works? His wife's name?'

Helen sighed. She knew Jess was probably right. She gave her as much information as she could from the few exchanges she'd had with Ralph so far.

Ten minutes later, Jess had an exacting profile of Ralph Potter accompanied by photographs of his flat, his late wife, his three children, the school he'd worked at, a summer concert he'd organised and his dog.

'Ever considered a career with MI5?' asked Nikki.

'Who says I'm not already working for them?' Jess flashed back.

'How do you do this?' asked Helen, intrigued.

'There's always a trail. You start with Facebook or LinkedIn or Instagram. I googled his phone number. Look – his number's on the website of the local Twin Town Association. Along with his address. From there you check out the address on Zoopla and you can see his house. Local paper for obituaries – there's his wife's name, then you google her.'

'You're scary.' Nikki couldn't help admiring her.

'If there's something he's hiding, I'll find it.'

Helen crossed her arms, part fascinated, part horrified. 'Well, I hope his kids haven't done the same on me.'

'You've got nothing to hide, Mum. You're squeaky clean. But don't tell him too much.'

'Of course not.' Helen put her hand to her chest. All this analysis was making her panic.

'Don't worry, Mum.' Nikki cast her eye over everything Jess had found so far. Ralph looked as if he had a nice life. Nothing too flashy but very comfortable. A decent-sized flat converted from a big old house in Somerset. His clothes looked lived in but good quality. He looked as if he'd fit in at the table here. He looked kind, she thought. As if he'd always have a packet of Polos on him. 'I'm sure he's above board.'

Jess wasn't so reassuring.

'You want to know everything about him, and for him to know nothing about you when you first meet. You can't be too careful. There's loads of scammers out there. You've heard the stories. Women falling in love and then getting taken in by a sob story and handing over their cash.'

'I'd never do that.'

'You say that. But these con men can be very clever.' Jess was still typing, scanning the information, processing it. Nikki had to feel sorry for Ralph Potter. By the end of it, Jess would know his inside leg measurement and which way he dressed.

Finally, Jess came to a halt. 'OK,' she said. 'If you want to meet him, I think he's legit. But we'll have rules. We need to know when you're going. And where you're going.'

'You're not going to stalk me?'

'No,' said Jess, but Helen didn't look convinced.

'I think he looks lovely,' said Nikki.

'Make sure he pays, as well,' said Jess.

Nikki and Helen exchanged amused glances.

'What are you like?' asked Nikki.

'What am I like?' Jess put her hands on her hips. 'Not an idiot. That's what I'm like. Nothing gets past me anymore. I've learned from bitter experience that people have to earn your trust. Even those close to you.'

Nikki felt her heartbeat falter for one moment. She closed down her laptop. 'If I don't make a move, I'm going to be late for my meeting. See you on Friday, at the bar opening?'

'I'll see you there,' said Helen. 'I'm going to drop in for ten minutes to see what it's like.'

'I'm on duty so I'll miss it,' said Jess. 'No peace for the wicked.'

Nikki tried not to show that she was relieved her sister wasn't going. Sometimes life was easier without Jess to compete with, even now. And her conscience was pricking. But she hugged her sister just the same. She loved her. She always had and always would.

26

'This is out of this world.'

Phoebe and Alec stood arm in arm in the middle of the field, gazing at the cobalt sea in the distance. The breeze rummaged amidst the grass and flowers – cornflowers and poppies and red campion shimmered in its wake. Overhead a buzzard wheeled across a pale blue sky, spying on proceedings, ready to report back as to why there were four people standing in the meadow when usually there was no one.

'It'll be a challenge, pulling this together,' Nikki told them. 'And it's a bit of a risk but because you've got the budget, I think Tamsin and I can make it work.'

They were in the middle of arguably the most picturesque farm for miles around. Perched high on a cliff overlooking the ocean, Nikki had been trying for years to persuade her oldest friend to diversify into weddings. Tamsin was standing next to her now, in her trademark jodhpurs and boots and a big fleece, looking part doubtful, part optimistic.

Contrary to popular belief, holding a wedding in the middle of a field was not a cheap option. Customers often wanted a festival feel for their nuptials, and thought sticking a marquee up and serving street food would be half the price of using a big hotel or wedding venue. The opposite was true. There were no facilities here, so everything would have to be hired in and transported, from loos to a mobile kitchen to water for washing up. But because Phoebe and Alec had given her a generous budget, Nikki thought she could make it happen. Then she could prove to Tamsin that it might be worth investing in all these facilities.

Tamsin had also lost her father the night of the disaster. They had both found it incredibly tough, losing their wonderful dads, but they'd been equally determined to follow in their fathers' footsteps, even though they'd had big shoes to fill. As an only child, Tamsin had been catapulted into running Windcutter Farm. Over the years Tamsin had tried various schemes to make money alongside the sheep that had been the Amory livelihood for generations, and because of its glorious location, tourism had been her friend. Her biggest earner was riding holidays, but it was becoming more and more difficult to make a profit as the cost of looking after the horses had shot up.

Nikki felt a surge of affection for her brave, hardworking friend and was determined to make this wedding work as a blueprint for the future. She prayed that Alec and Phoebe would fall in love with the location and give her plan the go-ahead.

She drew breath, ready to begin her pitch.

'As you can see, we've got a beautiful wild-flower meadow here with the sea as a backdrop. So, I want to keep everything as close to nature as we can. And the best thing is this site has very little light pollution. Obviously, it'll be summer, so it's not as good as autumn or winter for stargazing, but the moon is a waning crescent on the night of your wedding, so the sky will be at its darkest. My idea is to get a marquee with a clear roof, so everyone can look up and see the constellations. I've sourced some powerful telescopes, and I've found an astronomer who can come and mingle with the guests after dinner and show them what to look out for. All very relaxed, but I think it could be very special and a bit different.'

'I can't believe it.' Phoebe looked shell-shocked. 'This is better than anything we imagined.'

'Do you really think you can organise it in time?' Alec asked.

'I'm pulling in a few favours.' Nikki grinned. 'And it will be nerve-wracking. But for me. Not you.'

'It'll be the first wedding we've ever had here,' added Tamsin. 'But if it works, then maybe it'll be the first of many.'

'Windcutter Weddings,' said Nikki. 'That's my vision. And if you don't mind being the guinea pigs . . .'

'I completely manifested this,' said Phoebe, her eyes shining. 'Every day I thought about my dream wedding and here it is. It's *beyond* my dreams.'

'It's a miracle,' agreed Alec. 'Given how little notice we've given you.'

'There's a lot of practical stuff we need to sort,' Nikki warned. 'But between me and Tamsin, I think we can manage it. If you trust us.' Was she mad? This was a massive challenge, with lots of potential for disaster. But she and Tamsin would be a formidable team. If anyone could make this work, they could. 'Obviously, I'm not going to go mad with the budget. I'll keep in close touch and get your approval on everything before we green light it.'

'Whatever it takes,' said Alec.

'It's got to be within reason, if we're going to trial it as a business model. So don't worry. We'll keep it real. Anything else you can think of that you want, just ping me an email.'

Phoebe was looking at Tamsin. 'I've always had a fantasy about arriving at my wedding on a horse. Do you think that would be possible?'

Tamsin looked at Nikki, who nodded her approval. 'I don't see why not. Can you ride?'

'I used to, when I was a kid. Every holiday, I'd beg to go riding. I don't know why I stopped. Time, I suppose. And it's weird. I put a horse on my vision board yesterday.'

'Well, there we go,' said Nikki. 'Proof that manifesting works. I guess?'

Tamsin looked a bit puzzled. She was very practical and down to earth and wouldn't have the first clue about manifesting.

'Maybe you should get back in the saddle first?' Alec looked anxious.

'If you've got time to come down before, I can give you a few lessons,' suggested Tamsin. 'Take you out on Mercury. He's very calm but very beautiful. Gold, with a white mane and tail.'

Nikki smiled to herself. Tamsin was really getting into the whole wedding fantasy and running with it.

'I could be like Daenerys Targaryen, from *Game of Thrones*.' Phoebe clasped her hands, overwhelmed with excitement.

'I'm no Kahl Drogo, though.' Alec looked a bit crestfallen. 'I'll have to get a personal trainer or something.'

Phoebe threw her arms around him. 'Don't be silly. You're perfect as you are.'

Nikki's heart melted. They were so sweet. It made her more determined than ever to make this wedding a day to remember, even if she didn't end up making much money. It was more important to her for the bride and groom to drive off into the sunset happy.

As Nikki was about head back to her office, with Phoebe and Alec following behind, Tamsin leaned in through the car window.

'I've got a good feeling about this,' she said. 'Though it's kind of ironic. Us single girls in charge of a wedding.'

'Maybe it'll be one of us one day,' said Nikki lightly.

Tamsin shook her head. 'I'm married to the farm,' she said. 'And Andrew is married to *his*.' Andrew was her long-term boyfriend, a gentleman farmer from Exmoor. 'I'm not holding my breath.'

'It's never too late.' Nikki grinned. 'Anyway, we've got Bali to look forward to. I'm counting the days.'

Tamsin was coming with her to visit Bill, as she was his godmother. An exotic holiday for the two of them after a summer of hard work. Nikki couldn't wait. As she waved her friend goodbye and drove back along the drive, she reflected that the two of them didn't see each other often enough, even though they didn't live far apart. They remedied this once a year, at Christmas time. They'd book a twin room at a boutique hotel in Exeter, nail their present shopping, dress up, drink cocktails and then go dancing. A ritual night of carefree indulgence that reminded them they weren't all work and no play.

Once, after one too many espresso Martinis, the two of them had gone back to their hotel room and flopped onto their beds. Tongue loosened by the unaccustomed alcohol, Nikki had felt a terrible urge to spill her secret to her friend. She was tired of the burden and longed for a chance to talk it over. And perhaps even be told she wasn't as wicked as she thought she was. She imagined Tamsin saying, 'You're only human, Nik. Good people do bad things sometimes.' She relished the sweet relief that would bring, and the comfort of knowing she wasn't evil. Perhaps it would silence the voice in her head, the one which endlessly reminded her of her transgression and told her she didn't deserve happiness.

But Nikki knew once her secret was out, she couldn't untell it. It was too much of a risk. And their friendship was more important to her than absolution. So she'd stayed silent. And now, she was glad she hadn't ever said anything, for this venture could be a gamechanger. As her car rattled over the cattle-grid, her mind was racing with all the little details she'd need to snag to make this dream wedding a reality.

Back at the office, Phoebe and Alec tasted their way through the samples Nikki had organised through her caterer, all spread out on the antique table on big platters. She'd sent them the menus in advance, and now they were double-checking they were happy with their choices. Bruschetta with fresh peas and mint and local burrata, crab tartlets with aioli, trout with watercress and nasturtium vinaigrette, then venison drizzled with wild garlic pesto, new potatoes, and sugar snaps and purple sprouting broccoli. A gorgeously seasonal summer menu which would look beautiful on the plate.

And for pudding, îles flottantes, pillowy mounds of meringue floating in a passionfruit crème Anglaise, decorated with pistachios and gold leaf.

'That's a very pretty menu.' Nikki nodded in approval, producing a bottle of sparkling rosé. 'Now, this is my recommendation for the toast. Hints of strawberry with a creamy finish, if you'd like to taste it. It'll go perfectly with the cake you've chosen.'

They'd gone with the moon-topped fondant fancies, with a strawberry buttercream filling.

'Oh yes.' Alec leaned forwards and took the bottle. He removed the foil deftly and began to untwist the wire. He popped the cork and the bottle gave a gentle sigh. 'Would it be cheeky to propose a toast? To you? Our miracle wedding planner?'

Nikki didn't usually drink on the job, but today she thought she deserved a celebration. This had the potential to be the most triumphant wedding she'd ever organised. If that didn't deserve a glass of fizz, then what did?

27

She was still on a bit of a high when she sailed into Salacia with Adam on Friday evening. She felt on top of the world. A match for Tamara and her glitzy friends. She'd dug out an emerald-green lace shirt dress to show off the fact that her legs were brown and toned from climbing up and down the steps to the secret beach for a swim as often as she could. She and Adam had walked into town together along the cliff path, basking in the evening sun. She could tell from the glances they were getting that they looked the part as she walked in on his arm. He had on a pale blue lawn shirt, and yet again she was conscious of the warmth of him underneath the soft fabric.

'Blimey,' he said, 'I wasn't expecting this kind of joint around here. This is something else.'

'Speedwell's changing. There's a lot of new money here in summer.' Nikki looked around, impressed. Tamara and Duke had made quite a statement. The bar was decorated in eau de nil and gold, with a huge mural of Salacia emerging from the waves and a chandelier made from a tangle of green glass, like Medusa's hair. The floor tiles glistened like fish scales, and private booths with velvet banquettes lined the walls. Outside, the water in the harbour shone like newly polished silver. It felt glamorous, more Côte d'Azur than Cornwall. The usual Speedwell uniform was jeans or shorts and sweatshirts, but tonight everyone had dressed up and the air crackled with excitement.

'I keep expecting Liz Taylor and Richard Burton to walk in.' Adam took two glasses of champagne from a passing waiter and handed her one. Then he held his glass up to her. 'Cheers. And thank you for asking me to be your plus one. I haven't been out on the town for ages. I miss it. Though I am slightly dreading it.'

'It must be difficult. I'm so sorry.' Nikki felt mortified that she'd babbled on about work on the walk in when he had probably been battling his nerves.

'The funny thing is, I'm fine about it. It's other people who find it hard. I always hate the look of panic on their face when I explain I'm widowed. Some people hide it better than others but I can see them wondering what they should say. And I don't want them to say anything much. I want to have a normal conversation, about whatever. Global warming or Miley Cyrus or whatever . . . Anyway—' he took a glug of champagne – 'a bit of Dutch courage and I'll be fine.'

'Come and meet my brother,' suggested Nikki. 'He's pretty easy to talk to. He'll break you in gently.'

Even Graham had dressed up. He was usually in sportswear and trainers, for when he wasn't working, he was playing football or going for a run, but tonight he was in dark blue jeans and a pristine white shirt and proper shoes.

'Don't say anything,' he said as she approached. 'It was Suzanne. I wasn't given any choice.'

'You look great. Unrecognisable, but great. Graham, this is Adam. My neighbour. The one who's looking for office space.'

'Good to meet you.' The two men shook hands. Moments later they were deep in conversation about Arsenal – they were both supporters – and Nikki felt she could leave Adam's side. Across the room, she saw Suzanne arrive, in a Grecian-style white dress with a gold belt around her waist. Nikki could sense her mixture of anxiety and anticipation, obviously hoping to make an impression on Tamara as she pushed her way through the crowds towards her.

'God, this is amazing. They must have spent a ton. That chandelier must have cost gazillions.' Suzanne was gabbling. 'Do you think Speedwell is ready for this kind of thing? I mean, I love it but it's way too scary for the locals.'

'I guess once people know about it, it'll become a destination. We'll find out this summer.'

'Oh God.' Suzanne tensed. 'Tamara's coming over.'

'It's fine. She needs you more than you need her, remember.'

'She does?' Suzanne looked baffled.

'She needs us locals on side. She knows we could make or break her. If we don't get on board with this place, no one else will. It's going to be us who keep this place going over the winter.' Nikki was bullshitting slightly, but she wanted Suzanne to have a bit more confidence about her pack position. And it worked. Suzanne stood a little taller as Tamara joined them.

'So what do you think?' Tamara looked from Nikki to Suzanne.

'It's stunning,' said Nikki.

'Completely stunning,' agreed Suzanne.

'You don't think it's a bit over the top?' Nikki was surprised by Tamara's uncertainty. And her candour. 'The designer went a bit nuts. We didn't have enough money left to do the loos properly and you know how important loos are.'

'Oh dear,' said Suzanne, with the smugness of someone who wouldn't have gone overbudget.

'I think we made a mistake not using someone local.' Tamara smiled at Suzanne. 'We won't make that mistake again.' Suzanne didn't know what to say. Was that a hint? 'Have you got time for lunch here this week? I'd love your feedback.'

'Sure. Just say when. I'm pretty flexible.' Suzanne saw Nikki staring at her meaningfully. *Don't seem too available*, her look was saying. 'Except for Tuesday and Wednesday,' she added hastily. 'Oh, and Friday's not good either.'

Nikki tried not to laugh. Tamara wasn't fazed.

'Thursday then?'

Suzanne pretended to check her calendar. 'I think that's good for me.'

'Great.' Tamara typed the date into her phone. 'I'll see you here at one?'

'She's either going to bin me or sign me up,' sighed Suzanne as Tamara walked off. 'I don't know if I can stand the stress.'

'Don't let it wind you up. It might be the project from hell. If you don't get it, you might have dodged a bullet.'

'I want the challenge.' Suzanne wrinkled her nose. 'And

it would be big money. The little jobs are just pin money, really. I want to go large. I want to be someone, not just a small fish in a small pond.'

Nikki felt a ripple of fear that Suzanne might get her fingers burnt if she was too ambitious. But she didn't want to clip her wings by being negative. 'The universe will give you what you need,' she said in the end.

Suzanne looked at her, puzzled. 'What?'

'I'm doing a wedding for a manifester. I think it's rubbed off on me.'

Suzanne laughed. 'I'm going to do a bit of networking.' She took in a deep breath. 'Wish me luck.'

She pushed her way into the fray. Nikki thought how far she'd come from the shy teenager who'd been on holiday down here when Graham met her in the Neptune. Suzanne had been the quiet one amongst all her rowdy mates who were celebrating after finishing their A levels. She hadn't wanted to go back to the tent, because it was all getting very messy and out of control. Graham took her back to Mariners, installed her in one of the spare beds and she'd never gone back to the campsite.

Adam tapped her on the shoulder.

'I'm going to slip off. I'm not used to circulating. I've kind of hit the wall.'

Nikki hesitated. Should she offer to come with him? She imagined them walking back along the cliff road, the night air cooling around them, the scent of sea and honeysuckle blossom mingling with his cologne. Then she realised he probably wanted to be alone with his thoughts after his first public foray into Speedwell life.

'No problem.'

'Will you be OK to get back on your own?'

'Yes – I'll get a lift from someone, I expect.'

'See you soon.' He kissed her cheek, touched her elbow in a gesture of appreciation, and was gone.

The room felt strangely empty once he'd left. Even though nearly everyone was still there, and the chatter was loud, and the glasses were still being filled. Nikki couldn't summon up the energy or enthusiasm to talk to anyone else. She should have gone with him.

Then she saw her mum arrive, in a white linen dress with denim espadrilles, her hair loosely pinned up. Her mum was *glowing*, she thought. Was it down to Ralph Potter?

'Mum! You look amazing.'

'It's this new bronzer.' Helen patted her cheekbones, but her eyes were sparkling.

It was weird, Nikki thought, seeing her mum come to life after so many years. Not that she'd been a downtrodden drudge, but she spent so much time looking out for other people and never put herself first. Maybe now was her time?

She heard a ting from the depths of her mum's handbag and saw her jump, then grab her phone, reading the message hungrily.

'Mum. You're like a teenager.'

'I know. It's embarrassing.'

But Helen couldn't wipe the smile off her face.

28

Helen couldn't wait to get home from the party to answer Ralph's message. It was something she wanted to savour in private. Not that there was anything salacious in his messages – far from it. But they were warm and funny and descriptive and they made her feel giddy with happiness. So she made her way around the room, saying hello to everyone she knew, then hotfooted it home as soon as was polite.

She knew she had become slightly addicted to the sound of her WhatsApp notification. A dopamine hit that made her heart leap and her blood fizz. She and Ralph were exchanging messages on a daily basis, and the more she read the more she looked forward to hearing from him. It was very light-hearted. He was very easy to communicate with. She didn't feel self-conscious about her replies, which she found surprising, for she wasn't used to writing her thoughts. He always seemed to appreciate what she said, and took an interest in her opinions.

And it was strange. She didn't feel in the least bit guilty, or as if she was betraying William. It felt easy and right. Of course, at this point it was only a tentative friendship.

And perhaps the fact that Ralph was a widower helped. For they had both confessed to each other how much they had adored their other halves, and how no one would ever replace them. And both had agreed that both William and Eleanor (Ralph's wife) would have wanted them to find someone new.

She poured herself a small glass of wine and sat down to reread his latest message:

> *I've been stumping around the park in my duffle coat like Paddington Bear,* he wrote, *for there was a chill breeze here in Taunton today – one of those spiteful unexpected ones that take you unawares if you head off without a coat. And now it's time for Heinz tomato soup and a crumpet with melted Stilton on top. The height of my culinary skills – I'm no cook, I'm afraid, but I love comfort food. Scrambled eggs, porridge, kippers, shepherd's pie (is it shepherd's or shepherds' – does the pie belong to one shepherd or many?). Custard on anything, of course, and also rice pudding with a blob of strawberry jam. And, of course, toast and marmalade, like the bear himself – and to be brutally honest with you, our figures aren't that much different. Paddington, Winnie the Pooh – I'm of a generally rotund physique, though I like to think of myself as cuddly rather than obese. I thought I'd be honest about this, as these things seem to matter. I'm not a slob, though. I do my ten thousand steps a day, but it doesn't seem to do much to offset the roundness. So there you are. I'm a tubby bear, but with excellent blood pressure and good stamina.*

Helen found herself laughing at his description. She liked him for his honesty.

I'd really love to hear your voice, he went on. *I hope that doesn't sound creepy, but I'm not sure how else to say it. If you think you could bear a phone call, I feel as if that could be the next step. If you want a 'next step'. You might be recoiling in horror at the very thought. I find this all quite difficult. Not talking to you – that's the easiest thing in the world. But how to navigate this process without causing offence or putting pressure on. Please be assured that is the very last thing I want to do. Ever. The thought of causing you to feel awkward makes me cringe inside. I'll leave it up to you. If you'd like to speak, just call. If not, I understand. Oh God, bring back the olden days when you met in real life, on the top deck of a bus or at the tennis club. On second thoughts, don't, because I would never have met you. The ball, as they say, is in your court.*

Helen sat in the silence of the kitchen, pondering his proposition. This was the next step, but it was daunting. At least he hadn't suggested a video call. That would be terrifying. She sipped her Sauvignon and considered his proposition. Should she call him? Was now the right time? It had been a couple of hours since he had sent the message, and it was gone nine o'clock. She ought to put him out of his misery – though was it presumptuous to think he was desperate for a reply?

She might as well do it now. Otherwise, she was going to torture herself all night, weighing up the pros and cons and plucking up the courage. Nothing terrible could happen. The worst-case scenario would be that she didn't like the sound of him – that he would have a grating voice or a manner of speaking that wasn't as appealing as the way he wrote. It was easy to fall into the trap of creating the perfect person from a few clues. The chances of him being the man of her dreams were slim. But if she didn't call him, she might never know. Or he might get bored of waiting and find someone else on Sunshine After the Rain. Someone braver than she was, who wasn't afraid to pick up the phone.

She reached out her finger and pressed the little phone symbol on her iPad, putting him on speaker. She squeezed her eyes tight shut as she heard the ring begin. One. Two. Three.

'Helen.' He answered on the fourth ring. 'I thought I'd frightened you off. How lovely to hear from you.'

There was a lightness in his voice, which was brimming with warmth and pleasure and a convivial eagerness. A cosy, BBC sort of a voice, that might narrate a *Book at Bedtime*. Or read the shipping forecast.

'Hello,' she said in reply. 'I'm sorry it's taken me so long to ring.'

'Oh golly,' he said. 'I saw you'd read my message a while ago and I thought I'd blown it. The dreaded blue ticks.'

Helen knew the agony – the blue WhatsApp ticks that indicated your message had been read, and the agonising wait for a response.

'I was out when I picked it up. Someone's opened a new bar down by the harbour.'

'Sounds very glamorous.'

'It was, actually. But not really my scene nowadays. I

just showed my face and came home again. I much prefer to stay in on a Friday night these days.'

'How lovely,' he said. 'So, are you still in your marital home? If you don't mind me asking?'

'Yes. My kids would riot if I sold up.'

'I bit the bullet and downsized.' He gave a small sigh. 'But I found a very nice flat with room for the piano and decent soundproofing so the neighbours don't mind if I bang out Chopin at unsociable hours.'

'That must have been hard.'

'It was agony. But it's done. When I pop off, the kids won't have much clutter to sort through. It was therapeutic, in a funny way. But I waited two years. I couldn't have done it straight away.'

'I can imagine,' said Helen, not wanting to admit that barely anything had been thrown out in the twenty years since William had gone. She found it hard to get rid of anything he had touched. And because there was plenty of room in the house, she didn't have to. But perhaps it was time. The thought of one neat row of kitchen utensils hanging up, instead of drawers full of clutter you had to root through to find a vegetable peeler or a tea strainer, was very appealing.

'Anyway,' he said, 'I've got to get an early night. I'm adjudicating tomorrow so I need my wits about me.'

'Of course,' said Helen, immediately worried that she had bored him, that he wasn't interested in her, that he was desperate to get her off the phone and get back to whatever was on the telly.

'Nighty night,' he said cheerfully, and rang off.

She sat for a moment, not sure what to think. Then, a moment later, a message popped up on her screen.

Sorry to be boring. But I know myself too well – I could happily rattle on for hours and then I'd be fit for nothing and it's not fair on the kids who are doing their exams. It was lovely to speak to you. I'd love to speak again soon.

She smiled. She could go to bed reassured now. *Night, Ralph Potter*, she thought, imagining him in a tartan dressing gown. She wanted to meet him. She really, *really* wanted to meet him. Should she make the first move or wait for him to suggest it? Maybe she should ask Nikki or Jess? It felt a bit teenage, to need advice. But it had been a very long time since she'd been on her first date with William. More than fifty years. Oh God, that made her feel old.

There was another ting.

What do you think about meeting up? I'm terrified, of course, but it might be nice. No need to answer now. Think about it. R

And then, five seconds later, *x*.

29

Nikki was woken at two o'clock in the morning by someone banging on her front door. She leapt out of bed and rushed to the window of the front bedroom to see who it was, not wanting to answer the door in her pyjamas to a random stranger.

It was Jess. Still in her uniform. She felt a rush of fear. Had her poison pen postcard writer let out her secret? Had Jess come to confront her? Her mouth went dry and her palms felt clammy. She couldn't pretend not to be here. She had to face up to her sister, and what she had done. And Jess was banging the knocker again. She had to let her in, or Adam would start wondering what the racket was.

She ran down the stairs, her heart pounding, wondering what to say if Jess had come to have it out with her. She opened the door to find her sister distraught, tears streaming down her face.

'He didn't make it.' Jess stumbled inside and fell against Nikki, throwing her arms around her neck. 'He didn't make it, Nik.'

'Who?' Who was she talking about? Rik? Their father? Horrible flashbacks came into her mind.

'It's so unfair. I can't bear it. We tried and tried.' Jess was crying so hard she could barely hear her words through the sobs.

'Calm down. Tell me what happened.' Nikki tightened her arms around her sister.

'He was only seventeen. There's a bunch of them here on holiday. He took some ecstasy in Tawcombe.'

'Oh God.' An overdose. It happened, from time to time. Kids coming down to celebrate the end of their exams and overdoing it. There was temptation and they couldn't resist.

'I can handle it most of the time. And I don't know why it got to me. Maybe because he reminded me of Bill.' Jess put her face in her hands. 'I can't face going home. I don't want Juno to see me like this.'

Nikki realised the place was a mess and there was nowhere comfy to sit, only her dining chairs.

'Why don't you go upstairs and lie on my bed? I'll bring you up a cup of tea.'

Jess nodded, wiping the tears from her face. She was a little calmer. 'OK.'

Five minutes later, Nikki came into her bedroom to find Jess curled up into a little ball, staring blankly into the middle of the room. Nikki handed her a cup of tea, then sat on the edge of the bed.

'I'm exhausted, Nik,' Jess said in a small voice. 'And I'm so sick and tired of pretending I'm all right. When I'm not. Not at all.'

Nikki was alarmed. This wasn't like Jess. She was usually so bouncy and upbeat. 'What do you mean?'

There was no spark in Jess's eye when she answered.

'Do you know how much I get paid for what I do? Bugger all, really, considering every day I save somebody's life. Or sometimes, I don't, but I give it a bloody good try. And I don't know how much longer I can do it. But I can't afford not to, because I've got a mortgage and a car loan and a credit card, and none of them are going anywhere. And that's all I know how to do. Save lives.'

She blew on her tea. It was too hot to drink just yet.

'All I want is a holiday. I don't mean a week in Lanzarote that's almost over before you get there. I mean a month, or six weeks, so I can actually unwind and think about what I want to do with my life without the drama of someone going into cardiac arrest or organ failure on my watch. I want to feel the sun on my skin and swim naked in the sea and drink cocktails out of coconut shells and meet someone gorgeous and have fabulous, uncomplicated no-strings sex and then find out that actually, they are the love of my life and be swept off my feet. And then be looked after. Not in a sexist kind of a way. Just in a *can I make you a gin and tonic while you cook supper* sort of a way.' She was choking on her words now. 'Like Dad did for Mum.'

'Oh, Jess.'

'I want to jack in my job for a bit and go somewhere hot. And then come back and be an agency nurse or something with no responsibility. Because I *can't* do it anymore. I'm tired, tired, tired right down to my bones.'

'I'm so sorry.' Nikki reached down and swept Jess's hair out of her eyes. 'You should have just asked me for a loan.'

'I didn't want a bloody loan.' Jess sat up, indignant. 'I've got enough loans.'

Despite herself, Nikki laughed.

'What's so funny?' demanded Jess.

She couldn't tell her it was relief. But it was. The terrible fear that she'd been found out had receded, and selfishly, totally selfishly, the burden of guilt was lifted. For the time being, anyway. Nevertheless, she was concerned about her sister.

Jess never complained about her work. And she supposed none of them ever really acknowledged what she did, and just took it for granted. They didn't see her, with her uniform on, at the cliff-face, making decisions that were literally life and death, all the blood, sweat and tears, having to deal with distraught relatives, keeping morale high. No, they just saw the other side of her. Jess with her party face on, glass in hand, jokes at the ready.

'Right,' said Nikki. 'You are going to go into work, and I don't care how you do it, but you're going to organise a month off in the autumn, even if you have to hand in your notice or go off sick. And you're coming with me and Tamsin to Bali to see Bill. He'll find us a villa, or one of those huts on stilts on the beach, and we're going to do absolutely nothing. And it's on me. My extension can wait. I don't even need an extension.'

'Oh wow,' said Jess, brightening. 'Can you imagine how much fun we'd have?' She had her arms round Nikki now. 'I'm sorry for waking you up. I think I'm probably a bit mad at the moment.'

'It's our age,' said Nikki drily. 'Hormones are not our friends.'

'Watch out, Bali. Three peri-menopausal old bags are

going to hit you like a hurricane.' Jess took Nikki's hand. 'Can I crash here? I can't face driving home.'

'Of course.' She rummaged in the pile of clothes on the floor and found her a spare nightdress. Jess always had a toothbrush in her bag. She used to say you never knew when you were going to get lucky.

Minutes later, Jess was curled up fast asleep. Nikki lay next to her, wide awake, agonising over what a terrible sister she'd been. She hated herself for what she'd done. Even if it was partly Jess's fault in the first place, for stealing Rik from under her nose. Though was it? Did Jess's transgression excuse hers? Of course it didn't. She lay in the dark, one arm curled over her sister to protect her, as her mind wandered back to the past, asking herself if things could have been different, if there had been a moment when she could have altered the future for all of them.

30

Then

It had been Jess's idea for Nikki to organise her wedding to Rik.

She stood in the middle of the kitchen at Mariners on a Sunday morning, clasping her hands in mock prayer – a classic Jess gesture when she wanted something. Nikki was eating toast and strawberry jam, trying to ignore her. Helen was immersed in the Sunday paper, enjoying her second cup of coffee, but looked up to listen to her daughter's pleas.

'You'd be so brilliant. You're so organised, and I'm totally useless,' Jess wheedled.

It was true. If Jess had any hand in arranging the wedding, it would be chaos. She'd probably forget to post the invitations. She'd have no interest in feeding her guests. All she'd worry about would be keeping the wine flowing and hitting the dance floor. Nikki would make sure everything was perfect and everyone was happy. It was what she always did. It was obvious she was the person for the job.

It made absolute sense.

Privately, it was Nikki's worst nightmare. To be in charge of the one thing she was dreading. The very thought of Rik and Jess at the altar made her feel sick, but refusing to organise the wedding would cause uproar. She could imagine Jess enlisting Rik to try to persuade her, and that she couldn't handle. She still hadn't been alone with him since Jess had dropped her baby bombshell and they'd announced their engagement. Now the pressure was on to get the wedding organised before Jess got too big for the photos.

All she could do was agree, and pray that in the meantime fate would intervene and she could find a way not to be there.

'OK,' she said. 'Give me a budget, and a guest list.'

The less she protested, the easier it would be to step away.

'All I know is I want a red wedding dress,' said Jess.

'Oh, Jess,' said Helen, alarmed. 'Really?'

'Yep. That's the only thing I care about. Everything else is up to you, Nik. I don't care about food or seating plans or any of it, really.'

Nikki and Helen exchanged glances.

'Married in red, you'll wish yourself dead,' murmured Helen.

'That's rubbish, Mum. There is no way that the colour of your wedding dress can affect your future.' Jess didn't subscribe to superstition.

Helen sighed. There was no point in arguing. And Jess would look stunning in scarlet, even with her baby bump, which was just starting to show.

'Oh, and there is one other thing,' said Jess. 'I want you to be my bridesmaid.'

'What?' Nikki looked at her in horror. She had planned

on hiding herself away behind a pillar during the ceremony.

Jess slid her arms around Nikki's neck and planted a kiss on her cheek.

'I know I don't say it very often but you're my best friend as well as my sister.'

'I am?'

'Nobody understands me better than you do. And I need you right there beside me.'

She was going to have to stand next to Rik and Jess, in full view of everyone, while they exchanged their vows and try to hide her emotions.

'I'm going to be too busy organising. I can't be bridesmaid as well.'

'Nik, you've always been able to do twelve things at once. You can handle it. I'm not taking no for an answer.'

Nikki looked to her mum for support but Helen was clearly charmed by the idea of Nikki as bridesmaid.

'You'll be lovely. As long as Jess doesn't expect you to wear red too. I'm not sure it's your best colour.'

'She can wear whatever she likes. But I just need her there in case I pass out. I'm going to be so overwhelmed at the prospect of marrying Rik, I might swoon.' Jess put a hand to her forehead and did an impression of herself fainting at the altar.

'Don't worry. I'll be there to catch you,' Nikki told Jess, loyal and stalwart to the end. She could refuse her sister nothing. None of them could.

Two days later, Nikki bumped into Rik in the passage that led to Mariners. He leaned against the rough stone wall and smiled at her just as a watery sun deigned to make its appearance after a stormy night. He was bathed in a golden light so bright it dazzled her. He seemed really pleased to see her.

'Hey.'

Nikki managed a smile. 'Hey,' she echoed, embarrassed by her lack of eloquence.

'I hear you're organising the wedding.' His gaze swept up and down her. She felt sure she could feel it through her clothes. 'That's really kind of you.'

'She's my sister.' She tried to keep her voice light.

'It sounds like it's going to be quite a big deal.'

'Jess has already counted up about a hundred guests.'

Jess had invited everyone she knew and their dog. She was a social creature and a party animal. There would be no restraint with the guest list.

Rik pulled at the sleeves of his shirt, looking awkward. 'I was hoping for more of a quick tying of the knot then a couple of drinks at the Neptune.'

Nikki tried to laugh. 'Not a chance. You know Jess loves being the centre of attention.'

'I guess so.'

There was an awkward silence. Neither of them wanted to mention the last time they'd been alone. Rik looked down. He drew a circle with his shoe on the wet granite cobbles while he thought. Then he looked up again.

'I had to ask her to marry me, Nikki. I never forgave my dad for not marrying my mum. It ruined my childhood. I spent it wishing they were together. Wishing we had a proper family. Once I knew Jess was pregnant, I couldn't put our baby through what I went through.'

'No. That would be cruel.'

'I just worry that I'm not going to be able to make

her happy. I'm not sure she really wants this. Or me. Sometimes it feels like a game.'

Nikki swallowed. Was this her chance to put the knife in? She wouldn't have to lie. Jess was bloody impossible. She moved the goalposts all the time. She manipulated people to get what she wanted and then moved on when she got bored. Should she reassure him? Or plant further doubt in his mind? Her heart was thudding as she gazed at him. His cloud of golden hair like a halo, backlit by the sun. The sharpness of his cheekbones. The soft, full lips she had once felt on her skin, fleetingly, so warm she could still imagine their heat if she tried hard enough. Did she have it in her to betray her own sister?

'I've never known her so happy,' she managed at last. 'Honestly.'

He looked relieved. 'I'm so envious, of what you all have. Your family. Your house. It's all I've ever wanted and I hope me and Jess can . . .' He was overcome with emotion. 'I hope we can have something like that.'

He was almost in tears. Nikki wanted to step forward and take him in her arms. To comfort him. But she knew that would be disastrous. She could still feel that attraction, thrumming backwards and forwards between them, a zip wire of electricity.

'You will,' she reassured him. 'The wedding's going to be beautiful. I'll make sure of it. And you'll be happy.'

She tried to smile but she could feel her lips twisting, and tears gather in her eyes. He reached out a hand and touched her shoulder. He couldn't speak. He just nodded. She could feel his fingertips burning through her shirt. And then he turned and walked away, and she gazed at his retreating figure, those long legs, that slight swagger, the way he shook his hair out of his eyes. She wanted to call out to him to come back. Tell him to walk away from Jess while he could. Tell him that she, Nikki, was the one who could give him what he craved. Love, a family, a place to call home. But she couldn't.

She watched him disappear through the archway and head out into the street and it was as if the sun had gone in, even though it was still shining down on her.

31

Now

Nikki woke the next morning at five, as sunlight draped itself over the two sisters like a silken coverlet, and sweet birdsong crept in through the crack in the open window. She couldn't remember the last time she'd been so close to Jess. They used to fall asleep on each other's beds all the time when they were teenagers, listening to CDs when they got back from the beach, gossiping, laughing. Jess would smoke out of the window then spray CK One around the room. Nikki could never smell that scent without remembering warm summer nights and secrets and Jess spread out on three quarters of the bed, just as she was now. Jess took up space, in bed and in your head.

She turned to see her sister was wide awake, staring at the ceiling, yesterday's mascara still smudged under her eyes. She gave her a nudge with her elbow and sat up.

'Let's go for a swim.'

'What?' Jess looked unimpressed with the suggestion.

'Come on. You'll feel amazing after. It'll wash all your worries away. And it's good for you.'

Jess had always been less enthusiastic about getting in

the water when they were growing up. For her, it had been about posing in her bikini, especially as the salt water made her hair wild and untameable. So Nikki suspected trying to persuade her now would be a losing battle. But to her surprise, Jess threw back the covers.

'Come on, then. Let's go skinny-dipping.'

Nikki laughed. Jess always had to push it.

'I'll lend you a costume.'

'Nik. It's not called the secret beach for nothing. No one will be there.'

This was true. Nikki didn't think she'd ever seen anyone on the secret beach at this hour. She was caught up in Jess's enthusiasm. She couldn't remember the last time they'd done something spontaneous together. They used to when they were young. The North girls had been known for their *joie de vivre*. Jess was the wilder of the two, of course, but it was the two of them who had made things happen: a beach barbecue, a moonlit rave, a bonfire party.

'OK, then. I'll grab us some towels. Let's go.'

They must have looked slightly mad, rushing out of the back door still in their night things, down the garden, over the wall and along to the steps. Slightly out of breath, because she wasn't so fit these days, Jess stopped at the top and looked down at the beach below. The tide was on its way in, scampering over the sand, edging closer with each set of waves. The cliffs were pin-sharp against the sky, the landscape almost as pristine and perfect as a model railway, the trees placed carefully along the skyline by some unknown hand.

'Rik always loved coming here.'

'Did he?' Nikki tried to make her voice light. Could Jess hear the tension?

'It was his happy place, he said. He used to come here to think.'

'Oh.' Nikki couldn't look at her. Her chest tightened, knowing he hadn't come here to *think* at all. 'What about?'

'I dunno. Stuff. He was quite deep, you know.' Jess sighed. 'Way deeper than me. He had a bit of a dark side. I think it was his upbringing. His parents. It made him sad, how they couldn't ever make it work, and how lost he was because of it.'

Nikki rummaged for a platitude.

'Poor Rik,' she said in the end, which sounded incredibly lame.

'I sometimes wonder,' said Jess, 'what would have happened if I hadn't got pregnant? If life would have been different. If he hadn't been on call that day, or had got to the station later.'

Nikki watched the waves crashing down below. She remembered them the afternoon of the storm. The way they'd loomed over her. The moment she'd wanted to call him back.

'We wouldn't have Juno,' she said softly. 'I can't imagine life without Juno.'

'No.' Jess was staring at the horizon. Was she wondering the same thing Nikki had wondered for years? What had it been like, out there on the sea in that terrible storm? How long before they had known they had no chance?

'Why are you thinking about this now?' Nikki asked, her voice tight. The black words swam into her mind. *Who else knows . . . ?* There hadn't been another card for a while, but the menace still hung over her.

'I don't know.' Jess shook her head. 'Maybe it's the twenty-year thing? Everyone keeps going on about it. Zak

Glazier. Like it's bloody Glastonbury or something. Like it's a celebration.'

'It is,' said Nikki. 'It's a celebration of their lives.'

Jess shrugged. 'I guess I just always feel guilty, even though I know it wasn't my fault. They died because they were brave, not because of something I did . . .' She sighed. 'I don't know. I guess it's impossible not to feel guilty. Don't you?'

She stared at Nikki again. Did she know something? Nikki felt the blood rush to her cheeks.

'I feel lots of things. Every day. But it was nothing to do with us. That storm would always have happened. Dad and Rik would always have gone out to rescue that boat. That's who they were. There's no point in torturing yourself thinking you could have changed things.' Nikki knew that well enough. How many times had she said to herself *if only . . .*

'I know,' said Jess. 'But I didn't make him happy. Not because I was horrible. But because I wasn't . . .'

She seemed to be swallowing her words, to have thought better of what she was about to say.

'Wasn't what?'

Jess didn't answer the question. Instead, she grabbed Nikki's arm.

'We're supposed to be going for a skinny dip. Not wallowing in the past.'

As quickly as she had plummeted, Jess seemed to have snapped out of her melancholy and raced down the steps. Nikki followed and they leapt onto the beach at the bottom, scrambled out of their pyjamas, threw them on top of their towels, then pelted stark naked into the sea.

'Oh my God!' screamed Jess. 'It's bloody freezing!'

'Of course it is!' laughed Nikki, and dived under the water. Jess, to her credit, followed suit and the two of them swam into the oncoming waves, pulling themselves through with the strong strokes they'd been taught by their father when they were tiny. When they got to the calmer water behind the surf, they lay on their backs, gently sculling their arms.

'You're right,' said Jess. 'This is doing the trick. I'm so bloody cold I can't *feel* any emotion.'

Nikki was treading water. She felt deliciously weightless, almost graceful, relishing the tingling chill on her skin. She looked back towards the beach and saw a figure coming down the steps.

'Oh no.' It was Adam. Climbing behind Gatsby. Out on his early morning walk. 'There's my neighbour,' she told Jess. 'We'll have to wait till he's gone.'

'Well, I need to head in. I've got to be back at the hospital at nine.'

'We can't!'

'Why not?' Jess's eyes lit up with defiance and she started to swim breaststroke back towards the shore. Nikki followed, protesting.

'You can flash him if you want but I'm not. I've got to live next door to him.'

'Like he's never seen a naked woman before? What's he gonna do?'

'I'm going to wait. I just can't.'

They were back in their depth. Adam spotted them and raised a hand. Jess stood up, her torso clear of the water, her boobs proudly on display as she began to stride towards the shore. Nikki kept herself under the water and tried to stop herself laughing as Adam realised Jess was topless. Gallantly he turned away before she revealed her entire body. Undaunted, Jess carried on until she reached the sand. Nikki secretly admired her sister for her boldness as she glided over to their towels, catwalk confident, her hair streaming down her back as Gatsby raced up to her in delight and Adam tried whistling to get him back.

Poor Adam, she thought. He was probably mortified at having interrupted them. She'd have to apologise to him later. Or should she? Was Jess right? Did it matter?

Jess nonchalantly draped her towel around her then grabbed Nikki's and headed back into the water to give it to her so she could cover herself and make a more discreet exit.

'You're a nutter,' said Nikki.

'Isn't that why you love me?'

Yes, thought Nikki. It absolutely was. And that was why she felt unnerved, because she didn't want to lose her sister. Her crazy, brave, impossible sister. She just had to pray that whoever had sent her the cards wasn't intent on driving a wedge between them.

32

Zak Glazier lived in an ancient farmhouse along the coast. To get to it, you had to drive down a tiny, twisting road amidst ancient woodland. Nikki drove carefully, for it was tortuous and treacherous, with a terrifying drop to one side: a steep cliff leading to jagged rocks and crystal-blue water that looked heavenly but was deadly, the site of many a shipwreck. It was a magical spot. The locals had watched with interest as Zak restored the house with surprising sympathy. His obsession, according to rumour, was renovating the old walled garden and growing his own organic vegetables, which seemed like a very un-rockstar preoccupation.

'Your mum and I used to come out here,' she told Juno. 'Some old hippies owned it and they used to have parties every weekend. Anyone could rock up. They went on all night and everyone watched the sun come up.'

Nikki remembered being in the back of someone's car, terrified as they drove at speed, Jess laughing in the front and turning up the music. How they survived she didn't know. They were all young and reckless, with the insouciance of youth.

'Sounds wild.' Juno was nervous, but pretending not to be. She was heading out to meet Zak for the first time. Nikki had offered to drive her as Jess was at work. There was no way Juno could get to his house otherwise. There was no public transport anywhere near his house, especially not on a Sunday.

Nikki stopped in the driveway for a moment. She could sense Juno's apprehension. She'd made a big effort with her appearance while trying to pretend she hadn't, but Nikki could see she had refreshed the dark blue dye on her hair, and her make-up had been applied with even more precision: perfect dark red lips, immaculate arched eyebrows, contoured cheekbones. She was clutching the notebook she used for song-writing. It was covered in pictures of her musical idols, and wrapped in sticky back plastic: Debbie Harry and Nina Simone and Joni Mitchell.

'You're going to be fine,' Nikki told her. 'And remember, Zak was like you once. He wasn't born a star. He knows what it's like.'

Juno gave something between a shrug and a nod. Nikki reached out to squeeze her shoulder. Her fingers met the fabric of the dress she was wearing, and she started in sudden recognition. Now she looked she could see it wasn't a dress, but a man's shirt, hitched in with a wide belt over Juno's fishnets and lace-up boots.

A billowing collarless shirt, white with a thin black pinstripe.

'Is this new?' Nikki asked.

'It's Dad's,' said Juno. 'Mum gave it to me. She thought it would bring me good luck. That it would be like having him with me.'

'Oh, darling.' Nikki hugged her, rubbing her cheek against the soft cotton for a moment, remembering him in her arms, the feel of him, the warmth of him. 'Whatever you do, it will be amazing. Your dad would be so proud of you.'

'Do you think so?'

'I know so. How couldn't he be? You're clever and talented and beautiful. Zak is lucky to be working with you.'

'I bet he can't wait,' said Juno drily. She was too down on herself, thought Nikki. But maybe it was her age. Maybe they'd all been like that. Uncertain of their place in the world. She thought it had been easier for them, though, growing up without the pressure of social media, the micro-scrutiny and the fake worlds to which they were taught to aspire. Though Juno didn't buy into it so much, and was assiduous about teaching the M and Ms not to be taken in by Instagram and Snapchat and TikTok.

They rattled up the driveway as the farm came into view. It looked almost unrecognisable from the tumbledown old wreck Nikki remembered, with its ramshackle outbuildings and sagging roof. It had smelled of damp and weed and woodsmoke from the big old fire that was the only heating. Now it glowed mellow in the sun, immaculately restored, as splendid as the day it had been built three hundred years ago, not a brick or a window out of place.

And here was Zak, coming out to greet them with a wide smile in what looked like his gardening clothes, followed by an Australian sheep dog with bright blue eyes.

'Look at him,' breathed Juno, and as ever Nikki knew that her head was not being turned by the chart-topping heart-throb but his canine companion.

'Hey,' said Zak, holding out his hand to Nikki. 'I'm Zak. It's good to meet you.'

'I'm Juno's aunt,' said Nikki, trying not to be too starstruck. It was weird, seeing someone you'd watched on the telly at Glastonbury right in front of you. 'And this is Juno.'

He turned to Juno. 'I can't wait to work with you.'

'Same,' said Juno, with a shy smile.

'Come on in.' Zak nodded towards the house. 'You can wait inside, if you want,' he told Nikki. 'There's a bar and coffee and a TV.'

'Oh gosh no, I'll come back later,' said Nikki. The last thing she wanted to do was cramp Juno's style. 'Good luck, both of you.'

She watched them head off towards the studio. The rock star and the nobody. She felt a curious mixture of pride and protectiveness for Juno, but something told her she would hold her own. She had her own star quality, even if she was reticent about sharing it with the world. Maybe this was a turning point for her? Maybe Zak could give her the confidence she needed?

33

Two weeks later, Mike and Jason cleared away their tools from the cottage. All Nikki needed to do was paint the house from top to bottom and get her things from storage. To spur her on to finish the decorating she decided to throw a housewarming party before her furniture was moved in. She only had one Saturday without a wedding, which she'd deliberately kept free, so she texted invitations to her closest friends and family. Tacos, cocktails and dancing – something easy that wouldn't take much organising. She felt uplifted by the thought of a celebration that belonged to her and no one else, something to mark the kind of life she wanted at Number Four: free and easy, an open door, as welcoming in the height of summer with the sun blazing as it would be in the depths of winter with a log fire on the go.

Meanwhile, she drove Adam to look at a couple of office spaces on an industrial estate on the edge of town. Graham had given him the heads up as North Property Management had been pulled in to tart them up before they went back on the rental market. Adam signed up on the spot for the smaller one, and Nikki could feel his elation at making the decision.

They headed back down the long hill into Speedwell. As they turned the corner, the harbour came into view, the buildings along the quay shimmering in the midday sun. It was almost high tide, the boats rising higher and higher as the water trickled in. Only last week, the *Sunday Times* had run a review on Salacia, which was packed to the rafters night after night:

> A newly built dual carriageway and superfast broadband have turned this faded seaside town in North Cornwall into a glittering hotspot; the place to work remotely and enjoy the coastal life we all dream of. Imagine paddle-boarding around the bay in your lunch hour, and ending your day with a gin and tonic in Salacia, a sexy, luxe glass-fronted bar that has opened to serve the influx of former city dwellers who've chosen a new way of living.

Adam sighed as he looked at the picturesque sweep of the bay. In the distance, on the other side, they could see their little cottages, perched on the clifftop like birds on a wire.

'I haven't had a moment's regret about moving down here,' he said. 'It's perfect. Well, except for the obvious.'

Nikki lifted her hand to touch his arm, in sympathy, then took it away to change gear, worrying the gesture would be too intimate. She cleared her throat and tucked her hair behind her ear. It was warm in the car, and her head was filled with the scent of his cologne – it was both clean and dirty at the same time, citrussy yet musky, lime and pepper and honey, male yet feminine; complex, hard to pin down, hauntingly sexy. She found it incredibly distracting. Dangerous while driving down a steep slope in a narrow lane.

Eventually they reached the outskirts of the town and she drove towards the harbour, managing to find a space. It was getting harder and harder to park nowadays. They headed back along the quay towards the Neptune, walking past the memorial that had been commissioned for the fifth anniversary of the disaster. Forged in shining stainless steel, it was twenty feet high. A tangle of hearts, each one representing one of the lost men, were entwined with each other. From a distance, they looked like a huge cresting wave. It was simple and symbolic, slicing through the blue sky, glittering where the light caught it.

Seven hearts. Seven men.

Underneath was a white marble plaque with their names carved on it in black. Nikki's eyes rested on her dad's – William North – and then the one above his. Rik Mahoney-Chambord. She had learned not to flinch.

Adam reached his hand out and touched the marble reverently, tracing his fingers along the letters of each name.

'I imagine it never gets any easier,' he said softly.

Nikki couldn't answer. She just shook her head. He dropped his hand, then wordlessly took her arm, hooking his in hers in an easy gesture of comfort. It filled her with warmth, for the memorial always chilled her inside, and there was the added icy fear that hit her as she remembered her persecutor. The horrible recollection that she wasn't the person everyone thought she was.

There was always something there to remind her.

She composed herself as they walked towards the pub.

'Shall we sit outside?' She disentangled herself from him and edged towards the best table. There was a light breeze tap-dancing across the water, just enough to whip little white tips onto the surface, but the sun was gaining confidence as if it had been practising for its summer performance.

'Definitely. What do you fancy? I'll go and order.'

Nikki slid onto the bench. 'I'll have what I always have,' she said. 'Salt and pepper calamari and dirty chips.'

'Oof,' he said, grinning. 'I mean, there's no point in even looking at the menu. That ticks all my boxes.'

They nursed two glasses of icy Muscadet while they waited for their food. Then Gloria headed out with two bowls of chargrilled calamari and two bowls of triple-cooked chips topped with crispy bacon, spring onion, red peppers, sour cream and melted mozzarella.

'Hey, Nikki,' she said, 'thanks for the party invitation. Me and Belle will try and get over after service, if you think you'll still be going strong?'

'Oh,' said Nikki, pretending to wince, 'I don't know. I've got my grumpy neighbour to worry about.' She turned to Adam. 'Do you think he'll be OK with noise after midnight?'

'He might complain to the police.' Adam played along. 'Maybe you should invite him? Then he can't complain.'

'I don't know if he's a party person.'

'People can surprise you.'

Gloria was watching their exchange, bemused. Then she pointed at him. 'You're the grumpy neighbour.'

'I am.' He held out his hand. 'Adam. And don't worry. It will still be going until the small hours, I'm sure.'

'I'll see you then,' Gloria said, and headed back inside.

'These chips aren't just dirty,' said Adam, digging into his. 'They are absolutely filthy. You're a temptress.'

'Blame Gloria, not me,' laughed Nikki. 'Once you've tasted them, you're done for. She and Belle totally turned this place around when they moved in. You wouldn't have risked eating here before.'

They ate in silence for a few minutes. This was bliss, thought Nikki, sitting in the sun with a glass of wine, sharing delicious food with someone who really appreciated what they were eating and where they were sitting. From time to time, someone would pass by the table and she would introduce them to Adam.

'You really do run through this town like letters through a stick of rock,' he said admiringly.

'I've lived here all my life. There's not many people I don't know. Though there are a lot of newcomers these days. Second-homers.' She made a face, then realised he would be classed as one of them. 'Sorry, I don't mean you.'

'I'm guilty as charged,' he said. 'Though not anymore. I like to think I'll be putting back into the local economy, and contributing to the community. Especially now I've got my office.'

'Of course.' Nikki felt mortified that she'd judged him, and hoped he wasn't offended. He didn't seem to be.

He nodded over to the lifeboat station. It was on the other side of the quay, perched by the slope where the boats were launched into the harbour when a shout came in. The front was always open so passersby could see in, and have a look inside if they wanted. Speedwell was proud of its lifeboat. 'Would you show me around when we've finished?'

'Of course!'

'I was thinking,' he said. 'About volunteering. Not as crew – I'm probably too old, for a start, and I'm too much of a land lubber. But there must be other roles. And it feels like the best way to get to feel part of the town.'

'We always need help with fundraising. You should talk to my mum. Or Graham. And there are other roles that come up from time to time.' She clicked her fingers and pointed at him as if she'd had a brainwave. 'Oh – hang on a minute. We always need someone to dress up as Sammy the Seal in the summer. He's our mascot.'

'Right.' Adam looked doubtful.

'You'd be amazed how much money he collects from the tourists. He's one of our most lucrative fundraising tactics. That might be worth thinking about.'

Adam smiled politely. 'Maybe.'

She burst out laughing. 'I'm only teasing. The kids all take it in turn to be Sammy over the summer. Even if you wanted to don the seal suit, you'd have to fight them for it.'

'I'm going to pay you back for that.' He reached out to try to poke her in the ribs with a finger. She squeaked, and tried to dodge out of his way, but he was too quick for her, making contact, a teasing gesture of reproach. She gasped slightly at his touch, but turned it into a laugh, letting her hair fall over her face to hide her blush.

Was this neighbourly banter, or were they flirting?

'Come on, then,' she said, draining the last of her glass. As they headed over to the lifeboat station, she felt light-headed, from the wine, the sun, his lingering cologne, the bubbly thrill of their badinage that was so light and so easy. It felt completely natural. Was there some sort of chemistry between them, or was it because Adam was so effortlessly charming? Was she special, or did he make everyone feel that way?

She felt proud as she showed him around the station. The all-weather lifeboat sitting in the middle of the boathouse, splendid in its royal blue and orange paintwork, its high-tech equipment gleaming. Next to her, the inshore boat seemed almost insignificant, but Nikki explained how nimble it was, how it was often used to reach locations impossible for the bigger boat to get to.

'They want me to train as helm,' she told him. 'But I'm worried I'd be taking on too much.'

She still hadn't decided what she was going to do. She had to make up her mind, because Archie Fowler wouldn't wait forever.

'It's part of who you are, though, isn't it?' Adam was looking at the photographic displays on the wall, of all the rescues they'd done since the station was opened in 1860, and the boards carrying the names of lifeboatmen who'd been given awards for bravery over the years. 'Don't you want to do it for your dad?'

'Of course.' How perceptive he was, thought Nikki. 'But the weddings are taking over my life. I could book myself three times over in the summer. And it's all year round now. I'm booked up all the way through, except November. That's when I'm going away to Bali, to see Bill.'

'Maybe it's time to take a look at how you run things? Take on someone to help? You must have people working for you already?'

'Yes, but mostly I take people on for the day itself, or to help set up or take down. I don't trust anyone to do the other stuff.'

'Ah,' he said. 'Well, that's a mistake. You'll be a slave to your business until the end of time if you can't find someone you can rely on. I always thought like you. That no one could make decisions or run things like I could. But, of course, they can.'

'Really?' Nikki shuddered at the thought.

'It was the only way I could move down here. I had to get someone in London running things for me. It took me a long time to find the courage to do it, and to find the right person, but it's been a real game changer. The business is more efficient, I'm not tied up with minutiae, we keep in close contact and everything runs really well.'

'I can't imagine delegating. I guess I'm a control freak. I have to know that everything's been done my way. That it's all perfect. I can't afford an unhappy client.'

'Nor me. And that's what I used to think. You have to train them to think like you. But also listen to their ideas, because it's very easy to get stuck in your ways. Honestly, it's been a revelation. My clients love Marina. Almost more than they love me.' He grinned. 'Almost.'

They were in the kit room, where rows and rows of yellow waterproof gear and boots and helmets were lined up, ready to be jumped into at a moment's notice. Nikki wondered how many times she had clambered into the heavy kit, either for training or on a shout. She remembered coming here with her dad as a tiny girl and putting on a pair of boots. They'd come halfway up her thighs and she'd clumped about proudly to much raucous laughter.

'She's born to the lifeboat, that maid,' one of the crew had shouted.

'I think I'm going to do it,' she said.

Adam nodded his approval. 'You've got to make room for what you want to do in life,' he told her. 'And not get weighed down by the stuff you don't need to do.'

He was right. She supposed over the years she'd always had her mum to bounce off, or to help out when everything got too much. But it wasn't fair to expect Helen to share the burden now. The cakes were enough responsibility, and it was time for her to put herself first now, with the online dating. She didn't begrudge her mum a romance for a millisecond. But who could step up? She'd have to advertise and train someone.

On the drive home, she reflected on how much she had valued Adam's advice, and how useful it had been to have someone to discuss her options with. If she spoke to Graham, or her mum, or even Jess, about Archie's proposition, they would have views that didn't necessarily take her into consideration. Not that they'd force her into anything, but there might have been an underlying pressure – a sense of family loyalty, maybe even sentimentality.

'Thank you,' she said. 'For your advice. I really appreciate it.'

'Any time,' he said. 'It's always easy for someone else to see the big picture, though, isn't it? It's tough getting the balance right in life. Work. Home. Love.'

Love. The word resonated inside the car. Hung heavy in the air.

'And dogs,' he added.

'I'd love a dog,' sighed Nikki. 'But that really would be a step too far. Even with Juno to help me out.'

'Gatsby was the saving of me,' said Adam. 'I had to keep going because of him. Even on the days I didn't want to.'

This time Nikki did reach out and touch his arm. She held it there for as long as she dared. As she dropped her hand, he reached out and took her fingers, squeezing them, just for a moment. What was he demonstrating? Appreciation? Affection? She couldn't be sure. But it felt good to be touched like that. She didn't want him to let go.

34

On Thursdays, Helen often babysat for Suzanne and Graham so they could have a date night. This evening, they'd gone out to Salacia with Tamara and Duke. Suzanne had heard from Tamara that she had got the contract to do the Pier, and this was a celebration to seal the deal.

Suzanne had been on cloud nine when they came back. Tamara and Duke had fêted them with champagne and said how excited they were by her plans.

'She said they were fresh and witty with a nostalgic twist that didn't take itself too seriously. Way more uplifting than the pitches from her London designers. And I'd captured the spirit of Speedwell, instead of trying to turn it into something it wasn't.'

Helen was thrilled for her, but also a tiny bit afraid that it was a big challenge.

'Don't worry, Mum,' said Graham, who could sense her anxiety. 'Suzanne's got me to bounce off. We went over and over her quote with a fine-toothed comb and I sent my guy in to do a massive survey to make sure there's no nasty surprises. There's nothing she can't handle. This is going to be good. For both of us.'

Helen felt reassured. The two of them made a great team, with a combination of Graham's experience and steady hand, and Suzanne's creative flair. She went home with a sense of pride and satisfaction. All her children were settled and doing well, and as a mother, she thought, you couldn't ask for anything more. Graham and Suzanne were making the most of the opportunities in the town, Jess was hugely respected at work and Nikki was going from strength to strength with the weddings. OK, so Jess and Nikki were both single, but she knew they were that way because they were strong and independent, not because they couldn't get a man. In time, they might each find someone, and it was worth waiting for the right person.

No one knew that better than she did.

She slipped into the silk nightdress that she'd ordered online. Was it ridiculous, to buy glamorous nightwear for a man she hadn't even met, and might not even like, and might never share a bed with? No, she thought. Because actually, it wasn't for him at all. It was for her. She deserved to slink about in something gorgeous, even if it was for her own benefit. She looked at herself in the mirror and nodded approval. It was deep navy with splashes of hot pink flowers and suited her, perfect for her skin tone and her hair and her eyes, and in the lamplight there was no sign of a crepey cleavage or bingo wings, just smooth, glowing skin.

It gave her confidence as she slipped under the duvet and picked up the iPad that was charging on her bedside table. Even though he wouldn't see it – they hadn't progressed to video chats yet – he would hear something in her voice. She loved the way he made her feel. It wasn't seedy or sleazy. She just felt . . . recognised. Seen. Appreciated. Not just as a mother or granny or committee member. For herself.

She smiled as she pressed the WhatsApp icon and began to type.

You awake?

The answer was immediate. *Nope. Fast asleep.*

She grinned. *Ha ha. I've just got back from babysitting.*

Talk? he asked, and she felt a skitter of pleasure.

Sure.

She only had to wait a couple of seconds for him to call. She gave it three rings so as not to seem too keen, then answered.

'So you're in bed already?'

She blushed and smiled. 'I am.'

'I wish I could learn from you. I'm hopeless. Never in bed before midnight. Sometimes one or two. I get *embroiled*.'

'What are you up to, then?'

'Digging out pieces for an autumn concert at a local stately home. I'm in charge of the programme. It's getting the balance right that's the bugger. Familiar but not too clichéd. Crowd- pleasers but nothing hackneyed. It's quite a challenge.' He gave a theatrical sigh. 'Woe is me.'

Lying back on her pillows, swathed in silk, Helen suddenly felt emboldened.

'So what do you think about meeting up then?'

There was silence for a moment. Had she been too forward? They hadn't discussed meeting since he'd suggested it the other night. Should she have waited for him to mention it? Eventually he spoke.

'I can't think of anything I'd like more.'

Helen felt relieved.

'Perhaps just for lunch. Nothing too formal.'

'Well, why not? But where? I mean, I'd happily come down to you, if that's easiest. Or we could meet halfway. Maybe on the edge of Dartmoor.' He laughed. 'You can tell I've given it some thought.'

'Halfway makes sense.'

The idea excited her. It would be an adventure. Besides, all eyes would be upon them if he came to Speedwell. She wouldn't be able to relax. On the edge of Dartmoor, she would be unlikely to see anyone she knew well. She could meet whoever she liked, safe in the knowledge that it wouldn't be reported back.

'How about next Friday? Something to look forward to at the end of the week.'

'Perfect. I'll book us a table somewhere and let you know.'

She had a date. And it had been so easy. Everything was easy, with Ralph. She prayed it would be when they met in real life. Perhaps an online relationship was a bit of an illusion, and reality would be different? But if she didn't try, she'd never know. And what was the worst that could happen? She'd lose the price of a pub lunch.

'I suppose I should let you go now,' Ralph said, interrupting her thoughts.

'Would you play something for me?' She couldn't believe her boldness. Two overtures in one evening. 'Something dreamy to send me to sleep.'

'Well.' He seemed to be giving it some thought. 'Let

me call you back in a moment, then. I'll have to take you into the living room.'

'OK.'

He rang off. She lay there, smiling. How romantic it would be, to be serenaded from afar. She imagined him, moving through his flat, heading for a piano in the corner of the room, pulling out a stool, leafing through his music.

A few minutes later, he rang again.

'OK. I'm going to get no prizes for originality, but this is gorgeous. Debussy's *Rêverie*. I guarantee you will float off to sleep with a smile on your face. Ready?'

'I am.'

She waited for a few seconds, then a delicate arpeggio began, to be joined by other notes dancing around it. She imagined the gentle touch of his fingers as he moved up and down the keys, perhaps with his eyes closed as hers were, perhaps swaying in time. Her breathing slowed and her mind drifted. A sense of calm settled upon her; a peace she hadn't felt since William had gone.

This music was for her. Just for her.

35

When her pager went off early the next morning, Nikki came to with a groan. Truly, what were the chances of getting a shout at six o'clock in the morning?

She jumped out of bed. The morning was one of those pearly, misty ones, delicately pretty, the sea a cool pale grey beneath a matching sky. The sun might burn through later, or a thicker mist might roll in, obscuring everything for the rest of the day. Either way, for now it was chilly. She pulled on her Uggs and ran outside to the van in her pyjamas.

At the station, she was one of the first to arrive.

'It's a dog,' Eddie told her. 'Early morning walker. It's gone over the cliff about two miles round the headland.'

This was a surprisingly common occurrence. The team took canine crises as seriously as they took human ones, and came to their aid without question. Nikki pulled on her kit as quickly as she could, grateful for its weight and warmth, and was on board the inshore lifeboat less than quarter of an hour after her pager had gone off. She loved the adrenaline and the sense of purpose, all her earlier annoyance at her pager vanishing as they launched.

The morning air was cool and damp on her skin as they headed out of the harbour and hugged the cliffs along the coast. Minutes later they passed beneath the house she'd just left and she looked up for a moment, wondering if Adam was awake yet, wondering if he'd look out of his window and see her passing. Wondering just what that moment of closeness had meant in the car. A squiggle of pleasure zipped through her at the memory.

'OK, we've got some more info coming through,' Eddie told her. He was on the radio. 'We're looking for a Vizsla. A wire-haired Vizsla.'

Nikki froze. A wire-haired Vizsla? They weren't that common. Could it be Gatsby? She knew, from her swim with Jess, that Adam sometimes got up early to walk him. And Gatsby was a city dog, not all that used to the coast. He could easily have misjudged the cliff path and fallen. She looked up to the top of the cliff, then started to scan the rocks beneath as they reached the area where the fall was supposed to have happened, peering into crevasses and gullies and inlets. It was tricky to get close, because of the rocks just underneath the surface of the water as the tide started coming in, but they were in the best boat for the job.

And then she saw a bundle of fur, slumped on a flat piece of rock just above the shoreline. The cliffs soared more than twenty feet above that, so he must have taken quite a drop. She recognised him by the turquoise of the collar.

'It's Gatsby,' she told the others. 'My neighbour's dog. At least he knows me.'

Ed drove the boat into the deep ravine between the cliffs, getting as near as he could, so Nikki and Dan could get out and start climbing over the rocks. Nikki's heart was racing as she scrambled over the slippery surface, praying Gatsby wasn't too badly injured; that he might have bounced and rolled as he fell, not landed too awkwardly. As they reached him, he stared at her, looking sorry for himself.

'Hey, boy,' she said, pulling on a pair of protective gloves. Even though he knew her, fear might make him hostile. 'What have you done to yourself? It's OK. We've come to get you.'

There was no blood, no obvious injury, but he was shaking. Probably through shock, and the stress, but she knew it could also be an internal injury and at this point only a vet would be able to assess him. They needed to get him there as quickly as possible. She fed him a couple of the treats she'd brought in her pocket to calm him and gain his trust as Dan attached the oars of the boat to the ambulance pouch to make a makeshift stretcher. Gatsby nuzzled at her hand for comfort, and she murmured reassurance. She wondered where Adam was. He must have had to run back along the coast path to make the emergency call. There was no signal here, she knew that.

'It's OK, baby. I've got you,' she murmured.

It took the two of them a while to manoeuvre him safely into the pouch, but at last they were able to climb back over the rocks to the boat and get him safely on board.

'Good work,' said Eddie. 'Let's get him to the vet.'

And he turned the boat out to sea and set off back to the station.

Nikki had no idea if Adam knew Gatsby had been rescued. But they would radio back to the coastguard who could relay the message and get him to head to the lifeboat station. She reassured Gatsby as they powered back through the waves, burying her fingers in his rough fur, feeling his heart beat beneath her fingers, looking at his confused face as the breeze sent his eyebrows and whiskers and ears flying backwards. She could feel the relief on the boat. Everyone loved a successful rescue, even when it was just a dog. Perhaps especially when it was a dog.

Back at the station, the vet's van had arrived to whisk him off to the surgery where Adam was apparently waiting. The crew headed back in for a debrief, then Nikki got undressed from her heavy kit and slid back into her pyjamas, shivering with fatigue and exhaustion. All she wanted to do was go back to bed. She could steal an hour. She had a site meeting at Windcutter Farm at two, with all the technical crew. Electricity, lighting, sound. Her least favourite part of the job, as she could never predict the problems. She needed all her energy.

She waved her comrades goodbye and plodded to her van. At home, she made herself a hot milky chai, spicy and sweet for comfort and to warm her through, then headed up to bed. She climbed under the duvet and fell asleep before even starting her drink.

A while later she heard someone knocking at her front door. It must be Adam, with news of Gatsby, and she cared too much to ignore him even though sleep was luring her back. She staggered out of bed and down the stairs.

On the doorstep, Adam looked shaken.

'He's going to be all right,' he said. 'They're keeping him in, for observation. But he's going to be all right. I can't thank you enough. They told me at the station it was you who rescued him.'

'It was me and Dan,' she said. 'Teamwork. I'm just glad he's all right.'

She reached out to give him a hug. It seemed like the right thing to do. He held onto her for longer than she would have expected, but she realised he was struggling to keep a check on his emotions.

'Losing him would have been too much to bear,' he said into her shoulder. 'I should have had him on a lead but I didn't think he'd go towards the edge. It was a bloody rabbit. He can't resist chasing them. One minute he was there and the next minute he'd gone over.'

'It's OK,' Nikki repeated, not sure what else to say.

He gathered himself together and let her go.

'Let me at least make you some breakfast. To say thank you.'

The prospect of breakfast with Adam was irresistible. He was still in his early morning walking clothes – a light grey merino sweater that hugged him, and a pair of faded jeans. The smell of him as they'd hugged had stirred something in her.

'French toast?' he said. 'And freshly squeezed orange juice. And coffee.'

She couldn't say no. 'Can you give me ten minutes?'

He nodded. 'Just come straight in.'

When she headed into his kitchen, having showered, cleaned her teeth, slapped on some moisturiser and pulled on some clothes, she was overwhelmed by the scent of vanilla, cinnamon and crispy bacon mixed with fresh coffee bubbling on the stove. She realised she was starving.

She sat at the island and he carried over a plate with the fluffiest French toast she'd ever seen.

'There you go,' he said. 'A rescuer's breakfast.'

She went to take it from him.

'Hang on.'

She watched as he dressed it with a drizzle of maple syrup in the shape of a heart. She could barely breathe. What was this? A declaration? Had he felt something in the car yesterday? Had he been thinking about it too? Had her rescuing of Gatsby cemented his feelings and given him the courage to declare himself?

He smiled into her eyes as he put the plate in front of her. She could feel herself falling, falling, as if she'd lost her footing on the rocks earlier, her heart following on behind—

'That's from Gatsby,' he said.

'Oh!' Her voice came out as a squeak and she hoped it sounded like an exclamation of pleasure.

She'd got the wrong end of the stick. Hopefully he hadn't seen the mooning look of anticipation on her face. Hastily, she picked up her knife and fork and began to eat to cover her confusion. What was she thinking? Of course he wasn't going to declare himself to her. She'd read far too much into everything – all those little moments she'd thought there was a frisson or a connection had been part of her fevered imagination. She was his neighbour, for goodness' sake! Of course he wasn't going to get embroiled with her. It was completely inappropriate.

'By the way,' he said, thankfully oblivious to her racing thoughts. 'I'd love to do something to help for your party.'

She managed to recover her composure.

'Well,' said Nikki. 'Inspired by your burritos, I was

thinking of doing a taco bar. You could help me with that.'

Adam circled his thumb and forefinger with a smile. 'Perfect. I'll bring you round a vat of my guacamole. And I could make Palomas? With tequila in them this time.'

'Amazing. Shoot me a shopping list and I'll get everything you need.'

Nikki finished her French toast and put her knife and fork together. She was sure she could transform what she'd now identified as her crush on Adam into something she could handle by putting him firmly in the 'friend/neighbour' box. She could look him in the eye without blushing and no longer have to tussle with her fantasy of them falling in love over the garden fence.

Later, as she headed out to Windcutter Farm, she realised it was all for the best. Now, she wouldn't have to battle with her conscience about whether to tell him the kind of person she really was.

The kind of person who kissed the man who was going to marry her sister.

On their wedding day.

36

Then

The bungalow was in chaos. Perched on the outskirts of town, which made getting to the hospital in Tawcombe easy, it belonged to Jess's friends, two other A & E nurses and a hairdresser, and the three of them cheerfully admitted that you needed a tetanus injection before crossing the threshold. It was a house full of laughter, lipstick stains and empty glasses, for they worked hard and partied harder. Today, the lounge was being used as a beauty salon-cum-changing room as the bride and her attendants were prepared for the most glamorous wedding ever seen in Speedwell. Niamh had been doing Jess's hair for over ten years, and was armed with curling tongs, hair straighteners, false eyelashes and a bag of tricks that promised to disguise any blemish. Only perfection was allowed today.

She had already worked her magic on Nikki. Nikki, whose make-up routine consisted of a smidge of tinted moisturiser, mascara and lip-gloss, had sworn to make more effort with her appearance from now on as she gazed back at her reflection, her shoulder-length hair smoothed into a glossy mane, her eyes come-hither, her mouth a luscious pout of caramel.

'Come to the salon one day and I'll show you how to do it,' Niamh offered. 'You don't have to spend hours. It's all about the product.'

Niamh practised a kind of witchcraft really, Nikki decided.

Half an hour later, she saw that magic worked on her own sister. Niamh had transformed her into a Gothic fairy-tale princess. She was swathed in a sea of scarlet silk, the fabric cleverly cut to disguise her bump, her dark hair rippling over her shoulders as Niamh put on the finishing touches, applying a sticky coat of something to her lips that would make sure she didn't leave a smudge on anyone's cheek or a mark on the side of a glass.

By midday, she would be Mrs Jessica Mahoney-Chambord.

'Damn right I'm taking his name,' Jess had said in a flash of anti-feminist defiance. 'I mean, that's half the reason for marrying him.'

Nikki wasn't sure how she was going to get through the ceremony. Envy was gnawing at her insides. With luck, after today her yearning would fade. Once they had tied the knot, Rik would be out of bounds. Any hope that he would have a sudden change of heart and declare his undying love would be extinguished. She couldn't wait for the madness to stop. It was turning her into a shadow of her former self. She'd stopped going out with her mates, stopped going on all those silly outings that punctuated working life – shopping trips to Exeter, or clubbing in Tawcombe, or days out on Exmoor, ending up in a remote pub drinking cider. No matter how hard she tried, she couldn't stop thinking about him.

It was making her utterly miserable, no matter how

sternly she spoke to herself. The worst thing was there was no one she could talk to about it. She wasn't going to admit to being obsessed with her sister's boyfriend . . . fiancé . . . to anyone.

'Will I do?' Jess was standing in front of her, arms out.

'You look perfect,' said Nikki, and was horrified to find tears springing into her eyes.

'What are you crying for?' Jess looked puzzled.

'Because you look so beautiful,' gulped Nikki. 'I'd better go and get ready. The car's coming to Mariners at half eleven.' Nikki and Jess and their dad were going to the church together. Rik had stayed the night at the Pier Hotel with his mum, who had flown in to Bristol the day before.

'I'll be there.' Jess stepped forward and put her arms around her sister. Nikki could feel her warmth, and her head was filled with Jess's overpowering perfume, the familiar but unsettling scent, erotic and dangerous. It didn't smell like that on anyone else. Nikki had tried it once, and it had been harsh and bitter on her skin. 'And thank you. For everything. I'll pay you back one day. I don't know how, because I'm not an angel like you. But I promise I will.'

'You don't have to thank me,' said Nikki, stiff with guilt at her treacherous thoughts, wriggling out of Jess's embrace. Unlike her sister, she hated attention.

Nikki raced home through the streets, feeling a bit foolish with her hair done and her face fully made up, with jeans and a T-shirt on. Inside the house, she could hear her parents in the kitchen. She popped her head in. There they were, all dressed and ready to go, sharing a pot of tea as if it was a normal day. They seemed excited, but calm. Nikki had made sure that there was no pressure on them: she had wanted them to enjoy the wedding. Apart from William walking Jess down the aisle, they had nothing to worry about for the whole of the day.

'Oh, Dad!' she said. 'Look at you.'

William had a new suit, dark grey with a white stripe, and he looked so handsome, with his hair cut and his beard trimmed.

'Isn't he the bee's knees?' said Helen. 'I've told him we need to go on a date every week so he can get some wear out of it.' She was in a tight-fitting coral shift dress and staggeringly high suede shoes. A wide-brimmed hat lay on the kitchen table, ready to go on at the last minute. Her mum had always had a good eye for what flattered her, and a figure that meant she could get away with anything. But life in Speedwell didn't often call for dressing up.

'You both look a million dollars,' said Nikki. 'Mum, the car's coming for you and Graham at a quarter past, so you can get to the church early. Then it's coming back for us, Dad.'

William gave her a thumbs-up. 'I'll be ready.'

'Graham's not wearing trainers, right?' Nikki hated being nit-picky about clothing but this was a wedding, not football practice.

'I've told him.' Helen gave her a reassuring smile.

'I'm going upstairs to get ready.'

'Can I make you a sandwich? It's going to be a long day. You should eat something.'

'We had doughnuts.'

That was a bit of a fib. There had been doughnuts but she hadn't had one. There was no room for anything in her stomach besides nerves and dread.

'Hey, Nikki.' She was just about to leave the room when her dad called her back.

'Yes?'

'We're both so impressed with how you've handled this, love. Don't think it hasn't gone unnoticed.'

'What?' For a horrible moment, Nikki thought they were referring to her obsession with Rik. Was it that obvious?

'Organising the wedding.'

'Oh!' She laughed in relief.

'It could have been a nightmare for all of us, and I don't think anyone else could have done it except you.'

'You've done Jess proud,' her mother added.

'You deserve a medal.' Her father's eyes were twinkling.

Nikki didn't know what to say. She finally found her voice. 'She's my sister. I'd do anything for her.'

She left the kitchen and headed for the stairs. All she had to do now was get everyone to the church on time. She dashed into her bedroom, ripped off her clothes, rolled deodorant under her arms and squirted herself with perfume, then stepped into the bridesmaid's dress that was hanging up on the wardrobe. It was a strapless sheath in pale green satin – not Nikki's usual style at all, but Jess had talked her into it, and she had to admit she rather liked its sophisticated glamour.

Halfway into it she realised there was no way she could do up the long zip on her own, so she opened the bedroom door to shout down to her mum to come and help.

She came face to face with Rik, who was standing in the corridor.

'Oh God,' he said, embarrassed. 'I wasn't loitering. I was about to knock on your door.'

'Oh!'

'I just wanted to come and say thank you. For everything you've done for today. I don't think Jess would have got through it without you.'

'It's been fun.' Nikki tried to downplay it.

Rik looked even more extraordinary than ever, in a white linen suit, with a shirt made from the same scarlet silk as Jess's dress, and he'd done something to his hair that made it look even more tousled and ringlety and golden.

Could she ask him to do up her zip? She was standing there, clutching the top of her dress so it didn't fall down. Staring at him, transfixed.

'I thought you were getting ready at the hotel?' she managed eventually.

'Your dad asked me up for a drink. He thought I might be nervous.'

'Just a small one,' warned Nikki. She hoped that since she'd left the bungalow, Jess hadn't opened any more prosecco. She'd allowed everyone one Buck's Fizz, but she suspected the minute her back was turned, the corks would be popping. Jess and her mates were wild.

'Don't worry. I'm actually going to wait till afterwards. But I guess it's your dad's last chance to tell me to look after his daughter.' There was a strange expression on his face.

Something in the tone of his voice alarmed Nikki. 'Are you OK?'

He didn't speak for a moment. Then he took in a deep breath. 'I don't know if I should be marrying her.'

'Oh my God. Seriously?'

'I need someone to talk to.'

Nikki hesitated. 'You'd better come in.'

She told herself this was part of her job as the wedding planner. To calm the groom and make sure he got as far as the altar. As he stepped inside her room, she shut the door behind them.

He was here, inside her childhood bedroom, with all its personal possessions. Her unmade bed. Her clothes on the floor. Books, posters, make-up, CDs. She felt as if she was on display, as if he could now find out everything he needed to know about her.

But this wasn't about her, she reminded herself.

'Of course you're nervous,' she told him. 'You're bound to feel panicky just before you walk down the aisle. It's a huge thing. Jess is nervous too, though she won't admit it. But once you're up there next to each other, it'll be fine.' She was still clutching the top of her dress and he was staring at her. 'What?'

'I can't stop thinking about you.'

She froze. Had he really said that? What should she do? Laugh it off, she thought. So she tried a laugh, but it was slightly too high to sound convincing. 'Don't be silly.'

'Honestly. I woke up this morning and the first person I thought of was you.'

'Why?' Nikki couldn't imagine for one minute why this would be the case.

'Because you're kind and calm and sweet and funny and . . .' He swallowed. 'And I'm scared.'

'You can't do this.' Her voice was low and level. 'Not today. You have to be at the church in half an hour.'

'I don't *have* to be.'

How could you be thrilled and horrified in the very same moment? To want something so much but know you couldn't have it, even though it was right there in front of you? This was awful, thought Nikki. She had to think quickly. This might be her dream come true, but it couldn't go any further. Even though his words made her feel as if she'd been dipped in sugar crystals, she could think clearly enough to recognise that what he was suggesting was impossible. She was not going to be responsible for ruining her sister's wedding. Her sister's *life*. For all Jess's bravado, the humiliation would kill her.

And there was the baby. If it wasn't for the baby, then maybe. But it was there, the bump under Jess's scarlet satin dress. A tiny creature who needed a family. A whole one, not a fractured one. She would have to put on her sensible head. Be brisk and no nonsense.

'Well, that's by the by because even if I am all you can think about, it's not as if I'm interested.' She hoped she sounded suitably priggish and off-putting. She couldn't look at him, though. If she looked at him, she would crumble.

'Really?' He reached out and touched her bare arm and she jumped at his touch. 'Look me in the eye and say that. Look me in the eye and tell me there's not something between us.'

Why now? Why was he doing this now? It wasn't fair, to close in on her like this on his wedding day. It took all her will to inject a cold steel into her gaze as it met his. 'There's nothing between us, Rik. I'm sorry if that's what you think. I mean, I like you very much, of course. But as a—'

He took one step closer, bent his head and cut off her words by putting his mouth on hers. His hot, sweet mouth. And of course she should have pulled away. And of course she didn't. Instead, she shut her eyes and let him kiss her, letting go of her dress and putting her hands up to his hair. And then he stopped, and rested his forehead against hers with a groan.

'What are we going to do?' he asked.

She tried to steady her breathing. She grabbed the top of her dress and pulled it up again. He looked as if he was going to cry, his expression full of anguish as he looked to her for answers. More steel, she thought. More iron.

'We are going to pretend that never happened. You are going to zip up my dress and go and have a drink with my dad. And I am going to see you in church.'

How she managed to get the words out with such a firm voice she had no idea.

'Are you sure? You could grab some things, come with me, get on the boat. We could be halfway round the coast by—'

She turned around. 'Zip me up, would you please?'

She trembled as his hands shifted the fabric into place and he found the zip at the base of her spine. Halfway up it stuck, and she held her breath while he struggled to get it back on track. At last the zip reached the top.

'There's a hook and eye,' he said. 'Will I do that too?'

'Yes, please.' Her voice was a whisper.

As he finished, he put a hand on each of her shoulders. She didn't say or do anything. She stood stock still until he took them away and left the room. Then she collapsed onto the edge of her bed, not sure where to put any of the feelings that were whirling around inside her. Where on earth was she going to find the strength to get through the day?

37

Now

As Nikki headed down the drive to Windcutter Farm, it began to rain. Swathes of water swept across the horizon, turning everything to grey: the sky, the sea, the sand. Wet rain, they called it – not the gentle kiss of a summer shower, but a deluge. This kind of weather always unsettled Nikki. She headed out in her wellingtons and floor-length waterproofs and a hat. Tamsin made coffee in her kitchen for the team and the plans were spread out on the table. Nikki gave her usual welcoming talk to everyone who was going to be involved in Phoebe and Alec's wedding.

'This is a blueprint for the future, so we have to get it right. If we can make this a success, there's a future here at Windcutter for all of us. I want you all to work together to make sure there are no glitches. I've created a WhatsApp group for us, so we can check in with each other on any queries. Communication is the key. And I'm available twenty-four-seven to make sure everything joins up.'

Armed with umbrellas – Nikki had a stash of them which she used for wet weddings – she and Tamsin led the procession out to the field in the downpour. It took nearly an hour for everyone to mark out where everything needed to go – the marquee, the toilets, the mobile kitchen, the parking, the generators – but eventually Nikki had a site map she felt happy with.

Afterwards, Tamsin made tomato soup and they went over the details, making sure there was nothing they had forgotten.

'You can have all the flower clouds and grazing platters you like, but if we run out of power or water or the loos don't flush, that's what everyone will remember.' Nikki was feeling that cocktail of adrenaline and panic she always felt when she was committed but everything hadn't quite been ironed out.

By four o'clock, the rain had stopped and the sun popped out as if it had just gone to the shops. Nikki and Tamsin took their mugs of soup back to the field and sat on the fence. As the sea in the distance turned from dreary battleship to aquamarine, and the sky turned to periwinkle, the flowers in the meadow opened and the air smelled sweet, of heady blossom with a sprinkling of salt.

'What do you think the dads would think, if they saw us?' Tamsin asked. 'Two old spinsters sitting in their gum boots, plotting world domination?'

'Spinsters?' Nikki wrinkled her nose. 'We're strong, independent women. No one tells us what to do. We're amazing.'

It was the talk she gave herself when her confidence failed her. And it was true. Everything she had got, she had got for herself. She didn't answer to anyone. And nor did Tamsin.

'By the way,' she said, 'I've invited Jess to Bali. You

don't mind, do you? I know she's full on, but I think she needs a break.'

'The more the merrier,' said Tamsin. She'd grown up with Jess so she knew her ways. 'It'll be fun. A girls' trip. Though I kind of hate that expression. Always makes me feel as if I should have my nails painted and put fake tan on my legs.' She looked at her hands. Farming hands, a bit rough and chapped, with ragged nails. 'I'm looking forward to a massage, though. And a few cocktails on the beach. And seeing my godson.'

Nikki laughed. 'He's making plans already.' Goodness knows what Bill would have up his sleeve, but it wouldn't be boring.

She felt a sudden wave of tiredness, after the drama of the early morning rescue and the stress of the site meeting. She should go back to the office and consolidate the morning's decision by sending out follow-up emails, but the thought of going home was tempting. Though she wasn't sure how she felt about seeing Adam.

'I made a bit of a tit of myself with my neighbour this morning,' she told Tamsin. 'Not that I think he noticed.'

'Your neighbour?'

'Yeah. I thought we were heading in a certain direction, but turns out we weren't.'

'Nik! You dark horse. You've kept this quiet.' Tamsin loved a bit of gossip.

'He's really lovely. He's . . . everything. Smart and funny and kind and . . . hot. And a brilliant cook.' Nikki couldn't keep the smile off her face. 'But obviously it's ridiculous. We're neighbours. And he's widowed. His wife sounded amazing. She was a consultant anaesthetist. And really talented. One of those women who can do everything.'

'Like you, you mean?' Tamsin glared at her. 'Honestly, Nik – you don't give yourself enough credit. You're a legend. You keep everyone together. You've got a super successful business. And you're seriously hot.' She looked at her. Nikki was in a hoodie and leggings and wellies, her site-visit uniform, still bedraggled from the downpour. 'Well, when you make an effort.'

Nikki put her hand up, laughing. 'OK, OK. But I'm pretty sure he's not interested.'

'He's probably just nervous. It's probably a big deal for him. Maybe you need to make the first move?'

'Oh my God, I couldn't. But he's the first person to make me feel . . .' Nikki drifted off in a reverie.

'Feel what?'

'Well, anything, to be honest. Since . . .'

'Since?'

Nikki shrugged. 'Since forever. I don't know. He's just . . . special. He's got a glow.'

'A glow? Right. OK. Is he going to be at your party?'

'Yes. He's doing tacos. And Palomas.'

'Does he have a name?'

'Adam. Adam Fitzroy.'

Tamsin looked thoughtful. 'Nikki Fitzroy.'

Nikki bashed her friend on the arm. 'Stop it. I told you. It's not going to happen.'

'Why not? I haven't seen that light in your eye for a long time.'

'Honestly. Nothing is going to happen.'

Tamsin jumped off the fence. 'Well, I don't know how he could possibly resist you. You're gorgeous. And successful. And kind. I mean, what more does the guy want?'

38

Nikki reflected on Tamsin's words on the way back home. She wasn't a consultant anaesthetist with a talent for painting and interior design, but she was a lot of other things and she should remember that. She realised the postcards she'd been sent had knocked her confidence. They'd reminded her of the version of herself she liked the least, and brought out her insecurity. It was unsettling, thinking someone might know the truth. But there hadn't been any more since the second, so maybe she didn't have anything to worry about. She should focus on the future, not the past.

She remembered the advice Adam had given her, about making room in her life for the things she wanted to do. And she thought about Phoebe, and how she had made her dream wedding come true, golden horse and all. Maybe she should stop listening to her inner critic and start manifesting? Although really, that was just positive thinking and being proactive. Thinking about what you wanted and making it happen.

She was going to make it *all* happen.

As soon as she got back to the office, she started to draft an advert to put online.

ASSISTANT WEDDING PLANNER

I run The Seaside Wedding Company, a successful wedding planning business in beautiful Speedwell by the sea in North Cornwall. I'm already nearly fully booked through to the end of next summer. I'm looking for someone to come and help make these weddings unforgettable. You will need to be super organised with a good head for figures, an eye for detail, a great imagination and excellent people skills. A sense of humour would help too.

If she found the right person, this would make a huge difference to her life. Yes, it would cost money, but she would make more money, by taking on more weddings. At the moment she could never do more than one in a day. Once her assistant was fully trained up, they could take on their own. Why hadn't she done this before? she wondered.

As she posted it onto the local Facebook noticeboard, she set off for the lifeboat station for training night. It happened once a week without fail, and she always looked forward to it, because, somehow, she got so absorbed in whatever task they'd been given that all her worries faded into the background. She loved the camaraderie too. Rescues could only work through teamwork and she realised she needed to incorporate that into her working life. By taking on an assistant, she might feel less alone and more supported.

When training had finished, she headed into the station to find Archie Fowler. He was on the computer in the crew room, fine-tuning the rotas for the coming months. He reminded her so much of her dad, his tanned wiry legs sticking out of his baggy old shorts, his slow Cornish burr. And the kindness. Oh God, the kindness.

'I'm going to take you up on your challenge,' she said. 'I'm going to go for helm. I know it will be tough, but I think I can do it. I think I *should* do it.'

As soon as she said it, she knew she'd be really disappointed in herself if someone else stepped into the role.

Archie gave her his slow smile, the one that showed the creases in his weather-beaten face and lit up his powder-blue eyes.

'I'll see you through it,' he promised. 'I wouldn't have asked if I didn't think you were up to the job. You know that.'

'I know,' she said. She was the one who had to believe in herself. Everyone else already did.

Just before she went home, she got a text from Jess.

I went to see my manager. She's suggested I take a career break for a few months. They don't want to lose me. She suggested a bit of therapy too. I've been carrying all this grief around with me for years, and it would be good to talk it through with someone. Then maybe I won't behave like such a fuck-up all the time.

Nikki smiled and texted back. That's great news. And you're not a fuck-up. Or maybe we all are, to varying degrees.

Jess's reply was a line of emojis. A cocktail, a sunset, a wave, a heart.

Nikki FaceTimed Bill straight away, and told him to add his aunt to the guest list along with his godmother.

'Oh my God. Is Bali ready for Jess?' Bill had laughed. 'Don't worry, Mum. I'll find you guys somewhere super cool. You're gonna love it.'

She felt good. She felt confident. She felt she could handle anything life threw at her. She remembered Tamsin's words, about having to make the first move with Adam. Of course he was tentative. Moving on after grief was a big deal. She didn't have to be predatory. She didn't have to jump on him. Just have a bit more confidence in herself.

It was just after eight as she swung back into her drive. It had turned into a beautiful evening after the earlier deluge and the sea beckoned, so she headed straight round to Adam's to see if he fancied a swim. Life was going to get even more hectic as the wedding season hotted up, so having the time to take advantage of a dip when the sun was shining was going to be rare.

'Definitely,' said Adam. 'Apart from anything I need some human interaction. Zooms do my head in.'

He was in Levi's and a tight white T-shirt, a Celtic band tattoo peeping out from under his sleeve. How had she not noticed that before? Suddenly it was all she could look at.

'Nice tattoo,' she said, because there was no point in trying to pretend she wasn't staring.

He looked down at it proudly.

'I got it because it makes me work out. There's nothing worse than a tattoo on flabby skin.'

Nikki swallowed, then grinned at him, hoping she wasn't looking too inane.

'See you at the top of the steps in five?'

The cliffs had greened up in the past couple of weeks, and were studded with yellow and purple flowers that filled the air with a faint trace of blossom, all mixed in with dear little daisies tinged with pink. As they clambered down, Nikki felt a leap of pleasure. Even if this was just two neighbours making the most of what was on their doorstep, this was as good as it got.

Ten minutes later, they stood at the edge of the water, the pale aquamarine of an Alpine glacier, and she felt the familiar squiggle of nerves she always had before plunging in. It never left you, that moment of trepidation, for the icy cold was always a challenge. But that was why she did it. To build her courage.

She took a deep breath and dived into the foamy sea. She was in control.

Afterwards, they sat in the garden and shared the remains of a bottle of Pecorino Nikki had in the fridge. Adam whistled in admiration at her garden. The last thing Mike and Jason had done before they left the site was give it a make-over – in just one morning they'd transformed it by laying some chippings outside the back door, digging out a couple of flower beds and replacing the old fence panels. Her mum had brought over a few plants from the garden at Mariners. Something she'd put by the bench smelt out of this world – sweet and heady and sensual.

'My mum did the planting for me. She's got green fingers but I haven't inherited them.'

'Jill designed ours. We kept it simple, for maintenance,

but I think it could do with a bit more character. I'd like it a bit more jungly. But, like you, I don't have a clue.'

'Mum could give you some advice. She's coming to the party.' The bottle of wine was suddenly empty. 'Shall I open another?'

She didn't want the evening to come to an end. Neither, it seemed, did Adam.

'Definitely.'

Nikki stood up. 'You can help me make a playlist for the party.'

'I love a playlist!' Adam beamed with enthusiasm. 'Let's do it.'

She went inside to grab another bottle from the fridge, topped up their glasses, and brought out her portable speaker. Adam was already on his phone, scrolling through Spotify.

'What's the theme?'

'Theme?' Nikki frowned. 'I don't know. Do I need a theme?'

'You could have different themes for different parts of the evening. A bit of Latin American for the tequila cocktails while everyone arrives. Then a yacht rock vibe for later?'

'Yacht rock?'

'You know, cool seventies classics that old dudes with yachts would play. It's kind of cheesy but everyone loves it. A bit of Hall and Oates, Doobie Brothers, The Eagles . . .'

Nikki laughed. 'I love it.'

The next bottle of wine went down easily as they spent the next hour bouncing suggestions backwards and forwards on their phones, laughing at the long-lost tunes from their distant past.

'Oh my God. "Baker Street" by Gerry Rafferty.' As the saxophone poured out of the speaker, Nikki remembered imagining Baker Street as some sort of glamorous boulevard, then being a bit disappointed when she went up to London and saw that the most interesting thing about it was a queue for Madame Tussauds.

'That came out in 1978,' said Adam. 'You can't have been any age.'

'Yeah, but it's a classic, right? Everyone loves it.'

'Did you know he was in Stealers Wheel?' Nikki looked blank. ' "Stuck in the Middle with You"?' Adam pressed play on the track and started singing along.

Recognising it, Nikki sang along with him. They sat there as darkness fell, yowling their way through a slightly drunken duet. At one point Adam slung an arm around her shoulder as they swayed together in time to the music. She felt warm and happy and silly and fuzzy and—

The next song came on. It was 'Brandy'. Rik's song. In a split second she was taken back to the harbour the day he arrived, remembering how he'd sung the words to her.

'We should definitely add this,' said Adam.

'No.' Nikki was sharper than she intended. 'I don't like that one.'

He looked startled by her vehemence. 'OK.'

He turned it off and the silence felt ominous. It was suddenly cold in the garden, and there was a sense that their party for two was over. Nikki grabbed her jumper and pulled it on.

'I'd better get some sleep,' she said. 'I need to be up early. I shouldn't have had all that wine.'

'Famous last words. But it was fun.'

'Yes . . .' It really had been. Until the past had intruded like an unwelcome guest.

Adam was getting up out of his seat, putting his phone back in his pocket, picking up the bottle and the glasses to take them back into the kitchen because of course he had to go through her house to get back to his. She followed him in, feeling her mood plummet.

'Thanks for the wine,' he said, plonking the glasses in the sink. 'I'll stick the bottle in the recycling on my way out.'

He raised his hand in farewell and disappeared out of the door. Nikki stood in the kitchen wondering if things could have turned out differently if fate hadn't intervened. She couldn't remember the last time she'd had such fun, and they hadn't even been doing much, just sinking a glass of wine or two and listening to music. Adam was one of those magical people who made everything special, because he knew how to have a good time. He had a big heart and a warm embrace. She remembered his arm around her. She could still smell his cologne.

She pulled off her jumper and the shirt underneath. The last thing she wanted was to be haunted by his scent all night, giving her disturbed dreams. She'd been there before, after all.

She was determined not to go to bed dejected. Today had been a good day. Adam wasn't the last item at the bottom of a check list that she'd failed to tick off. She'd had a brilliant site visit, advertised for an assistant, taken up Archie Fowler's challenge and sorted out her sister. That made her a success, surely?

And she hadn't had time to revel in the fact that the house was now finished. She had to admit Mike and

Jason had surpassed themselves. The rooms seemed twice the size now, with the walls glowing snow-white and the floorboards gleaming like honey. The fireplace had been opened up, and there were fresh logs stacked either side. In the kitchen, there was a row of navy-blue cabinets with copper handles, beech work surfaces and rows and rows of rustic scaffold shelving. It was modest compared to Adam's, but it was a million miles from the dreary kitchen she'd viewed a few months ago.

And she had a houseful of all the people she loved descending on Saturday. She didn't have time for regret.

39

Helen knew exactly what to put on for her lunch date with Ralph: a floral shift dress in pinks and oranges, with her platform sneakers and a coral cardigan. She felt like herself, she felt comfortable, she looked as if she'd made an effort but not overdressed. It was just a casual lunch in a country pub, after all.

She set off from Speedwell just before midday. It was an hour's drive to Chagford, where they were meeting, so that would give her enough time to find a parking space and nip to the loo before he arrived. On the drive, she found that she wasn't at all nervous. On the contrary, she rather enjoyed the heady mix of excitement and anticipation, turning up Elton John and putting her foot down on the winding roads, singing along to 'Tiny Dancer'.

Was this a turning point? she wondered. Was she about to embark on something life-changing and exciting? By the time she drove back this afternoon, she would know if Ralph held the key to a new future. She reminded herself not to be disappointed if he didn't live up to expectations, but she couldn't help feeling excited as she went over all their conversations, the little clues that suggested they had a connection. The way he played something different for her every night, her own private lullaby.

She arrived on time at a quintessential English country pub, with the requisite log fire, oak settles and a sprinkling of customers with Jack Russells and Labradors. She nipped to the loo, touched up her lipstick, then settled herself at the table by the window that Ralph had booked – she liked that he had taken the initiative. Not that she needed a man to take control, but it showed a certain chivalry.

By a quarter past one he still hadn't arrived. She tried not to keep checking her phone, but instead sipped at the mineral water she'd ordered. He was coming from Taunton. It only took a tractor or a farmer trying to get his sheep across the road to hold you up. She ordered some sourdough and nibbled at it to give her something to do. Twenty-five past. He wasn't late, she thought. She'd been stood up.

She signalled to the waiter. 'My lunch date isn't coming,' she said, without explanation. 'Can I settle up?'

'That's fine. Don't worry,' said the waiter, and she realised he was being kind, trying to compensate for her humiliation. It was only then that she felt a twinge of disappointment, bending down to get her bag so he couldn't see the trace of a tear in her eye. It had been too much to hope for. She'd built Ralph up into someone who was going to swoop in and add another dimension to her life. She'd allowed herself to dream of trips away, perhaps to the Lake District, or even Prague. She'd imagined them slumped on the sofa barking the answers to University Challenge, or trying to guess the valuations on *Antiques Roadshow*. Little moments of togetherness.

Of course it wasn't that easy. Of course you didn't find The One with a single click on the internet.

'Helen.'

She looked up, her keys in her hand, her sunglasses on. And there he was. Ralph Potter. In cream chinos and a checked shirt, looking extremely nervous.

'I had a last-minute wobble,' he said. 'I didn't think I could do it, because I'd built you up into something so momentous, I didn't think I was worthy of you. I was half a mile down the road, calling myself everything under the sun for being such a coward, trying not to think of you sitting here knowing I'd let you down. Then I heard that song on the radio. 'Rise Up'. Do you know it?'

'I do,' said Helen, and stood up. They stared at each other for a moment.

'And I turned straight around. And I'm sorry I'm late. And would you still have lunch with me?'

There was a muscle twitching under his right eye. And a slight sheen of perspiration on his forehead.

'Of course,' she said. 'Sit down.'

He flashed her a grateful smile for her understanding. She felt the warmth of his cheek on hers as they exchanged a polite kiss of greeting, and it felt right. She breathed in his after-shave – something impossibly English and discreet and not overwhelming, just a faint drift of moss and ferns. They sat down and she passed him the menu.

'I think I'm having the fishcakes.'

He didn't pick it up. He still looked anxious.

'There's something I have to tell you. Before we start. I should have told you before, but there wasn't a right time.'

Her heart sank. He was seeing someone else. That must

be it. He'd met someone else on Sunshine After the Rain and had chosen them over her. Oh well, she thought.

'Go on.' She couldn't quite hide the wariness in her voice.

In answer, he lifted his hands and rested them on the table.

It was all she could do not to cry out in surprise, for every finger was twisted and bent out of shape. She looked up and met his gaze, unable to hide her shock. He gave a sad smile.

'I've been crippled with arthritis for five years now. Obviously, it ruined my career, though I've carried on with what I can. Teaching, adjudicating, composing – but not playing.' He looked down at his hands, clawed and disfigured, then looked up again. 'I wasn't playing to you, all those times I said I was. But it wasn't a complete lie. They were recordings. Of me, when I was still able to play. I'm so sorry. The first time I did it, I should have told you, but I got swept up in the romance, the idea of playing to you each night. And once I'd done it once, it was hard to tell the truth. So I kept up the pretence. But obviously now we've met in real life, I can't hide it.' He held up his hands again. 'I understand, if that's it. If you don't want anything to do with me now.'

'Oh Ralph.' Helen lifted up her own hands and took his in hers. She rubbed them gently, every bump, every nobble, every swollen joint. 'I am so sorry. It's so unfair.'

'You're not angry?'

'Angry?' She looked puzzled. 'Only that you've had to go through this. I'm not angry with you at all. It was still you playing. It didn't take away from the pleasure.'

'Goodness.' Ralph blinked in surprise. 'I've been lying

awake all night for days, imagining you walking away from the table.'

'It's OK,' said Helen. 'Let's put it behind us. There might be a million reasons you don't find *me* your cup of tea. But let's have some fun while we find out more about each other.'

'You're an angel.'

Helen laughed. 'We're too old to be judgmental about silly mistakes. We seem to get on pretty well. We're very different but we've got the same values. Life's too short to pass that up. Let's see what happens.'

He pushed the menu to one side. 'I think,' he said, 'I'll have the fishcakes too.'

A fishcake person like me, thought Helen. That was as good an omen as any.

40

On Friday, Nikki didn't finish work till eight o'clock. She wanted everything off her desk so she could have a clear head to prepare for the party tomorrow. Twenty-five of her nearest and dearest would be arriving from seven o'clock onwards, and although her job meant she was the queen of party planning, she couldn't remember the last time she'd done one for herself, and she was a tiny bit apprehensive as to whether she'd get everything done in time. She wondered if she was mad to put herself under this extra pressure, but this was her chance to thank everyone who had helped her with the house: Joel, of course, and Mike and Jason, and Suzanne, who'd given her endless advice. And her family. The list was endless and she was grateful to all of them.

She took with her all the candles and lanterns and fairy lights in her store cupboard that had been left over from previous weddings. Woody was coming round in the morning to help her string everything up. She wished Bill was going to be there too. She imagined him padding around in a T-shirt and boxer shorts with his tousled hair in his eyes, trying to be helpful but being endlessly distracted by his phone, his skate board, his need for food. Infuriatingly, frustratingly adorable.

On the way home, she stopped off at the supermarket to get wine and beer and tequila, and all the ingredients for the tacos. The avocados, by some miracle, were perfectly ripe. Maybe this manifesting lark did work? She felt invincible, as if everything was there for the taking, despite her minor wobble the night before. She blamed the Pecorino. Too much white wine always opened the emotional floodgates. She'd be more careful tomorrow.

Back at home, with her arms full of shopping, she unlocked the door and pushed it open. Bingo! The dress she'd ordered on impulse earlier in the week was there on the doormat. She still wasn't sure about it – it was a floaty chiffon A-line in jade and turquoise swirls. Very seventies, very sheer, very short. She thought she could get away with it as long as she wore flat shoes and not high heels. She bent to pick up the parcel and froze.

There was another postcard underneath. This time it had a picture of the sculpture on the harbour – the seven entwined hearts. She turned it over to read the message:

Twenty years this August. The perfect time for the truth to come out.

Nikki threw her shopping into the kitchen and ran back to her van. Pure panic propelled her to the pub. Woody always went there on a Friday evening. She needed to catch him before he was too many pints in. As she pulled into the car park she looked out across the boats in the harbour. She shivered, remembering that terrible night, the crowds gathered along the quay waiting for news, the driving rain, the howling winds, the foreboding sky as the next day dawned . . .

She jumped out of her van, headed into the pub and scanned the interior, trying to avoid catching anyone else's eye, praying Jess wouldn't be in there. Her luck was in. There he was, a half-drunk pint of Safe Harbour in his right hand.

She sidled up to him.

'I need to talk to you.'

'What's up?'

'I've had another card.' She felt self-conscious. Suddenly, she worried that whoever had sent it was in here, watching her and enjoying her discomfort

'Let's have a look.'

'I can't show you in here.' That would be awful, for the sender to witness her showing the card to Woody. 'Can you come back to mine?'

He hesitated. 'Sure. I'll just text Katya but I'm sure she won't mind.' Woody had a new girlfriend he'd met at Tawcombe parkrun. It was early days. 'Let's get a curry. My treat.'

The thought of food made her stomach curdle. But she hadn't eaten since breakfast, so maybe a takeaway was a good idea. They always used to have one on a Friday night, when they were together. Then, the only curry in town came from the chippy, swimming in yellow grease. Now, the Bhaji Shack had opened, and its beautifully aromatic dishes were seasoned to perfection with zingy fresh herbs and served with pillowy nan breads.

'OK,' she agreed as he finished his pint. She drove them to the other end of the high street where they ordered onion bhajis and vegetable samosas, then chickpea, smoked aubergine and potato curry for her and beef rendang for Woody. They headed out of town as night finally curled itself over the coast road, and it was getting dark when Nikki pulled up outside Number Four. There was the soft glow of golden lights coming from Number Three, and for a moment she wondered what Adam was cooking in his kitchen of dreams. Under another set of circumstances, she might have brought a takeaway home and offered to share it with him.

In the kitchen, Woody put his hands around his face and peered out of the glass door to the back garden and the darkness of the sea beyond.

'I bet you can see forever on a clear day. To the edge of the world.'

There was a wistfulness to his tone. Woody worshipped the sea. He'd be in it every minute of the day if he could. She thought for a moment how much he would love having the secret beach on his doorstep.

'What are the neighbours like?' He broke into her thoughts.

'Young couple in Number One. Middle-aged couple in Number Two. Widower next door. Just moved down from London.' She had to stop herself giving too much detail about Adam.

'Do you want me to run a check on him?'

'No! He seems fine.' She put plates and cutlery on a tray. 'Come on. We can eat in the dining bit. I can't call it a dining room. Dining area?'

She ushered him through to the table at the bottom of the stairs. Woody unpacked the containers from the brown paper bag and peeled off the lids. The air was filled with the scent of ginger and star anise and coriander. Usually, her mouth would be watering by now, but the dread in her stomach made her feel slightly nauseous.

Woody eyed her thoughtfully.

'You have to eat,' he said. 'I know you're stressed. But everything seems much worse if you starve yourself.'

She sighed. 'I know.' She flopped herself down in her seat and obediently began to fill her plate. Woody had picked up a quartet of Cobra beers from the off-licence and flipped the lid on two of them. She knew Woody wouldn't let her talk until she'd eaten. And once she began to dig in, the food pushed away the flickers of fear.

'OK,' he said, when the last container was empty and their plates had been scraped clean. 'Let's have a look.'

The very sight of it filled her with panic again. Just a couple of sentences, but they seemed so threatening.

'OK,' Woody nodded thoughtfully, 'I guess combined with the other two messages it does seem like they know something.'

'Oh God.' Suddenly Nikki felt as if she had lost control of everything. 'What do they want, though? And who is it? And how do they know?'

Woody shrugged. 'What do they *think* they know? I mean, what proof could they possibly have?'

'Shit. I don't know. I don't know!' Nikki wanted to cry. Frustration and panic were toxic bedfellows, enough to make anyone lose their mind.

'I mean, short of being in the room with you, and taking a photograph, which presumably you'd have noticed, no one can prove anything. So it's just an educated guess.' He stared at the phone. 'Assuming they're referring to . . .' He made a face. 'Matey boy. Or have you got other dark secrets?'

He was teasing, but Nikki wasn't up to being teased. 'Stop it. I don't know. It must be that. It's the only thing I've ever done wrong.' She *was* going to cry. She could feel herself crumbling.

'Stop it!' Woody jabbed a warning finger at her. 'You need to hold your nerve. We need to look at the evidence. Try and build up a picture. But you need to stay calm. What are they banking on? What have you got to lose?'

He looked at her, his eyes wide. Those eyes she knew so well. It was the laughter in them that had drawn her to him when he turned up that first day at school. He exuded mischief and warmth, always happy to play the clown yet always there for her, through thick and thin.

Now, Nikki tried to answer his question with logic. 'Everything. My relationship with everyone in my family. Which is the only thing that matters to me. Jess, obviously.' She gave a wry smile. 'She'd probably kill me on the spot. Mum would be horrified. And Juno . . .' She shut her eyes at the thought of her niece knowing the truth about the aunt she held in such high esteem. 'Graham's a bloke, so I guess he wouldn't be so bothered, but he wouldn't be impressed.' In her mind, her family stood in front of her. She could see their expressions. Disgust, mostly. 'The whole town would turn their back on me. Think of all the support they gave me. All the kindness. After dad. And all the time I was living a lie . . .'

'Nikki.' Woody's voice was calm and kind. 'It was a lifetime ago. And you're only human. Everyone makes mistakes. You're being too hard on yourself as usual.'

'It's easy for you to say. It's not your reputation that's going to be in shreds.'

He flipped the lid on a second bottle of beer.

'Let's look at who it could be.' He took a quick slug and wiped his mouth. 'The only person you've ever told is me, right?'

'Yes. And I have to hope it isn't you.' She managed a half-laugh.

'It's a risk. Have you got a paper and pen?'

'Yep.' She cleared the plates and took them into the kitchen, where she grabbed a pad of paper and a biro, then put them in front of Woody.

He picked up the pen and wrote: *WHO KNOWS?* And underneath he put three names. *NIKKI – WOODY – RIK.* Then he drew three lines under Rik's name.

'That's the weak link right there. We don't know who Rik might have told.'

Nikki put a hand to her mouth. 'He wouldn't have told anyone, surely?'

'He might have. Easily. He could have had a confidante. Someone he'd known for a while and thought he could trust.'

'Oh my God.' Nikki sank back into the chair. 'I'd never thought of that.'

'I've told you before, Nik. You're too trusting. People say one thing and do another all the time.' Woody tapped the nib of the biro on the paper. 'We really don't have much to go on until they make their next move. We don't know what they want, so we don't have a motive. It'll be one of two things though. Money. Or revenge.'

Nikki shut her eyes. Revenge. The thought pumped ice through her body, leaving a cold chill around her heart.

'Or both,' he finished.

'Don't sound so bloody cheerful about it.'

He ruffled his fingers through his hair so it stuck up in a little tuft. 'You'll be fine. I'll get you through this.'

Suddenly Nikki didn't want to discuss it any more. She was going round in circles, and although Woody was trying to help, he was adding to her anxiety. She needed to sleep. It was the only way she could escape the questions whirling around her brain. She put one hand on top of one of his and squeezed it gratefully. 'Thank you. Either way, I need to get an early night. I've got a lot to do tomorrow.' She paused. 'Shall I get you a cab?'

'I'll jog back,' he said. 'I missed my run this morning.' He looped a long arm around her and dropped a kiss on her head. 'Try not to worry. I know you will, but worrying is playing right into their hands and making you vulnerable. We'll fix this, one way or the other.' While he was standing there in her house, his warmth around her, with his certainty that truth and justice would always win the day, she believed him. 'Whatever happens, you've got me. You know that, don't you?'

He was very intense and serious, for Woody, and she looked up at him, startled.

'Of course,' she said. 'That's what we agreed. That we'd always be there for each other.'

He disentangled himself and grabbed his jacket, sliding it on and heading for the front door. He held a pretend phone to his ear as he opened it.

'Call me any time,' he said, and she gave him a thumbs-up.

Twenty minutes later she lay in bed, curled up under the covers, going back over everything Woody had said, wondering if perhaps he was right about Rik telling someone. But he couldn't have. He wouldn't have. If anything, he was the one who wanted it kept a secret. She should have left town, after the wedding. That would have changed everything.

41

Then

Somehow, she'd got through the wedding. Somehow, she managed to smile in all the right places. Watched as her sister turned to Rik at the altar and repeated her vows, watched him slide the ring onto her finger, watched as they shared their first kiss as husband and wife. Somehow, she managed to dodge the bouquet as it flew through the air, letting Niamh step forward and catch it to cheers and clapping. Everything was perfect. Of course it was, because she'd made sure of it, down to the last rosebud tied onto the napkins with gold thread. She'd given her sister the wedding she'd dreamed of. There had only been one detail she'd got wrong, and that hadn't been of her making.

All she could think about was what Rik had said to her. His lips on hers, the pounding of his heartbeat through his red silk shirt. She had no idea where she'd found the strength to send him away. Time and again she replayed a different ending. The two of them flying through the streets hand in hand and jumping on his boat. Jess arriving to an empty altar. Jilted.

A week after the wedding she came down to the secret

beach to try to escape the scenes that played themselves on repeat in her head. The alternative ending that would never be. It was freezing, but she enjoyed the way the cold air sliced through her, the way the damp got under her coat and swallowed her up. She sat on the icy rock, remembering its summer warmth soaking into her limbs that first day, and Rik's body next to her, the rise and fall of his chest as he slept. It seemed impossible, that he had been there for her to take. Why hadn't she had the courage to reach out and touch him, to roll onto him, to kiss him and claim him as hers?

Gelid tears slid from her eyes. She shivered, the cold biting at her bones. She lay down and the rock felt like a deathbed, hard and unforgiving. Gradually she got used to the temperature, slipping into its depths as her breathing slowed. It was getting dark. The tide was on the turn and she could hear it getting closer. She wanted to fall asleep and wait for the sea to cover her up. In her mind, she could smell him, feel him, taste him. In the end, she went home, curling herself around a hot-water bottle in an attempt to defrost her frozen heart.

Afterwards, she should have put what happened on the wedding day to the back of her mind. Put it down to a moment of impulse on Rik's behalf. He'd been testing himself, perhaps. Or her? Either way, she should have tucked the memory away somewhere and got on with her life, leaving Rik and Jess to get on with their marriage.

But because she was on high alert, she began to see the cracks.

Jess was not suited to marriage. She wasn't used to taking someone else into consideration on a daily basis, or putting them if not first, then at least on an equal footing. It left Rik bewildered and hurt. He wasn't clingy or controlling, but he wasn't expecting a wife who carried on behaving as if she was single. And he worried about her, because she was pregnant, but she endlessly forgot to tell him where she was, or when she was coming home, or what she was doing. They were still living half at Mariners and half on the boat, with a view to getting a proper place of their own, but Jess didn't seem interested in finding somewhere. Twice Rik set up a viewing on a flat and she didn't bother turning up.

When Nikki chided her, Jess couldn't see the problem. 'It's how I am,' she said. 'I live in chaos. I always have. I need my space. He's got to understand that.'

Rik tried his best, but he found it difficult.

'I just want to look after her. Make the most of our time together before the baby comes.' He looked bewildered. Nikki didn't know what to say. It was unlikely that Jess would change. Maybe she would when she became a mum?

Things came to a head one night in the Neptune. Ironically, it was because Jess thought Rik was spending too much time talking to someone else. Jess had always insisted she wasn't a jealous type, because it suited her for other people not to be jealous when *she* flirted with someone else. But perhaps that night she was feeling vulnerable, conscious of her thickening waist, the fact that she couldn't sink three glasses of wine in quick succession, the fact that the girl in question was an Alanis Morisette lookalike in a slip dress and cowboy boots and was getting the attention Jess craved.

When Jess remonstrated with him, Rik protested.

Despite his magnetic looks he wasn't a flirt, but he did like talking to people.

'So it's one rule for you and one rule for me, is it?' Jess shouted.

'No, Jess. There are no *rules*.' Rik objected to her making out he was some kind of monster.

Jess stared at him for a moment then stormed out of the pub. Rik went to go after her but Nikki stopped him.

'I'll go,' she said. 'I'll calm her down and take her home. See you back there.'

Nikki pushed through the crowds and headed outside. Her heart sank as she saw Jess at the end of the quay, getting into a car with a bunch of local lads who were heading off to Tawcombe to go clubbing, which was the ritual after closing time. Nikki ran towards the car, waving at Jess to get out, but Jess just laughed and put two fingers up out of the back window as the car sped off.

Nikki stood at the end of the quay watching the Fiesta disappear up Speedwell high street. She could hear the pounding of the bass long after it had gone. Her sister was proving a point. Nikki knew she wouldn't do anything completely irresponsible. She'd probably dance for a while then grab a taxi home. But she was too old to be behaving like a spoilt brat. She was married. And pregnant. With a responsible job. Her behaviour was disrespectful to Rik. And quite honestly, exhausting for everyone else, picking up the pieces and worrying. She knew Jess would be living in the moment, urging the driver to turn up the music even louder, totally focussed on the people in the car with her, not giving those she'd left behind a second thought.

Nikki decided to head home. There was nothing else

she could do until Jess came home. Rik was in the kitchen, and jumped up as soon as she came in.

'Did you find her?'

'She's gone to Tawcombe.'

Rik shook his head in despair.

'I'm scared,' he said.

'Jess'll be fine. The boys will bring her back safely.' This was true, at least. She knew they all took turns to be the designated driver. Losing your licence in Speedwell was too much of a pain for anyone to risk drink-driving.

'I was only talking to that girl. What did Jess think?'

'She's feeling a bit vulnerable.'

'But I wasn't interested in her.'

'No, I know. I know you'd never—' She stopped. He was gazing at her as if he was trying to commit her to memory. 'What?' She swallowed, not sure what was coming next.

He shut his eyes, and she was astonished to see a tear, just one, roll onto his cheek.

'Oh, Rik. Honestly. She'll be back. Don't worry. It'll all be fine.' Instinctively she stepped forward to hug him. A chaste hug, the sort of hug a sister-in-law would give her brother-in-law. But as she put out her arms, he opened his eyes, and time slowed down, and *that* was the moment she should have stepped back, should have done something sensible like put the kettle on, but something pulled her towards him. And sliding into his embrace again was like nothing she had ever felt. Warm and tingly and so wrong but so right, and she felt the tight clamp she had been keeping around her heart to protect it loosen. He buried his face in her hair, murmuring her name, and she felt every strand ripple. She turned her face to his, shivering with the shock and the anticipation, and she was the one who went in for the kiss, who put her hands up and slid her fingers into his tangle of blond hair and pulled his head towards hers.

Hot honey filled her blood, pumping its way to her heart, her belly, further down. He was rough but gentle; fast but slow. Right but wrong. So many contradictions.

'We shouldn't be doing this,' she whispered eventually, when they broke away.

'We should have done this a long time ago,' he contradicted her, and there was nothing like the thrill of realising that he really did want her. That perhaps he'd always wanted her.

And so it began. An ill-advised affair, as most affairs are. A cobweb of lies and subterfuge and intoxicating lust but also the magic bubble of two people together who shouldn't be, which is so potent and makes you blind to danger or the harm you might be causing. It was like falling into a whirlpool. Terrifying, disorientating, and the more she struggled to get out, the more she was sucked in. And so, after a week or so, she stopped fighting it.

'We're in too deep to stop,' he said, holding her face in his hands. They shared endless stolen kisses in passages, doorways, corridors; kisses filled with urgency, sweet but sharp, like passionfruit. His hand between her legs, his lips on her neck, her fingers in his hair. She was weak. Weak with longing. Weak as a kitten as he dropped her onto her bed, her own bed, and she wriggled out of her jeans and let him inside her and had to cover her mouth to stop herself from crying out as she exploded into a million pieces, rocked to her very core.

Somehow, she managed to carry on normal life, even

though she thought it must be written all over her, her pupils huge with lust, her legs trembling wherever she walked, her blood sweet and hot as a pan of strawberry jam, ready to boil over at any moment. Her mind ran on parallel tracks. Invoices, estimates, pro formas, schedules, timetables in one half. Him him him in the other – his marshmallow mouth, the salty tang of his skin, the tautness of his muscles like a leopard or a cheetah, coiled beneath her fingers. She would catch the drift of his scent on her and it would take her somewhere else.

Infatuation. It was a disease, with seemingly no cure. She had no choice but to go back again and again. And he felt the same. It was an impossible situation. They had three options. To stop. To carry on with their subterfuge. Or to run away together.

'We can't stop,' said Nikki. For they had tried, time and again, but Speedwell was too small for them to avoid one another, and the minute they came into close contact, they were magnets. 'And if we carry on, we will get caught. I know we will.' It was far too dangerous. Again, Speedwell was too small.

'So do we run away?' They were at the secret beach, hiding in the caves behind the rocks. He'd brought a flask of spiced rum. It was gold and sweet and potent. It wrapped her up in the artificial glow of safety that only alcohol can give.

'How? Where?'

He pulled something out of his pocket. A paper boat, made from thick blue paper.

'We can take my boat. Sail over to Ireland. Live in Kinsale, where my father's from. I'll get work. You can have lots of babies who'll grow fat on thick cream and black pudding.'

Nikki imagined it. A small white-washed cottage surrounded by hedges stuffed with fuchsias, the Atlantic crashing in the distance, the air sweet with the smell of dairy cows by day and sharp with burning peat by night. Patting out rounds of soda bread. Pegging out small clothes on a washing line. A donkey, perhaps.

She turned the boat over in her hands. The paper was soft, like sugar paper.

'What about Jess?' she asked in a small voice. It would be the ultimate betrayal, for your husband to run off with your own sister. 'What about the baby?'

A bleakness flittered across his face. 'I don't know.' It was almost as if he'd forgotten that detail. As if he was getting carried away with his own fantasy. 'There is no answer,' he said in a flat voice.

Nikki pushed the paper boat into her pocket.

The weeks slipped by, in an eternal loop of agonising soul searching and clandestine assignations at the beach, as Jess grew bigger and now there was no mistaking her bump. Six months. Seven. Nikki and Rik spent hours tangled up in each other in the caves at the beach, painting pictures of an imaginary future together with words that came easily, fantasy and reality blurring in a fevered frenzy. She could never be certain of him, for sometimes it was too dangerous and he wouldn't be there, and she'd learned not to complain or accuse him of losing his nerve. He would be there if he could, but he wasn't reckless. Not in the way she could be. Sometimes she didn't care who knew, or if they were caught. Sometimes she longed for that day, for she thought it was inevitable. Small town. Sharp eyes. Loose tongues.

Other times, her biggest fear was him putting a stop to it. She could tell when guilt played heavily on his mind, and that was when she had to make sure he lost himself in her, and by the end of the afternoon he would gaze up at her, his eyes glazed, his guilt forgotten.

Most of all, though, she knew it was madness. It had to stop. She wanted to be normal again. To live with certainty, and without fear.

'We have to decide,' she told him. 'Before the baby comes. Because once the baby's here, we can't do this. We just can't.'

'Shhhhhh.' The sound came out of him like a sigh. It was a command, not reassurance. He was silencing her. He didn't *want* to decide. In that moment, she knew he never would. That it would be up to her to dictate what happened. He would go on like this for ever. Getting away with it. Two sisters, like chalk and cheese. Snow White and Rose Red.

She remembered the story. And the immortal line: 'Whatever one gets, she shall share with the other'.

42

Now

That night, Nikki barely slept. And when she did, she dreamed of paper boats and flasks of rum and threats written in black writing on the side of the lifeboat for everyone to see. She would have to cancel the party. She was exhausted. She didn't have the strength to go through with it.

Woody wasn't having any of it. By nine o'clock, he was standing on a kitchen stool fixing dozens of white paper lanterns left over from Christmas to the living-room ceiling. They spun in the air like out-of-season snowflakes.

'I feel sick.' Nikki looked down at the card again. 'What if they're coming here tonight? What if I've invited them and they're going to come right into my home?'

'It's just bullshit, Nik.' Woody jumped down off the stool and took the card from her. 'You've got to hold your nerve. They could be bluffing. We don't know what they know or what proof they've got or how they would back up any accusations. And who would believe it if they did say something?'

'Who would believe I could do something so terrible, you mean?' Nikki was in despair.

Woody crossed his arms while he considered his next suggestion. 'You're not going to like this, but the only way to devalue your secret is for it not to be a secret anymore.'

'What do you mean?'

'You should tell Jess the truth.'

Nikki stared at him. 'Are you mad?'

'No! That way, you control how much detail she gets. Tell her it was a moment of madness between the two of you, and it meant nothing. But at least it would be out in the open and no one can threaten you anymore. End of problem.'

'She'd go ballistic. She'd kill me.'

'You can play it right down. No one can possibly know what you did. Unless they were stalking you.'

'Someone knows something.'

'But not everything. Only you and Rik know everything. Well, and me.' Woody laughed. 'And it's not me.'

Nikki looked down at the card again. It was so matter of fact. So confident it had the upper hand. She wanted to crush it, but she didn't want to destroy the evidence.

'Would it help if I told you Jess made a pass at me once?' asked Woody. 'At Bill's third birthday party. When you and me were still together.'

Nikki sighed. 'No. Not really.'

'What – so it's OK for her to do it, but not you?'

'She wouldn't have meant anything. She was probably bored. She wouldn't have gone through with it.'

Both Woody's eyebrows shot up. 'Don't you believe it. She went into pretty exacting detail about what she'd do to me.'

'It's totally different.'

Woody came over and wrapped his arms around her. 'I

think you should stop worrying. Enjoy the party tonight. Think about telling Jess.'

'And Mum. I'd have to tell Mum. Because Jess would go straight to Mum.'

'Your mum is pretty wise. And she wouldn't hold something against you from twenty years ago.'

'But they'd know what an awful person I am.'

'Why is it all your fault? There are always two sides. You told me yourself that Rik and Jess were having problems.'

'That doesn't make it OK.' Nikki shut her eyes as if she could hide from the truth.

'You were young.'

'Twenty-four. Hardly a child.'

'Vulnerable.'

'Vulnerable how?'

'You've always had a vulnerable streak because you're so kind. And nice.'

'Not so nice, it turns out.'

'You don't think Rik took advantage?' That had always been Woody's point of view. Nikki had always insisted they were equally complicit.

'I'm not blaming him, Woody. He's not here to defend himself.'

The argument was getting heated. Woody hated conflict. His natural instinct was to defuse a situation. And it ate him up to see Nikki so distraught. He clenched his fists in frustration.

'I didn't judge you, did I?' he asked. 'We ended up together even though I knew what an *awful* person you are.'

He was teasing her, but she couldn't take it, and looked

at him reproachfully. Over his shoulder, she could see Adam out of the window.

'Shit. It's Adam. I'll have to tell him the party's off.'

'You are not cancelling,' said Woody, clamping his hand on her shoulder, his voice firm. 'You're guilty of nothing except being human.'

She sighed as she headed to answer the door. If only that were true. She loved Woody for being so supportive and staunch. And now here was Adam, ready to help her with the catering for tonight. She didn't deserve either of them. But Woody was right. She couldn't cancel now. She'd have to put on a brave face and smile her way through it.

43

By six o'clock, the paper lanterns Woody had put up were spinning gently in the breeze from the open front door. Dozens of pinprick fairy lights were hung around the walls, with a few extra strings balled up and put in the fireplace. There were chunky pillar candles on the mantelpiece and windowsills, to be lit later, and terracotta pots planted up with marguerites.

Nikki did her best to take a breath and put her anxiety to one side. She was so proud of her little house, and how she had turned it around, with everyone's help, to be a place filled with light. And hopefully love and laughter. Next week, the rest of her furniture would arrive and she could start to nest, letting her home evolve as she moved things around from room to room, put up pictures and hung curtains. But for now, the house was ready to throw open its doors and let everyone in. She felt a little stronger, as if she could face the evening.

In the kitchen, the taco bar was laid out on a trestle table, and next to it were metal dustbins full of ice – one containing Sol, the other bottles of white wine. There were pitchers of Palomas chilling in the fridge.

'Hey!' Adam was standing over a vat of chilli on the Everhot. He was in a tight white T-shirt and jeans, with a full-length apron, and she could see the toned muscles in his arms as he stirred. He'd completely taken over the catering and she wasn't going to complain. That was the part of entertaining that stressed her out the most. He was quite happy in her kitchen, though he had brought round most of his own equipment – knives and chopping boards and a huge casserole dish.

'Taste,' he ordered, holding out a spoon. She blew on it for a moment, then tried it. It was deep, rich and smoky, with a sweetness to it.

'Oh my God,' she said. 'That's out of this world.'

'Lots of different chillis,' he said, 'and a few squares of dark chocolate.'

'It's sublime. Thank you.'

He just smiled. 'Right. Guacamole time.' He picked up two avocados, threw them in the air and caught them deftly. 'And don't worry – I'll put lime juice on top so it doesn't go brown.'

'That's why I'm useless with food,' said Nikki. 'I'd never have thought to do that. I'd have ended up with a bowl of brown muck.'

He picked up a knife and began to slice the mound of avocados she'd bought.

Nikki went and stood at the back door for a moment, taking in several calming breaths, reminding herself that she had earned this party, that all the people she loved and who loved her – well, except Bill – were coming, and she mustn't let one twisted person ruin her moment.

The sun was drifting down, nearly touching the horizon, throwing a wide band of light across the sea, like a silvery gold carpet. She felt as if she could step straight onto it and walk towards the edge of the world.

'Isn't it beautiful?'

She jumped to find Adam at her elbow.

'It's called a glitter path,' she told him. 'The rougher the sea, the wider the path. So although you might think it looks calm out there, it's not.'

'A glitter path. I've never heard of that before.'

They stood for a moment, lost in their thoughts, watching the sea sparkle and shimmer until a single cloud drifted over the sun and the glitter path disappeared.

'I'd better go and get ready.' Nikki looked at her watch. 'People are going to start arriving in half an hour. I don't think I've given myself long enough.'

'You'll look great whatever,' Adam told her, and she thought how nice he was to say that, even if he didn't mean it.

Upstairs, she dithered over what to wear. She wasn't sure she was confident enough to wear her new dress. Were her legs thin enough? Brown enough? Was it too attention seeking? Her instinct was to put on her denim shirt dress instead. It was safe. But when she tried the new dress on, out of curiosity, the chiffon glided over her limbs, and shimmered when she moved, and she looked . . . absolutely fabulous.

It was her party. Why shouldn't she look like the belle of the ball? If anything was going to give her confidence, it was this dress. She pulled on her cowboy boots, put on emerald-green eyeliner, hot-pink lipstick and dangly earrings. She was ready for anything.

*

An hour later, family and friends were pouring in through the door. Graham and Suzanne with the M and Ms, who were allowed to stay until ten, when Helen was going to take them back to Mariners for the night. Woody and Katya. Tamsin, in an actual dress, the first time she'd seen her out of wellies and jodhpurs this year, with Andrew. Joel, who blinked in amazement at the transformation, hardly recognising it as the house he'd sold her. Mike and Jason, accepting congratulations whenever she pointed out that the hard work had been done by them. Other people would be turning up later – Gloria and Belle, hopefully, after they'd escaped from the Neptune. The house was full of all the people she loved.

'You didn't tell me Stanley Tucci was catering,' Jess hissed at her, her eyes wide, clocking Adam in the kitchen. 'Where did you find him?'

'Right next door.' Nikki laughed at the expression on her sister's face. 'You saw him, remember? On the beach? He probably won't recognise you with your clothes on.'

'Is he spoken for?'

'He's widowed,' said Nikki hastily, not wanting Jess to unleash her charms on Adam. Her sister was in a halter-neck dress spattered with red cherries: it would be impossible not to be knocked sideways by her.

'Oh. Well, we have something in common, then.' Jess eyed him from a distance. Adam was talking and laughing with everyone as they lined up for food, making sure their tacos were properly loaded, adding a squeeze of lime and a smattering of fresh coriander. He had on a beautifully laundered white shirt untucked over faded jeans, and pale grey suede Chelsea boots. His cuffs were undone, revealing a very nice Swiss watch.

Yet again, Nikki felt a shoot of warmth at the sight of him, like chilli in her veins.

'I'm going to go and introduce myself,' said Jess, and she sailed off, her dress swirling round her as she walked. Nikki turned and headed back into the living room, where Woody raised an eyebrow at her, as if to ask if she was OK. She raised her beer bottle to him with a smile, but she felt on edge. Was the blackmailer here, watching her, enjoying the power they had over her, knowing that she couldn't possibly feel as relaxed as she was pretending to be, relishing the anticipation of their next move? She hated them for it. Hated their cruelty, their slow torture of her, the way their threats tainted her every waking hour.

And then she felt her mother's cool hand on her cheek.

'Darling, are you all right? You look awfully anxious.'

'Oh – you know what it's like to host a party. I'm just worrying whether everyone's having a good time.'

'Of course they are. It's perfect. Just the right size and everything looks gorgeous and those tacos – that is one special neighbour.' Helen gave her a knowing look.

'Yes. He's a very good cook.' Nikki wasn't going to be led into a debate about Adam's qualities. Thankfully, her mum knew when not to push it.

'By the way, I had a lunch date yesterday,' she said instead.

'With Ralph Potter?'

'The very same.'

'Why didn't you say? Why didn't you tell us?'

'Because you'd have made me nervous. And because if he'd been awful, I didn't want to have to tell anyone.'

'So . . . ?'

'He is absolutely lovely. Twinkly and kind and funny. We didn't finish lunch till gone four. They had to throw us out of the pub.'

'Oh my God, Mum. This is epic. You should have brought him tonight. You should have said.'

'It's far too early to throw him in at the deep end, poor man.'

'When are you seeing him again?'

'Tomorrow, actually. We're going to Hestercombe House to look around the gardens and have tea. I know that doesn't sound very thrilling but I'm really looking forward to it.'

'Mum, I'm so happy for you.'

'It's early days. But he's easy company.'

Her lovely mum, thought Nikki. She'd waited a long time for this. She had scooped them all up and gathered them to her, when William and Rik died, even though her own heart had been shattered. She had kept them close, kept them warm and safe, making sure there was always a warm stew to dip into or a cake to cut. Perhaps that had been her only way of coping, making sure she served a purpose by focussing on their needs rather than her own. And now, maybe she would have someone who would look after her. The family all did their best to look out for Helen and spoiled her when they could, but there was nothing like having someone who was there just for you.

Later in the evening, everyone gathered around as Juno sat on a stool with her guitar.

'I hope you don't mind,' said Juno. 'But I've written a song. It's for my dad. And I want to play it to you all, to see if it's any good.' Her fingers danced over the guitar strings, letting out a plangent chord. There was a smattering of applause and she smiled, then began to play.

'He's there in my eyes
The man I never knew
A hint of gold
A splash of blue
Like the blue of the sea
That took him away
Before I could say
Hello . . .'

She was so assured, so unselfconscious, pouring out her heart in words that held meaning for nearly all the people in the room, for they had all lived in the shadow of what happened. And although Juno hadn't been born at the time, it had a huge effect on her life too, and somehow she'd managed to capture that longing and that sadness in her song.

Nikki watched, spellbound, her heart filling with pride. And then she turned her head and saw Jess standing in the doorway, tears streaming down her face. As the song ended, Jess flew over to her daughter and the two of them held each other. And then Juno disentangled herself from her mother and turned to her audience, smiling through her tears.

'You reckon it's OK, then?' she asked, and everyone cheered and clapped.

Jess wiped away her smudged mascara and for a split second, Nikki saw the grief on her face, as raw as it had been on that terrible day. How on earth could she tell her the truth, even if it was to stop someone else from telling her?

She turned to leave the room. She needed some air, to breathe in the sea, to clear her head. Adam was standing in the doorway. He was gazing at Jess, the shimmer of tears in his eyes and sorrow etched on his face, for he understood her pain. Nikki sidestepped him. In that moment, she wanted to run away, far away, to a place where nobody knew who she was, or what she had done.

In the garden, Nikki sat on the bench, her fingers curled round a glass of neat tequila. The night air was chilly and damp, and she could feel the mist creep its way around her and settle on her skin. The sky was moonless, starless, a blanket of grey. The waves pounded the beach like an ominous metronome.

There was no one she could talk to. No one she could tell her secret, and ask for advice. Woody, bless him, was so staunchly loyal, so determined that doing the right thing would make it all OK, but he didn't understand how terrified she was of losing everything, everyone she loved.

Why hadn't she walked away earlier? She could pinpoint the moment. You could often home in on that split second where the wrong choice was made, and your future was like a runaway train headed for certain disaster. It was the time they'd met in the caves at the secret beach, after they'd kissed in the kitchen at Mariners, for that was when it had become an assignation, deliberate and calculated rather than a moment of recklessness. The memories were so vivid, only instead of the thrill of it all, the shame made her skin crawl, and all she felt was remorse.

She finished her drink. She couldn't stay here all night, alone with her thoughts. All her guests were inside and she was the hostess and soon someone or other would notice she had gone and would wonder what was wrong with her.

Inside, the music was up and the living room was filled with bodies dancing away to Basement Jaxx, everyone's heartrate rising in time with the beat. The atmosphere was just what she hoped it would be. A wonderful christening for the house she hoped would bring her peace and happiness. Nikki downed another tequila shot to keep her anxiety at bay. It was always there, needling at her. Drink wouldn't help in the long run, she reminded herself. It made her vulnerable. She wouldn't have any more.

'Darling, I think it's time for me and the girls to slip away quietly.' Her mum slid up to her. 'It's been a wonderful evening, but I can feel my bed calling. If I'm not tucked up by midnight, I'm done for.'

'Thanks for coming, Mum. I'll round up the girls for you.'

Nikki moved around the room, extricating the M and Ms who were in their element, showing off their moves. There were protests but Nikki was firm.

'Come on, girls. You knew the deal. And it's not fair on Granny.'

Outside, they all hugged her goodbye as they got into Helen's Mini. Nikki smiled at her mum's generosity in allowing Graham and Suzanne a night off and a lie-in. She'd been worth her weight in gold when Nikki was bringing up Bill. After she and Woody had split, he'd always been a brilliant dad, but there were times when back-up was needed. Helen could always be relied upon, to do a school pick-up, to drop off a lunchbox, or step in when there was an illness. Neither Nikki nor Jess would have survived single parenthood without her.

She wandered back inside. She could hear Amy Winehouse singing 'Back to Black' and froze slightly. It was Jess's anthem. When it came out, a few years after Rik died, Jess played it on repeat, for the darkness of the words spoke to her.

In the living room, she saw that Jess had taken the floor and everyone had moved back to watch as she shimmied and twirled to the music, her arms in the air, her hips swaying, her dress moving with her. And then she saw that Jess had a partner, their eyes fixed on each other as they moved to the music. They were mesmerising, taking their cues from each other in perfect synchronicity, as if they had been rehearsing for weeks.

Which they couldn't have, for the partner was Adam. He was a natural dancer, his feet moving in perfect time to the beat, his body sinuous as he bent and swayed with her, entirely confident about performing with a woman he didn't know. Their performance had a wantonness that was mesmerising, and the chemistry between them was palpable as Jess dipped and swayed and twirled, building to a finale where she leaned back and put one toned, tanned leg in the air, her dress riding up, her hair falling onto the floor behind her. The crowd whooped and stamped their approval, and she stood up, fell against Adam's chest, laughing, then turned and kissed him full on the mouth. And he looked more than happy about it, one arm around her shoulder, wiping the sweat from his brow with the back of his hand, his chest rising and falling as he tried to get his breath back. They looked like stars. They looked so right together.

For a moment, Nikki remembered the karaoke night. Jess and Rik on the stage, everyone transfixed, everyone recognising that this was the start of something that was meant to be.

Adam and Jess, thought Nikki. What did they call it? Divine retribution? An eye for an eye, maybe? Of *course* that was her punishment.

44

It was half past one. The house looked like an abandoned movie set – half-drunk glasses and half-burned candles everywhere, and the fairy lights still valiantly blinking to an empty room, as if the cast had gone off for lunch, and would reappear any minute and take their places to talk and laugh and drink and dance until dawn. But everyone had drifted off not long after midnight, and the party was definitely over.

Nikki was determined to get all the clearing-up done before she went to bed. The last thing she wanted was to come down to a bombsite in the morning. Besides, she was used to military clean-up operations. She wandered around with a bin bag, chucking in paper plates and napkins and collecting glasses. Her head was throbbing and she felt slightly sick with a cocktail of tequila and tension as her resolution not to drink any more had been forgotten. Jess and Adam had disappeared not long after their extravagant performance, and were presumably getting it on next door. She couldn't bear to think about it. She wasn't sure if she could carry on living here, if the two of them were going to embark upon some steamy romance. The thought of seeing Jess tumble out of Adam's house tomorrow morning all dewy-eyed and glowing filled her with dread.

She reminded herself she had no claim on Adam. They'd had a few drinks, a few chats, a few swims. Jess had hardly broken up a meaningful relationship. But Nikki had to admit to herself that she had really liked him. He was smart and kind and interesting and confident and creative; successful but not a show-off – the ideal mix. The first man to have captured her interest for a very long time.

Oh well. She found a broom and began to sweep the floorboards in the living room. Cinderella to the end. And she couldn't even cast Jess as an ugly sister. She was the beautiful one. The one no man could resist.

She looked up as she heard a tap at the front door. Should she open it? It was very late. Who would be wandering around here at this time of night. Maybe someone had left something behind? A phone or house keys? She went to the window and looked out into the darkness. She could just make out a shadowy figure on the doorstep.

It was Adam. What on earth did he want at this time? She answered the door. He was shivering in the night air.

'I could see you were still up. I wondered if you wanted a hand? There's nothing worse than coming down to a mess in the morning.'

'Thank you. That's kind.' Nikki looked behind him. 'Where's Jess?'

He looked puzzled. 'She went ages ago.'

'Oh.' She stood aside as he walked in. 'I thought—'

She wasn't going to say what she thought. Adam looked at her.

'Oh God. Did everyone think we'd got off with each other?' He laughed. 'I was showing her Jill's paintings.'

'Oh. Right.'

'Then we got a bit maudlin and were swapping notes. The widow and the widower. Did everyone get the wrong end of the stick?'

'I don't think so,' said Nikki, which was true. It was just her who'd assumed the worst.

He looked around the room.

'So what can I do? Though to be honest, it looks like you've nailed it.'

'I think I've nearly finished.'

'Right, then. Let's go and have a hot tub.'

'What?' She laughed. 'At two o'clock in the morning?'

'No better time. The sky's cleared. The stars are all out. And it's the perfect way to see off a hangover. Sweat it out.' He grinned. 'Come on. I'm going in even if you don't. It's really warm.'

'OK. I'll just get my costume.' Did she sound a bit prim? She wasn't sure of the protocol. Should she be leaping in naked, without a care in the world? But Adam seemed happy with her plan.

'I'll leave the front door open. Just walk through to the back,' he told her.

Ten minutes later they were sitting opposite each other, immersed in luxuriously warm water, staring up at the night sky. The hot tub was made of cedar, set into decking made of the same wood, with tiny pin-prick lights mirroring the stars above. They chatted idly. About who was who at the party. And what a success it had been.

'It must be hard, hosting on your own,' Adam said. 'I haven't done it yet.'

'The trick is to get people to do all the things you don't like doing.'

'Exploit them, you mean. Chain them to the kitchen and get them to make tacos.'

'Oi!' She flicked the surface of the water with her finger to wet him. 'Honestly, though, I really appreciated it. Catering's not my forte.'

'So I've heard,' he said.

'What?' She was indignant, then realised he was teasing her again. 'I'm not rising to the bait.'

After ten more minutes, they decided to call it a night.

'I'm getting prune fingers,' said Adam.

'You were right, though. It was the perfect end to the evening. I feel all relaxed and sleepy.'

'Good.'

She clambered out of the tub and pulled on her fleecy robe. Next to her Adam was towelling his torso then pulling his sweatshirt back on. She turned away at the sight of his abs, stuffing her feet into her Crocs, very aware that yet again she wasn't that enticing a prospect. They hurried back up the path, for the air was sharp out of the balmy warmth of the water. Somewhere nearby an owl hooted as they reached the doors at the back of the house and headed into the kitchen.

'I haven't stayed up this late for a long time.' Adam looked at the clock. It was gone three.

'Me neither. And I'd better go.' Nikki was starting to shiver. The wet bathing suit under her robe felt as if it was made of ice.

'I didn't mean for you to get cold.' He reached out and

began to rub her arms briskly, as you might a child. 'Is that better?'

She laughed. 'Much.'

He stopped rubbing her arms, just held her in place with his hands. 'I don't want you to go.'

She wasn't sure what to say. What did he mean?

'I'm so happy to have met you,' he said. 'I was scared to come here, after Jill. But I didn't want to stay in my old life without her. It felt wrong.' He sighed with the effort of his revelation. 'Oh God, I hope this doesn't sound mad. And it's not the tequila talking . . .'

He looked away. A bit emotional.

'Hey. It's OK,' Nikki said. She put a hand up to his cheek and turned his face back to hers.

'I wake up in the morning and I want to do things. I haven't felt like that for a long time. I want to go swimming, or go for a run with Gatsby, or go to the harbour to buy crab, or learn how to paddle board in the harbour. Last night was the first time I'd been to a party since she died. It felt good. It was *fun*.'

She wasn't sure what to say. 'You know what they say. Time . . .'

'I don't think it is time. I think it's you.'

Nikki stood there, in her robe and Crocs, her hair damp and flat, her make-up long gone, the least glamorous she had ever felt in her life. 'Me?'

'You've made me feel as if anything's possible. You've made me realise that I can start to live again. And every day I hope . . .'

He trailed off.

'Hope what?'

'That I'll see you.'

Her eyes widened in surprise. 'Oh!' And she smiled. 'Me too. I hope I'll see you, I mean.'

She stepped towards him. And she felt his arms reach around her, and she was filled with warmth, not just from the contact of his embrace but from his words.

He was going to kiss her. He was going to kiss her. He was going to kiss her.

And then she remembered. She didn't have the freedom to fall into his arms. To fall in love with him. She was being threatened, by someone who knew the kind of person she was. She couldn't just reinvent herself and waltz off into the sunset with Adam, because the truth would come out and ruin everything.

She pulled away from him.

'What's the matter?' He looked at her, puzzled. She looked into his face. Those warm smiling eyes, filled with concern. The faint grey smattering of three-o'clock-in-the-morning stubble against the tan of his cheek. The deep laughter lines grooved into his face, either side of his mouth.

'I need to tell you something,' she said.

'Oh God.' His face fell. 'It's never good when people say that.'

'I just . . . want to be honest. About my past. It was all a very long time ago, but I need you to know. And then you can make up your mind about how you feel about me.'

She knew she was taking a risk telling him. But she didn't feel comfortable keeping it a secret. It had been part of her for so long. And if she and Adam were meant to be, he would be able to see past it. And if not . . . well, that was the price she would pay.

He looked thoughtful for a moment. She shivered as she waited for his reply.

'OK,' he said. 'Let's get you into something warmer first. And then you can tell me everything.'

Ten minutes later, he had lit a fire in the grate and she was sitting on the sofa, wrapped up in a pair of his pyjama bottoms, a jumper and thick socks. His clothes were like a warm embrace, comforting, and they gave her the courage to do what she needed to do. She started at the beginning and she finished – well, she finished with the day it all ended.

45

Then

Nikki stood at the top of the steps. They were precarious at the best of times, let alone in a high wind with the rain almost horizontal, driving little needles straight onto her eyelids. The television and radio had been rife with severe weather warnings all day. No one with any sense was out in it. You'd have to be mad. Maybe she was? She sometimes thought so. But she hadn't seen him for over a week, what with one thing and another, so here she was, scrambling down, her sneakers slipping on the wet stones, the shale at the edges providing no purchase, nothing to cling on to but a few scrubby branches of gorse.

When she'd left town earlier, the waves were coming up over the harbour wall, hurling themselves over the railings in a spectacular display of petulance. The wind careened around the winding streets as if hunting someone down, relentless and unforgiving, letting out a high-pitched moan. Speedwell was battening down its hatches, shops shutting early, sandbags in doorways, cars moving away from the edge of the quay. Everyone knew the drill. No one ignored the warnings.

No doubt tomorrow, it would be as if nothing had happened. The sun would come out and the sea would be tranquil and nonchalant. The tourists would emerge, eager to make up for a day spent indoors on jigsaws and holiday paperbacks. The tills would ring merrily again: postcards and fudge and ice creams.

But for today, the storm raged on.

At the bottom, she jumped onto the sand. The sea was a murky, bruised blue, swirling and surging at random. It didn't seem to know where it wanted to go, as dangerous and unpredictable as a drunk at throwing-out time. She put up a hand to wipe her face. It was impossible to know what was rain, what was salt spray and what was her tears. When had she started to cry again? She mustn't. She had to hold it together, or he would take her in his arms and kiss those tears away and her resolution would crumble.

She'd made up her mind. It was the solution with the least collateral damage. He wouldn't be able to argue with her logic. Sometimes in life you had to make a sacrifice. You had to do the noble thing.

She took in a gulp of air to try to calm herself, pressing her body against the cliff as she edged along towards the rocks that formed their hiding place. She knew the shoreline like the back of her hand, even though it changed with every turn of the tide, every phase of the moon, the sand and the rocks shifting and morphing, the colours melting into each other. She knew its smell, that hit of briny, brackish air like opening an oyster. The feel of the sand that branded the soles of your feet in the midday summer sun but would be cold and hard as iron if she stepped on it now. The noise of the waves: now a menacing boom, but on a warm night they would whisper gently as you drifted off to sleep. She tried not to think about the fact that this was the last time she would see him like this.

In secret.

On their secret beach.

She looked back at the steps to see if he was there yet. That was the price of being early. You were always the one waiting. She'd never been the kind of person to leave things to the last minute. To saunter in without a care in the world, like her sister Jess would.

Jess . . .

She tucked herself in behind a rock, its surface studded with rings of bright green lichen, wondering where he was, panicking that something might have happened to stop him coming.

There! There he was, standing at the top, his hood up but offering him scant protection. His hand was shielding his eyes from the rain as he scanned the beach below, looking for her. He didn't know yet that this was the last time they'd be together. Maybe she shouldn't tell him? Maybe she should slip away quietly into her new life? No. She needed to say goodbye. Look into his rockpool eyes. Feel herself become part of him as she put her mouth on his. Let their heartbeats mingle, dancing out of time with each other, his always slow and steady, hers out of control.

He was jumping off the last steps, light on his feet, almost balletic, bounding onto the beach and across the sand until he reached her. She felt the usual leap of joy, her face lighting up, but he was frowning.

'We shouldn't be here.' He tugged at her elbow. 'It's dangerous. Come on.'

'It's fine.' She pulled him back towards her.

'It's insane. No one should be out in this.'

'Rik.' She spoke urgently, trying to capture his attention. 'We need to talk. I've made a decision.'

He looked at her, puzzled, as if life was perfectly straightforward and there was no need for any discussion. As if they didn't spend half their time together agonising over what to do.

'I'm leaving Speedwell.' Three words. There was no need to say any more, really. Not when, or where. Certainly not why.

'No.' He shook his head.

'We don't have a choice.' She was surprised how calm she sounded. 'I've got a job on a cruise ship. Leaving Southampton on Tuesday.' The thought of setting sail in less than a week was terrifying. But if she went to sea, he couldn't follow her. She'd been amazed how easy it had been to get a job. Two phone calls. They'd been impressed with her admin skills. Offered her a post as a junior purser. In less than a week, she'd have a uniform, a cabin, a whole new life. Without him.

He slumped back against the rock, shutting his eyes. She pressed herself up against him, putting her hands on his cheeks.

'Don't make it harder for me than it already is.'

He nodded, without opening his eyes. He couldn't look at her. She wiped a runaway tear from his face with her thumb, pressed her mouth onto his, warming his frozen lips with her kisses, feeling the strength of his arms as they wound around her waist, relishing the hardness of his thigh between her legs as they became entwined. She wanted to breathe him in until they were one person.

Maybe that was the answer? To shape shift into another life?

Suddenly something vibrated against her hip. She jumped back as he went to grab the pager in his pocket.

'Shit.' He punched the rock with his fist. Then he looked at her, and pushed the pager back into his pocket. He didn't move.

'Rik?'

'I'm not going.'

'What do you mean?'

'We have to talk about this.'

'You can't not go!'

'There'll be others on call.'

'You've *got* to go.' The thought that he might ignore the pager filled her with horror. It would be sacrilege. It would undermine everything. She grabbed his arms, shaking him as if to wake him up. 'You've got to!'

In answer, he pulled her to him so tightly she could hardly breathe, holding on to her for two, three, four seconds, his face buried in her neck.

'I love you,' he said, his voice muffled. 'I love you. You must never forget that.'

Before she could answer, he let her go and raced back towards the steps without a backwards glance.

She stared after him, her heart in free fall as she watched him taking the steps two at a time. She wanted to shout up to him to stop. She had to tell him she loved him too. But there was no time. Duty overrode passion. Duty overrode everything. That was the rule.

She turned away, but the sea provided no comfort. If anything, it was taunting her. She looked out at the swell, a massive wall rising and falling almost in slow motion.

How high was it? Thirty feet? She shivered. How had that happened, in the few minutes they'd been together? What was the sea plotting behind their backs?

She put her hands to her lips, as if she could lift his last kiss off them and put it in her pocket. Then she pulled her coat more tightly around her, put her head down against the wind and headed back up the steps.

She crawled into bed when she got home. Sleep usually brought much needed respite from the whirling in her brain, but not today, for the ungodly noise outside interrupted her slumber: the rattling windows, the squeals as the wind got in through the cracks, the barrage of rain like tiny bullets on the roof. Amidst the pandemonium, she heard the rest of her family come back as the afternoon dragged into evening. Except her dad. Usually by now she'd be able to hear his voice through the floorboards. Had he been on call today too? Were he and Rik both out on the lifeboat? The thought unsettled her. She tried to go back to sleep, but she was too anxious, listening for the bang of the front door and the reassuring sound of male voices.

And then, the doorbell went. A long, persistent ring that made her leap from her bed and run downstairs. Somehow, she knew whoever was at the door was the bearer of bad news. She arrived at the top of the stairs just as her mum answered. It was Archie Fowler, head mechanic at the lifeboat station.

'Coastguard's lost contact with the lifeboat,' he said, terse with tension. The look on his face told them all they needed to know.

Her mum grabbed her coat from the hook. Nikki ran

down the rest of the stairs. This meant her dad must have gone out in it too. He'd have gone from work.

'Is it Dad?' Graham appeared in the kitchen doorway.

'There's five of them gone out, in the all-weather boat.'

And then there was Jess, in a flowered dress, holding her bump. She had barely a month to go.

'Did Rik go?' she asked.

Time stood still for Nikki. She couldn't say anything. Of course she couldn't.

'Yep.' Archie gave a brief nod. 'Helicopter's on its way out there. There's fifty-foot waves.'

He didn't need to say any more. Nikki stood on the staircase and watched as they all pulled on their coats and Archie stood waiting for them, head bowed, hands in his pockets, waiting to escort them back to the harbour where they would wait for news, hoping, praying.

Her mum looked up at her. Her expression was bleak, as if she feared the worst had already happened. 'You're coming, aren't you?'

Nikki jolted herself out of her catatonic state. Her dad was out there. And Rik. The two most important people to her in the world. Nikki adored her dad. They worked together nearly every day, and she had learned so much from his calm, quiet demeanour, his way of getting the best out of people. Which was why he would be such a great member of the lifeboat crew. He'd be out there now, taking orders, keeping his head, galvanising the team, a reassuring presence.

How would Rik be? She couldn't be so sure. Doubt niggled at her. He'd be lithe, quick, practical, surefooted – but was he a team player? He had almost refused to go earlier. Who would he put first? Of course, she was questioning him because she knew his morals were questionable, because of what they were doing.

They were not good people.

She felt a sense of impending doom as she ran down the stairs and pulled on her waterproof coat. Her mum looked pale, her eyes strained, her mouth in a knot of worry as she put her arm around Graham, ever the protective mother, then grabbed Jess's hand. Nikki followed behind the three of them, led by Archie, a funny little parade of humans with their heads down in the driving rain. There was no question that any of them would stay at home to wait for news.

Conditions at the harbour were terrifying. They had to stand well back, for the sea was still determined to hurl itself onto the quay. The few remaining boats anchored in the harbour were being tossed around like toys, their masts flailing, backed by a thick mist the colour of week-old skimmed milk. It was impossible to see; it was impossible to hear. It was impossible to imagine anything but the worst.

The Norths joined the clusters already waiting for news. They gathered in front of the Neptune, and Keiran sent out a steady stream of trays with mugs of coffee, even though most people were too distracted to drink it. Nevertheless, it was a kind gesture, indicative of the way Speedwell looked after its own without question.

Gradually the Norths gleaned information. The lifeboat had headed out to rescue a crabbing vessel with engine trouble. It was being swept towards Devil's Teeth, the deadly rocks after Devil's Cove between Speedwell and Tawcombe, when the captain radioed for help late afternoon.

A helicopter had been despatched to help try to lift the fishermen off, as the lifeboat couldn't get close enough to send out a line. The winds were too high for the winch man, the mists too thick, so the helicopter had abandoned its efforts, the pilot grim-faced with frustration and despair as he headed back inland.

It was just the two boats now, one desperately trying to come to the aid of the other in terrible conditions. No one on shore had any way of assessing the success of the mission. They just had to wait, and hope. Everyone on the quay was linked to someone out there: a husband, a father, a brother, a son.

A lover. Nikki looked down at the wet cobbles and drew her coat round her. She was shivering with shock, not knowing where to direct her prayers. She looked up to see Jess, her face wet with tears and rain. She had to stand by her sister. People would think it was strange if she didn't. She walked over and tucked her arm in hers. Jess turned and there was an expression on her face that Nikki would never forget as long as she lived. Terror and anticipatory grief and bewilderment: this was the woman who took control in A & E when there was a crisis, who kept a cool head, rallied her troops and dealt with casualties with swift and good-humoured efficiency. But now, she was at a total loss. Everything was beyond her control. She had no resources to deal with the crisis. Nothing she could do or say would change the outcome. They were all at the mercy of the weather and the sea: a co-dependent duo whose mood could turn on a sixpence. Only they could choose who to save.

They waited all night. Along the coast path, rescue services and groups of local men roamed the clifftops, shining their beams out in the hopes of catching a glimpse of someone or something to give them hope. The wind toyed with them, merciless and cruel, aided and abetted by the rain, a pair of bullies, hellbent on some pointless mission with no benefit to them or anyone else.

With every hour that passed, hearts grew heavier. Sending another craft out to help would be senseless. They all knew that if rescue was possible, the crew already out there would make it happen. They had the gear, the knowledge, the skills, the courage.

All they needed was luck.

A churlish dawn arrived, dragging a reluctant sun onto the scene as the wind left in a fit of pique, as if it had found something more interesting to do. After a while, the rain stopped too, as if it had needed the wind as its ally. Lifeboats from further up the coast were launched.

Nikki waited, shivering, arm in arm with Graham.

'I wanted to join the lifeboat,' he said. 'But Dad wouldn't let me. Said it wasn't fair on Mum, for us both to be in it. He said I could join when he retired. If he's gone,' he said, and Nikki's eyes filled with tears as her little brother tilted his chin up defiantly, 'I'm joining straight away. No one can stop me.'

'No one will stop you,' Nikki whispered. She glanced over to her mum and Jess. The dread on the harbour was palpable now. Keiran had been up all night and was sending out tea and more coffee and bacon rolls. They went largely untouched.

As calm descended, the sea began to offer up clues as to what had happened. The broken hull of the fishing vessel. An empty life raft, still buoyant, bobbing around as if offering help, too little too late. And finally, the first of the bodies. Seth Pickering, the youngest member of the crew. A keening sounded on the harbour as his relatives were told. Above, seagulls mimicked their cries, heartless.

A terrible roll call unfolded throughout the morning. A tight band squeezed itself around Nikki's heart. How was she going to survive this? She had to, for her mum was going to need her. And Jess too. She felt her father's presence, his kind, reassuring voice in her head. 'You're going to have to look after them all for me, Nik,' he told her. 'You're the strong one.' And as much as she felt his presence in her soul, she knew he had gone, for he would be here by now if he could be. He wouldn't keep them all waiting like this. He was solid, redoubtable, their rock.

And then she saw the police car glide along the quay, and the chief constable get out, his face carved from stone, only his eyes moving as he searched amongst the crowds. And she saw her mother turn and catch sight of him. Helen drew herself up and set her shoulders square, holding her head high as he began to walk towards her, her fists bunched to stop her hands trembling.

Nikki grabbed Graham's hand and pulled him along until they reached Helen's side just as the chief constable reached out and touched her on the shoulder in a gesture of condolence.

'They've found him,' her mother said to them. Only for a second did her composure slip. Her eyes flickered for a moment, her lip gave a slight quiver, then she steadied herself. 'They've found your father's body. We should be proud for what he did.'

'My sincere condolences,' said the policeman. 'He was a true hero.'

Helen reached out to Graham and pulled him to her. Her son. Her baby.

'Where's Rik?' Jess demanded. 'You've got to find him. You've got to find Rik.'

'We are doing our best.'

Jess began to whimper, her face in her hands, and Nikki grabbed her, wrapping her up in her arms, holding her as tightly as she could. Only by burying her face in her sister's shoulder could she smother her own emotions. Her father, her wonderful father, gone. And Rik out there somewhere, his beautiful body being tossed around by the waves. Both of them, dying a hero's death, never questioning their duty. Nikki imagined them on the deck of the lifeboat, working as a team with the others against all odds, the men on the fishing boat their only concern, braving impossible conditions, never giving up.

She looked up and met her mother's gaze. 'Let's go home,' she said to her, and Helen gave a nod. Mariners was waiting for them.

They linked arms, the four of them, Helen, Nikki, Jess and Graham, and walked all along the quay, passersby reaching out as they saw the unmistakable grief on the North family faces: a squeeze of a hand, a murmured condolence, a bowed head.

Mariners was ready. It knew. It had warmed itself in anticipation and drew them into its heart. Somehow the kettle was boiled, the brown pot filled, mugs appeared. Graham curled up in his dad's armchair, his shoulders shaking as he wept silent tears.

'I can't do this,' said Jess, standing in the middle of the room, her hands at her sides. Her voice was desolate.

For a moment, Nikki wondered if Rik had escaped,

somehow. That he was going to use the disaster as cover to run away. That he would eventually send a message to her from somewhere, to come and join him. So they could be together without anyone ever knowing what they had done.

She was horrified by her thought process. How selfish could she possibly be, thinking of herself at a time like this? Even if it did happen, she could never leave them all. Not now. Not now William had gone. She felt a wave of grief engulf her, more powerful than any of the waves she'd seen the night before. She took in a deep breath, and Helen turned to see what the noise was, for it came out as a low moan, and the sobbing followed, uncontrollable, wrenched from deep inside her. It took over her whole body, turning her inside out, and she could barely stand, almost sinking to her knees before her mum came to catch her.

She breathed in Youth Dew and Persil and the last hug her dad had given her mum, traces of him still lingering on her jumper, for they had endlessly embraced each other, her parents. And she tried to remember the last time she'd hugged him herself. Had she hugged him yesterday morning before she'd left the office? She couldn't remember because at the time all she'd been full of was anticipation, the thought of that lean, brown body on hers. Panic clawed at her as she tried to remember their last exchange. Was it when she'd handed him a coffee in his *Doctor Who* mug and he'd asked her when the new set of ladders was going to arrive? She'd promised to chase them, and then forgotten. How could that have been their last conversation?

She was never going to see her dad again.

The doorbell drilled through the house. Jess jumped up and flew out into the hall before anyone could stop her, as if she expected Rik to be at the door. And of course he wasn't. His body, too, had been found by one of the lifeboats. It was being brought back in.

Nikki buried her face in the coats on the peg in the hall and let out a silent scream as Helen rushed to her eldest daughter's side. How was she going to bear this double loss? How was she going to hide her secret grief? Could she hide it behind her father's death? The reality of what she had done, and what she was going to have to face, made her tremble with fear. You deserve this hell, she told herself.

The others didn't deserve it. Not her mum, or Graham, or Jess, who was suffering the same double blow: the loss of her father *and* her husband. Was that part of her punishment? Knowing she'd dragged them all to the brink of misery with her? Was that how it worked?

Life became a grey fog of despair and distress with no respite, beginning with that awful moment in the morning when she remembered, and her heart folded in on itself. She would start the day by taking tea in to her mum, lying on the bed next to her while she drank it, curling into the space left by her father.

She was in awe of her mother. Every day Helen got up as soon as she'd finished her tea, would shower and dress and put on her make-up and go out into the town to see who needed help and support. Seven men gone, but so many more people affected: there was barely anyone in Speedwell who hadn't lost a relative or a friend. Tributes were flooding in: flowers lay piled up on the quay with heartfelt messages, and money was pouring into the lifeboat station. Cheques and five-pound notes and postal orders. The committee couldn't process them fast enough.

And the press were crawling everywhere, trying to get to the heart of the matter, eager for personal tales of loss and the effect it was having on a small community. The nation was gripped by the tragedy. Somehow, with help from the chair of the lifeboat committee and the chief constable and the editor of the local newspaper, Helen called a news conference.

'Everyone who died that night is a hero. They were each as brave as each other, whether rescuing or being rescued. They went down together, and they will be remembered, together, by all of us here in Speedwell. But it's time for us to be left alone to grieve, to start our new lives without our loved ones by our side. We have each other, but what we would like now is privacy. To be able to heal without the eyes of the nation upon us. We truly appreciate all the messages of support, and the kindness that has been shown, but we want some time for quiet contemplation. We hope our wishes will be respected.'

Then she read out the names of the men who had been lost. Her voice didn't waver, not even when she came to William's. She stood at the front of the hall in her blue coat, cameras whirring, flashes popping, microphones waving, and spoke for the whole town. She was on every news station that night, and every front page the next morning.

As proud as Nikki was of her mother, she feared for her sister. Jess cried so much she made herself sick. Her skin was sallow, her hair greasy. The baby was less than a month away, so she couldn't take any sleeping tablets.

Nikki had been to the doctor for some for herself, for the nights loomed, so many hours to be filled with sleeplessness or nightmares – Nikki wasn't sure which was worse.

William's funeral had almost broken her heart. Graham had wanted to help carry the coffin, along with two of William's brothers and the remaining crew from the station. Nikki had felt her mother's hand squeeze hers at the sight of him, dignified and serious in the suit they had bought him from Medlar Brothers, the gentleman's outfitters in the high street. Afterwards everyone went upstairs in the Neptune for egg sandwiches and scones and William's favourite tea loaf thick with butter. Helen had spent the days before the funeral furiously baking, stirring bright glacé cherries into bowls full of currants and raisins and sultanas.

Jess had barely spoken or eaten for days.

'I'm having my wedding dress taken out, for Rik's funeral,' Jess told Nikki. 'And shortened.'

'What? But it's red.'

'It's what he'd have wanted,' Jess insisted.

Nikki couldn't bring herself to wear anything to his funeral that might draw attention. She wanted to be as inconspicuous as possible. She was already panicking about how she was going to cope with the service. She imagined it again and again in her head to numb herself, so that when she actually saw his coffin at the front of the church, she would feel nothing.

It was Nikki who went to collect Rik's mother from Bristol airport. It was Sabine who helped her keep it together, because how could she fall apart when Sabine had lost her only child. She was determined to be strong for her. It was hard, listening to Sabine talking about Rik, all those little details that made it impossible to believe he was gone. It was agony, sitting next to her in the church, but she held her hand tightly and kept her tears in check, somehow, through sheer effort of will.

It was the next day before she was able to go down to the beach and howl into the waves, screaming and raging until she exhausted herself, her own private ceremony for the man she had loved so desperately but hadn't had the right to keep.

46

Now

As her story finished, Nikki sank back into the depths of the sofa. She was exhausted. By everything. By work, by the renovation, by the worry. The constant whirling in her head: clients, checklists, planning. And the menacing postcards reminding her that her come-uppance was long overdue. Was this it? The moment when everything would come home to roost, and her chance for something wonderful would be snatched away. Her teeth chattered. Reliving that time had brought a chill to her heart. She could almost feel the thick sea mist on her skin. The driving rain. The icy dread.

Adam didn't say anything for a moment. Then he stood up. She couldn't read his expression. It was grave, but what was underlying it? Disappointment? Disapproval? Disgust? Eventually, he smiled at her. A kind smile, but perhaps it was the kind of smile you gave someone you had misjudged while you thought about what the hell you were going to say to them?

'Wait there,' he said, and headed off into the kitchen. Nikki wondered if she should slip away quietly. Spare them both the agony of the post-mortem. They need never speak of it again. They could simply revert to being polite neighbours, taking in each other's bins and signing for parcels with perhaps the odd social occasion when they could dilute each other with friends or family.

Just as she was about to make for the door, he came back in with two big mugs.

'Here,' he said. 'It's got a bit of a kick. Chilli and cinnamon and cloves. I call it White Witch hot chocolate. Like the drink she gives Edmund, in *The Lion, the Witch and the Wardrobe*.'

Oh, thought Nikki. He is so perfect. That had been one of her favourite childhood books. And she did feel as if she was being bewitched as she drank. It made her feel drowsy, but strangely comforted. All she wanted to do was curl up and go to sleep. But Adam had begun to talk.

'You do know,' he said, 'that everyone has stuff they're ashamed of? Stuff that makes them squirm when they remember it. Stuff that makes them feel like a terrible person.'

'Yes, but—'

'Shhh.' He put a finger to his lips, but he was smiling. 'When I had one of my first jobs, at a big ad agency in Soho, I had a fling with a married woman. It was so intense, and we didn't think about anyone else. My girlfriend, her husband, her kids.'

'Her kids?' Nikki looked shocked.

He gave a wry shrug. 'You see? I'm not very nice, am I?'

'But it was—' She stopped.

'It was a long time ago? Is that what you were going to say? It was, and I was young and foolish, and she wasn't having a great time at home and for a few months we had a very passionate and intense affair even though we knew it was wrong.' Adam paused, choosing his next words carefully. 'And I'm not trying to excuse either what you did or what I did, but we do mess up sometimes, especially when we're young. You're driven by your emotions. Even though you might know something is wrong, common sense goes out of the window.'

'Yes,' said Nikki, remembering how often she had tried to apply logic to the situation, but somehow the intensity of her passion had always won. 'But I betrayed my own sister.' Despite his comparison, she still felt her crime was worse.

He shrugged. 'It wasn't your finest hour. But there were lots of things at play. It doesn't sound to me as if Rik and Jess were happy. That's not an excuse. But it does explain why he might have turned to you for comfort. And there was a spark between you, right from the start, until Jess swooped in and grabbed him.' He shrugged. 'Two wrongs don't make a right, but guess what? You're human. You made a mistake.'

'There were so many times I could have stopped it.' Nikki shut her eyes. Talking about it was overwhelming. 'And I did stop it, in the end. I was going away to sea. I'd made the decision, and sorted everything out. It was all over. And then he . . . then he went and died.'

In that moment, she was there, at the bottom of the steps, watching Rik bound upwards as the sea crashed onto the beach behind them. She could have stopped him going. But how would he have felt, had he not gone, knowing he should have been there to help with the rescue?

'Hey.' Adam came over and sat next to her. She wanted to sink into him but she was rigid with remorse and unshed tears. 'I think because of what happened, you've blown it all up into something huge and never forgiven yourself. Maybe you should?'

He was too near to her for her to think straight. All her thoughts and memories flew around like the bats at dusk in the garden as she tried to put everything into perspective. Gradually they began to settle. Maybe he was right? The endless self-flagellation never seemed to change anything, after all.

'You've convinced yourself you don't deserve love, or happiness.' His voice was gentle, washing over her, soothing her. 'But you do. Oh, you do. You're a good person, Nikki. A wonderful person. I've seen how much you care for everyone. Not just your family, but your friends, and your clients. And your new neighbour . . .' He touched her arm, and she felt a tingle. 'You've made me feel . . .' He trailed off for a moment. 'Warm again. I felt so cold when Jill died, all the time. Deep inside. But when I think about you, when I see you . . .'

She stared at him. He had a smile on his face that seemed to be getting wider and wider as he spoke. His eyes were shining with something: they sparkled and glittered and she felt spellbound, as if she'd been drugged, like Edmund. All she wanted was to lean into his warmth and his light. And in that moment, she forgave herself, for every mistake, for every wrong decision, and suddenly the black shadow she'd been under flittered away into the night air, and she could breathe again.

As he opened his arms it felt like the most natural thing in the world, to fall into his embrace. And then they were kissing and it was perfect. She could taste the chocolate they'd been drinking, feel his warm fingers on her skin, smell that scent which had haunted her since the first day they'd met.

Eventually Adam disentangled himself. He stood up, taking her by the hand and leading her upstairs. She slid out of his pyjama bottoms and pulled his jumper up over her head, dropping them onto the floor, where they lay in a crumpled heap until morning.

47

The next morning, Nikki woke and found herself staring into a pair of pleading eyes topped by bushy eyebrows, paired with hot breath and a lolling tongue.

Gatsby.

'Hey, boy,' she said. 'Do you want me to let you out?'

She could hear his tail thudding against the floor. She turned to see Adam waking, saw the smile on his face when he realised she was there. Her heart looped the loop as she took in his toned arms, his tattoo, his stubble, his laughing eyes full of mischievous glee. They had finally fallen asleep in each other's arms as a thundering dawn chorus serenaded them and the sun ventured into the room.

He reached out and ran a finger down her arm. She lay there for a while, enjoying his exploration of her bare skin. Despite her swimmy head, light from lack of sleep, she knew what she needed to do.

'I've got an errand to run this morning,' she whispered. 'Do you want me to bring you up a cup of tea?'

'Lovely. But why are we whispering?' he whispered back.

'I don't know.' She fell onto him, laughing. He danced his fingers over her back and it made her shiver with delight. But she pulled herself away, rolling off him and grabbing his borrowed clothes from the floor. Gatsby stood patiently, curious but non-judgmental.

'I'll be back in an hour,' she said. 'Shall I bring croissants from the Co-op?'

Adam had his arms behind his head and was gazing at her. 'Amazing.' He looked ridiculously happy. 'A-mazing,' he repeated, and she wasn't sure if he meant her or the prospect of patisserie for breakfast.

It was hard to tear herself away, but there was one thing she had to do before she could allow herself to move forwards completely. Woody was right. She had to come clean to Jess. It was the only way to be free of the threats that were shadowing her. The only way she could take control of the situation. Whoever was sending the postcards had nobody's interests at heart, and Nikki was determined to protect Jess as far as she could, even if that meant telling the truth.

She let Gatsby out, made Adam a cup of tea and nipped home to change. Then she jumped in her van and headed out to Jess's house on the outskirts of town. She let herself in the back door, wondering if Jess would be up yet after the party.

Inside, the house was a mash-up of a Moroccan souk, a bordello and an eighties cocktail bar; a riot of colour and an explosion of *stuff*. Extrovert, over-the-top, chaotic, it was pure Jess from floor to ceiling, which, of course, had mirrored tiles. 'Like the Hotel California,' she used to say. A life-size flamingo, backlit glass shelves with every bottle of alcohol she'd picked up in duty free, flashing fairy lights, feathers, fake flowers, suede pouffes in candy colours, a neon sign that read: *Save Water; Drink Champagne*. And always a pulsating soundtrack – Madonna or Chaka Khan or Lady Gaga. Something empowering and uplifting that said *don't mess with me*.

'Hey!' Jess bounced into the room in a zebra-skin dressing gown. She looked glowing and youthful and decidedly unhungover. Jess's ability to recover from a late night was legendary. 'Alexa, play Harry Styles.'

'Actually,' said Nikki, 'I need to talk to you, so could we have silence?'

Jess stopped in her tracks and frowned. 'Silence?' she said as if she'd never heard of such a thing. 'OK. Forget that, Alexa.' She jumped onto a red velvet sofa shaped like a pair of lips, and crossed her legs. 'What's the matter?'

Nikki walked over and sat in the cracked leather armchair facing Jess. It was smothered in cushions, and she grabbed one, holding on to it for comfort.

'You're not ill?' Jess asked, and Nikki was touched by the concern in her face.

'No, nothing like that.'

'So what is it? You're not moving away? You've only just bought that house.'

Nikki shut her eyes and put up her hand. Jess was talking at her, and it was making her feel panicky. 'Shush. Slow down. I'll explain. Just hear me out for a minute.'

'OK. Sorry.' Jess put her arms round her knees and tried to look obedient, like a disruptive pupil who'd been told off and was doing her best to restrain herself. On another day, Nikki would have found it amusing, but she wanted to get her confession over and done with.

'The first thing you need to know is, if I don't tell you

this, someone else is going to. And I'd rather it came from me.' Jess opened her mouth then shut it when Nikki darted her a warning look. 'And I've never told you before because . . . well, I won't need to explain why, once you know.'

Of course she'd never told her before. She would never have been so cruel. It wasn't because she was a coward. It was to protect Jess, and her memory of Rik. And at least by being the one to tell her now, she could limit the damage. She took in a deep breath. She'd rehearsed this bit, over and over.

'It's about Rik.'

'Rik?' Jess looked startled.

'We had a . . . bit of a fling. Just before he died. It was just a flirtation, really. Honestly nothing serious. But I can't keep it secret any longer. And I want you to know that even though he was having a bit of a wobble, he absolutely adored you. And if it was anyone's fault it was mine, because I . . . was in a bad place and I liked the attention and I knew he was . . . a bit insecure . . .'

This was agony. Telling the truth, but protecting Jess from the absolute truth, the intimate details that would crucify her.

Jess was sitting bolt upright, staring at her. Nikki couldn't read the expression in her eyes. They were blank. She seemed hypnotised by what she'd been told. She ploughed on.

'Somehow, somebody else knows about it. I don't know who, or how, but they're threatening me. Threatening to tell. And they might try and turn it into something it wasn't. So that's why I'm telling you. So you don't read too much into it. So that you know how insignificant it was. You were the love of his life and I think he always lived in terror of losing you and he turned to me for reassurance and I was so bloody needy I thought he wanted something else and I ended up kissing him.'

There was still no response. Nikki realised she had been bracing herself for an explosion. But the only sign Jess had even heard what Nikki was saying was her chest rising and falling a little faster, and a slight flush on her cheeks.

'Rik loved you very much,' Nikki went on. 'He was in total awe of you. And he was mortified by what we did. He made me swear never to tell anyone, and I didn't. But somehow someone knows. Or has guessed.' All the stress and the panic from the threats were building up inside her. She tried to stay calm, because getting hysterical was only going to make her look more guilty. 'This was the only way I could think of to make sure they didn't hurt you more than was necessary.'

Jess's eyes were boring into her. Nikki couldn't tell what was going through her mind. Or how she was processing what she'd been told. Which was the greater shock? Nikki's betrayal? Or Rik's?

'Say something,' Nikki whispered.

Finally, Jess blinked. Now, her eyes were swimming with tears.

'I knew,' she said.

Nikki frowned. 'What do you mean?'

Jess gave her a twisted smile, her chin trembling as she shrugged. 'I knew all along.'

Nikki fell back in her chair.

'What?'

'It was so bloody obvious. You couldn't keep your eyes off each other when you were in the same room,' she told her. 'In the kitchen at Mariners. In the Neptune. You lit up like a Christmas tree whenever he was anywhere near you, and he wouldn't let you out of his sight. I could feel the electricity between you.' She put up a hand and jerked it, as if getting a shock from an electric fence. 'And I could always tell when he'd been with you. He was so happy. His smile reached his eyes in a way they didn't when he was with me.'

'You *knew*?' Nikki finally found her voice. She would never have guessed that Jess knew in a million years.

Jess turned and looked her straight in the eye. Her gaze was intense. Searching. What for? Nikki wondered, feeling uncomfortable under her scrutiny.

'You must know I stole him from you, in the first place,' Jess said eventually.

'What?'

'I knew you two had something right from the start. It was there, in the room, a connection between you. He was so dazzling, so seductive, so out of this world, I wanted him for myself. And I knew clicking my fingers wouldn't be enough. It usually worked. It still does, sometimes.' Jess gave a laugh. She did have a way of hypnotising men. It was her confidence. 'But I could see he wasn't enough of a bastard to turn his back on you.'

'OK,' said Nikki, not sure where this was going.

'So I had to think of another way to snag him. I told him you and Woody were childhood sweethearts. I told him you were as good as engaged. And so I was able to steal him. Right from under your nose. And I'm sorry.'

'He told me—' said Nikki, remembering Rik standing in the passageway outside Mariners – 'he told me he'd got the wrong end of the stick about me and Woody. But he never said it was you who'd told him.'

'Well, he wouldn't have, would he? Because he was a good guy. He wouldn't have dumped me in it.' Jess's eyes were glistening, as bright as sea glass. 'I was never the person he wanted.' She flailed about for the words. 'He thought he liked me at first, but I was too much for him. I thought if I calmed down, tried to be more like you, kind and calm and caring, he would come round, but it didn't work. In the end, I resorted to the oldest trick in the book.' Her face crumpled. All her bravado evaporated, and she put her face in her hands. 'I knew getting pregnant was the only way I was going to keep him, because who wouldn't choose you over me, given the choice?'

Nikki put down her glass, jumped out of her chair and flew over to Jess's side, taking her sister in her arms as she broke down. They breathed together for a moment, both acclimatising to the truth being out after so long.

'We weren't right for each other, me and Rik,' said Jess eventually. 'Not at all. And the sad thing is I think you were. You're both kind. And gentle. And you care about people.'

'You care about people.' Nikki's voice was insistent. 'Look at what you do! You save people's lives every day.'

'Not because I'm a good person. Because I'm good at my job. I do it automatically. With my head, not my heart.'

'You couldn't do it if you didn't care.'

Jess shrugged off Nikki's words. For all that she craved attention, she didn't take praise well.

'I don't understand,' said Nikki, 'why you didn't say anything afterwards?'

Jess wiped her tearstained face with her sleeve. 'Because I didn't want everyone to know he preferred you. That the only way I could keep him was by using the old trick women use to trap men who don't want them. And the other thing was because when Rik died, and when Dad died, I needed you. I needed all of us. Our family.'

Both of them were crying now. It felt good, to have the secret out in the open. Even though it hadn't been a secret after all. And whoever it was who'd been sending the notes had no power anymore. The relief was immense. Nikki felt as if she could breathe for the first time in weeks. The heaviness in her heart and the burning sensation in her stomach had lifted, and her mind felt clear.

Afterwards, she went back to Adam with a bag of warm croissants.

'Apricot jam,' he said. 'We need apricot jam.' He went over to the cupboard.

They sat at the island while she told him about Jess, Gatsby sitting at their feet catching stray croissant crumbs. Adam listened carefully, occasionally asking a question.

'The thing is,' said Nikki when she'd finished, 'I still don't know who's behind the notes. But it doesn't matter now. They can't hurt me or Jess, and we're the ones who cared about Rik, even if it did all get in a terrible tangle. And he loved us both too, in different ways.'

'So who do you think it is?'

Nikki shrugged. 'It could be anyone in Speedwell, I guess. Anyone who was around at the time. Which is most people, because nobody ever seems to leave.' She laughed, a little shakily because she was still getting used to the idea that she didn't have to live with her secret any longer. She and Jess had discussed what they would do if whoever was sending the cards tried to cause trouble.

'We stick together and we deny it. To protect Rik, and his memory. Bollocks to them,' Jess had said. 'No one intimidates my family.'

She was so loyal, thought Nikki, and felt a burst of love for her sister.

She couldn't believe how lucky she was. She sat there with the sun streaming in on her and Adam. They had the whole of Sunday ahead of them.

'What do you want to do today?' he asked, sensing she'd probably quite like to change the subject. 'I was thinking maybe a swim? Then lunch at the Neptune? We could walk there with Gatsby along the coast path, then we can have a glass of wine. Then come home and sleep it off?'

'Sleep it off?' said Nikki dreamily, but her eyes were laughing as he put his arms around her.

'Yeah, we can sleep it off,' he said, kissing apricot jam off the corner off her mouth. She melted into him. 'In fact, why don't we go and *sleep it off* now, before we go swimming. The tide's not in for another hour at least . . .'

48

After the party, everything seemed to fall into place. Nikki was flat out with two weekday weddings but somehow she floated through them without any mishap, and even managed to take delivery of her furniture on Wednesday. Graham brought it all over in one of the company trucks, and he and Jason delivered everything to the right room. Her little house became a home.

On Thursday, she asked Adam round for supper. She'd bought fresh crab from the fishmonger in the harbour and made him crab linguine strewn with chilli and flat-leaf parsley and lemon zest. They sat in the garden as the sun went down.

'I thought you said you couldn't cook,' he said.

'You've inspired me,' she replied.

'Bloody delicious,' he said, raising his glass to her. 'It turns out that you're actually perfect.'

She grinned and sipped her wine, gazing at the sunset, enjoying his appreciation. Her heart felt as light as a balloon, now she was unburdened. Occasionally, she would wonder about the postcards – she still felt a moment of trepidation when the postman arrived – but the threat would be an empty one. Of course, it was disconcerting to think there was someone out there who was targeting her, but they could no longer do her any harm.

Otherwise, she and Adam trod lightly on each other's lives. They did their own thing, coming together to walk Gatsby or go for a swim or share a meal. And while they inevitably ended up in bed, Nikki often found herself retreating to her own for the night. She needed her sleep to function. Waking up in his arms was a treat she would reserve for a day off, when they could lie there gazing at each other, unable to wipe their smiles away.

'You're a terrible distraction,' Adam told her, teasingly. 'I've hardly done any work. How are you so disciplined?'

'I can't let people down,' said Nikki. 'I've got their dreams in my hands.'

The next weekend was Phoebe and Alec's wedding. Nikki was at Windcutter Farm just after dawn. There was barely a cloud in the sky, just the odd powder puff bobbing along like an errant bridesmaid, and the sun wore rose gold, confident in its role as the most important guest.

Tamsin was on site already. She'd been instrumental in making sure everything went without a hitch, co-ordinating all the deliveries, supervising the marquee, getting the adjoining field mowed for parking, grooming Mercury until he shone ready for the bridal entrance. He was in his stable now, waiting patiently for his moment of glory.

'I've even organised the sun for you, Nik,' she said, unscrewing the lid from a flask of tea and pouring them each a cup. 'Oh, and come and look at the pièce de resistance.'

She led Nikki into the adjoining field, to a shepherd's hut parked in front of a glade of trees. Inside, the walls had been painted a cobalt-blue that was so rich and deep it almost glowed, sprinkled with golden stars. There was a bed piled high with goose-down and velvet coverlets, and over it was written 'Alec and Phoebe' and their wedding date.

'The honeymoon suite,' said Tamsin proudly. 'There's a telescope outside, for stargazing. And a fridge filled with champagne and strawberries and cream, because that's all you need on your wedding night.'

'Who knew you were such a romantic?'

'Aren't we all, deep down?' said Tamsin with a sigh.

Nikki put her arm around her friend as they walked back to the main site. The caterers and the florist had arrived to set up and the tech team were doing a sound-check. This was the nerve-wracking bit, when potential disasters suddenly revealed themselves. But if Nikki had learned anything it was to have a back-up plan. She hadn't encountered a problem she couldn't solve yet. By ten o'clock, everything was set fair and the air was filled with expectation and excitement. Everyone on her team was passionate about delivering the dream wedding, right down to the parking attendant. She made sure of it.

'It's going to be perfect,' she said to Tamsin, and as if on cue her phone rang and Phoebe's name flashed up.

Her heart sank as she heard Phoebe sobbing.

'I don't think I can do this.'

'What?'

'What if the same thing happens? What if Alec runs out on me after we're married?'

'Phoebe. He's not going to do that. He can't wait to marry you!'

'That's what Charlie said! On the morning of our wedding, he said I was his dream come true. Six months later he was gone.' Phoebe was hysterical, gulping on her words.

Nikki looked at her watch. Phoebe and Alec were due at the registry office at midday. Only two hours away.

'Are you at your hotel?' She'd checked them into different ones, so they could be apart the night before the wedding and get ready separately.

'Yes.'

'Wait there. I'll be as quick as I can. Go and lie down on the bed. Breathe. It's all going to be fine. I'm on my way.' She hung up. 'Shit,' she said to Tamsin. 'Cold feet. Do you know, I've never actually had this. Nerves, perhaps, but not total panic.'

'Oh God.' Tamsin held out her phone. 'Shall I send her a photo of Mercury?'

'It might make her panic even more. Forward it to me. And can you hold the fort here? Text me if anything crops up.'

'Of course.'

'Wish me luck.'

She ran back to the van, praying that nothing would go wrong on site while she was away, then drove hell for leather back into Speedwell. Luckily the Saturday traffic hadn't built up yet, so she screeched into the car park of Phoebe's hotel and ran to her room.

Phoebe opened the door in her dressing gown, looking as if she hadn't had a wink of sleep.

'Where's hair and make-up?' asked Nikki. 'They should be here by now.'

'I sent them away.'

'What?'

'Don't worry. I'll pay them anyway. But I can't do this. I was awake all night worrying. I can't live with the fear, that Alec's going to leave me like Charlie did. I can't go through that again.'

'Have you spoken to him?'

'No.' Phoebe looked shamefaced. 'I want you to do it. Because that's how much of a coward I am. He'll find somebody else. He'll be fine.'

'Phoebe.' Nikki led her over to the window and sat her down in a chair. 'Alec adores you. And he's far, far too honourable to ask you to marry him unless he knew he was completely committed. The problem with your previous marriage wasn't you. It was Charlie. There is absolutely no reason for history to repeat itself. It wasn't you. It was him.'

'Do you think so?'

'Yes. And it's quite normal to be nervous on the day. Especially if you didn't sleep. Everything seems a bit daunting. But look.' She got out her phone and showed her the photos Tamsin had forwarded her, of the meadow, and Mercury standing in his stable. 'All that is waiting for you.'

Phoebe wiped the tears from her eyes as she looked at the pictures.

'Now listen. Let's do some manifesting. Breathe in and say to yourself "Today I'm going to marry the man of my dreams and we're going to have a perfect day".'

Phoebe shut her eyes. She was shaking. Her voice was wobbly as she repeated Nikki's words.

'Today I'm going to marry the man of my dreams and we're going to have a perfect day.'

'Good. Now say it again.'

Nikki made her say it three more times, and the third time Phoebe seemed to have some conviction. Out of her emergency bridal bag she found eye drops and Rescue Remedy.

'Take these. Go and have a shower. I am going to get you to the altar on time if it kills me.'

She looked at her watch. Just under an hour. She was going to need help. Hair and make-up was out of her skill set. But she knew just who to call. How many times had the M and Ms pleaded with Juno to make them over? She'd watched in awe as her niece transformed her cousins into shining stars, almost unrecognisable. Nikki didn't always feel comfortable with their transformations, but she knew Juno could work wonders with her box of tricks.

She dialled her number, praying she'd be able to help, and that she wasn't out with a pack of dogs somewhere. 'Can you get to the Fairmount? I've got an emergency bride scenario. Get a cab. I'll pay you back.'

Twenty minutes later, Phoebe was out of the shower and Juno had arrived, carrying her extensive make-up kit and state-of-the-art hairdryer. They had thirty minutes to make Phoebe altar-ready and get her to the registry office.

'This is Juno. She's my niece and she'll make you look beautiful,' said Nikki.

Phoebe sat in the chair Juno had put ready for her. 'I'm

so sorry. I'm such an idiot. I completely panicked.' She had a bit more colour in her cheeks.

Nikki patted her shoulder. 'It's OK. It's normal to feel overwhelmed.'

Phoebe took hold of her wrist. 'Will you be my witness?'

'Me?'

'Yes. I don't think I can go through with it unless you're there.'

Nikki hesitated. There wouldn't be time to get back to the meadow and double-check everything. The guests were due to start arriving at one, an hour after the ceremony, in time for Phoebe's grand entrance on Mercury.

But if she didn't get Phoebe to the registry office, there would be no point to any of it.

'OK. I'll just have to make a few calls.'

She left Juno putting primer onto Phoebe's face with a big brush, and headed out into the car park to ring Tamsin. And she'd better call Alec. Make sure *he* hadn't had a change of heart. She didn't want to find out he'd done a bunk overnight.

He was there. In a three-piece-suit with a window-pane check and blue suede shoes as Nikki walked Phoebe in on her arm on the dot of midday.

'You look beautiful,' she whispered to Phoebe, and she did. Juno had pulled out the stops in record time, even managing to dry her hair and do an elaborate loose plait with some crystal beads woven through.

'I can't thank you enough,' Phoebe whispered back. 'I was just about to get in the car and drive home when you arrived.'

And then the music began, the gentle strumming of a bright guitar and soft female vocals, and Phoebe walked down the boardwalk to 'The Sea of Love' by Cat Power, and Alec turned to look at his bride. The look of joy on his face was unmistakable. Fifteen minutes later, they were married, and Nikki felt proud to sign the register, trying not to worry about what was going on back at the farm. It didn't matter if the generator had exploded or the marquee had fallen down – she'd done the most important part of the job.

The rest of the day went in a blur. All her meticulous planning paid off. Mercury behaved impeccably as Phoebe rode into the meadow side saddle with Alec leading him. The guests applauded. They were young, beautiful and dressed up to the nines, in a rainbow of silk and velvet and tweed, statement hats and vertiginous heels. In the marquee, flower clouds studded with peonies and old roses hung over the trestle tables. Later, as night fell, the astronomer wandered amongst the tables, pointing out the constellations. But none of the stars shone as brightly as Alec and Phoebe.

At one o'clock in the morning, Nikki and Tamsin sat on the fence at the bottom of the meadow, their hands curled around mugs of tea, scoffing the last of the miniature wedding cakes Helen had made.

'Well, that's that, then,' said Tamsin. 'Windcutter Weddings it is. I should have listened to you years ago. I'd be planning my retirement now.'

Nikki licked the last of the buttercream from her fingers. 'If you get your skates on, you could be up and running next summer.'

'I've got all those bloody barns falling down. We can

do a proper kitchen. Proper loos.' She laughed. 'I don't know what Dad would have thought. He didn't have a romantic bone in his body.'

'I think he'd be very proud,' said Nikki. 'You've worked yourself to the bone keeping this place together. Most people would have sold up.'

'This farm's in my blood. I'll do whatever it takes to keep it. And I just want to thank you, for giving me the inspiration. For making me do it.' She reached out and took Nikki's hand. They sat there on the fence, taking a moment to reflect on the success of the day, and what that meant for them, each of them grateful for their friendship, each of them aware that they were conjoined by tragedy, yet it was something stronger that kept them together now: the future, not the past.

49

On Sunday, Nikki drove Juno back out to Zak's for another rehearsal. It was the last time he was going to be in Speedwell before the anniversary next month, so it was their final chance to fine tune their performance. Juno seemed very sanguine about the fact she was performing with him, and by all accounts Zak had been very laid back about them sharing top billing, not at all starry.

They pulled up outside Zak's house. 'I'll come and get you in a couple of hours,' Nikki told her. 'Text me if you finish sooner, or want a bit longer.'

Edith was sitting on the back seat, and Nikki planned to explore the nearby woods with her. She watched Juno go, in a long fishnet cardigan over tiny denim shorts and clumpy suede ankle boots. She was so talented, so self-assured in some ways – she had completely transformed Phoebe the day before without breaking into a sweat – but Nikki still worried that she had no conviction or self-belief. She'd been monosyllabic about her first rehearsal with Zak, just saying it had been fine and not going into any detail even though they were all longing to hear the minutiae.

She looked down and noticed that Juno had left her notebook on the floor of the car. It had all her lyrics in it, and she usually guarded it with her life. Nikki bent down to pick it up – she could run it into the house as she'd probably need it. As she picked it up, a piece of paper came loose. It was torn from a spiral-bound notepad, like the ones they had always used at North Property Management. She went to tuck it back inside, but as she glanced at the words, written on it in blue biro, she froze. *I've been thinking and thinking about how to get us out of this mess*, she read.

Should she read it? This was Juno's private notebook. But something drew her in. She had a feeling this was something she needed to read. And as soon as her eyes fell on the first paragraph, she knew this note had been intended for her.

I'm going to take Jess and the baby to Ireland.

The note was from Rik. She read on, even though she knew this was one of those moments which would redefine everything. The past and the present.

> I think we could have a good life there. I can get work in the harbour and Jess could work at the hospital when the baby is bigger. There are good people in Kinsale. They looked out for me when I was young, and they'll look out for her. Your mum can come and visit as often as she likes – she can fly to Cork from Bristol.
>
> It's the best thing for all of us. We can't go on like this. It's not fair on your sister, or the baby. It will

break my heart, and I know it will break yours, but it's the only—

The note ended there, as if he'd been interrupted and had hidden it away.

Nikki spread it out on her lap with shaking hands. She didn't know what she was most shocked by. The revelation that Rik had a plan that he'd never shared with her, or the realisation that it must have been Juno who had sent the postcards. Her own niece. She felt sick. All that time they spent together – Juno helping her with the house, Nikki organising the rehearsals with Zak, her performance at the party, coming to help her out yesterday. How could she have done that, knowing she was threatening Nikki behind her back?

She looked up to see Juno running back out of Zak's house. Nikki met her gaze as Juno ran towards the car, then slowed to a halt.

Nikki opened the car door and held out the notebook. Juno took it wordlessly, her eyes not leaving Nikki's.

'Where did you find the note?' Nikki tried to keep her voice calm and non-accusatory.

Juno sighed. 'Mum gave me a load of Dad's albums. It was inside one of them.'

'OK.' Nikki nodded. That made sense. She could imagine Rik scrawling away, then tucking it away hastily out of sight inside a record sleeve. When had he planned to give it to her? Would he have revealed his plan that last day, when she told him about the cruise ship? They had both come to the same conclusion. They had both independently decided to leave Speedwell, but only Nikki had had the chance to voice her decision.

It didn't matter now.

'So was it you? The postcards?'

Juno nodded. Her lips were pressed tightly together. She was trying not to cry.

'Why, Juno? Why didn't you come and talk to me?'

'Because I was angry with you. How could you have done that to Mum?'

'It was—' What? Complicated. Difficult. Impossible. How could she put those months of turmoil into words Juno could understand?

'I used to think the world of you,' said Juno. 'You always seemed to have the answer to everything. And you were so kind to me. To everyone. But it turns out you don't care about anyone else at all. You're a liar.'

'I know. I know . . .' There was nothing she could say in her own defence.

'I wanted to make you suffer. I wanted to give you sleepless nights. But I also wanted it not to be true. Because it's made me think everything is a lie. I don't know what to believe about anyone or anything anymore.'

Nikki felt a wave of tiredness wash over her. It was all too much to take in. And Zak was inside waiting for Juno.

'You'd better go back inside. Zak's waiting.'

'What?'

'Go and do your rehearsal. We'll talk about it when you're done.'

A myriad of emotions flickered over Juno's face. Guilt, confusion, anger. Contrition? Even, perhaps, relief that she'd been found out. It was going to take a while to untangle this situation and Nikki needed some time to think about how to handle it.

As Juno headed back to the studio, Nikki leaned her head back and shut her eyes. She didn't blame Juno for what she'd done. It must have been a terrible shock, to find that evidence, and not to be able to tell anyone.

She remembered when Juno was born. A month after Rik's funeral, Jess had asked her to be her birthing partner.

'I'm going to be a terrible patient,' Jess had told her. 'And I know I won't deal with the pain. I'm going to hate everyone seeing me for the big fat wuss that I am. I'll be screaming for an epidural before the first contraction is over. I know I will.'

Surprisingly, it had been an easy birth. Nikki steeled herself for tantrums, drama and confrontation with the midwives. She brought in soothing face spray and wine gums and a tape she had compiled. A baby girl popped out in the middle of 'Angel' by Massive Attack, and it was all Nikki could do to stop Jess calling her that.

'It's kind of a lot to live up to.'

'Juno, then,' said Jess. 'Juno Brandy.'

'Brandy?'

Jess sang a few lines of the song. 'Rik always used to sing it. He said if he ever had a daughter, that's what he'd call her.'

'Oh, Jess.' Nikki squeezed her hand, remembering him singing it the day he arrived.

'Do you think Mahoney-Chambord-North is a bit much?'

'I think you've answered your own question there.'

'Chambord-North?'

Nikki shrugged. 'Why not just North? She's one of us.'

'You're right. Juno Brandy North.' She flexed the

muscles in her right arm. 'That's a super cool, strong name for my baby girl. My fine girl.'

And when the nurse came back in to check on them, she found the two of them singing 'Brandy' and laughing and the baby gazing up at the two of them in apparent wonder at the two women who were going to be such a big part of her life.

Juno had never been short of people to care for her, but Nikki had always made a special effort to look out for her. Was it because Juno was her only flesh-and-blood connection to Rik? Of course not. It was because Jess was vulnerable, and being a single mum was tough, and Nikki was her sister so of course she would have done anything she could to help. And when she and Woody had Bill, the two cousins were as thick as thieves, almost like brother and sister, so Juno often used to come and sleep over or accompany them on days out.

They were one big messy complicated family. What other secrets were swirling around in the background? Nikki supposed everyone had stuff they didn't want people to know. But some secrets were better out in the open. It took away their power. Otherwise, they were like unexploded bombs, and you didn't have any control over when they might go off. By detonating them, maybe you limited the damage?

After the rehearsal, she and Juno walked Edith through the woods near Zak's house. Dappled sunlight fell on the path in front of them, the woods silent with reverence, just allowing the merest rustle of leaves in the afternoon breeze and the occasional burst of birdsong.

'I totally understand, why you sent them,' Nikki told her.

'I didn't know what else to do. I couldn't talk to Mum. I didn't want her to know. And I was too scared to talk to you about it. I didn't understand who you were anymore. Every time I saw you, I wanted to say something, but it didn't seem possible, that you could be that person.'

'It wasn't something I was proud of, Juno. You must understand that. It was torture for both of us.'

'At least it was me who found the note. What if Mum had?'

'She knows. I told her. I couldn't risk someone else telling her.'

'Oh my God.' Juno looked horrified. 'I didn't mean for that to happen.'

'It's OK.' Nikki put her arm around her. 'She already knew.'

'She knew? All along?'

'Yes.' She sighed. She didn't want to blame Jess. Tell Juno that her mum had stolen Rik from her in the first place. It seemed petty. 'I don't know how much to tell you. I don't know how much you want to know. It was so complicated. It was everyone's fault. And no one's. If that makes sense.'

For a while, there was nothing but the sound of their footsteps on the soft path, and Edith's panting.

'Just tell me again what he was like.' Juno broke the silence. 'That's all I really want to know.'

Nikki thought back, to the very first time she'd seen Rik as he stepped off *The Lady Stardust* and her eyes had followed him every step of the way along the pontoon, transfixed.

'Whenever he walked into a room, people looked at him. He had a sort of radiance. A special light. But he wasn't aware of it. He could have been big-headed, but if anything, he was unsure of himself. Sometimes. He had so much to give but sometimes he held himself back. And sometimes, he made mistakes.'

As she spoke, Nikki realised she could have been describing Juno. Radiance and reticence.

'Do you think I'd have liked him?' asked Juno.

'Liked him?' Nikki could feel her heart buckle. 'Darling, you would have adored him. And I can tell you, hand on my heart, that he would have adored you too. Whenever he spoke about you, even though you hadn't been born, he was so proud. So excited. You were the most important thing in his life.'

Juno walked on, her hands in her pockets, looking at the ground. Edith padded along next to them, occasionally stopping to snuffle at the roots of a tree. Eventually she spoke.

'Zak's asked me to go on tour with him next year. As a backing singer.'

'What?'

'I don't know what to do. I mean, I've been to France on my own, to see Granny Sabine. But this would be twelve countries.'

'Juno, that is the most amazing opportunity. And you might never get another one like that.' Nikki felt a thrill go through her at the thought of what this could mean.

'He says it's not all glamour. Sleeping on a tour bus with everyone's smelly feet and snoring.'

Nikki knew with Juno it was best not to put her under pressure. Gentle encouragement was the best tactic. 'I think,' she said carefully, 'you might regret it if you turn it down.'

'That's what I thought.'

'And the M and Ms would kill you.'

Juno laughed, then went quiet. 'You were the first person I wanted to talk to, when he offered. But I felt like I didn't know you anymore. I didn't trust you.'

'Juno, you can always trust me. It was all a very long time ago, remember. And you know the most important thing to me is family. My mum, Jess, you . . . everyone.'

Juno bit her lip as she considered Nikki's reply. 'What would my dad have said to me, do you think?'

Nikki didn't hesitate. 'He would have told you to follow your heart. To take wing and fly. To make all your dreams come true. And he would have been very, very proud.'

Juno seemed to flinch, blinking, then she stood very still as she took in the words. Nikki was about to try to rephrase her encouragement – had she been too forceful? – when Juno suddenly flung her arms around her. The two of them stood there, in the middle of the mighty trees, clinging on to each other, and they were both crying, but laughing too, as the sunlight trickled down through the branches, drenching them in gold as the shadows of the past finally fell away.

50

A month later

The day of the anniversary, Speedwell was looking her very best. Tamara had a crack team getting the harbour ready. The pavements were swept clean of litter and dust, the shop windows were shining and bunting was strung from every lamp-post. A stage had been set up in the car park, ready for the ceremony and the performances. Both the inshore and all-weather lifeboats were on proud display outside the station. Belle and Gloria were already prepping in the Neptune kitchen, and mobile food trucks began to arrive.

At Mariners, Helen was icing trays and trays of cupcakes bearing the lifeboat logo which would be sold in the shop. Ralph was packing them carefully in boxes as she finished each dozen.

'I think,' he said, 'I should make myself scarce during the ceremony itself. I'll join you all this evening.'

Helen stared at him, her palate knife held aloft. 'Oh no,' she said. 'I want you with me.'

'But grief is a very private thing, don't you think?' Ralph looked concerned. 'When Eleanor died, I didn't want anyone except family around me.'

'Ralph,' said Helen, 'whether you like it or not, you are family now.'

'I am?' He went pink with pleasure. They had only been together a couple of months, but it felt like forever. They were so comfortable with each other, yet never in each other's pockets. And he got on like a house on fire with the rest of the family. He and Graham already had a plan to restore *The Shrimp* when she came out of the water in the autumn. She had seen better days, and Ralph loved nothing better than tinkering and fettling.

'I can tell you, William would expect you to be there. He would be glad that there was somebody there for me.' She firmly believed that. Nevertheless, her voice faltered for a moment, and she blinked back a few tears. 'It would be wonderful to have you by my side. I don't think anyone would expect me to face it all on my own until the end of time.'

'Oh, Helen.' Ralph stepped towards her and put his hands on her shoulders. 'That makes me very proud. It will be an honour.'

She looked up into his dear face. How lucky she was, to have had not just one but two wonderful men in her life. William was a tough act to follow, but Ralph was caring and considerate and affectionate but never smothered her – she wouldn't have been able to stand being smothered.

'Let's get these cupcakes finished,' she said, a little overwhelmed by her emotions, turning away and sticking her palate knife into the icing.

Nikki had fully intended to sleep in her own bed the night before the anniversary. She'd wanted to go to bed early to be alone with her own thoughts and not wake up next to Adam with a heavy heart.

'It's not that I don't want to be with you,' she told him. 'I'm just not sure how I'm going to feel. I want to sit with it all without worrying that I'm being morose.'

But somehow, she hadn't been able to resist going to sleep in his arms. She'd meant to slip away before midnight but had fallen into a heavy, dreamless slumber and woken just before dawn. She was surprised to find she felt the most at peace she'd ever felt on an anniversary. Usually in the run-up she would have vivid, unsettling dreams and a low-level anxiety would buzz through her, compounded by concern for her mum and Jess and Graham and how they might all be feeling.

This year, something had shifted in her. She felt a lightness, a kind of acceptance, a coming to terms. The ache would always be there, of course it would, but it wasn't as cumbersome.

At six, she climbed out of bed and pulled on her clothes without waking Adam. Gatsby jumped up onto the bed and wriggled into the warmth she had left behind, snuggling up to his master. She smiled at the pair of them, entrenched in their snooze, headed outside, jumped over the wall, down the steps and onto the beach. It was bright and freshly laundered, with not another soul in sight. She headed to the water's edge, pulling something out of her coat pocket. She'd had it in there for weeks, waiting for the right moment. Now seemed the perfect time.

It was the paper boat that Rik had given her. The blue was faded almost to white. She imagined his fingers folding it up, and wondered what he'd been thinking when he made it. Their little boat, to sail away in. What would have happened, if the sea had been kinder that day? Would she have ended up on the cruise ship? Or would Rik and Jess have headed to Kinsale, as in the letter Juno had discovered. She would never know now, how they would have negotiated the next step. Perhaps they would have both gone back on their resolutions and carried on? There were so many possible outcomes. She resolved not to give any more time to wondering as she walked down to the water's edge. It was time to let everything go. The past, the memories, the last vestiges of guilt.

She lay the boat down on the water. The wet paper soon grew dark and it bobbed up and down valiantly for a few moments. She couldn't bear to watch. Tears filled her eyes, but she brushed them away as she turned and walked back up the steps. The past was floating away. She had said her final farewell to the man she had loved so passionately. Her future was hers now, not tangled up in remorse and what might have been.

As she got to the top of the steps, she could see someone approach the cottages. It was too early for the postman. Who was it? She screwed up her eyes against the sun. Definitely a male – a tall, slender one. Young, she thought.

Then she stopped in her tracks, her heart pounding. She knew the tilt of that head, the slope of those shoulders.

'Bill!' She ran as fast as she could and met him just as he reached her front door. 'Bill!'

'Hey, Mum.' His eyes were full of mischief as he reached his arms around her. Oh God, he smelled the same, her boy. She couldn't hold him close enough, feeling his skinny ribs, his heartbeat.

'What are you *doing* here?'

'I couldn't miss the anniversary,' he told her. 'I know how much it means to you all.'

'Did Dad know you were coming?'

Bill gave her a sheepish grin. 'He picked me up from the airport last night. I'm here for a fortnight.'

'You absolute beasts.' Joy bubbled up in her heart, and she thought she might sob with intensity. Now she'd felt him in her arms again, she realised just how much she'd missed him.

The two of them walked arm in arm up the path to the front door.

'Nice crib, Mum,' Bill said approvingly as they went inside. She'd gradually been putting up pictures, rearranging books and ornaments and buying the extra bits and pieces that made it a home: a rug to go in front of the fireplace, a vase for flowers on the mantelpiece, a velvet lampshade for the light fitting. It felt as if she'd been here forever.

'There's loads more I want to do. But I want to live here for a while before I get too ambitious.'

As they walked through to the kitchen, he whistled in amazement.

'Mum! This has got to be the best view in the world. This knocks the socks off Bali.'

'I never get tired of it. And I know I'm very lucky. Tea?' she asked, reaching for the kettle.

'Why not?' He smiled at her. 'It's good to be home.'

She loved that he called it home, even though he'd never set foot inside the house before. She guessed it was because she was in it, and it made her feel happy, that he felt it was his too.

'Well, your bedroom's upstairs. I've put your stuff in it.' She'd thought at the time she was being silly, choosing blue-grey paint and denim curtains with a matching duvet cover and putting his clothes in the chest of drawers, and even his old teddy on his pillow. But even if he only spent half the time he was here in her house, it was worth it to know he was there, another heartbeat.

'Hello!'

It was Adam, calling from the front door which she'd left open. They wandered in and out of each other's houses all day long, but he never just barged in.

'Adam! Come and see who's here.'

Adam appeared in the kitchen doorway. He was dressed in navy linen trousers and a white shirt – quite formal for him, but this was obviously a nod to the occasion. A mark of respect. His face lit up.

'You must be Bill,' he said, heading straight for her son and taking his hand. 'I have the good fortune to be your mum's neighbour. I hope she doesn't have too many complaints.'

'None at all,' said Nikki, but she loved him even more for not making it obvious they were an item, for keeping his distance in case she didn't want to reveal that yet. Not that Bill would mind, but she wanted to give him a moment to breathe, to take in the new house, to settle back in. 'He's here for a fortnight. He came back for the anniversary.'

'And because I was missing you,' Bill admitted. 'Bali is wild, but I just kept thinking about summer in Speedwell, and everything I was missing. Our sea. Our view. Fish and chips.'

'Well, we're doing a barbecue on the beach tonight,'

Adam told him. 'I'm just off to the butcher so put your order in.'

'Sausages,' said Bill. 'I've been eating way too healthily. I don't want to eat a single piece of grilled fish while I'm here.'

'Sausages it is. I'll catch you later.'

When Adam had gone, Bill looked at Nikki, who blushed.

'Me and Adam, we're kind of . . .'

'I know.'

'Who told you? Dad?'

Bill rolled his eyes. 'It's totally obvious, Mum. And it's cool. He seems great.'

He took the cup she was holding out. And they went outside to the bench, and drank their tea, and chatted over everything and nothing until it was time to get ready and go into town for the ceremony.

At midday, Helen took to the stage to give her annual speech. There had never been so many people. She looked out at the throngs gathered on the quayside, at the boats in the harbour, at the lifeboat station in the background, and the memorial glinting in the midday sun.

'It's hard to believe it's been twenty years,' she began. 'Sometimes it feels like yesterday. Sometimes it feels like a lifetime. The memories and the sadness might have faded, but we still carry those seven hearts in our own hearts. They are all still there, in our children and our grandchildren, and we are still proud to have called them our fathers, our husbands, our sons, our brothers, our friends. And their legacy lives on, in the courageous team who still man the lifeboats, who still make sacrifices, who will stop what they are doing to save lives at sea. Speedwell is eternally grateful to everyone for their contribution, whether it is time or support or money, for without the lifeboat we are nothing.'

Afterwards she stood, head bowed, while the lifeboat crew sang 'For Those in Peril on the Sea', backed by choirs from the local church and the local school. She could see both Nikki and Graham in amongst them, Nikki in her all-weather gear, Graham in his suit, and she caught sight of Ralph in the crowd, giving her a nod of reassurance. And as the last notes of the hymn came to an end, she took the huge wreath of flowers Tamara had organised and went down the steps at the front of the stage, walked along the harbour's edge and laid it at the foot of the memorial. There was a reverent silence until she stood up, and then someone began to clap. A thunderous applause of recognition and gratitude and remembrance broke out and seemed to go on forever, until the marching band struck up and filled the air with stirring nautical tunes.

Helen stood there, overwhelmed, not sure what to do. And then Ralph was there at her side, taking her by the arm, leading her through the throngs as people reached out to touch her on the shoulder or shake her hand. He led her straight into the Neptune, where Gloria whisked them to a private table. There was a bottle of champagne on ice in a silver bowl.

'For you to propose a toast,' said Gloria, opening it deftly.

And then Nikki and Graham were there, and Adam, and Bill, and Suzanne and the M and Ms, and Jess and Juno.

'We'd better get another bottle,' said Helen. And there

they all were, the Norths, their glasses charged, and Graham raised his and said, 'To William and Rik.'

'To William and Rik.' Everyone echoed him, and they all clinked glasses with each other and drank, each with their own thoughts and their own memories of the two men who had meant so much, even those who had never known them.

Later, in a bedroom upstairs that Gloria had lent them, Nikki and Jess got Juno ready for her performance with Zak Glazier. She was quiet, because Juno always went in on herself when she was nervous. She was staring at her phone. Zak had sent her a text saying, You're going to be a superstar, Juno. I'm so proud to be performing with you.

'This is surreal,' she said.

'This is just the beginning,' Nikki told her.

Jess was standing at the window, uncharacteristically quiet. Nikki worried that of all of them, she was the one who hadn't moved on. Nikki had Adam, Juno had her exciting future, Helen had Ralph. But then Jess had always been so certain. She had always had the ability to get just what she wanted in life. So maybe she was happy with where she was; what she was. Nikki reminded herself that they had Bali to come. She could spend some down time with her sister. Get underneath her skin and find out what she really wanted.

'It's five to two,' said Juno, her eyes wide. She and Zak were on at two o'clock. The band were already on stage tuning up, the chime of guitars floating across the water. 'There's so many people.'

Jess was looking down over the crowds. The car park and the quay and the streets around were rammed. She could see camera crews. She walked over to her daughter and put her arms around her. 'This is your day, Juno. You deserve this. And I can tell you one thing, your dad would have been right there in the front, cheering you on. He would have been so proud.'

Jess was proud too, Nikki realised. Maybe that was enough for her, for now, to know that Juno was finding her place in the world, that she had an incredible opportunity.

'Wish me luck,' said Juno, disentangling herself from her mum and heading for the door.

Jess and Nikki looked at each other. 'He's there in her, you know,' said Jess. 'I can see him. She's going to be a star.'

At two o'clock, Tamara took the microphone. Nikki might have felt prickly about her at first, but Tamara definitely knew how to pull together an event and get great PR. And, of course, her biggest coup was yet to come.

'As a newcomer to Speedwell, it's an absolute honour to organise this special day to remember all those brave men who were lost, twenty years ago. I didn't know them but I feel as if I did, for I've met so many of their families and shared memories with them. They truly do live on. And today, I'm delighted to announce that we have a very special guest to help us celebrate their lives. Well, two very special guests, but I shall let Zak Glazier do the introductions.'

The crowd went wild as Zak jumped onto the stage, his wild red curls flying, sun glinting off his aviator sunglasses. He kissed Tamara, then took the microphone off her.

'It's a massive honour to be doing this gig today, in

memory of all those amazing men who I can't even begin to live up to. Their courage has been an inspiration to me, and it's made me proud to be a local. If I'm allowed to call myself that yet?' He gave a wry grin. 'I've also had the honour of working with an incredible young lady. She lost her dad and grandad in the disaster before she was even born, so this day is really important for her. We're performing some songs together. I hope you like them. Ladies and gentlemen, would you put your hands together for Juno Brandy North!'

Nikki felt a lump in her throat as Juno came out in a white crocheted dress with a big straw hat, her feet bare. She looked like a star, a natural performer with the audience in the palm of her hand, completely at home on the stage as she walked over to Zak with her microphone.

'Thank you, Zak. It's been so great working with you, and thank you for giving me a voice. And um . . .' She gathered herself together for a moment. 'This is for you, Dad.'

Nikki felt Jess squeeze her hand so tightly it hurt.

Juno and Zak sang three of his songs, their voices dancing around each other, his gravelly, hers sweeter but with a husky edge, and it was as if they'd been born to perform with each other.

Then Zak brought out a stool for Juno to sit on, and handed her a guitar, and the stage was all hers. She sang the song she'd written for her father, the one she'd first performed at Nikki's housewarming.

'He's there in my eyes
The man I never knew
A hint of gold

A splash of blue
Like the blue of the sea
That took him away
Before I could say
Hello'

For a moment, Nikki imagined *The Lady Stardust* in the harbour behind, and a figure on the deck watching his daughter. She looked at her mum, with Ralph standing behind her, and Jess and Graham with Suzanne and the M and Ms dancing along, and she thought *we're all OK, Dad. We miss you as much as we ever did, but we're all OK.*

As the last notes of Juno's song faded away, the crowd burst into applause. Zak came over and put his arm around her, beaming with pride, and Juno managed to take a bow, unable to believe the reception she was receiving. And then the band began to play the intro to another song, and Jess and Nikki recognised it straight away as Zak began to sing, with Juno doing the backing vocals. It was 'Brandy'. Rik's song. The Neptune anthem. Within seconds, the whole harbour was singing and dancing along, and Juno and Zak couldn't wipe the smiles off their faces as they serenaded the little town. Nikki and Jess stood arm in arm, swaying, singing, crying, filled with pride and memories and the love for each other that had ridden out a twenty-year storm.

Later on, the Norths headed down to the secret beach, laden with picnic bags and coolers and rugs. Adam and Bill took over the barbecuing and soon the air filled with the scent of sizzling sausages. Nikki sat on the flat rock with a bottle of beer and thought her heart might burst with the joy of all her family in one place, and friends too, for Tamsin had come with Andrew, and Woody and Katya were there. Tamara and Duke were coming by later. A proper beach party.

She lay down on the rock and felt its warmth through her shirt. For one split second Rik was there, smiling down on her, and she smelled the scent of oranges, then he was gone. A fleeting memory. She felt a shadow fall across her and opened her eyes. It was Adam.

'OK?' he asked, and she nodded.

'More than OK,' she said, reaching out her hand, sliding her fingers between his, closing her eyes with a contented smile. She let the chatter and laughter wash over her, the last of the heat from the setting sun, the smoky wood of the barbecue.

There was nothing she could do to change the past, but there was nothing, not a single thing, she would change about now.

Acknowledgements

My huge thanks to Lucy Lo-Vel, who is a volunteer for the lifeboat crew of her local station in Appledore. She was a big inspiration for Nikki's story and I am in awe of her courage and her zest for life. Whether dangling from a helicopter or hand-making the most beautiful lampshades, she grabs life with both hands and I hope some of her spirit is reflected in *The Secret Beach*.

Any mistakes in the protocol and procedure of the Speedwell Lifeboat are entirely mine.

Discover your next uplifting read from

VERONICA HENRY

Because Paris is always a good idea . . .

Years ago, Juliet left a little piece of her heart in Paris – and now, separated from her husband and with her children flying the nest, it's time to get it back!

So she puts on her best red lipstick, books a cosy attic apartment near Notre-Dame and takes the next train out of London.

Arriving at the Gare du Nord, the memories come flooding back: bustling street cafés, cheap wine in candlelit bars and a handsome boy with glittering eyes.

But Juliet has also been keeping a secret for over two decades – and she begins to realise it's impossible to move forwards without first looking back.

Something tells her that the next thirty days might just change everything . . .

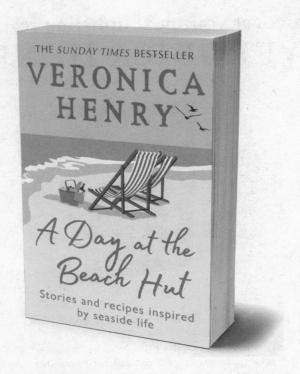

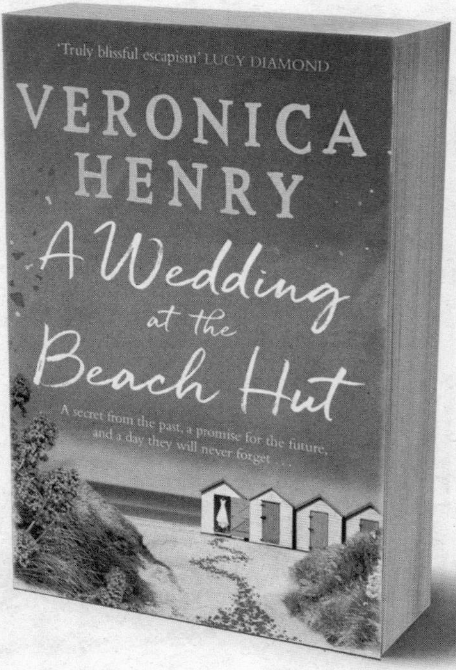

Return to Everdene Sands, where the sun is shining – but is the tide about to turn?

Robyn and Jake are planning their dream wedding at the family beach hut in Devon. A picnic by the turquoise waves, endless sparkling rosé and dancing barefoot on the golden sand . . .

But Robyn is more unsettled than excited. She can't stop thinking about the box she was given on her eighteenth birthday, and the secrets it contains. Will opening it reveal the truth about her history – and break the hearts of the people she loves most?

As the big day arrives, can everyone let go of the past and step into a bright new future?

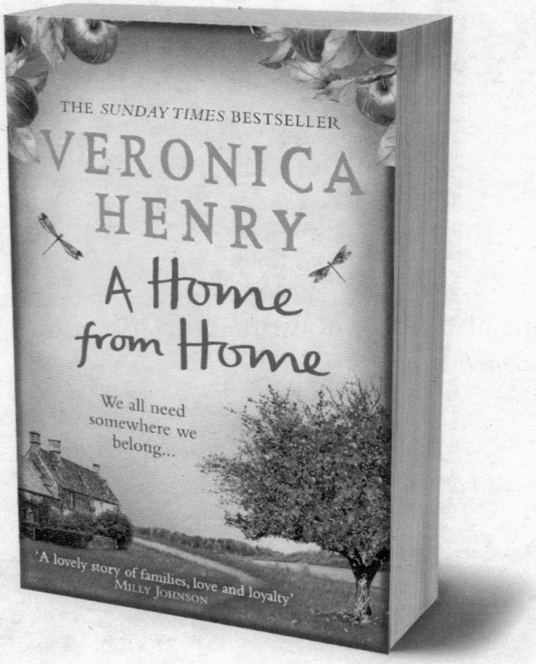

Sunshine, cider and family secrets . . .

Dragonfly Farm has been a home and a haven for generations of Melchiors – archrivals to the Culbones, the wealthy family who live on the other side of the river. Life there is dictated by the seasons and cider-making, and everyone falls under its spell.

For cousins Tabitha and Georgia, it has always been a home from home. When a tragedy befalls their beloved Great-Uncle Matthew, it seems the place where they've always belonged might now belong to them . . .

But the will reveals that a third of the farm has also been left to a Culbone. As the first apples start to fall for the cider harvest, will Dragonfly Farm begin to give up its secrets?

Credits

Veronica Henry and Orion Fiction would like to thank everyone at Orion who worked on the publication of *The Secret Beach* in the UK.

Editorial
Charlotte Mursell
Sanah Ahmed

Editorial Management
Charlie Panayiotou
Jane Hughes
Bartley Shaw

Proofreader
Linda Joyce

Audio
Paul Stark
Jake Alderson

Contracts
Dan Herron
Ellie Bowker
Alyx Hurst

Design
Charlotte Abram-Simpson
Joanna Ridley

Copyeditor
Marian Reid

Finance
Jasdip Nandra
Nick Gibson
Sue Baker

Marketing
Helena Fouracre

Production
Ruth Sharvell

Publicity
Leanne Oliver

Sales
Jen Wilson
Esther Waters
Victoria Laws
Toluwalope Ayo-Ajala
Rachael Hum
Ellie Kyrke-Smith
Sinead White
Georgina Cutler

Operations
Jo Jacobs
Dan Stevens